BLOSSOMING DESIRE

"I can't," Christina breathed. "Don't . . . not here . . . not anywhere!"

"Anywhere you like," he said. "Lie with me."

A breeze picked up making the dark leafy shadows of the greenhouse shush any response. And he kissed her; her mouth trembled as his lips took hers.

A strange tension began to vibrate through Christina. Like the distant, persistent buzz of bees over the citrus blossoms, down the corridor of plants.

She tried to turn her face away. "I can't do this—" But his fingers slid against her cheek, his thumb bracing her resisting jaw. And what began as a protest on her lips somehow became muddled into soft exclamations of pleasure. . . .

STARLIT SURRENDER

STARLIT SURRENDER

JUDY CUEVAS

ZEBRA BOOKS

KENSINGTON PUBLISHING CORP.

ZEBRA BOOKS

are published by

Kensington Publishing Corp.
475 Park Avenue South
New York, NY 10016

First Printing: January, 1988.

Printed in the United States of America

Prologue — July, 1789

The gown was extraordinary. It made Christina laugh, deep down inside herself, all the time she moved in it. How beautiful — and how very noisy — it was! Taffeta. Yard upon yard of rustling, churning taffeta; the woof and warp of different colors so that it changed and shimmered. A pale and iridescent blue that wasn't blue, but silver. Christina went down the terrace stairs and watched it froth among her petticoats, delighted with the dress, with herself, with the night.

She laughed aloud when she remembered what she'd overheard in the powder room. "Christina is such a pretty young woman. I wonder why she isn't married yet."

As if nineteen were the age of an old maid! Christina wasn't married, and she didn't plan to be for quite some time. She'd missed one Season because her father had insisted on an extra year of schooling. She'd missed last Season because she'd been ill. But here she was at last. And no young lady had ever more warmly embraced the pleasures of London social life. She felt more than happy to be where she was: She felt blessed.

Christina believed in the magnanimity of Fate as only someone very young and privileged can. After all, did she not bear marks, tangible reminders — a scar by her ear, two on her shoulder — of how amiably Fate smiled on her? She'd survived a siege of smallpox with relatively little damage.

5

Fate had seen her rich. Fate had given her beauty. Even her illness seemed to have worked to her advantage. Following her recovery, her face had become all eyes. An already delicate face, it was dominated now by hollows, by deep-socketed eyes that shone out like the bottoms of polished copper pots. These eyes were round, enormous, and thick-lashed. They were almost artificial in color, too exact a match with her light, burnished hair. Some termed her in redhead, others called her a blonde. But all called her beautiful. She was alive in a way that made people stare. Incandescent. Like a star. And this was her heaven. She couldn't imagine a life any lovelier than the one she led. And she certainly had no intention of letting any one gentleman make dramatic changes in this.

Christina had two very good reasons for this attitude. First, there always seemed to be something wrong with each young gentleman she knew. Vain. Or self-conscious. Babbling. Or too quiet. It didn't matter. She could find the particular variety of fault — put her finger on it with a kind of off-putting specificity at times — in each man. There was not one she would want to marry. Then, second, there didn't need to be: She was her father's only heir.

Christina's father was not terribly rich, but his money was solid. Winchell Bower was a barrister of some stature. He'd married well, though he was a widower now. He'd made good investments. He had a house in London, a house in the country, and some rental property in Bath. There had even been rumors in the last year of the honors list for him, though no title had yet materialized. Still, he was "well fixed."

"Well fixed" was the word her good friend, Thomas Lillings, had used. He'd said it sadly. Though the idea had quite cheered Christina as she'd thought on it. "Your old man won't be looking for money. He'll be looking for a title for you."

And look, he may. In fact, Christina thought this looking

business was wonderful fun. Gentlemen calling, awkward and polite, trying so earnestly to make a good impression on her. Tea in the parlor. Chaperoned dancing in the music room. And then there were lovely parties like this one.

The whole situation, Christina thought, was well fixed. This was where she belonged. And with God's grace and her father's backing, this is where she would stay. She intended always to be pursued and never to be caught. She intended to go to parties and wear gay, fluffy dresses and gossip behind fans with girls who whispered and giggled. This, she was sure, was what she'd been made for.

She leaned against the terrace gates and tried to catch her breath; tried to put things in proportion. This night seemed so unreal. She crossed her arms, hugged them to her. She could see the evening whiteness along her arm, her dress casting a blue glow on her skin, on her bare shoulders. Whiter than white. "Like an alabaster statue," Richard Pinn had said tonight.

She laughed. Richard Pinn was young and handsome, the eldest son of a baronet. And he was interested in her, ever so properly. Bowing and nodding. Voluble and tongue-tied in turn. She enjoyed his attentions. Her heart beat so hard, so happily, she could scarcely breathe.

And this was why she had escaped to the terrace. She had needed the night air. The gallant Mr. Pinn was too close, too attentive. The dining room had become overwhelming. So many people. The warm, picked-over food. With heavy steaming puddings coming out now on more silver trays. She had eaten too much perhaps. Or laughed too hard. Or perhaps drunk a little too much wine. Whatever the reason, the cure was cool, fresh air. And, of course, after the cure, she would have the pleasure of making an entrance again—

Above her, party lanterns swayed, hung from eave to eave. They gave an artificial but wonderful illumination to the evening. Christina's thoughts, too, swayed on a breeze of delight. They were as gay and as unfocused as the shadows that shimmered in her dress.

The wind picked up a little from a different direction. It brought a wisp of hair against her cheek. And suddenly, from above, the sound of voices carried out onto the night air.

Surprised, Christina looked up. There were people on a balcony overhead. She stared up. At the same time, the people above her grew silent. They stared down.

The moment held. Inside, someone at the dinner table made a crystal glass ring with a fork. "May I have your attention. Another toast . . . " Yet here, on the terrace, seemed of another world. The men above her—for they were all men—were clearly defined. Light came from behind them, from inside their upper-story room. The party lanterns danced over their heads. And on two pedestals, part of the parapet at each corner of the balcony, two large oil lamps burned brightly. The men were illuminated as if on a stage. And they looked as if caught in the act—

"Christina Bower! Is that you?"

"Thomas?"

"What are you doing down there alone?"

"Nothing of your business." Thomas Lillings was not speaking to her in his usual pleasant tone. She would have to remember that, she thought, and snub him when they all went in to dance.

"Well, you gave us a start. We didn't know you were down there."

"And what are you up to? That one woman can send a start into—how many?—six men?"

Her curiosity focused suddenly. She gave the balcony her full attention. There was a man there she didn't know. This she considered truly unusual, for she felt she knew everyone worth knowing. He was tall, somewhat angular, and rather beautifully turned out. The sort of build that wore clothes well. The sort of clothes that spoke of a love of style and

8

Thomas replied in a voice infused with some of its old gentleness, its humor. "Actually, we were up here having a smoke. The hostess was rather nasty about it downstairs. I don't think her old man ever gets a smoke with his brandy, poor fellow." She thought she saw him smile. Then looked again. Five. She could only count five men now.

She hesitated. Had she imagined—?

She abandoned Thomas Lillings and the terrace with a rush. She heard Thomas calling as she hoisted her skirts through the doorway, tilting to get their width through the french doors. Just in time. She hadn't been mistaken. A gentleman was coming down the far stairs, two steps at a time. And he was more than well turned-out. He looked royal. Blue velvet coat and breeches, several inches of Mechlin lace bouncing against dark fingers. Rings, watch— several watches crisscrossed his coat! He glittered. His very shoes sparkled—diamond buckles! She had never seen anything quite like him before. He was a dandy. Of the first order. But a very rich and elegant one. She tried to see his face, only he was traveling too quickly. She caught just the impression: dark skin against volumes of white neckcloth. Black hair—Shining, thick, clean—The hair curled over the cravat to lie against the velvet, jet-black against azure-blue.

He avoided the dining room and made straight for the entrance way.

She called to him. "Wait!"

He turned at her call, a kind of graceful pivot. He walked three steps backward, staring at her. He seemed taken by surprise. There was a rare gentlemanliness to him. Gentlemanliness that was not merely polite, but was a vocation, as with diplomats and kings. This politeness, ingrained, innate, held him there for her.

She had stopped by the stairs, her hand on the banister. He was only a few feet from the front door. The length of the foyer separated them. But their eyes held. Christina could not look away.

He was perhaps thirty. With the most beautiful eyes she had ever seen. They were fair — trumping his dark coloring with an unreal arresting blue. He had a sharply planed face; a broad jaw, a wide mouth. His body was slender, loose — long-limbed rather than compact. He was strikingly handsome. And a little eccentric: His clothes were fussy, excessive, full of pomp. They were more showy than just upper-class. The odd thing was he somehow carried this off. Another man would have looked ridiculous; he looked extraordinary. Christina could understand how this man — if he was who she thought — should easily live the reputation he had.

He stood, waiting. She, with timid curiosity, closed some of the distance. Then, quite surprisingly, he spoke to her.

"Will it do, then?"

Christina blinked. His voice was deep. Perfect vowels, the intonation of tutors and university. "Will what do?"

"I'm not sure. But I can't remember when I was last inspected so closely." When she appeared awkward at that, he shook his head, "No, no, I rather liked it. Are you finished?"

"I — I didn't mean —"

He raised his brow, "I am not offended."

She frowned. As if offense to him were something to be avoided.

He glanced toward the door. An eagerness to go manifested itself briefly. Yet it didn't take him away. His face came back to her. He tilted his head. "Come closer. Let me look at you."

She was wary. The bloom of self-assurance, all over him, rankled. Yet it was also terribly attractive. She walked toward him.

He held out his hand, inviting hers. In the dining room behind them, the quartet began to play again. Soft music, the deceptive tones of a single violin before the other

10

instruments descended on it. Why she gave him her hand, she couldn't imagine. Or did he just take it? But the sensation was devilish. His hand was much warmer than hers. And it did not touch her delicately. Richard Pinn had touched only her fingertips when greeting her tonight. This man's thumb pressed into her palm, while his very long fingers wrapped around the back of her hand. It was the sort of grip that was gentle yet would brook no resistance. Then, he didn't kiss her fingertips as Richard had done, but instead drew the hand straight up over her head.

Alarmed, she tried to pull her arm down. But a hand touched her shoulder and turned her under his arm, as if the music in the distance were for them.

"Very nice," he said as she came around. Still he held her hand in the air. Then, with his other hand, he took her chin and lifted her face to him. "You're very pretty. Why don't I know you?"

"Do you know every pretty woman?"

"Yes." He smiled.

His smile didn't seem wicked. It was very nice. Even, white teeth; creases at his eyes that softened some of the blistering arrogance of him.

"Should I have your name, then?" he asked. The question was a politely phrased demand.

"No."

She lifted her chin from his fingers. When she tried to free her hand, he would only let her lower it. He was frowning, staring at her so hard—

"Why don't I know you?" he repeated.

"I was at dinner."

"Were you?" His smile showed a trace of surprise. "I came late. And, alas, am leaving early." Much more sincerely now: "Won't you tell me your name?"

"No." She smiled. She liked this game.

"Are you someone's cousin come to London? Someone's sister?" He raised a brow. "Someone's wife?"

11

This made her laugh. "No."

"If you don't say, I won't know where to find you. I'm going to France tomorrow. But I will be back and would like to call—"

"No. You mustn't call."

"Why?"

"My father wouldn't permit it. He doesn't approve of you."

He was taken aback. "You have me at a disadvantage— Or am I taking the blame for another man?"

"The Earl of Kewischester." She said it as she'd heard it, *Kester*, with not only letters but whole syllables unpronounced.

He took a breath. "And do you share your father's opinions?"

"Not all of them."

"Then meet me."

She looked at him. "What?"

"Tell me a place. Get me a message. Meet me."

Another small laugh escaped. "You're daft. I don't know you."

"But you've just said you do."

"No, I don't." Yet she was still laughing. Why did this amuse her?

Then less amusing: He drew her by the captured hand up against him. His arms dropped around her back.

"Sir," she protested. But she liked the feel of him, the warm, rushing sensation he caused in her. She could feel a broad, muscular chest pushing against her palms.

"I've never kissed a total stranger," he said. "In fact, I think I prefer you don't tell me your name." He bent his head toward her. She could smell the brandy and cigars of the upstairs room.

"No—" It was mildly alarming, this nearness, this forwardness. But what could he do with fifty people in the next room? "I shan't permit you to kiss me," she murmured.

12

But she knew that she was going to.

She waited. Seconds stretched out, delicious in their slow deliberation . . . .

And he let her go. She almost fell from the sheer surprise of it.

His laughter was quiet, more breath than voice.

Christina looked away sharply. "Am I so funny?"

"Yes. Are you really so ruffled that I didn't do what you wanted?"

"Wanted?" She glared at him. "Do you imagine I wanted—?"

"No, I didn't imagine it. I understand a token resistance when I am holding it."

She huffed at that. "And you, sir, are exactly as they say. A cad."

"But not enough cad for you." He laughed aloud.

"You're horrid."

"I know what I am," he said. Then he leaned and sent words back at her, articulating each one, like little stings. "And you are a Hot. Game-playing. Little Baggage. Whoever you are." He laughed again. "But a very beautiful one."

At the door, he turned toward her again. "I can find you, you know. I fancy you're not unknown, and you're hardly difficult to describe." His eyes glanced down the length of her. "You are really beautiful, do you know that? And I did want to kiss you. I still do. But not here. And not now."

Christina let out a little sound of shock, dismay. How dare anyone speak to her in this manner—! Yet she stood mute, flushing in waves and turns; angry, frightened, flattered, confused. She struggled for a retort, a clever last word to fling at him. But the door clicked behind him.

His footsteps tapped out onto the portico, down the steps, then disappeared at a run out onto the soft earth of the front garden. All was quiet. There was only Christina, standing alone in her pretty dress . . . .

She'd been holding her breath. It came out as a huge

sigh, almost a sob. She looked around her. No one. No one to be any wiser, she told herself. Behind her, she could hear that dinner was over; everyone had moved into the ballroom to dance. Yet the entrance room where she stood felt hollow. The room echoed with a kind of loneliness she had never felt before. Something had happened. Her cheeks were glowing with heat, her hands, clenched in little white fists, were tingling cold.

And she was not happy. That awful man had ruined it. He had ruined a perfectly good evening by his silliness. She would never forgive him, she thought, never. And tears began to come down her face. Hot, bitter tears that tasted salty as blood.

On the day following her encounter with the earl, flowers were delivered to her father's house in London. A great many flowers: It took eight vases to accommodate them. All morning, Christina looked at them with a strange, confused delight. Though she wasn't certain she should enjoy the idea, the Earl of Kewischester had indeed found her. He knew not only her name but the whereabouts of her home — and had had the nerve to confront her there with this huge, florid display. He had sent roses. The biggest, fattest, reddest ones she had ever seen.

Just what Christina might finally have thought of all this, however, became a moot point. It was the reaction of Winchell Bower, King's Counselor, that achieved a tangible effect.

He came in from court that afternoon and was, at first, delighted. He believed Richard Pinn had sent them. Which made them, at that point, "a jolly, fine display." Then he saw the note.

"Respectfully, to Miss Christina Bower. From the Honorable Adrien Hunt, seventh Earl of Kewischester." The message was engraved. A plate had been cut just for her.

At this point, the flowers, the entire gesture, became "an ostentatious show of superiority." But this was not enough. The card had been signed, in ink, in the man's own hand — and here was the *coup de grâce* when her father saw the single initial: *A*

"What is this *A?* How well do you know this libertine . . . this . . . this dissolute . . . this . . . this . . . ? Do you use his given name? Just his initial? How familiar are you? By God, daughter, I can see I have been too free with you . . . ." Winchell Bower was livid. "Where on God's earth did you meet this man?"

She explained she had only spoken to him briefly at the Baysdens' party the night before.

"When? I never saw you speak to him. And he sends you flowers — so many flowers! — the next day?" A crescendo was building. "My dear young woman, do you know Pinn's son is interested in you? A future baronet. And there's been talk of marriage. A marriage which, I must say, would see me content to the last of my days." He took a breath. "But may I tell you that that family — any decent family — would not even so much as turn their head your way if *this* got out!"

This? "I don't see how —" But there was no defense allowed with the counselor.

"Open your eyes! You're not a child any longer. An earl, especially that earl, is hardly likely to offer you marriage. My God, girl, are you a fool? He doesn't approach me. He sends you flowers — many too many flowers. Then he signs his name . . . like a . . . like a . . . like much too familiarly." He drew himself up. "If he has laid so much as one finger on you —"

And, thus, there began a kind of revision of fact. For Christina was called upon to give details of the meeting. Over and over. It seemed neighbors, as well as every servant in the house, knew of the arrival of the bouquets of flowers. It had taken three of the earl's men — liveried — and a carriage — crested, of course — to bring them. And the contents of the note, no doubt also through servants, became common knowledge. Circumstances made it necessary for Christina to express her shock and recount—in a slightly tidier, more modest version—the incredible cheek of the man.

Circumstances also made it possible. For, as it turned out, only Christina's version of the evening would ever be heard.

On July 11th, the morning of the flowers, Adrien Hunt crossed the English Channel. From there, it took him almost two days to get from the coast into the southeast of France. To the province of Dauphiné. Exhausted from travel, he went to bed in the wee hours of the morning and was still sleeping soundly at midday on July 13th when the commotion broke out.

Unbeknownst to him, all night a group of farmers had been gathering near the manor house where he slept. By mid-morning, feelings were high. United by hunger and a sense of injustice, they rioted. Local manor houses were burned and chopped. Whatever damage could be wreaked with sticks and rocks and the tools of a farmer was meted out with whatever was at hand. Only later would this be recognized as the preamble to the French Revolution—the provincial equivalent of the storming of the Bastille in Paris.

France that evening stood on the precipice of enormous social change. A hundred years before, the English had had their revolution. Their king had lost much of his power to Parliament—and in the bargain lost his head. But France had continued on under the old notion that the French king ruled by Divine Right—that the king and all his vassals, the French nobility, had by God's will the absolute authority to live better, freer, and without compunction for the lower classes. This social order had worked for hundreds of years. But industry and economic change, growing since the turn of the century, gave birth to a new social group: *La bourgeoisie.* The middle class. The whole future notion of three classes rather than two — and the power of the business class — would be built on events and ideas that came from these turbulent times in French history.

France was not oblivious, at least to the rhetoric of these ideas. French writers — Voltaire, Rousseau, Diderot — gave words to the new spirit breaking over the world. French treasuries helped finance, across an ocean, the largest experiment in liberty, equality, and brotherhood: America. The surprise was, however, that these ideas could ignite so violently in France herself.

Three things in particular made this possible. First, a foolish king, Louis XVI, followed a profligate one. Louis' father, Louis XV, had indulged himself at the expense of the people. He had taxed heavily. He and his noblemen — exempt from these taxes — had grown accustomed to living overly well and passing the bill on. The son, Louis XVI, ascended to the throne and saw both the high taxes and empty coffers of his treasure. Yet he refused to make reforms or live more frugally. Eventually, there was simply no money left — either in his treasury or in the poor peasants' pockets. Then, the *coup de grâce:* crops failed. There was no wheat, which translated for the poor man to no food. Bread was the mainstay of his diet. The masses, great in number, poor and hungry, had everything to gain and nothing to lose by uniting with the more articulate and financially savvy middle class. Voilà. The organism had a brain and a huge, massive body; a revolution came to life.

And Adrien was there on the morning this violent force — which would shake a continent for ten years — came screaming and wailing into cohesive existence. He, along with his hosts in a manor house in Dauphiné, were roused from sleep and dragged from their beds. Neighbors — poor men, farmers — were their enemies. With whatever weapons these peasants could find — stones, rocks, shouts, fists — they began their war on the upper class. Then, another stroke of enormous bad luck: In Adrien's corner of the fracas, the weapon to hand was a scythe.

He sustained what were considered mortal injuries, the curved blade making a neat and remarkable incision from under his arm, down and across his belly, around to his flank. No man, the doctors said, could ever have been more artfully sliced from one end to the other. The poor ailing lord was doctored in France, then carried on a litter, very gently, across the water and back into England. He was brought home to die.

When the news came of the earl's "accident," Christina felt a guilty sense of relief. Her small lies were secure. But she felt also, as the days moved on, something else. She *had* lost something. And she had to deal with this tiny bit of grief alone. Her spirits became subdued. She became restless and hardly up to the social commitments expected of her. No one had the first inkling or understanding of it, but she went into a kind of mourning. Not specifically for the earl himself. But related to him, she knew, in a way she could not pinpoint. She went into mourning for herself. For something the earl had represented to her. And for a romance with life she had suddenly realized was based too much on her own whim, too little on reality.

Part I

Shadows in the Sun

Chapter

1 — May, 1792

Christina Bower Pinn arrived at the country house in a rented carriage. She stepped firmly into the mud of the driveway, wrested her own bags from the rear box (Was the driver a lout? Or did gossip spread so rapidly, even among a boorish class of strangers?) and faced the front door. It was, she realized, the front door of a "gentleman friend," that is to say, a kind of back door to her cousin Evangeline's happy existence. But it was nothing less than what Christina expected, and she was grateful. Thank God for Evangeline. Who else could she have relied on, on such short notice.

She pulled the door chain. Then pulled it again. And again. It was a preoccupied cook who answered at last, covered at this early hour in the makings of the day's bread. The housekeeper, it was explained, was with the fowler haggling over a catch of wild birds. There was no one else save a lazy gardener who could never be induced to leave his dirt, not even to answer the door.

The master of the house was, as promised, in London. But Christina was welcome; they were expecting her.

"Faîtes comme chez vous." Make herself at home. The cook

was French.

Christina was left to get her own bags into the entrance way.

Directions to her rooms were flung over a shoulder at her, in the air, accompanied by a mild dusting of flour. *"Vous comprenez?"* But the woman didn't wait for an answer; she rushed on. "You weel be make more comfortable *plus tard. La femme de charge* weel be up *tout de suite."*

And with that, Christina was alone.

She stood in a huge entrance room, a room so large it seemed almost impossible to describe the feel it had: It was cluttered. Pictures, tapestries, objects of art. Glass-fronted vitrines filled with a miscellany of tiny figures, vases, dishes. Every variety of furniture crowded in on each other. And along one sideboard were enough roses, heavy and wilting now, to have denuded every bush in Hampshire — the gardener wasn't entirely lazy. The air reeked of their scent. The enormous room was made to feel close, made oppressive with the call to bees and pollination.

Naturally, Christina's mind would turn to pollination. She remembered suddenly that Evangeline herself would be looking a little pollinated when she next saw her. Christina hoped she could deal with that gracefully.

On this note, Christina heaved up her first bag and threw herself into continuing on — a phrase which lately was beginning to annoy her for how often her mind seemed to resort to it. She carted up her belongings as directed. Up the stairs, second landing; her apartments were on the right — or were they straight ahead? — the two words in French were so alike. And two years of French at an English finishing school did not make one exactly fluent.

Straight ahead. It must be correct, for the rooms were wonderfully devoid of all the busyness of the rest of the house. They were stark. They longed for someone to move into them, to occupy them. The sitting room and bedchamber pleased Christina immensely for their spaciousness and

21

simplicity.

The bed was large, open. Its bright brocade canopy-drapes were tacked back to admit light. Christina set down the last of her bags. The bedroom was full of light; wonderfully pleasant. There was a night table, a wardrobe, a large, comfortable chair; and there was the most magnificent mirror — gilt, at least seven feet high and four feet wide. Then, as she turned, Christina came face to face with the best feature of the room: Its windows looked out over what had to be the best prospect of the whole of the back estate. The view was magnificent.

Or perhaps it wasn't all one estate. Christina frowned. Could this all belong to this one man?

Out the window she could see an open, formal garden; lawns, plantings, statuary. Beyond that, set into a patch of higher bushes, was a fountain; defunct, not in use. After this, grassy meadow. The meadow was green, vividly luminous in the morning haze. Dotted with little black-legged sheep, it ran all the way to the horizon, as far as the eye could see. Then, at the horizon, trees; a woods. This final, distant thickness of trees seemed to enclose the property like open arms. It gave the land a sense of entirety, an integrity all its own; as if this land could hoist a flag and declare itself sufficient unto itself.

"And a woods," Christina whispered to herself.

Only royalty and a handful of the peerage could afford their own private woods for hunting. Did those trees belong to her cousin's friend? And everything in between? Exactly who was this man? Where had her cousin sent her?

Christina was suddenly aware of how little she knew about her new circumstance. Evangeline's note had been brief. It had said the house would be vacant and that it would be entirely all right with its owner if she sent a visitor to it — it seemed Evangeline had that privilege. Christina knew, or at least suspected, that Evie was involved with some gentleman here in her own region. She

22

imagined this was his house. But Christina didn't question the offer. She had embarked knowing its drawbacks. And Evie had said, in a sentence, its advantages: It was comfortable, less than a night's ride, and available on immediate notice.

This last qualification had been particularly important. Christina had dashed off a note to her cousin only last night. In it, she had asked—begged—for refuge and immediate help. Christina was grateful that Evie had given these so promptly. It wasn't everyone who came willingly to the aid of a wife leaving her husband.

Christina took a deep breath and began to unpack.

The housekeeper appeared after a time. There was no maid to spare; it was hoped Mrs. Pinn would understand. The housekeeper was a starchier, more dour woman than the cook. And strange. While she said her piece she fought, from the moment she entered the room, a somehow inappropriate smile. Not one of welcome, but the sort that glimmered suddenly at one end of her tight mouth and, as quickly, flickered out.

"You've found your towels?

"Do you require another lamp?

"Shall I help you unpack?"

The woman had a whole list of inane, superfluous questions. And all the while she asked them, she fingered Christina's possessions.

Christina wished to finish unpacking, to undress, yet she became reluctant to do so. She supposed that her unusual and sudden arrival, with no maid and only a few belongings, amused the woman.

They lapsed into uncomfortable silence.

"I hate to keep you—" Christina said at last. "I know you are busy—"

"Not at all. I'm having my tea."

Indeed. Me—you're having me for tea, Christina thought.

"Look at that!" the housekeeper said suddenly. Christina glanced. The woman pointed out the window.

"He's not from here, you know." This was meant to explain a great deal.

"Who?"

"The man, the gardener down there." The housekeeper gestured with emphatic distaste. "If you can call 'im that. All he does, endlessly, all day is meddle with God's work. A devil be more his name. Blasphemous. Look. He's at it now."

Directly below them, a man in a broad hat had walked into view. He stood at the base of the sweetbrier that climbed the three stories almost into Christina's room. The plant was still holding some of its spring bloom.

"How lovely," Christina said.

The gardener, unaware of either woman, had brought out a small pair of shears. He was working so carefully over one stem he looked more a surgeon than a groundskeeper.

"Ugly," the housekeeper spoke forcefully. "He makes orange roses." As if this were the ugliest color in the world. "And every one of them has been sterile. Every one. It is pointless." The woman turned. A sly smile stole across her face.

Christina stood open mouthed as the woman, with seeming satisfaction, left the room.

Such deliberate malice, from a stranger, left Christina a little shocked. But, surely, this woman couldn't have have known—

Then, of course, Evangeline did like to talk—

Christina slumped onto the bed. The woman had eyes, she thought. Perhaps it showed. She had never thought of herself in those terms before, but she was feeling oh so orange now. Didn't the sun bring out pale orange freckles on her face and arms? Didn't it streak the bundle of orange hair that weighted her neck. Her eyes—she closed them—were so light a brown as to almost be orange . . . . Well, no, she refused to believe she was ugly. Rejected perhaps. Cast off. But not ugly. Her "orange" features were her strength, her immediate and visual uniqueness. She would carry them as if they were beautiful — mostly because she still believed they were, but partly because she was perfectly willing to bluff if they were not.

But sterility was another matter. It was not ugly precisely. Just completely out of order; the last thing one expected to question to oneself.

Obstinately, even now, Christina's mind would not let go of a sense of being whole, of feeling normal. There was the depressing sense of everyone having got it all wrong. She wasn't just a breeding cow. Why should it matter so much if she couldn't bear children?

Yet it had mattered to Richard. And because of it she was going to hear another humiliating word applied to her: divorced. She hadn't been able to stay in the house a moment more, once Richard had told her: A baronet needs heirs — and a wife who can provide them.

"Honest to God, Evie! The Earl of Kewishchester! How do you expect me to get my father's help when he finds this out?"

"I don't. You are a big girl now, Christina. You can handle Richard without holding Papa's hand."

"You've stabbed me in the back!"

Evangeline laughed. "I haven't. I have given you a shove in the right direction. Besides, where else would you have gone?"

Christina turned from the window to look at Evangeline Sloane. Her cousin was slender — except for a large, round, pregnant belly. And she was very pretty. Evangeline was the sort who looked lovely in ruffles and curls, her brown ringlets hanging sweetly on the pink shoulders of a voile dress. She had wide, innocent eyes and, in general, a look that let her get away with a great deal of less than innocent behavior with hardly a raise of brow.

The two cousins, Christina standing by the window, Evangeline sitting on the sofa, were talking in the earl's front library.

Christina sighed. "Evangeline, don't mistake me. I appreciate your help, and I understand what you're saying to me. But this is too important. I want — I *need* — Papa's help. He can be a little demanding, I know. A little too fond of his own way of doing things. But I know how to handle that."

"Anyone who can handle Winchell Bower —"

This flustered Christina. " 'Handle' is the wrong word. I don't manipulate him. I don't want to manipulate anyone. I only want to protect my own. I've enjoyed a certain amount of independence since my marriage. I've grown used to that —"

Evangeline laughed. "Yes, and don't we all know it. You know, that is the real reason Richard wants shed of you. Not this stupid excuse. He is afraid of you, Christina. He can't control — predict — you." With a fresh breath, Evangeline seemed willing to change the subject. "Well. So let me see if I understand: Somehow, someone has given Richard the idea you will never bear children."

"Doctors, Evangeline. Three of them."

"How on God's earth could they know?"

"I got an infection. Two summers ago. It was really nothing, a little pain, but then I started to bleed. When my regular doctor left, he was shaking his head. He said I had to stay in bed, that I would probably get well if I rested, but that my infection would damage things inside." Christina heaved a sigh. "Richard seemed very concerned. So I let him call in another doctor. Then another. They were unanimous. I was forming scar tissue in the Fallopian tubes."

"In the what?"

Another sigh. "I've heard it often enough; I ought to know how to say it." Christina sat her bottom on the windowsill. She looked at her cousin. "But what it means, Evie, is I can't conceive."

Evangeline patted her tummy with a sly grin. "I'm not certain that is so bad." At twenty-eight, she had five children. And now a sixth— There was a pause. Then: "So what is the plan?"

Christina mugged a look. "The plan *was* to get my father to help. Though I have no idea what he'll make of all this now." She bowed her head. "I don't know. I suppose it is all right to be barren. Only I can't stand the thought of everyone gossiping about me before I have had a chance to understand what is happening to me first. I want time. Papa could do something for me. I know. He always can."

"And Richard? You've talked to Richard?"

"For hours. Before I left. But he wants it. He really wants it. I can hardly believe—" She made a dry laugh. "Do you know what he had the nerve to tell me? He wants to be able to remarry. He doesn't want to come off in a bad light. I am not to make 'a thing' of this. 'We must both think of the future.' " She let out a contemptuous breath. "Every time I think of the future, I want to throw up." Then she shook her head. "He's really not being very nice."

"He never has been."

Christina frowned. "I used to think he was." But then she recanted, "No. I suppose you're right, he never has been." She sighed. "He just had all the right appearances. And, of course, he pleased my father's sense of upper class. A title."

"You should have let your father marry him." Evangeline made a sniff. "And only a baronet at that." Then she laughed more wholesomely. "Now if you want a title, why not Adrien? Remember the flowers? How your father went on!"

Christina hadn't thought of that. Not for a long time. She groaned. "Please. I'd rather not—"

But Cousin Evangeline was off and running. "A full, blooming earl. And the Prince of Wales has slept in this very house. In fact, he's gotten drunk in this very room." Evangeline's eyes always danced when she spoke of such things.

She reached for the teapot over a pile of scones and cream and cake with honey. Quantities of such things were being prepared for the master. He was due back by the end of the week. Like so many of the *ton*, the Earl of Kewischester was retiring to the country for the summer.

Evangeline edged forward as much as her increasing girth would allow. "There's so much I could tell you. Adrien looks wonderful. And he's every bit as naughty as he has always been." She laughed. "And I think he tells me every wicked thing he does just especially to fan his reputation. He flirts with me abominably. Even like this!" She patted her belly and laughed. "And this past winter, even as I was beginning to show, he stopped me in the antechamber of Haverings' main dancing room and kissed me full on the mouth."

This shocked Christina. For almost three years, she had been living in the world of marriage and rules and responsibility. She shook her head at her cousin. "There is talk, you know, Evie. Of you and, I think, this man."

"Just talk."

Talk which Christina, from her own experience, was inclined to believe.

Her cousin clicked her tongue. "Christina. Don't be such a prig. He's very charming. You will like him. Honestly." She tilted her head, "And I, of course, would never really be unfaithful to Charles. But Adrien makes me feel so —"

"Loose," Christina finished for her.

Evangeline laughed. "No, you ninny." Then, more laughter. "Well, yes." She mocked the unsmiling young woman across from her. "It's a game, Christina. It's only a game to play. And Adrien plays it quite hard. And quite well." Then

28

she grew more sober, more affectionately admonishing. "Sweet coz, I wouldn't ever really ... you know. You *must* know that. Adrien could never take the place of dear Charles. He is much too—well, full of himself. Adrien comes with all the drawbacks of someone who has had way too much for way too long. Selfish. Self-centered. Shallow, but fun. And he can be perfectly obnoxious when he wants to be. But one puts up with him. Partly because good-looking, rich, well-educated men can be so amusing to have around. And partly because"—she winked—"the Prince of Wales sleeps here occasionally, and it is a tickle to be so near the blood." Evangeline teased with her eyes as she reached forward to drop an enormous mound of clotted cream onto a split scone.

Evangeline knew everything about everyone, usually the day before they knew it themselves. She also didn't always tell the truth or toe every moral line. But she was a loyal friend.

"Well, for all your recommendations"—Christina gave a sidelong look at her cousin—"I don't think I can continue to stay here. Not after he comes home. It would hardly strengthen my position with my father, let alone the rest of respectable society."

"Don't be silly. He'll be coming with a whole group of people. And he's said he doesn't mind. Besides, what would you want with some 'respectable' man, by which I assume you mean some boring little banker somewhere. Or another baronet. Auggh! When the best of eligibles will be traveling with Adrien here!"

Christina groaned. "Oh, please don't start on that. I just meant normal people. I couldn't possibly tolerate all the awkward politeness and boredom of courting again. Besides, who wants a wife who can never produce children?"

"I wasn't thinking strictly of marriage—"

Christina stood up suddenly. "Ah! Evangeline. You are incorrigible."

29

"Richard would be green." She laughed. "I think I shall see to it that he hears you are living with an earl."

"Don't you dare." Christina wandered back toward the front window. "I hear the Marshalls are looking for a governess."

"He pinches bottoms."

Christina looked at her. "Who?"

"Felix Marshall. That's why they are looking for a governess. Perpetually."

Christina made a face, then folded her arms and looked back out over the drive and front lawn. "I've got to find someplace, Evie. Someplace to belong, to stay. And I don't want to live with my father. Which means I shall certainly have no more money than what little trickles in through my trust. What in the world shall I do? I need some fertile place where I can take hold again." Bad choice of words; why had she used the word "fertile"?

"If you would like to live in the nursery until . . ."

"And crowd you still further? No, dear. Charles is right. There isn't room."

"I could get you a bit more money perhaps . . ."

"I have taken too much from you already." Christina could feel the heat behind her eyes. She tilted her head to balance the self-pity before it slipped down her cheeks in tears.

"Richard is such a rotter," said Evangeline from the sofa.

Christina gave a breathy laugh. "Fine. Richard is a rotter. But where does that leave me? I don't know what I'm going to do. I don't know where I'm going to go. I only know I'm being divorced. For something I have no control of, that will make me . . . strange to people. Different. I don't know if I can cope with all this."

"I don't have a doubt in the world that you can. Admirably."

"I think I'm going to cry, Evangeline. Do you want to watch, or do you want to leave?"

"Christina—"

"I know, I know—"

"Poor, sweet Christina."

"Oh, don't, please don't." Christina had to wait a moment to gain control over her voice. "Badger me. Tell me more of your neighbors, of your wretched earl. But don't call me 'poor' or 'sweet,' please."

Chapter 2

Evangeline made a strong case for Christina's becoming an official house guest of the Earl of Kewischester. In a few days' time, he would arrive, but with many other people. In the summer, the upper class frequently traveled together in groups. From one grand house to another. From Kent to Hampshire to Bath to Lyme. They moved from watering hole to watering hole, trying to entertain themselves. The earl's house would merely be one stop along the way. Adrien Hunt would hardly know Christina was there. Besides, Evangeline argued, even Winchell Bower couldn't question company that was regularly the choice of the Prince of Wales.

But there was another, more personal reason that Christina stayed. In the time she had been on the estate, she had found unexpected consolation in her new surroundings. Something about the house and the land invited her to be part of it.

It was beautiful land. Christina loved to walk through it. And the joy of it was that she was unusually free to do so. The earl's property was extremely well protected. Not only did it have a forbidding forest at its back borders, but high iron palisades ran the full perimeter of the property, to the woods and behind. Gamekeepers patrolled the various sections. The earl had an uncommon zeal for privacy. But, happily, this made his property one of the few pieces of

England where a well-to-do woman could go off, for hours alone, without fear of becoming the prey of highwaymen, or worse.

Best, Christina liked to wander off on foot. And, most often, her feet led her to the periphery of the woods. A coolness emanated from the trees. The shade protected her from the heat; she had found that no matter how she customized her attire—no chemise, no stockings, a light dress that required no layer of quilted petticoats—she could still become damply warm if she trudged too far in the direct sun. But she liked the edge of the woods for another reason. It was remote. No servants. No cousins. Not a single reminder of civilization. Even the animals of the place—the sheep, the ducks, the geese—ignored it. She was alone there.

The first signs that this peaceful existence was going to be short-lived came on the eighth day of Christina's stay. A letter arrived. A lawyer wrote from London. The divorce was real. It would be final in five weeks' time. But it was the end of the lawyer's letter that Christina found alarming. She would be given "a very reasonable allowance from the Bower-Pinn Trust."

There was no Bower-Pinn Trust.

Was Richard planning on forming one? Was he planning to supplement her income? That would be very good of him, but was not very likely. Richard would inherit a title, but he and his family had little income. It was through Christina that money had been expected to flow eventually into the baronetcy. Richard was sensitive to this issue. He didn't like the fact that his wife came from more money than he did—he even came to resent the little trust her father had set up for her.

"I can take care of you without that," he'd say. "Besides, it's all coming to you in the end anyway, isn't it? Why must he make such a show of your having money that I mustn't have?"

Christina would often give him half her monthly windfall at that point. Which he always took. But, in fact, the money was only eight pounds. One *could* live on such a small sum — but not easily and not well. Most certainly, one could not live on it *and* keep a bevy of lawyers happy.

Christina was distressed. She couldn't imagine fighting Richard — and paying for the fight — on this. She had already borrowed more from Evangeline than her cousin could really spare. If Richard tied up her money in the courts, Christina didn't know how she would manage. She sent the matter under urgent cover to her lawyers in London. Then, bravely, she wrote to inform her father of the matter. He had intended the money to be hers — to be a small freedom from a husband's parsimony, not the object of it.

This made two letters now that Christina had written to her father. In the first, a week ago, she had tried to explain what had happened, where she was and why. Thus far, however, Winchell Bower had not acknowledged her letter, her divorce, or even her existence outside of her marriage. She wasn't optimistic he would communicate over this new matter.

Then, another misery. After fretting over her correspondence all morning, Christina was eager to be outside and off for her walk. She all but flew out of the house. And there, within the first hundred yards of the back terrace, she twisted her ankle in a rabbit hole. She railed at herself as she hobbled home. Stupid, clumsy, preoccupied, she simply hadn't been watching. But no amount of self-rebuke would cure the problem. The sore ankle kept her planted in the house for the rest of the day.

The next day, the house was frantic with activity. A barrage of new faces, servants, had descended upon the place. Floors were wet from washing. Heat and clamorous noises emanated from the kitchen; there were boisterous calls and chops. Smells wafted to the rafters. Marriages of

34

roasting juices and cleaning compounds. Roast duck. Vapors of lye. Beeswax and lemon oil mingling with the aroma of honey tarts. And all this with servants as intent on their business as if they were making the wax and honey themselves. The earl was expected to arrive by that evening or next. With "guests," as Evangeline had said. Christina's absent host was traveling in the company of an indeterminate number of "friends"—perhaps fifty to one hundred people.

Depressed at the prospect of this invasion, Christina tried to escape to her room. But, even here, the place was intolerable with activity. Furniture and parcels were even being brought into her own rooms! Then, out the window, she spied her deliverance. Horses. More than a dozen truly beautiful horses were being marched toward the carriage house and stables.

"Shall we leave?"

"Half an hour more?" Adrien suggested. The earl stood at the edge of the woods talking with Thomas Lillings. Several other men waited back near the trees.

Thomas nodded.

"If she doesn't come by then, we'll just have to give up." Adrien spoke to the men behind him. "We'll have to resume as if everything were all right. And wait and see."

Adrien watched the open grassland that separated the group from his house in the distance. He was smoking a cigar. It was dark and fat compared to the long fingers that held it. And it was also somewhat chewed. It had not been a good day. It had not, in fact, been a good twenty-four hours.

He bit down. Smoke puffed off the end of the cigar. "Who spoke to her last?"

A square-set man, Sam, grunted acknowledgment, then added, "But it was only a message: She would keep the

35

appointment as arranged."

"When was that?"

"A week ago. No, six days. In London. She still had hopes of rescuing her brother, the message said." He snorted. "She was hoping for the Englishman's help. That was all."

"Right." It was a clipped, sarcastic reply. But it was himself that Adrien was put out with. He paced a few steps, exhaled again. They waited.

They waited for a woman none of them had ever seen. But all of them, uniformly, were feeling the tension, a gnawing in the belly, from the effects of their contact with her.

Two weeks ago this unknown woman had begun making helpless pleas to friends of theirs, haphazard messages intended "to reach the right man." She had said she was a French aristocrat and that, like so many other French *émigrés* in England, she was trying to get her family out of France. Over the last two years, France had become a very dangerous place to live if one was a "former" aristocrat: All titles and privileges had been declared null. Any nobleman who didn't bow immediately to the new equality of the land was subject to imprisonment often followed by death. Political opposition to the reigning powers was silenced in the most efficient way possible—the heads of those who spoke eloquently for the aristocratic viewpoint were severed at the neck and discarded in a basket.

The woman in question had pleaded just that: She could not get one member of her family out of France without help. Her brother, she claimed, was a prisoner in La Force, a prison on the outskirts of Paris. He was being held as an "enemy of the revolution" and was on the list for the guillotine. Having had firsthand knowledge of the random violence across the Channel, Adrien had been very sympathetic to the woman's plight.

Unfortunately though, he had learned the night before

that the woman and her whole story was a ruse. There was no brother—though there most certainly was such a prison. It was the administrators of that prison who had sent the woman. She worked for them. Imprisoned French aristocrats had been disappearing from La Force for over a year. All escapes had been successful. All escapes were beginning to show the earmarks of a single mind. And all had left a trail to England. The woman had been sent out to find the source.

The source, very uneasy now, was smoking a cigar and rearranging, with the toe of his boot, bits of moss and leaves on the ground.

"Crazy," Adrien Hunt murmured. He had caught himself half hoping the woman wouldn't show up. Yet, this was an insane hope. If she didn't come, it meant she had already deduced whom she would be meeting. Not only would French authorities be making life difficult for him in that event, but there was now an English authority who would be, he marveled, a little upset with him. The Old Man, from whom he had inadvertently gotten the information about the spy last night, had made it perfectly clear he didn't like anyone interfering in foreign intrigues in France. As Minister of Foreign Affairs, he considered such matters his sole prerogative.

Adrien slowly raised his head to stare along the line of trees. He was idly playing with his cigar again when all motion in his body ceased. He stared off at a point in the distance, his head erect, his eyes narrowed.

A rider was coming. She—for the rider looked to be female by an abundance of skirt that rode to the side—had not been immediately visible because she'd been riding not across the grass as they'd expected, but keeping to the cool screen of shade, much as they had been doing.

"Thomas! Sam! There she is! Get to your horses and circle behind her. You four, cover the front, then Charles and Phillip pull out to cover her side. Herd her back into the clearing. The less we startle her, the easier this will be."

Christina had not been riding ten minutes when she realized that the shapes moving just beyond her, in the shade of her woods, were other human beings.

She stalled on her horse, mesmerized by their sudden appearance, then all the more fascinated by their sudden action. They were a very busy group, one minute restlessly milling about, the next pouncing to horses in great haste. Then, quite surprisingly, they were mounted and, it seemed, bearing down straight at her.

The horses they rode had coats that glinted in the sun. The men were all well dressed. Bright splashes of white lace pounded to the rhythm of a gallop as they closed in—

They were pressing down on her! She reined her horse in a half circle. More men were coming out of the woods just behind her. They, too, veered in her direction. She reined her animal around. Then back again. The horse reared in protest. But it was true. My God, she seemed to be somehow a target for these men.

The sound of galloping began to sound like thunder. Then a cracking. The glint and posture of a raised pistol. Someone had fired over her head. She needed no more encouragement. She bolted for cover. Into the woods.

The mare was a marvel. It surged into a gallop. Miraculously, it seemed to know its way. Into the thick of trees and vegetation they both plunged, at a speed that sent Christina's heart straight into her throat. But she could hear, by the sounds of her pursuers, that she had surprised them. She actually gained ground ahead of them.

Voices came into the forest after her. Cursing, calling to one another. "This way!" "Cut her off there!" But they were having difficulty overtaking her. Again, she blessed the animal beneath her. It was a miracle. It knew the woods. It leaped a fallen trunk, then jagged around a low branch that would have unseated her. She was going to get away.

Then a sharp explosion rang out.

It seemed so distant, the shot. But its effect was immediate. The ground beneath her began to give way. As if everything were caving to the center of the earth. Christina was suddenly aware of blood. Everywhere. Pouring, gushing. Wet and sticky at her knees. The mare's blood. The horse was going down.

Christina had to scuttle to keep from falling and sliding beneath it. The mare was screaming, screeching, deafening her eardrums. But there were other sounds. The men closed in. There was no time but for a brief look as Christina leaped. A ghoulish sight. The animal was flailing, its underbelly running red. Christina ran in mortal fear.

Mindlessly, she tugged and scrambled through any opening that materialized among the trunks and leaves. Her clothes caught, rent. The skin of her face and arms and palms became brushed with scratches. She didn't notice. A collision with a sturdier branch stunned her for a moment. But the calls of her pursuers — crisscrossing in front of her, behind her, from all sides now — added fuel to a kind of hysteria which drove her to more desperate impacts as the forest resisted her flight.

The woods were alive with crunching, rushing movements. Tears began to run and blind Christina's vision. Her breath was coming hard and fierce, dotted with tiny sobs of frustration. Her movement, she could hear, was being followed now by someone with agonizing efficiency.

"Arrêtez, madame! Ne bougez plus!"

She didn't understand. Futility began to weigh on her. She began to lag. Her lungs burned. Her side had developed a knifelike stitch in it. But it was her ankle that finally brought her down. The sore ankle got a jolt going over a gnarled root, and there was no recovery.

A mouthful of dirt. Her teeth snapped violently. A dull bounce of forehead. Cut tongue . . . Momentarily spots

. . . Dizziness . . . The earth pounded and roared in her ears. Feet running, tearing through the brush. Men. Shouting. Stomping. The distant shrill sound of an animal's moan piercing all of this, over and over. She could hear the mare dying.

Then the warm, metallic taste of blood in her mouth as someone rolled her over. Blue sky through treetops . . . A smatter of white clouds . . . A strangling headache tightened at a temple. Her whole face washed cold. Only bubbles of consciousness . . . Faces overhead, blotting, blackening out everything . . . A hot hand patting her cheek . . . Someone speaking in fragments, unintelligible phrases . . . Then, nothing.

Chapter 3

Consciousness spread slowly, as though only the surface of her mind were thawing. All was quiet. There was a slight chill, dampness from the ground, from her sweat-drenched clothes. But something had been wrapped around her to keep her warm. This was all the world Christina knew for a long time. This, and the slow rhythm of breathing, a paradoxical feverishness in her eyes, and a deep, contented lethargy.

In time, a soft conversation drew her head around. She unfolded further, turning on her shoulders to see behind her. Her tormentors were perhaps thirty feet away, standing by the dead horse. She was lying at the opposite edge of a small clearing.

Then she noticed, not all the men were standing. One was squatting by the dead animal's head. It seemed he was the one talking. He was somehow the center, the focal point for the rest. Every other man's face was turned toward his.

He was a curious man, the one man near the ground. Unlike the others, he was missing his coat. This gave his white shirt a dazzling conspicuousness. Billows of sleeves escaped from a snug waistcoat. Mounds of white neckcloth. And over his high collar lay hair as shiny and black as anthracite.

The man stood. And another difference. He was taller than the other men. Very slender, but somehow solid. And there was something a shade foreign about him. He wore the brown, dull colors of an English country gentleman, but there was an excessiveness of lace, of cravat that was not strictly English. Christina linked this, if her memory could be trusted, to the baffling French that had been spouted at her.

The man turned. He seemed to catch sight of Christina in her new position, and was on his way over. Christina had the strangest sense suddenly . . . déjà vu.

As he stooped down beside her, the slightly dandified impression was again evident. He smelled of a spicy sweet water, though the smell was somewhat subdued by scents of the outdoors that clung to him. Leather, horses, grass, sun, perhaps tobacco.

He smiled. "You're not in very good order after all this, are you? Can you stand?"

Again, the sense of something familiar flickered. But, uppermost, she was wary of his concern. "I doubt it. My ankle—"

His immediate and rather businesslike examination of her lower legs startled her. Though primarily for the loss of sensation in one foot.

"I'll cut the boot off if you have no objections," he said. He called back over his shoulder, "Someone find me a knife." Back to her: "Here, sit up a little."

She jerked away from him as he reached to help her.

He paused, gave a mildly put-out look. "Are you going to panic again?"

"Not so long as you don't kill anything out from under me."

"Yes." He made a pull of his mouth. "How *did* you get hold of that horse?"

It hit her. She had been a bit slow, but there it was. He looked different. Thinner. More tense. And something—what? More serious. Yes, the Earl of Kewischester looked infinitely more serious, sadder than when she had last seen him at the dinner party.

"Your grooms lent it to me."

He was taken aback. It was the same game all over again. He didn't know her . . . .

Then she thought perhaps he did. "You?" He gave a puzzled frown. "Oh God. You're the woman Evangeline has put in the house. Now I understand where you came from." He muttered and shook his head. "None of us could figure it out. I had completely forgotten —"

And it seemed, conclusively, he had. He did not know the woman he had almost kissed three years ago.

A knife arrived. The man who brought it remained, with downcast eyes. Like a convict awaiting his sentence. Or a chance to escape.

"Thomas," the earl addressed the one who had brought the knife. "Is this still the woman you think? It's a bit hard to tell, I would think, with all the bruises and swelling taking shape."

Christina looked up. She hadn't seen Thomas Lillings since her wedding. But it was a huge relief — and a puzzling sense of having misunderstood something somewhere — to see him now.

He ignored her. "It is," he answered. "It's not a mistake I could make." Then, with a painful sigh, a pained expression: "For God's sake, what are you doing here, Christina?"

"I should be asking you."

"You almost got yourself killed, you know."

"By you?"

"By your own insanity. You damn near made us all into murderers with your craziness —"

"My craziness! You idiot! You chase a woman down, shoot the horse out from under her, then have the nerve to suggest —"

"That's enough." Adrien interrupted. "You were set upon by thieves, and we came to your aid."

"What?" She pushed herself all the way up to look at

43

him. "You what?"

He looked her right in the face and said it again. "You were set upon by thieves, and we came to your aid."

Her fear and confusion turned slowly to anger. What kind of game was this? And Thomas, her friend. She could feel even his complicity against her somewhere. She looked around. The other men stood back. They wore hangdog expressions, a sense of wrongfulness that, though weary, seemed determined to stay wrong.

It was the earl who appeared to be their spokesman. She addressed him. "I know perfectly well by whom I was 'set upon.' And I don't intend to participate in any hoax to save anyone's good name. I want to know what is going on."

He eased the last of the boot from her ankle. The foot was swelling badly. She looked down at herself. Her clothing was ripped and torn. Her dress was askew. Her hair hung down in ratty knots from her rough handling. And there was blood on her skirts.

She pulled away sharply, as again the earl reached for her.

"Easy, my dear. I am only pulling the coat—"

It was his coat she'd been lying on. He brought it up over her shoulders.

"Now." He began to lecture as one might to a slow child. "This might all seem very unfair to you. But we are all going to stick fast to our story of thieves. The nine of us. If you want to try to concoct a different story, that is up to you. But no one will believe you." He made a tired, rather nasty facsimile of his former smile. "And I am a wonderful liar, madam. I know just the sort of details to lend a story credibility. So give up. We will take very good care of you, see that you are comfortable, and right this unfortunate incident as best we can. Don't ask for more. You won't get it."

He got up abruptly. "You talk to her, Thomas. And can you bring her back on your horse? I thought I might go

44

prepare the way." Then, once more, the earl turned to her. And with the logic that was now becoming characteristic of this encounter, he blurted something at her in French, something about a meeting; *un rendez-vous*. His face waited for a response.

Christina threw a rock at him. A fist full of leaves. Whatever was at hand. "What? Do you think you are a bloody prince! You pompous bully! If you think I am going to go along with any harebrained whitewash of what you've done . . . They should have finished you in France!"

He was watching her. "Should they?" Again, he said something in French, as if they actually might have a conversation in this language. What could she possibly know, she understood him to say, about the people in France?

But the use of the foreign language only infuriated her. Sometimes she understood a sentence in French, sometimes a word, and sometimes nothing at all in whole mouthfuls of the gibberish. "Speak the King's English, *s'il vous plaît*. I don't speak the bloody language."

He smiled then, possibly at her accent. She had a bad one, she knew. But in any event, this seemed to satisfy him. He turned, only speaking again as he mounted his horse. "I will see you all back at the house." To Christina, he made a mock bow from the saddle. "And you, madam. *Je vous souhaite la bienvenue*."

Welcome home.

Chapter 4

Birds somewhere had decided it was safe to sing again. The sun flickered through the trees above, making patterns, phantasms, on the forest floor. The woods were quiet. The other men had followed Adrien Hunt back to the house. Only Thomas remained, fixing his saddle, moving a travel bag around to make room for two.

Christina sat on the ground. Her head hurt. Her swollen ankle had begun to give off a dull throb. She was covered with scratches and bruises—there seemed hardly a place she didn't ache or sting. But what was hardest to bear was Thomas. Testy and secretive, her old friend was no better than the rest. He wouldn't say why—or even *what* exactly— had happened to her here in the woods. Worse, his mood seemed to say that he owed her an explanation—perhaps out of loyalty—but that it was all her fault that he should owe her something so impossible to give.

"Let it be, Christina. You've stumbled onto more than is good for you," Thomas said as he lifted her into the saddle. He looked up at her. "If I thought for a moment anyone would benefit by my satisfying your curiosity, I would empty my soul to you. But it would serve no one's best interests." He steadied her a moment, then swung up behind her.

"Especially not His Lordship's."

Thomas made an irritated sound. "You've not the first

46

inkling about him, Christina—" He paused. "Or do you? Do you know him from"—he made a gesture with his hand that supported her back—"somewhere?" There was an implied incredulity in the wave of his unseen hand.

"No. Why?"

"Nothing. It was he who picked you up and carried you to the clearing. I don't know." She felt him shrug. They began, at a slow pace, to make their way out of the trees. "It seemed to me he fussed over you a lot."

"Guilt."

"Perhaps." He paused. "Or he just liked messing about with your legs and skirts."

She didn't like that—the way Thomas had said it. "Actually," she said more honestly, "I met him once. But he seems to have forgotten. I suppose it was nothing."

They rode in silence.

Thomas broke the awkward quiet just as they were approaching the house. "I beg of you to cooperate with us, Christina. I can't explain. Only I wish you would trust me." He paused. "And Adrien really is a nice sort. Better than that actually. He's first-rate, top-drawer. I wish you would give us all a second chance—"

"Top-drawer people don't go about shooting horses out from under people."

"He didn't shoot the animal."

"He's taken the responsibility for it."

"Yes, he has, hasn't he?" His tone sounded as if he had won some sort of point on this issue. Then, a more pleading tone; the old Thomas. "Christina. If you only knew what all he has on his mind, what he has been through. He's handling some very touchy, rather complicated business, and doing damned well with it. Incredible, in fact. And more than just the eight of us are grateful and dependent on him for it—"

They were at the house. Thomas slid from the horse, then carefully took her from the saddle and into his arms.

Then something odd. His face came very close to hers. And he did an even more peculiar thing. He bent and whispered to her, "I had forgotten how beautiful you were, Christina." He laughed softly. "Even messed up a bit."

She sighed and turned her face into his shoulder. Yes, she had forgotten too. She only knew its absence when she felt, suddenly, its presence again: It had been a very long time, but in Thomas' arms she felt feminine and lovable again.

The real injustice was that everyone believed the earl's story of thieves, just as he'd said they would. By the time she arrived, it was pat; done. The house was swarming with friends. She was carried in, looking more like she had been dragged in by the cat, feeling awful. She was simply too tired to explain in the face of all the sympathetic strangers who seemed to "already know, you poor dear."

Yet, even this wasn't enough. When she told Thomas where her rooms were, he began cursing under his breath. Bloody hell. Carrying her in his arms, he stomped up the stairs in a silent fury, as if she were the worst traitor in the world.

Her sitting room now had a giant, carved desk planted awkwardly in its midst and yet more trunks and boxes. Then, the most surprising addition of all: Adrien Hunt was in her bedchamber. He turned as Thomas marched in with her. The earl's breeches were open; he was tucking in the tail of a fresh shirt.

"What is this?"

There was a brief moment where no one said anything. An awkwardness that seemed larger than the sum of three bewildered adults. Christina squirmed. She felt helpless somehow in Thomas' arms.

Irrationally, she demanded, "Put me down!"

Thomas, with equal reasoning, did so.

The ankle didn't even consider supporting her weight. She flinched and, with a small cry, toppled. It was the earl who caught her.

He held her weight against him. "What's got into you, Tom? Will you at least slide over that chair—"

Christina's hands gripped the man's shoulders. She tried to turn her face, too aware of him. Beneath her hands, she could feel the fluid movement of his muscles as he stretched across the length of her body—Thomas, irritatingly, had put the chair only within arm's reach. For an instant Adrien Hunt's hips—and the open pants—pressed against her. No amount of tucked and folded linen could quite obliterate the fact from her mind. The chair scraped on the floor. The muscles of his shoulder contracted; his grip around her waist tightened. Christina clung for an instant, her face muffled against crisp, fresh-pressed linen; his shirt gave off a warm, masculine smell. Then she was lowered into the chair.

Adrien Hunt drew away from her, leaving behind a flush of embarrassment that radiated over her skin. He felt so different, she thought. Different from Thomas, different from Richard. Why? His movements . . . The texture of him . . . Even the smell of him . . .

He turned away slightly and went at the buttons of his pants. He, too, seemed a little self-conscious in this regard. There was an unexpected shyness to him, an ill-at-ease quality which she at once liked in him. Then it was gone. He ran a hand around the waist of the breeches and looked from her to Thomas; back to her, back to Thomas. "So, what sort of problem is there now?" He extended his arms behind him.

A manservant appeared from the recesses of the room with a fresh waistcoat. He helped the earl into it. Then Adrien glanced over at Christina's meager little pile of trunks now standing in the corner. He looked at her.

"They're your things?"

She couldn't meet his eyes.

He laughed. "We couldn't be getting off to a much worse start, could we?" He shook his head. "I couldn't understand—When I saw the trunks and that sweet little nightdress—"

"I was told to come to these rooms," she said defensively.

"Not by me." He was still laughing. The quiet laugh she remembered from the entrance room at the Baysdens. "Though I don't mind if you stay. But as you can see these are my rooms, and I don't plan on vacating them."

It was Thomas who objected. "This isn't funny, Adrien."

The earl threw him a look. "Indeed."

He seemed relaxed again. More like the man of three years before. He turned and began taking watches that were held out to him on a tray. He tucked one, two, three into the pockets of his vest. His man came around, fastening the chains through buttonholes. The earl raised his arms.

"Chapman," he addressed the servant, "as soon as you are done here, find Lily for me. We'll get Mrs. Pinn another room. Then I want to speak to the housekeeper."

A coat was held out behind. The earl put his arms into it. The servant took up a set of brushes. With brisk, even sweeps, the man began to eliminate lint, any tiny speck of imperfection from the exterior of the Earl of Kewischester.

"Thomas, has anyone sent for the doctor? I think someone should look at Mrs. Pinn's forehead and ankle."

To Christina's surprise, Thomas answered in French. A burst of fast words said in anger.

Thomas had, she knew, studied art in France, but it had never occurred to her this meant he would speak the language.

The earl laughed. A pleasant enough laugh. He said something in return. There was an exchange. The word *elle*—she—was bandied about. But Christina couldn't find a key word. She was lost.

After a minute, Thomas seemed marginally pacified. "I'll see to the doctor," he said in English.

The manservant followed him out, presumably to find Lily. Christina was left alone in the company of Adrien Hunt. In his bedchamber.

"I think," he addressed her, "you should settle down in here for the afternoon. It will take several hours for them to open up another apartment. The other guests have spread out to fill all the available rooms. But I won't be here, and I wouldn't mind at all if you would like to lie down on the bed. Shall I help you?"

"I shan't lie on your bed," she said tartly.

"It hasn't bothered you till now. I don't see—"

"I didn't realize. I'll wait in the sitting room."

He was going to argue for a second, then changed his mind. He shrugged. When he bent toward her, she braced herself away, pushing herself up into the back of the chair.

"What are you doing?" she asked.

"I was going to take you to the sitting room." He slipped an arm around her back, the other under her skirt and thigh. "Now, if you will put your lovely hands about my neck once more—"

He lifted her. Again she was in his arms. She cooperated, but didn't in the end know really where to put her hands. She cast her eyes down. His back, his shoulders were so broad. . . . His hair felt cool and dry as it curled over the silk of his cravat and onto her fingers.

There was a French chaise in the sitting room, also a new item. He put her into it, but rose frowning, staring. He looked at her for several seconds before he seemed to collect himself from whatever bothered him. Then he moved out of sight. He returned a moment later with the cover from his bed.

"Why are you doing this?" she asked.

"I think I had something to do with putting you in this situation. It seems only right I should help a little to get

51

you out of it."

"I won't like you for it. It doesn't make it all right."

He smiled. "You don't like me much to begin with. So I won't worry."

A small man came into the sitting room, a balding man with a thick black book. Adrien acknowledged him. The book was opened, and the little man began to write as the earl spoke.

"Tell Mansville I'll need a carriage for tomorrow, Thursday, and Friday. Then draft a note to Prince George. Tell him we will have a group on the courts Thursday if he wants to play. Oh, and the Princess Flavia is hinting broadly at her birthday again. Is it this month?"

"The fourteenth, sir."

"Find her something nice, would you? Then let me know what it is." He went to a trunk, opened it, and threw most of its contents onto the floor, searching for something. Gloves. He found grey kid gloves.

"How much, sir?"

"Oh, I don't know, you decide." He was putting the gloves on. "Find out what her husband's giving her, then aim just under that. We must please one without offending the other. Anything else, Dobbs?"

"The gardener has asked for the third week in August off. His daughter is getting married."

"That will be fine."

The housekeeper had come to the doorway. She stood there, not entering without permission, yet staring into the room. Her eyes touched each piece and parcel of it, including Christina, in her peculiarly objective manner.

Adrien Hunt almost brushed by the woman as he was leaving. "Oh, Mrs. Jameson, there you are. I'm dismissing you. I will have a letter of reference ready for you by tomorrow, though I am afraid it will be rather brief and qualified. This incident of the rooms has been most embarrassing to Mrs. Pinn—"

The woman was open-mouthed. "I only thought—"

"I pay you to know, Mrs. Jameson. And if you don't know, to ask. But we both know this is not the first confrontation we have come to, is it?"

"I was being discreet." The woman was going to argue with him. "The last several ladies that have come on their own—"

Christina could not see his face, but she saw that he pointedly stopped to look at the woman. Her face lost all its defiance. She stammered and retreated into silence.

"Dobbs will prepare the letter. I will sign it in the morning. I have arranged for a carriage to take you to your daughter's or wherever else you'd prefer. You can have this month's wages. Mr. Dobbs will give them to you. Have you anything else to say to me?"

She had bowed her head, displaying a hitherto unknown meekness. She spoke very softly. "No, Your Lorship. That would be fine. Thank you."

"Good. Dobbs," he threw this over his shoulder, "you'd best set up some interviews. Meanwhile, Lily will have to manage. Oh, and Mrs. Pinn—"

Christina stiffened. She felt suddenly like one of the others, called to account.

"I am most sorry for your discomfort today," he said to her. "All of it. If there is anything I can do . . ."

He took perhaps three seconds, a pause designed to imply that she might, at this very moment, ask something of him and he would comply.

But then he was gone.

As he went down the stairs, Christina could hear more people stopping him, his laughter, his low, deep voice responding, joking.

She looked around her. The man, Chapman, and Mr. Dobbs had begun to go through the sitting room, deciding what should go where, discussing the earl's preferences as knowingly, as lovingly as if they were their own.

Through the afternoon she watched the room take shape. And, in the course of the next days, something parallel happened to the whole of the house. What had hitherto been a jumbled confusion of décor took on an unforeseen character. The number of "things" did not decrease; in fact, the earl added to them. But a loose, almost mystic coherence developed. The interior of the house, room by room, became more livable. It was busy — literally with people and figuratively in its design. It was occasionally overwhelming in its profusions. But it also became comfortable to move through, elegant to the eye. As if by some sleight of hand or optical illusion. The huge house was like a picture that had been hanging a few degrees off center. It came into proper focus — unique and rich, made up of myriad idiosyncratic details — only after it had been set at the right angle. Only after it had been touched by the right hand.

Chapter 5

One good thing about the arrival of the earl and his entourage was that they all seemed to have a great deal to do. They hunted. They played tennis — the earl had the use of the Royal Tennis Courts less than two hours' travel away. They played cards. They went off on little trips. In fact, most or all of the group disappeared together for many long hours at a time. Christina still had much the run of the house.

By the beginning of the week she was on her feet again. But the recovering ankle only allowed short walks. It was chiefly through this limitation — and a revitalized curiosity — that Christina began to explore the house itself. The house fascinated her since its owner's return. Room by room, corridor by corridor, she began to know its libraries, halls, and public rooms. Today, she stood in the upstairs gallery.

It was a magnificent room. Long mahogany tables were set against each window, each window rising high overhead, patterned in hundreds of lead-mullioned diamonds. Draperies hung, from twenty feet overhead, down the edges of windows, along the legs of the tables, to the floor. And light. The windows sparkled with it, as if they were made of cut crystal — though they were only clear and clean and catching an early morning sun. Window upon window ran along one wall of the upstairs gallery. It was literally a gallery. Christina stood—leaning her knuckles delicately on one of the tables—in a long, mirror-lined room. Behind her, in front of the mirrored wall and all along it, were Greek and Roman statuary; gods and goddesses in stony nudity. In front of her, through the window and below, was a view of Adrien Hunt and friends. They were up very early this morning, after the fox.

Thomas was at her shoulder. "You're invited to go."

"And decline."

"Are you such a coward?"

"No. I don't like killing animals as much as he does."

"Honestly, Christina—" For the hundredth time, Thomas refused to discuss the dead mare buried out in the forest. "That's not what I meant, anyway. Not the meet. Kewischester himself. You're rude. You jump when he speaks to you. You refuse all invitations to be part of things."

"I don't feel part of things."

"You make him feel like some sort of ogre."

"He is."

"Is not."

She smiled at him for a moment, at the game from their childhood. They were getting on much better as the days went by. Much of their old affection remained.

She gave her attention back to the movement and people below her. "Who's that?"

She pointed to a woman with blond, curling hair, blue velvet riding habit. Tiny, pretty.

Below them, everyone's breath—even the horses—blew visibly in front of them. There was a subdued excitement in the air as well. Many more people than just the visiting guests had turned out. Almost all of the countryside was there. Local squires, townspeople. Even farmers who couldn't afford the horses and equipment to participate came out to watch. Horses pranced. People jockeyed their animals as they greeted one another. Grooms milling. Dogs barking as they were held back in their pack. For the first

56

time, Christina realized, she longed a little to be with them.

Richard, very quickly after the marriage, had taken them "home" to south Kent. He was not as keen as Christina for social gatherings. Nor for her manner of socializing. Being the first on the dance floor was "calling attention to oneself." Laughing too loudly, speaking too loudly, saying outspoken things, these all fell in a similar category; tasteless display. It had been several years since Christina had seen so many people all come together just for the purpose of having a good time.

Below, the horse of the woman Christina had just pointed out jostled the earl's animal, for the second time. Both horses reared slightly. They were jittery, as eager as the people to be off. Christina watched Adrien stand in the stirrups and bend to calm the woman's horse. A servant, one of perhaps a dozen circulating among the guests, came by with a tray of shot glasses, brandy. The earl reached for two and handed one to the young woman.

"Cybil Chiswell," Thomas answered.

"Are they an item?"

"Who?"

She threw him a look over her shoulder; *don't be dense.*

"I don't know."

"Does he call on her?"

"Yes. I think he does."

"They spend time together? Alone?"

"How should I know?"

"You know, Thomas. I know you know."

"And why do you want to? For a woman who won't let him visit or inquire how she is doing while she is in bed for a week. For a woman who runs the other way when she sees him coming." He made a snort of a laugh at this. "Actually, it's rather amusing. He doesn't really know what to do with you. He leaves you alone since that seems to be what you want. But I get the impression he doesn't like it. I think he is a little offended."

"Are you going, then?" She turned fully. She leaned her arms on the table. Thomas was dressed for the meet but had followed her up here instead. The gallery was close to her new rooms.

"Would you rather I stayed with you?"

"Not particularly."

He made a glum mouth.

She laughed. "You know Evangeline and Charles are coming this morning. I can't wait to see her. Besides, she won't let me talk to you anyway—once she comes. You know how she is."

Something came over Thomas. His face changed. As if he hadn't heard a word she had said. His hands took the edge of the table on either side of her, effectively barricading her against the piece of furniture. It seemed impossible, an almost laughable non sequitur, but he drew closer. And suddenly she believed he was going to kiss her.

On the mouth. "Tommy—" She turned away.

His face found hers again. His mouth, dry and warm, pressed against hers. Then his arms came around her, and his mouth wanted something less chaste.

She let him finish. Then she pushed him back gently. She bowed her head. "Why did you do that?"

"I don't know. It's occurred to me several times before."

"That I'm fair game now?"

"No. But I know about your husband, if that's what you mean. And I wouldn't have kissed you if you weren't divorcing him. There would have been no point."

Her eyes came up, wide. "What did you say?"

"You would have probably hit me."

Her expression remained astonished.

He laughed. "Which I hope you are not still contemplating."

"No. The other. About the divorce."

"Evangeline told me. And I think you have every right to rid yourself of him—"

"Thomas." She was shaking her head. "You don't understand. It's not that way."

"I'm sure it's more complicated than that. I don't mean to oversimplify—"

She wanted to laugh, only she knew she didn't dare. Sweet, dear Thomas. He would always give her the broadest benefit of the doubt.

"No." She shook her head, smiling again. She placed both hands on his chest. "No. You don't understand at all."

"What then? Explain it to me."

She laughed. "Dead horses, Tommy. We'll leave it out in the forest; we'll leave this conversation here."

She turned, gave him her back again to watch out the window. The horns were sounding. And Adrien Hunt, she could swear, was looking straight up into the gallery window.

"Don't do this," she heard Thomas say behind her. "I'm not hiding things from *you* just on whim."

"Nor am I you."

"The other is not something I can discuss."

"I understand. I was half killed by you and some of your friends, and you can't offer me even a vague explanation. Fine. Neither of us needs to make explanations to the other." She sighed. "And now, if you want to catch up to them, you'd better go."

She stared out the window. And there, below her, stood an absolute certainty. Adrien Hunt, half wrestling his horse to keep it facing the right direction, was directly below the window, looking up at them. Christina's chest tightened. He was something to behold, she thought. He was beautiful.

Chapter 6

An hour later, Christina was still waiting for Evangeline and Charles. They were late, which was absolutely typical. Christina surmised she would have several hours on her own to entertain herself. This was not something she minded. With everyone out hunting, the house was empty—only servants were about. And in the back gardens there would be no one at all. The gardener had gone to town on errands. Christina set off happily to wander through the immediate back portion of the estate.

Everything was lush. Spring had been early. And though it was only the end of May, summer had arrived. The garden was high and bushy and full of carefully groomed flowers. Christina made her way through the pristine rows and patterns to the huge fountain. There, water shot out from the wheels of a careering stone chariot, giving the impression of great speed on the surface of the pool. It was just beyond the fountain that rows of high rosebushes began. Strange bushes. Not like those she knew. They grew thicker, straighter. Then, around one bush, she collided smack into someone emerging briskly from the other direction.

Adrien Hunt.

She was so taken aback she couldn't speak.

He more or less had to set her on her feet again. "Are you all right?"

"What are you doing here?"

He smiled. "I live here." He was still in his riding clothes.

"I thought you had gone hunting."

Again, he smiled. His face was censuring but polite—it said he was not going to account for himself to her.

"And your friend," Christina asked. "The one in the blue velvet riding habit. Is she with you?"

"Upstairs."

"How convenient." The casualness of his admission irked her. She was almost certain that, during the week since his arrival, he had not slept one night alone. The Chiswell girl had arrived the day before. And before that, there had been another woman, older, a woman who wore her hair swept off her neck in a chignon. "Well, then, run along. Don't let me disturb your plans."

He stood there, watching Christina. Quite softly, he said, "She's broken her arm. Her horse threw her."

"Oh dear." Christina looked into the folds of her skirts. "I am sorry."

After a moment, he snapped a rose off the bush beside them. "Here," he said.

She looked at it as he handed it to her. "What's this for?"

"To cheer you, I suppose." He paused. "You always seem to take everything so seriously."

She tried to give back the flower. "I have good reason." He wouldn't take it. "Life has been a little 'serious' for me lately." She bent her head and began to pick at the petals.

"Evangeline's told me," he said. "About your marriage, that is. I'm sorry it has been such a bad disappointment for you."

Christina glanced at him. "A 'disappointment'? Is that how she describes it? Thomas was saying something as well. What is she telling people?"

He laughed. "She only hints a great deal. As if being

61

very discreet. But I gather you are finishing it off with something of a frivolous skirt-chaser."

Christina laughed, too. The antithesis of Richard. But she did not want to think about Richard now. She touched a long stem on one of the rosebushes. "These are very pretty. Though strange. Not like anything we had at home."

"We grow them that way. It's a hobby. I've been crossing them for several years now. Playing with the color mostly."

She frowned at him. Liar, she thought. "Trying to make orange roses," she said.

He looked surprised that she should know. "Yes."

Who was he trying to impress with this? "It's your gardener's project."

He looked at her, perplexed but cordial. He contradicted. "They're my crosses. I write them out; he does them. He works for me." He stopped to look hard at her, as if trying again to understand the measure of her. "It's very much like Mendel's work, only we've not been as lucky. We've gotten some decent sorts of things, like these." He flicked something on a leaf—a speck, an insect— Then said quite innocently, "But every hybrid thus far has been sterile. The generations we need to refine color, shape, size, that sort of thing simply can't be produced." He shrugged. "A pity. Come, if you like, I'll show you my favorites."

She followed him, on a trace of guilt, a trace of curiosity.

He led the way deeper into the garden. Trees came up to the path here and there. The bushes grew higher, denser. And the air was warm and perfumed with roses in bloom. Butterflies—the outlined contrasts of Clouded Yellows, the brilliant color of a stray Adonis Blue—flickered in the shade or darted in an erratic pattern through the sun that filtered down to the garden path.

She felt a fool. He was polite. He wasn't disapproving or making harsh judgments of her. A gentleman, she realized as she followed him. Whatever else he was, he was that. Not a sham, no deceit, but something genuinely upper-class. Like the sound of his voice. She envied his speech. It had taken her so long, and several girls' schools, to achieve something similar. She chastised herself, Who was the liar really? All her life she had been masquerading, trying not to let people see . . .

They went around the last bend in the path, and, there, stood a little house. It was made of nothing but panes of glass.

"What—?" She halted.

He held the door open.

Inside, it was warmer. Though a gentle breeze cut through: Some of the panes opened out, hinged at the top.

"They're toward the back." He motioned, then guided, putting her in front of him. His hand touched lightly at her back. It sent a shiver through her. The first inkling she was out of her class, out of her league.

The glass house was not particularly small, but it was crowded with shelves of plants. Orange trees bloomed. Lemons. Pineapples. And at the rear, a wall of roses. Beautiful peach-colored blooms. He pointed to them.

"There."

"Oh—They're lovely!"

He moved around her, brushed her shoulder as he passed. She was more aware of him—of his body, its solidness, its peculiar grace—in the crowded quarters. She felt herself flush as he bent toward her. His chest came up against her arm and breast. He murmured an apology, as if this were perfectly excusable. He picked up some shears from the workbench.

One. Two. Three . . . A dozen. Methodically, he cut the flowers. When he offered them to her, she didn't know what to say. His smile, his pleasant friendliness, his sharp features were so magnetic. She damned all handsome men as she stood in a cloud of confusion. After a moment, she reached out. Then stupidly, promptly dropped the roses on the floor.

"Ah—"

Blood oozed from the tip of her middle finger.

His hand wrapped around hers. Smooth, dry fingers. He took her finger into his mouth.

She was stunned.

His mouth was warm. She could feel the gentle pressure, a drawing of his teeth and tongue. It took her much too long to retrieve her hand.

"Sir," she reprimanded softly. She looked away.

The floor of the house was raised, a solid foundation. Dirt and dried leaves were scattered about. Buckets half-full with water. Empty pots. Chaos on the floor. Then suddenly that thought seemed horribly prescient. As if he might throw her right there on her back, among the dried-out leaves. A stupid thought. But she couldn't quite get rid of the image. And worse, she couldn't quite decide if it repelled or attracted.

She looked up, blushing, tongue-tied; vaguely angry. She suddenly wanted out of the miserable little house. Why, in God's name, had she come back here? With a known philanderer? But she was anchored, without the first notion how to hoist free.

He bent and began picking up the flowers at her feet. A sudden ray of sunlight came over the workbench, cut across his head and shoulders. Then a butterfly, as if on that beam of light, made its way through the opening of the window. It swooped and danced over his shoulders. The broad shoulders. The arms that could pick one up as if one weighed no more than a feather pillow . . . .

The breeze died. The little glass room began to feel close, overly warm. He was picking up the flowers—six, seven, eight—and aligning them. Christina flattened her hand into her skirt to hold it back, to avoid stepping on his hands. She tried to take a step back, but a low shelf caught her, pressed into her bottom. It was strange, but this was somehow alarming. She felt agitated, fidgety. She looked at her finger. It had begun to throb lightly. There was a pinprick of blood.

He stood, the bundle of roses in his hand, and reached above her—his chest against her face. The smell of him again. Soap, tobacco, leather. Was he doing this on purpose? Christina felt suffocated by him. She held her breath, rather than breathe in his warmth, his humidity. She raised her hands. Lightly against his chest. Not knowing how to push him back without touching him. Then, on his own, he moved back. As if it were nothing. As if she weren't there. She was nonplused, a woman left in midair. She couldn't look at him. Yet, in nervous glances, couldn't keep from keeping track . . . .

He was wrapping a piece of paper about the stems of the roses. He set the tidied parcel on the workbench, then took another step back. He rested an elbow on an upper shelf and looked at her. There was a faint, ironical smile on his lips.

"I've frightened you," he said.

She was quick to shake her head. "Oh, no—"

He laughed. "Oh, yes. I'm sorry. I didn't mean to." He reached and caught her hand again.

She was half-flustered, half-piqued at the apology followed by the same trick. She flinched as he turned her hand over and studied it. Her hand was clammy. It shook slightly. His was steady, smooth.

He let go. She huffed a wounded breath and pressed her palm to her chest. "It will be all right," he said. He cocked his head to the side. "The cut, I mean." As if he could have meant something else. "And I am sorry for a moment ago. Only your finger just suddenly looked—" He shrugged, smiled—"It's what I do to mine. Honestly." His smile broadened—a flash of white teeth as brilliant as a bolt of electricity through the sky.

Christina blushed, turned her head away. She caught sight of the door, at the far end, down the corridor of plants. She really must leave, she thought.

Then she heard him laughing. "If you make a break for it, I'll drop you to the ground flat out. Wrestling team, you know, all the way through university. I'm a smash at a takedown."

Her eyes went wide to him.

His soft laughter again. "Sorry." He made a self-conscious apology with his shoulders. "Only pulling your leg. You look so bloody green." More soberly: "But I'm just a little insulted: What you must be thinking."

"I wasn't thinking anything."

"Only that I'd as soon rape you as look at you. Which is not true. I find looking at you exceptionally pleasant." He paused. "Why did you come out here with me if I frighten you so?"

No answer. Though it remained a very good question.

The breeze picked up. A long time seemed to pass with just the gentle movement, the soft brush of something leafy at the other end. Some of her tension dissipated down to something easier to cope with—the level of bees buzzing somewhere near the citrus blossoms. Then he broke the spell.

"Here," he said. He bent down, this time staying where he was. He brought out a book from beneath the workbench. He opened it. It contained entries in a neat hand. Latin names, cross-marks, lines. At the end of every page was written "will not set hips." Then, as he turned the pages, "sterile."

"It's my writing," his voice teased. "Shall I demonstrate?"

"No." She glanced at him. He seemed to be asking for something now; so sincerely, so guilelessly. She laughed. "You are a proper scientist, then. The new Mendel."

"No. A dilettante. With a hundred hobbies. But, yes, I would rather be taken a little more seriously than a simple cad. Thank you."

There was a nice moment. More silence. In which she

began to look at the book again. She turned a page, ran her finger down it.

"I'm barren," she said. It came out without design or reason. "The nonsense of my divorcing my husband is Evangeline's doing. My husband is divorcing me."

As soon as she had uttered it, she wished she could call it back. What a thing to tell someone. Why had she said such a thing to him?

But he seemed to understand too well. "He's a fool," he murmured. He touched her. His hand ran along her arm. It sent shivers through her; goose flesh. Then he took that arm, turned her by it, and pulled her to him. She found herself bracing her fingers on his abdomen. Her arms pushed. She held the distance.

He glanced down. "Am I supposed to force you?" he said. "Would that make it all right in your mind? I'm going to kiss you, you know."

"I wish you wouldn't."

He whispered in her ear, "No, you don't."

His lips were warm and sure. They knew what they wanted. They moved against her lips, feeling their shape, their softness. His tongue briefly tasted these edges—then, with perfect boldness, his kiss pressed her mouth open. His tongue went deep into her mouth, taking every square inch. Christina squirmed a moment. Everything seemed to be turning over on itself. A kind of horrible yet fascinating movement at her core; like oil rolling up over water. Something rose in her chest, sunk in her belly. Her breath felt tight, compressed. Her breasts tingled against his chest. She was suddenly aware of the texture of his silk cravat, of the smooth, soft wool of his coat, of her own cambric dress. As if, on their own, her arms, her breasts, her belly could take notice of such things. Her whole body, in fact, seemed to come alive in a way that made her feel a stranger in it. Her heart pounded. Her head swam. Her legs wanted to buckle—

After a time, his arms loosened. Just a hand ran down her arm. She exercised the option this gave her. She stepped back to lean against the workbench. Then, another touch; he had to steady her for a moment or she would have fallen against it. She couldn't speak. She couldn't breath properly. She put the back of her hand to her cheek — her hands were ice, her cheeks on fire — and looked at him.

He was frowning. His chest was noticeably rising, falling. He closed his eyes and made a noisy exhalation of air. "I keep underestimating you," he murmured. It took him several seconds more to continue, "You're so beautiful, no —" he actually took it back with a shake of his head — "much worse than beautiful. You feel —" he couldn't quite find words — "extraordinary in my arms."

She looked down. "Oh, don't do this."

"I want to make love to you."

She stared back up at him. "I wouldn't allow it."

His eyes were watching her so intently. She felt that he might look right through her, that something she wished not known might be on the edge of his perception.

"I think you might," he murmured.

She felt the blood rise in her face. She turned her head away as far as she could. "What incredible cheek —"

He exhaled a dubious breath at this, amused. "You tremble when I touch you," he said. "You face flushes easily. And you watch me. I hardly enter a room that you don't. Or from a window." He let this sink in. "I'm seldom wrong about such things."

"Yes, I can see you'd be expert on ladies' flushed faces. With this sort of conversation." She turned away. "I should go."

A boot came across the narrow corridor of plants — she collided against his leg. And, at the same time, collided directly with the first tremors of genuine alarm. He had braced his leg on the rim of a citrus pot, blocking her exit.

Her hands fell lightly on his thigh—lightly on the strong, solid muscle that, unabashed, could hold her where he wanted her . . . .

"Don't play games," he murmured. "I know part of you is interested. My God, you can't conceive. You're not a virgin. You're not married."

"And I'm not a trollop."

He sniffed at that. "I was suggesting something rather exclusive and private, not the Royal Navy."

She made an uncomfortable laugh. "I can't believe you're so frank in asking—I don't know what to do in the face of such presumption."

"Give in."

Again she laughed nervously. But the only response that would come was to shake her head *no*. She stared down at her own hands resting on his leg—then watched as his fingers closed over hers. He tugged her around.

Christina found herself standing directly between his legs.

Emotion surged. Apprehension. Anxiety. Something more . . . She felt trapped by the workbench, a wall of plants, and an aura—a spell cast by the most charming, most forward man she had ever met. While he stood so close . . . Then closer. He leaned a forearm on the elevated thigh, his face a breath away.

Christina glanced down at the barricading leg. Something about this must have amused him. He laughed.

"Do you see yourself struggling on the floor," he teased, "against my improper advances?"

"No," she said, too quickly.

"Good." There was a pause. "I would hate for you to struggle."

Her eyes grew wide. "But I assure you I would, if—" She couldn't finish. Again she couldn't look at him. A tension in her stomach knotted into something she couldn't quite define. God, he was so bloody attractive . . . . So damned close . . .

An arm smoothed down her back, tried to pull her to him. She put out her hand. "Don't—" she said. "I can't— Not here." Recognizing what she'd said, "Not anywhere."

"Anywhere you like. Lie with me."

"You're mad."

His head tilted; his look for an instant was vaguely mean. She could imagine him angry. It gave her a sudden insight into something that Evangeline had said; that all his charm had a mark of tyranny running through it. He wanted his way, damn anyone else; never mind that he was pleasant about it. What she hadn't understood though—a misjudgment that had put her where she was now, clearly in over her head—was that these words, *tyranny, too-charming, a menace,* had nothing to do with the cad proceeding against protest. They meant rather something much smoother; a gentleman—articulate, soft-spoken—proceeding to induce complicity.

Her mouth trembled as he leaned to kiss her. But she didn't turn away. She let him take her mouth. Dimly, timidly, she knew she wanted to feel this, sense this, taste this again.

But this kiss became different. His mouth accepted her submission, then twisted and took a kiss from her in a way she couldn't believe existed. His arms lifted her hard against him, the flat of his palm pressing her to him by the small of her back. Then, as his tongue came fully into her mouth, his palm rubbed downward over her buttocks—a slow slide of pressure. She could feel the whole length of his body against hers as he pushed her into him. And his body pushed back; a slow, deliberate movement.

Christina had never known a less innocent kiss. She tried to be appalled. Through the bulky layers of clothes—her petticoats and skirts, his breeches, a flap of coat—she could feel him. Male, tumid, hard; his blatant intentions were outlined solidly against her own fluttering stomach. Yet,

70

try as she might, she couldn't be offended by the way he kissed her or the way he felt. Rather, she found herself impossibly attracted. Without realizing, without consciously willing it so, her mouth opened up to his. His tongue penetrated deeply. While every female sense in her body responded to his sharp masculinity. Her arms wrapped around him. She rose up on her toes, letting his arm bring her up to help equalize their heights. Her legs parted slightly as he pulled her, tight, against his hips; he pressed himself against the rise of her bone. Christina's mind lost all coherent thought. His arms felt strong . . . . The muscles of his chest and shoulders were hard, contoured . . . . His legs had a muscular length . . . . And his hips, as they conveyed their small, suggestive pressure, were the devil's own . . . . Then a stray, outrageous observation: For all its grace, his body would be heavy; his weight would feel sublime.

Christina tore her mouth away from his, scrambling, trying to pull away from this thought. "Please — My God —" She turned her head away. She had never had such a strong reaction to just a kiss and the simple presence, through a dozen layers of clothes, of a man's body.

This time, however, he didn't release her. He let her pull her face away, but he kissed her throat. He held her to him firmly, his lips traveling into the soft, sensitive place behind her ear where her jaw met her neck. Christina groaned. What began as protests on her lips somehow muddled into soft exclamations of pleasure. It made no sense to allow this, but sensation by sensation, she found herself delaying, promising herself she would stop him in a moment . . . . In a moment. . . .

He found her mouth again, and, again, she didn't refuse him. He was so tender, with such an incredible touch . . . .His hand went to her face, his thumb stroking her cheek as his fingers went around into her hairline. Then, slowly, the hand began to travel down her spine.

71

A second later, a warm draft brushed across her shoulder blades. It felt beautiful. Then alarming. My God, she was coming literally undone: The hand, his fingers descending toward her waist, knew unerringly the pattern, the hooks and fastenings of a lady's dress.

The thought roused Christina. Yet, her responses were sluggish. "No—" She managed to get her hands around.

He stopped readily. But the damage continued to accumulate. The bodice felt no longer snug. Her breasts lay loosely against the opened neckline. And he eased the neckline down a little, just off her shoulders, and bent his head. He kissed her throat and neck and shoulder. Then his hand, through the fabric of her dress, pressed her breast. He pushed it high over the edge of the loosened neckline to where his mouth could find it.

"Oh, God," she murmured. She wet her lips. She couldn't seem to catch her breath.

His lips and tongue felt moist against her skin. They left a hot, heavenly trail that ran along the neckline of her dress, then dipped down between her breasts. While his hands went into the dress at the shoulders, sliding it downward—She caught her dress just as it fell to her elbows. Bare shoulders. Open down the back. Only her crossed arms saved any modesty.

She clutched these layers of fabric, her last defense. But this left her with no means—no hands—to stop him otherwise. His palms smoothed freely down her naked back, opening the dress further. She heard his breathing rasp, catch. He shifted. He had to brace himself against a low potting table; he was in no better shape than she. Christina began to stir restlessly in his arms. While Adrien's fingers reached into her hair.

Hairpins hit her shoulders, tickled as they brushed her bare skin on their way to the ground. The mass of copper-gold hair followed heavily to her shoulders, then down her back. Adrien buried his face at the curve of her neck as he

72

spoke a litany of soft phrases, none of them intelligible. None of them, in fact, in English. Then, as if it were the most natural thing in the world, he drew her arms down. The dress fell.

Bare breasts. High. Round. Faintly trembling from the rise and fall of her breathing. *"Mon Dieu, Christine—"* he murmured.

He said something more—soft, foreign—as he cupped his palm under a naked breast. His hand lifted, felt the weight of the exposed breast. Christina's body arched.

"Ay—" She called out as his fingers gently enclosed this soft curve of her body, possessing it, squeezing, tugging at the nipple . . . .

Halfheartedly, she raised her hand to his, thinking to pull it away. Yet, somehow, this seemed an impossible effort. His mouth began to plant wet kisses along her collarbone . . . . She moaned in frustration. If she could have quieted his movements for just a moment . . . But his dark head bent further. The smell of his hair, clean, warm, filled her senses. And he took the pink tip of her breast into his mouth.

She let out a half-sob and reached for him, taking his face into her hands. My God, she had to stop him from such indecent, unearthly pleasure . . . . But he took her hands and kissed their palms. Heat shot up her wrists like jolts of lightning. And he slipped the last of the dress from her wrists and shifted her around. The low table—full of pots he cleared off with one sweeping clatter—hit her in the backs of the thighs. He bent her backwards. She caught herself on her arms, fell to her elbows. And he pressed forward.

Distantly, Christina remembered she was trying to stop him, but the reason for her resistance had blurred into a glazed heat behind her eyes. He bent over her, taking her other breast into his mouth. Pleasure spun out on pleasure, darkened. Nothing existed but the feel of his tongue and

73

mouth making their gentle pressure on her bare flesh.

A soft breeze blew through the greenhouse. It cooled the wetness left behind on the abandoned breast, contrasting this—a mild irritation—with the warm sensations that enveloped the other breast as he covered it with his mouth. A kind of maddening feeling took hold; wanting him to be everywhere, to make her feel warm, liquid in every curve and crevice of her body. She arched slightly, offering her breasts, her nakedness to him.

He took it. His knee came onto the table, claiming a place between her legs. The weight of his hips came onto her. Christina let her arms slip out. She lay back on the table. She felt herself sinking . . . melting . . . . Let him, she thought. My God in heaven, let him. Whatever he wants. . . .

Then, suddenly, nothing. Nothing at all.

With an abruptness that left Christina floundering, the man above her became still. The moment stretched out, quiet, vacant. Vaguely, Christina became aware of the wind chimes by the terrace, far off. They clattered beyond the bushes and flowers and trees. While there, in the greenhouse, time itself seemed to have halted.

Adrien remained bent over her, half on top of her. She could feel his abdomen, alive like a warm animal against her, moving with the rapid rhythm of his heart, his breath. But his chest remained raised. He had turned to look over his shoulder.

She made a soft moan, "What's wrong—?"

He put his hand over her mouth. "Shhh."

"What?" She was in a fog of longing, a sea of confusion. What in the world was he doing now?

"We have company," he whispered. He took her by the arms, trying to gather her up. But she was limp as a doll. His mouth brushed her ear. "Tonight," he murmured. He folded up the front of her dress to cover her; a caress, a shiver . . . .

And this time, Christina heard it too. Evangeline's laughter. It carried on the wind. It blended into the sound of the odd bits of metal and piping that hung, tinkling, by the terrace steps.

"Thank you, then," Evangeline's voice said, "I'm sure I can find her now." Then a light little tune. She was singing. Evangeline was humming and da-da-da-ing her way down the path that led to the greenhouse.

Chapter 7

Evangeline's voice closed in on them. "Christina," she called, "Christina!"

But a voice close to Christina said her name differently. "Christina, stand up," Adrien whispered. "I can't get to the back of your dress." He was lifting her to her feet.

It was like coming up out of a drugged stupor. The air on Christina's face — on her bare shoulders and bosom — felt cold. Reality washed over her. And suddenly, she couldn't look at the man in front of her.

"Come on. Turn around," he whispered.

She did so, clutching the top of her dress.

He lifted her hair and draped it over her shoulder. His hands nimbly took hold of the back of her dress. The fastenings began to close, a precise movement at her waist moving upward. "Tonight," he spoke near her ear as he worked. "I have to speak to the doctor about Miss Chiswell's arm, then I have to get her home. But she doesn't live far. I'll be back by nine —"

"No —" The word was physically difficult to get out; as if she had lost the power to express her own will. "No," Christina reaffirmed. "I — I think we'd best leave things where they are —"

"I won't be late —"

"No." She turned, letting her dress remain incompletely fastened. She needed to stop the delicate touch of his hands, needed to move him away from her. She took his fingers in hers and pushed him back. In the distance, Evangeline could be heard, splashing in the fountain, calling in the wrong direction. Christina wanted to get through this as quickly as she could. "I've done a horrible thing, I know, letting you believe—"

"You're done nothing horrible—"

"I've let you believe I would"—she could think of no nice way to say it—"that I would be"—a pause—"available to you." God, what an awful way to put it. She bowed her head.

But his fingers took her jaw and brought her face up to look at him squarely. She glimpsed the angry tilt of his head, the querying brow that was trying to imagine any other explanation. "Available?" he asked.

"Don't make me explain. I don't understand it myself. But you mustn't touch me—"

His frown deepened. "Why?"

She became aware of a ring on his finger, the hardness of gold and stones pressing into the bone of her chin. She lowered her eyes. "Because there is a woman upstairs with a broken arm."

"I didn't break it."

"Not her arm."

"And what's that supposed to mean?"

"And there was a woman before that."

"You want to be the only one?"

"No—" she stammered. Is that what she wanted? "No."

Evangeline had at last found the right path. Leaves rustled. Footsteps tapped along the stones in their direction. While the two of them stood there facing each other.

He let her lower her face. "What do you expect from me, Christina? Love? I don't know you well enough to love you. I only know what I feel at the moment. I'm fascinated by you."

"Like a cat in heat."

He let out a breath. "Christina, you knew what I was when you came back here with me. In fact, I think that was part of the attraction—"

"All right," she snapped. "I was curious. It was wrong of me, but I was. I'm very sorry—"

"I want to sleep with you."

Her eyes flashed up at him. "Well, we don't all get what we want."

His jaw tightened. He drew himself up. And Christina experienced a moment of regret. She tried to mitigate the brutality of her remark.

"Honestly," she offered, "I would have no idea how to go about having an affair with a man like you. I would make a mess of it, saying, wanting all the wrong things—"

But his eyes had frosted completely.

And the next moment, there was a tap at one of the windows.

"Am I disturbing something?" Evangeline was coming around to the door.

She opened it, stepped in. She smiled a quizzical, almost mischievous smile. "There you are, Christina. I'm so sorry. John-John threw up this morning and there was no getting away from the house until he was quieted down—oh dear—" She looked from one to the other, Christina to Adrien. Then very sweetly, softly, she said, "I *have* interrupted something, haven't I?"

Evangeline smoothed a wrinkle from the shoulder of Christina's dress. She picked out a leaf from the ends of her hair. "Well, you *are* a dark horse. How long has this been going on?"

"It's not how you think, Evie. I have just offended him horribly."

Evangeline laughed. "By the looks of you, it's the sort of offense he's quite used to."

"No—"

"Well, never mind. He recovers quite quickly—and is not put off nearly so easily as you might imagine. If he fancies you, Christina . . ." Evangeline let her words trail off. She seemed to be looking at Christina in a new light. Then she shrugged and turned. She leaned against the door of the greenhouse. "He can be very persuasive, you know."

"Have you slept with him?" It wasn't a very polite question. But a whole number of rather impolite things were suddenly running through Christina's mind.

Evangeline paused, picked at the spines of a pineapple. "There's hardly a woman in fifty miles who hasn't."

"Then you have?"

Evangeline's face came up. Again, the full contemplation. "Then I have. Several years ago." More genially, she held out her hands—"Don't be an idiot, Christina. He won't be true love, he won't marry you, but he's lovely; I can tell you that much." She cocked her head. "What do you want, for God's sake? You've already tried Prince Charming and he didn't turn out to be very grand. Maybe what you need is a nice, pleasant Prince of Darkness who'll stroke your thigh for a time."

"Evangeline!"

"If I were less a friend, I wouldn't say it. And"—she paused—"if I were less a friend I wouldn't warn you: There's half a dozen women in these parts half in love with him. Don't give him a foothold there. I've seen what he can do, the kind of damage he can wreak. He's a nasty customer, Christina. I hope you understand what I'm saying. He's attractive, sweet, lovable, but absolutely selfish and self-centered. The only way you can deal with him is to be absolutely as perfectly full of self-interest as he is."

Christina had never heard Evangeline—any woman—speak like this. The philosophy seemed vaguely wrong, but she couldn't say where. It seemed also to have a bit of right to it.

79

"Evie. Another thing."

"Yes?"

"In French." She embarrassed herself, yet she wanted to ask this. "Am I losing my mind or does he make love in French?"

Evangeline gave a brief, wondering smile. "Why, yes. I think he does."

"Why—how?—would an English lord do such a thing?"

"His mother was French. He was raised there. He didn't come to England to live until he was sixteen or seventeen." She paused. "I think he's developed an English accent over it now. But he was, at one time, quite fluent." Then Evangeline laughed lightly. "Why? Has he said something filthy?"

"I don't know. I don't understand him most of the time."

Evangeline gave a wicked grin. "Well, I know *all* the dirty words. You must let me help you."

"Have you got a grammar? A lesson book?"

"Probably. Somewhere?" Evangeline looked puzzled. "But you're not likely to find what he has to say in textbooks."

"That's all right. I want to brush up anyway. It will be something to do."

Evangeline sighed and ran a hand back over her hair. She had forgotten. Her hair was a disaster, pins and pieces dangling. She groaned. "For all the damage, I half wish I'd sinned a little more thoroughly. There's not going to be a soul to believe I've been attacked by yet a second band of thieves."

"You mean you haven't?" Evangeline was coming to her rescue, picking up strands of hair, smoothing in pins. " 'Sinned thoroughly,' I mean." Evangeline threw her head back and laughed. "You are in a state, aren't you?" She was picking leaves off the back of Christina's dress as well. "But, my darling coz, I wouldn't give you a tuppence for your chances of staying clear of him in that case. Not if you got this messed up and still didn't finish the deed." Her laughter became uproarious. "Well. We are all about to see some very heavy courting. The mating dance of Adrien Hunt. It's been so long since anyone has bothered to make him go through it. Bravo for you, old girl." She patted her back. "Bravo for you!"

Almost immediately as he entered the house, Adrien was waylaid by Thomas Lillings, Sam Rolfeman, and Charles Sloane. Thomas and Sam had helped bring Cybil Chiswell back to the house. Charles, Evangeline's husband, had just arrived.

"Where have you been?" Thomas asked. "We've been looking all over for you."

"I went to the stables to see how Miss Chiswell's horse was faring. I sent a stable boy for the veterinarian. Has Dr. Willis arrived yet?"

"He's upstairs with her now. Adrien—"

"Yes?"

Thomas' anxious look seemed to accuse for a second. "I can't find Christina either."

"I just saw her out in the garden."

Sam broke in. "Mrs. Pinn isn't our main problem, you know. What's become of the woman we mistook her for? Have you heard anything more from the Frenchwoman we were supposed to meet that afternoon?"

All three—Thomas, Sam, and Charles—were in league with Adrien to rescue French aristocrats destined for the guillotine.

"Not a word," Adrien answered.

"Has she gone back home, then? Do the French know?"

"I don't know what's become of the Frenchwoman. But the French don't seem to know anything. Our friend in Paris has tested every likely vein in which the information would flow. No one at La Force, or anywhere else for that matter, seems any the wiser."

81

Sam was puzzled. "I don't understand it. Why would a woman come over here, spend seven weeks tracking us down to your very doorstep, then leave without contacting us or turning us in?"

"I have no idea."

"So, what do we do now?"

"Start up again, I suppose. Very cautiously."

"Then you still want to go the night after next?"

"It's either start again or be intimidated by this into ceasing entirely. Do you want to quit?"

Sam frowned. "No," he said quickly.

"Thomas? Charles?"

"I'm sure no one wants to quit," Thomas said.

"Good. You can ask the others. Unless I hear differently, I'll assume we're leaving Friday night, as planned. Meanwhile, I'll try to get hold of Edward Claybourne. He's the one who suggested that this woman was a spy working for the French. I'll see if he knows anything more."

"Oh—" It was Charles. "I'd forgotten. As I came up, a messenger brought this." He produced a note.

Adrien took it. It was from Claybourne himself, the English Minister of Foreign Affairs. He was demanding a meeting. Immediately. The note included directions to a not-too-distant house.

"So." Adrien sighed. "Claybourne must know—he must have realized the 'interloper' he was speaking to me about last week was, in fact, standing right there in front of him. I suppose, now, I'm to be called on the carpet." Only the week before, Claybourne had expressed a strong antagonism toward anyone 'meddlesome enough' to take French prisoners out of French prisons. He never liked anyone to cause the French more trouble than he did, having built an entire career on the age-old enmity between England and France. Adrien folded the note. "And I suppose I have to go. If I'm to pump any information out of him."

Reluctantly, Adrien went toward the stairs.

Halfway up though, out of the corner of his eye, he saw Evangeline and Christina Pinn come in the far terrace-doors. He stopped. Christina Pinn looked flushed. Her red-gold hair was a halo of tendrils and wisps — she had not gotten it up again too neatly. Her eyes were bright. Her skin glowed. She had never looked more ravishing, he thought. Adrien smiled to himself as he climbed the remaining stairs. Being gently fondled on a hothouse potting table seemed to agree with the woman.

Chapter 8

Claybourne made him wait. "Busy," a servant had announced. Adrien checked his watch: Three minutes past eleven. Then he resumed his pacing.

It had been dark when he had left the Chiswell house. He had taken the young woman home as soon as the doctor had finished with her arm. Then he had continued on to this place. The old minister's message had been explicit: "Come at once."

At once, indeed. Adrien checked his watch again. It was beginning to look as though he would see the sun rise as well as set before he was home in bed. The Old Man hadn't changed a bit.

Adrien strolled, paced, drummed his fingers on the wall. He was in a small, dust-ridden room, empty of furnishings. The remote manor house to which he'd been directed in the note was deserted. Except for the certain presence of the old intriguer. The place reeked of his sense of drama. It was one of the few indulgences of a thoroughly disciplined man. Edward Claybourne loved to lend his unofficial doings a sinister atmosphere. It had always aggravated Adrien and, at the same time, strangely charmed him that the old statesman should add such unnecessary trappings.

Adrien had made a neat path through the dust on the floor, turned for the hundredth trip across the room, when the servant who had let him in returned.

"Here." The servant was an unusual creature. He was huge, perhaps seven feet tall. He gestured with a small lantern toward a dark hallway. Adrien followed.

The giant and his lantern led the way down a corridor to light coming from under a door. As the door opened, Adrien was surprised to find that Claybourne had, indeed, been busy. Another man, a stranger in a hurry, brushed by him.

"I'll be with you in a moment." A familiar, gravelly voice spoke from the corner of the room.

But the place, not the speaker, commanded Adrien's attention. The room was a glowing tribute to Claybourne's mood-mania. Only the far corner of the room seemed to have any light. A fire was crackling in the hearth there, but a large desk blocked much of the radiance it might have given to the rest of the room. Two small oil lamps burned brightly on the desk. Yet their light diffused quickly. They barely illuminated a settee that sat only several feet opposite the desk. The rest of the very large room fell into a limbo of flickering darkness, with only sheet-covered lumps — presumably furniture — populating the void in occasional bursts of dim firelight. Macbeth's witches would have been happy here: a tiny corner stage playing to a vast audience of ghosts.

The director of this little drama was behind the desk, stirring papers, not caldrons. He motioned with a handful of them.

"Sit. I'll chew you out after I have a look at you." Yet he continued with whatever absorbed him on the desk.

Adrien came up to the back of the settee and stared at the other man. It was instant déjà vu to see him in this setting. Edward Claybourne. English Minister of Foreign Affairs. Old Plotter. Old Man. Adrien had last worked for him three years ago in '89.

Adrien's young life had had a span in it when dissoluteness, sheer excess, had threatened to claim him. Then, one propitious night, Edward Claybourne had found him—being sick into the back pond of St. James Palace. "I've been watching you for months," Claybourne told him. "I know everything about you." Claybourne knew—and more importantly could speak neutrally about—the sordid details that had led Adrien there, to that night by the pond. And Adrien had rolled over onto his back in the grass, sick at heart, sick in mind and body, and listened. "What you need," Claybourne told him, "is a sense of direction, a sense of purpose. I can give this to you."

Adrien had first gone to France for Claybourne eleven years ago. He was sent over as a kind of unofficial diplomat. Under the old monarchy, Adrien's mother's family and friends were highly placed Frenchmen—from simply being raised in their midst, Adrien was on a first-name basis with French aristocratic power. This made Adrien, from the beginning, an excellent unofficial resource for those situations that didn't lend themselves to more formal negotiations. But, eventually, Adrien became more: Claybourne liked it best when Adrien would hobnob with the purpose of accumulating subtle influence and privileged information. And Adrien had his own reasons for rebelling against the French, the culture that had loved and reared him.

Adrien found out quickly that he liked this sort of work. Claybourne had been right on that count. It was a challenge. A great game—which, on his own, Adrien made into a strange kind of balance sheet, a game of double-defection: He betrayed France by giving England confidential information. And sometimes, by not telling Claybourne the whole truth when he chose, he betrayed England. By the end, he was a trusted confidant of both countries—a courier of secrets who played off what he could find out about one country against what he knew about the other. Adrien had once or twice come very close to getting caught, in both quarters. But this was all part of the almost suicidal pattern, the total apostasy Adrien had embraced in his early and mid-twenties.

And it was all before the Bastille—before a revolution had forced Adrien to reconsider, at the wrong end of a scythe, whether he truly wanted to live or die.

Adrien had run into Claybourne last week, briefly, at a very crowded party. Other than that, he hadn't seen the man since the night Claybourne had met his boat in Dover, the night he had bent over his stretcher with the compassionate words, "Is it revolution? Will it reach the streets of Paris? Tell me quickly, before you die."

Presently, the Old Man looked up across the desk. The same disquieting eyes. Small, black pistol balls lost in the folds and wrinkles of an ageless face. It was uncanny. The man always looked exactly the same. Neat, compact. Even the same manner of dress, white wig included, forever frozen in some style of the 70's.

"Well, come around. I said I want to look at you. You hardly gave me a chance at the Haverings last week."

Adrien obeyed.

The Old Man scrutinized him, up and down. He frowned, then spoke. "They said you'd recovered completely."

"They?"

"How do you feel?"

"Fine."

"You look awful."

Adrien suppressed a laugh, somewhat unsuccessfully.

"Well, you do. You must have lost two stones. And your hair. Is that the fashion?"

"No."

"Then why did you cut it off?"

"I didn't. The doctors did. I got used to it, I suppose."

"Well, I don't like it. It looks—ostentatious."

"It was less ostentatious when I tied it with a silk ribbon?"

Claybourne seemed without a reply. He stared a moment

longer, then dismissed the issue by going back to the papers on the desk. He spoke without looking up.

"Well, it's good you've come. I didn't realize you were up and about again. It is high time we were in contact—"

"My dear Minister—"

And the old face came up like a shot. "Don't use my name or title here. And I shan't use yours."

"What do you want?" As to his own new French activities, Adrien had decided he would wait to see what Claybourne knew before he waded into explanations and apologies. Then he would broach the subject of the vanished Frenchwoman-spy.

"I want you to sit down." Claybourne gestured to the settee, then went back to the papers.

He sat as indicated, having to remind himself to be patient.

During their brief encounter at the Haverings, the week before, Claybourne had tried to interest Adrien in rejoining him this side of the Channel. Telling him there was a Frenchwoman in London posing as a countess, Claybourne had suggested Adrien help locate her, "to find out what she really wanted." Adrien had declined. But the woman Claybourne had described—"posing as a French *émigré* and planning to meet some damned Englishman who seems to be helping French aristos escape prison"—had sounded remarkably like the woman Adrien and his little rescue group were due to meet the very next afternoon—the woman for whom they had mistaken Christina Pinn. Adrien imagined Claybourne would now want to touch on this project again. If he wanted to stay on Claybourne's good side, Adrien would have to listen patiently, politely, before bearing down on the issue of exactly who and where this damned Frenchwoman was.

The Old Man was in no hurry. He brought forth a quill and slashed a paper here and there with ink.

"The man who just left"—he gestured to the door with

the feathery end of his pen — "said no one could find you." He added, "The dolt. Where have you been? I expected you hours ago."

"I had an errand."

"I said I needed to see you immediately."

"I came as quickly as I could —"

Claybourne sniffed at that. "You and I both know you went off to some woman's house first .. . ." Adrien opened his mouth to explain, then thought better of it. "Bad enough," Claybourne continued, "you still cavort like you do. But to put me second to some quick spill of a woman's skirts —"

"Edward, why don't you tell me about France. I am sure that is more to the point of this meeting."

Claybourne cleared his throat. "Well." He went back to the papers on his desk. He seemed to find something there to smile at, a little glimmer of triumph. "Why don't you tell me?"

"Pardon?" Adrien shifted on the settee, bracing himself for the worst.

"France. It is nice this time of year, isn't it?"

"Yes."

"I was so delighted to hear you'd gone back again."

"You were?" That wasn't the impression he had gotten the week before.

"Absolutely. I never thought you'd set foot on French soil after that incident in '89." He paused. "But then, you have relatives there."

"Dead ones."

Claybourne looked up. He set his quill down and sat back in the chair. "And one slightly foolish living one."

"Ah." Something made sense at least. A little.

Adrien's grandfather, despite all efforts, could not be induced to leave the country where he was born. It was unfortunate. But Adrien half understood. The man was very old. His memory failed him at times. The familiar was his anchor to reality, to life itself. He *couldn't* leave France.

"All right," Adrien responded. "I have one. But he is not exactly the sort that would do your schemes any good."

"Indeed."

"He's been ill."

It was the first out-and-out lie. Something was cautioning Adrien. He could feel the old man's mind pulling with all its energy at something so tangibly that he could almost imagine a vacuum being created in the room.

In reality, the door had opened. Several puffs of dust and cobwebs had rolled across the floor. And, Adrien noted, the colossus-servant had entered.

The Old Man pushed away from the desk as he rose. He was not prone to pacing, yet he did two short tours to the fire and back before he caught himself. Hands behind him, he turned to face Adrien.

"Your going back on your own meant I could ask something of you. That, and of course seeing that you are so fit again. I want to send you into France. Old times."

Adrien laughed. "Old times there are gone for good. They've hanged or decapitated most of the people I ever knew."

"But there is a just cause—"

"I'm not much moved by causes. You, of all people, should know that."

"Ah, yes." The old mind seemed to reminisce. " 'All ideals drawing life from their own opposition.' Am I right? Heraclitus, I believe."

Adrien dropped his eyes. "I was very young when we started, Edward."

"Yes." Claybourne laughed. "The grim cynic of age twenty-three. Though you were an idealist of sorts." He paused. Then he began afresh. "So. If you don't want to appear idealistic now, perhaps a little revenge. French politics all but murdered you. Wouldn't you like a little of your own back?"

"Not particularly. If I have any complaints, they are against fate, history."

Claybourne laughed. "Still philosophical." He shrugged. "But I think I can ignite your curiosity, as I always have—"

"I'm really not going to begin again, Edward. If this is the point of this meeting."

The old minister turned his back, holding his hands out to the fire. "There must be something," he spoke softly into the hearth, "that could convince you to venture, for just a short time, from your safe life?"

"No."

Adrien received a quick look over the Old Man's shoulder. It seemed a forewarning, a last chance to come along peacefully. He knew he was about to be pressured in some way. He wondered, briefly, if the giant at the door would be part of it.

He made a vague gesture in that direction. "Are my arms to be broken for me if I don't comply?"

The Old Man looked genuinely surprised. "Gregory?" He frowned. "No. Gregory is here for *my* protection. And, of course, I wouldn't want you to leave until I've had my say."

"Are you going to need protection?"

The old minister turned slightly, cocking his old head in an obscurely amused manner. "Yes," he announced, "I think I may."

He made a deliberate show of turning to Adrien, as if now braved for a fuller confrontation. "Your life is safe," he said, "but your grandfather leads a very dangerous life, don't you think?"

"My grandfather is blessed with political acumen and blind luck. He's in an absurdly safe position for a former nobleman in France."

"His luck could change."

"Could it?"

"I have it on the best authority."

There was a brief moment before Adrien could ask, "What are you implying?"

The Old Man raised his brow and left the threat unspoken. He seemed to be savoring some better secret. Then, like a child in the knowledge of how secrets are most wonderful—in the telling—he went to the desk and dug into a side drawer. He produced a carved box. A humidor that Adrien recognized.

"Cigar?"

"No, thank you."

"Give it up?"

"How did you get that?" The box belonged to the French grandfather.

"It was by his bed. But we'll put it back. I promise."

Adrien watched, puzzled at the foolish pranks of the English statesman. If this was more melodramatic "fun," he found it to be in exceedingly poor taste.

The papers on the desk were picked up. The Old Man tucked them neatly into the humidor. "I have it on the best authority," he repeated, "that this will be found on M. La Fontaine's armoire tomorrow evening, if his grandson does not prevent that."

Adrien stared at the box as it was dumped into his lap. The sudden, concrete feel of it made his spine prickle. "You're serious," he said, still not quite believing it.

"Open it," the Old Man encouraged. He took a small breath. "Read them."

"I don't need to." Incriminating papers. Treasonous correspondence with Austria. Something of that nature was in the box. The right words in the right hands could, indeed, reverse his grandfather's luck.

Adrien opened the box and withdrew a cigar. He rose and went to the fire to light it, using the papers to hold the flame to the tobacco

It took the Old Man several seconds to realize what he'd done, then several more to react.

"Gregory!"

The move was predictable. The giant had, also, been predictable. Slow. But breathtakingly strong.

Adrien made only the smallest effort to defend himself and the burning papers. Just enough to test the giant's reflexes. They were nothing special—nothing like the man's strength. Adrien allowed his arms to be pinned back. This ended the scuffle.

The Old Man looked disproportionately frightened, considering he was free—by several feet—of the brief fracas. "Do you have him?" he asked.

With almost comic confirmation, Gregory grunted affirmatively. He gave Adrien's arms a demonstrative pull for good measure.

Adrien winced. "This is unnecessary. Call him off."

The Old Man came forward, still cautious.

"Truly," Adrien re-petitioned, "he is dislocating my arms for no purpose. Call him off."

The Old Man looked puzzled, even mildly disappointed. "It's all right, Gregory. But what's wrong?" he asked Adrien. "What's become of the old, slightly violent temper?"

Free, Adrien rotated his shoulders. Then he began to straighten himself, the lace at his sleeves, a button at his waistcoat. "I lost it in France," he answered. "I had it surgically removed, if you'll recall, by a band of French farmers."

"Ahh . . ." It was a long, protracted sigh that reconsidered, reevaluated.

Then a small, old hand seemed to come from nowhere to Adrien's face. His chin was lifted just enough to align his eyes with the old ones that looked into them.

It was an odd gesture, uncomfortably incongruous with any stretch of Adrien's interpretation of his and Claybourne's relationship. The condescension in it he would have expected. But an inappropriate almost-affection was implicit in the touch. And it went beyond—too intimately

93

past—what liking Adrien himself could muster for the old man. Adrien felt himself, for an awkward moment, in the position of being openly cared for more than he could even pretend to care back.

Adrien jerked his head away.

"Ah, there we go." The Old Man chuckled. "Traces of temper."

He flicked the Old Man a look, ran his hands down his lapels one last time. "I think I'd better go." Something in this situation was making his skin crawl.

A frail hand on his arm stopped him. He would, for some reason, rather have grappled with Gregory.

"We could be friends again," the Old Man offered.

"That's not very friendly, offering to see my grandfather to the guillotine."

"You are perfect for this. There is no one else even half so good."

He saw the new tack coming. He would be flattered and cajoled, if he allowed it. "You need to find a different man, I'm afraid. You won't draw up more papers, will you?"

No reassurance on that point. Instead, the Old Man removed the hand-on-arm to point a finger. "That's it. I have you. There's a very *different* sort of lady involved." With triumph, the Old Man's finger arced upward. *"Cherchez la femme!"*

"Femme." Adrien corrected the pronunciation. It was involuntary.

"That's what I said. It means 'search for the woman.' "

"I know."

"Do you remember the Frenchwoman?"

"No." It was another involuntary response. Suddenly, Adrien didn't want any part of the Old Man's knowledge of her. He could all at once remember the relief of having his belly cut open: lying in a French courtyard, in a pool of comforting blood, lying there in the sure knowledge that he was out from under the Old Man's thumb. "I'm handling

94

my quota of woman, Edward. I need my cloak." He glanced toward the servant. "Does he fetch, too?"

The Old Man blocked his way; a silly two-step dance. "You're being difficult," he accused. "You're too perfect for this. I *have* to have you do it." He tacked back across what he must have thought was a terrific, strong point. "The woman spy is said to be loose, as well as beautiful." He crimped his old face. "A real tart."

"This may surprise you," he said, "but I'm not particularly interested in being pimped out to strange women."

"Well, you could do it. You're not shy."

Adrien let out a laugh. "Just what is it you're asking me to do?"

The wrong thing to say. The Old Man had now been invited to discuss the matter. His old face lit.

"Remember the French spy I was telling you about at the Haverings, the one claiming an Englishman was raiding French prisons? Well, the French have lost her, too. No one knows what has become of her. And they have asked—no, demanded—our help in finding her and the mad prison raider, who they insist is English—though I have my doubts—they never can take the blame for their own problems. Anyway, given our present relations with France, I can't openly give their demand the proper horselaugh it deserves. What I want is for you to go to France, track down the woman, if you can, and see what she knows. Then humiliate the authorities of the New Republic by capturing this madman before they do.

"There. I have you, don't I? It interests you, I can see it. You are so right for this! This madman works so much of your old stamping ground in France. I don't know why I didn't think of you sooner."

Adrien was standing, frowning, smiling. This was surely a joke. Adrien *was* the "madman" raiding French prisons. Was the Old Man actually asking him to go out and find himself?

"You see," the Old Man continued, "the French think the woman is now protecting the man for some reason." He snorted. "Leave it to the French to make it into *l'amour* . . . ."

He had pronounced it *la mort*. Death. Adrien blinked. The Old Man anglicized every French syllable he spoke. But in this instance, the mispronunciation made Adrien's stomach knot up. None of this seemed quite real. Adrien sat, with a *plomff*, back on the settee.

"Are you all right?" The Old Man halted.

"Yes. I'm fine."

Claybourne patted Adrien's shoulder. He beamed, pleased with himself beyond measure. "I've captured you, haven't I?"

Again, the sensation. He knew. The old goat was pulling his leg. This was only his way of getting even, an elaborate punishment for not asking permission. Adrien waited, expectant that he would be let off momentarily . . . .

But he wasn't let off.

Through the course of the rest of the night, Claybourne discussed the project quite seriously, point by point.

War between England and France was in the air. Both countries were in the antagonistic position of considering it without wanting to trip it off accidentally — before they'd tallied and sealed up every possible advantage.

The French were considerably more upset over their prison absentees than Adrien had believed. They had listed a reward for any information leading to the raider's capture, and they were tightening security at every prison and detention center. Prison rescues were going to become more difficult.

And England — at least the English Minister of Foreign Affairs — was equally unhappy with a free agent mixing into French politics and waving the flag of England over acts against the French government. "It could upset a very delicate balance between two nations trying to avoid war."

Then, there was the French informer for whom Adrien's band had mistaken Christina Pinn. The Frenchwoman was a wild card. No one seemed to know where she was or what she knew. This particularly bothered Adrien — as there seemed to be a woman somewhere who might have all the information needed to see him arrested in France — and what? reprimanded? in England?

All of this left Adrien very uneasy. This, and the fact that the Old Man had an incredible amount of implicating information. Adrien couldn't, for the life of him, understand why he wasn't being confronted as the mad prison raider rather than being sent off to go find him.

But the full scope of the disaster didn't hit until the end of the meeting.

The old minister had begun to reorganize the papers on the desk, as if looking there for anything he might have overlooked. Adrien sat with maps, diagrams, forged French identification in his hands — even a draft on a Parisian bank where money would be routed to him. It was like an afterthought that the Old Man stooped and opened another of the desk's drawers.

"Here." He offered Adrien something else from this strangely well provided desk.

"What is it?"

It was a woman's scarf. A red one. Adrien took it. It was silk, of very fine quality. He rubbed it between his fingers, then, almost without thinking, drew it to his nose. It was strong with the musky smell of a woman's heavy perfume. Too strong. Its brazenness offended, like the sly smile of a soliciting whore. But it attracted, too.

"Trashy, but nice?" The Old Man's smile wanted a confirmation.

"It's nice," Adrien responded. "What am I supposed to do with it?"

"Tuck it into your pocket. Remember it."

"To whom does it belong?"

97

"The disappeared Frenchwoman. It was all that was left of her by the time we tracked her down to the room she used in London." Claybourne sighed. "I have a sneaking suspicion that, if we could find that woman, we could unravel much of this."

"You think she knows who the man is you're looking for?"

"She said she did. In a one-line note we intercepted on its way to France. But there were no particulars, and she vanished before we could get hold of her."

"Is there a way to know her if I found her?"

The Old Man pointed. "For one thing, she might smell like that. But, no, we don't have a good physical description. I wouldn't count on finding her. We haven't turned up a clue. I would simply keep the idea in the back of your mind. In case she finds you."

"I see." Adrien had put the scarf in his coat pocket. He fondled it absently, fingering the smooth folds, the wad of silk. Even out of sight, the smell insinuated. It was overpowering, hypnotic.

Claybourne began to gather up his belongings. Adrien stood, as well. He picked up the humidor that lay open on the little table beside him. Then the oil lamps behind him whiffed out.

"Coming?" he heard the Old Man ask from the dark.

"I'm keeping this," Adrien said. He snapped his grandfather's humidor shut and tucked it under his arm. Not that it would make any difference in regard to Claybourne's threat. The little box was only an indication, a token, of what he could do. It was for himself that Adrien wanted the box. As a material reminder: Before anything else, he was going to physically drag his grandfather from France, out of harm's way. Then he would have to decide what to do about the "meddling prison robber" Claybourne seemed so desperate to have out of the way.

"This prison robber," Adrien asked as they entered the

empty waiting room. "After I find him, what do I do with him?"

"I thought that was obvious." The Old Man had been about to blow out the one oil lamp in the room. He looked up. He had cupped his hand about the lamp glass. His visage waxed hellish above the flame. He must have known the effect, for he held the pose for several seconds.

Adrien looked away. The game was wearing thin.

"After you find him," the Old Man said. He blew out the flame. "You simply alert me. I shall dispose of him."

'Dispose' sounded rather lethal. "I'm not going to kill anyone for you," Adrien said.

"I wouldn't ask you to. You leave that to me."

"You do intend to kill him?"

No reply.

"But suppose the man were cooperative," Adrien offered. "Suppose he would even fall under your—jurisdiction?"

They had reached the front door. Dawning light flooded suddenly bright over the Old Man's compact figure as he stood poised in the doorway. He seemed to think over what Adrien had said.

"I hadn't thought of that," he answered. More thinking. Then: "Yes. If you can convince him to that sort of arrangement, by all means, bring him to me peacefully, alive. I would love to talk to this man." Claybourne sighed. "What a fascinating mind. He reminds me of me. Yes, I should love to visit with him." He turned and spoke over his shoulder as he walked out of the dilapidated house. "Before I hang him."

"Hang him?" Adrien wondered how calmly he managed to say that. He walked quickly after Claybourne. "How can you hang him? He's done nothing for which to be hung?"

The old minister's carriage was waiting some yards away. Gregory stood by its open door—no driver, no footman, no other servant about.

The Old Man stepped in and sat, then leaned his head

out the doorway. "I applaud your humanity, but you must learn some crucial lessons—if you ever decide to be a regular in this business. First, one never lends credentials to a promising usurper. The man will be discredited—French, English, or Hungarian, he will be discredited and hung. And, second, power and good reputation allow one an occasional misdeed. I shall capture the man for English diplomacy, then hang him for myself. And get away with it. Because, with the reputation I have so painstakingly built for myself, no one will consider a selfish motive. When I say this madman is a traitor and an enemy of England, I will be believed."

The Old Man cleared his throat, letting what he'd said sink in. Then he added, a little sadly, "You, my young friend, unless you change your ways, will always be the victim of reputation to the other extreme. Your few good deeds—if there ever are any—will be mistaken for bad, your truths for lies. God's mercy on you. Good night."

With that ominous ending, the Old Man motioned for Gregory to close the door. It slammed, then the carriage wheezed down the drive. It disappeared into a low fog that was rolling in with the dawn.

Chapter 9

By the time he stomped up his own front steps, Adrien was tired and irritable. He was greeted at the front door by Dobbs, Chapman, and a kitchen girl.

Dobbs began immediately, reading from a list. "Lady Meldown wants a reply for a party on the nineteenth. We have heard from the Scottish estate; the agent says the tapestries are bid currently at 95 pounds each. Then, Captain and Mrs. Hall have returned from India; they're hoping you will come by and give your opinion on a piece—"

"That's enough. We will have to deal with all that this afternoon."

"But, Your Lordship, there are two other bidders on the tapestries. And Captain Hall—"

"I said that was enough, Dobbs."

The man closed his book, a slow gesture full of grave reluctance. "As you say, sir."

"Will you be wanting breakfast now, my lord?" the girl asked.

"I'll be down for dinner."

"Sir—" began Chapman.

"I have no need of you now. I'm going straight to bed. I'll ring for you when I wake up. What is this?"

There, by the door, were two small trunks. He recognized them before the answer came.

"Mrs. Pinn, sir. She has sent for a carriage. She is packed for London —"

Adrien had already picked up the larger of the trunks and started up the stairs.

Christina barely heard the knock. "Yes, yes, in a minute," she called. She was preoccupied with a letter she was writing.

She blotted it and began to fold it. Then, on a whim, she unfolded the correspondence. She dipped the pen into the ink again. A postscript had occurred to her, which she added to a letter otherwise written with careful forethought.

Five days ago, she had at last heard from her father. His letter had been brief, succinct. She was to come home at once — had she lost her mind? He had hired the best firm of solicitors in London for cases such as hers. If that scoundrel, Pinn, wanted to take it that far, by God, Winchell Bower himself would handle the matter in court. Also, there were some doctors he thought she should see. He had spoken to several, and such things were never so cut and dried . . . He had several other ideas . . .

Christina had not liked the commanding tone of her father's letter. She did not like the idea of more doctors. She was not even sure she liked the idea of more lawyers. She only wanted what was hers and the peace to adjust and try to understand what had happened to the happy life she had planned for herself. And, to this end, she had an idea of her own. Unhappily, she didn't know how to implement it without retreating to her father's household — he would never deal with her from here; that much was clear. And this, she judged, was perhaps for the best anyway. The greenhouse incident had frightened her. For a number of reasons, she was going home.

Yet the present letter she wrote was not to her father.

She was beginning to suspect Richard of being more venal than she had realized. She had heard from his lawyers again. There was mention of a "sum." They continued to assert that Richard did not wish to make a "thing" of this, that everyone involved must think of the future. But this was beginning to sound more like a threat than a desire for peace. Everyone knew her father—Richard's lawyers included. Winchell Bower was already mounting for battle, preparing for war. He would not have his daughter found insufficient in any way. At least not on paper, in black and white. The counselor set great store by such things.

Indeed, the problem did not seem to be getting her father's "help," but rather keeping him from giving it.

Her father meant well, Christina knew. He truly did care about the "principles involved." She just didn't want to become the focal point, caught in the midst of one of her father's battles for principle. The one obvious way to stop this would be to get—to pay—Richard to admit some trumped-up culpability, pay to have the divorce decree read the way her father thought it should. Oddly enough, Richard seemed amenable to such a possibility. She wasn't certain why, but Richard seemed suddenly less interested in "coming off in a bad light" and more interested in money— provided it should fall to him in sizable quantity. And what Christina was interested in, at this point, was more information.

Hence the letter. It was to a firm her father had used on several occasions. For a price, they would "gather evidence."

The knocking came again, almost a pounding. "I'm coming," Christina called.

She opened the door to her sitting room, thinking it was the man come for her last bag.

"May I come in?"

"No." She was stunned. And flustered.

She couldn't believe the look of him. Adrien Hunt was disheveled. His cravat was undone, his coat and vest

103

unbuttoned. He had a dark growth of beard. He looked frayed, raw at the edges. And rather touchingly all the more human for the state he was in. Accessible. Even perhaps a little vulnerable.

Yet his eyes, the piercing blue, didn't yield to this. They pinned her. "Where do you think you are going?" he asked.

"Home. To my father."

"Like a frightened child?"

She looked away. This offended. For this was precisely her fear. That all her resolve might just be an excuse. That she, in fact, was just a child, unable to cope and running to Papa. "I'm sorry," she murmured. "I must go. The carriage will be waiting." She tried to close the door.

His hand slammed into it. He braced the opening a foot wider. "Why?"

"You know why."

"Remind me."

She looked down. Her free hand had begun to play with the buttons at the neck of her dress. "You know why," she repeated.

He let the trunk go. It made a dull echo, thump-and-clatter. "Must I really speak to you out here in the hall?" He put pressure on the door.

She leveled a censuring look at his hand, then his face. This stopped him.

He heaved a huge sigh and ran his hand back through his hair. "Why are you being so difficult?"

"My leaving will simplify things." She wanted desperately to put distance between them. "Your Lordship," she added.

He made an insulted snort. "Adrien."

She shook her head, *no*.

"Christina." His voice sounded soft, conspiratory there in the hallway. "I've kissed you. I've done a lot more than kiss you. You can use my first name."

Again, she resorted to head-shaking. She couldn't speak. She couldn't look him in the face.

"What then?" he asked. "There was no intercourse, so your virtue is intact."

What sort of conversation was this? Her face glowed from the frankness he insisted on. She could barely breathe. "More or less," she murmured. She struggled for a coherent answer. "I don't know."

His hand touched hers. He stilled the fingers that played with the buttons of her dress. "Then let's eliminate the ambiguity."

"No—"

Again, he dropped his hand. As if he would wait for a better solution. Then he changed his mind. He touched her face. Her eyes went up to him. Dangerous. He leaned and kissed her. His hand went down her side, around her waist. He brought her to him. Then, he covered her other hand with his, lifted it from the knob and pushed on the door. He stepped through.

"Don't."

She shoved at him, a little angry, a little overwhelmed. Not twenty-four hours from the greenhouse, and he was backing her into the same position. He turned her around, a slow spin. And suddenly she found herself pressed against the other side, the inside, of the door.

She heard the key turn in the lock.

She tried to push him back. "Don't. I'm serious."

He took her face in his hands. His thumbs stroked her cheeks. Tender. All she could see were the blue eyes in the vaguely unkempt dark complexion. They traveled her face.

"So help me," she promised, "I'll scream."

She reached up and took his fingers from her face— trying to render them harmless. Yet he didn't move away. She lowered her eyes.

His cravat hung loose. The first few buttons of his shirt, she noticed, were undone. The shirt was open: She had had sudden knowledge of him she didn't want. The hair of his chest would be dense, black. It showed at the edge of his

105

opened collar. She could smell the warmth of him . . . . Mingled with another, heavier scent she couldn't quite put her finger to. . . . Then she realized her mouth, her chin were resting on his knuckles. She was still holding his hands.

She turned loose, pushed away. He stepped back, at arm's length.

She leaned her head against the door while he studied her.

"Would you really?" he asked.

"What?"

"Scream."

She nodded, very soberly. Yes.

He thought about this. Then he let go.

He turned and took in his surroundings. He didn't seem to know the room. Or he knew it only in an abstract sense: a room like a dozen others he had walked through. He glanced at her last trunk, standing upended in the middle of the room.

"So you were going to sneak off, without saying a word?"

Suddenly, it did seem awful. "I was going to leave you a note," Christina lied.

"Oh, fine, a note." He threw her a sarcastic look, tapped his fingers once on the trunk.

She didn't know how he was doing it, but he was making her feel guilty. As if *she* were somehow the cad. "You should go." She moved toward him, trying to physically start him toward the door. "My carriage will be here—"

He raised his arm indignantly as she tried to take it. He slipped by her in precisely the opposite direction she was trying to get him to go. "Is this my note?" he asked.

Christina was left standing, bewildered, in the middle of the room. Then bewilderment took on a little anger, a little panic. He had picked up her letter.

"No, it's not your note! That's mine!" She crossed the room.

She reached. He sidestepped. There was a little scuffle. The writing table chair grated, went over backward. The desk slid as she came up against it. Then against him. She leaned, reached, all but leaped up the length of his body, trying to get at the letter. But all she got for her trouble was a lordly glance—which quickly turned into the sort of sharp, speculative interest she wished he would keep to himself.

She backed off, raising her hands from his chest cautiously, as if they had touched something prickly: This time she knew the scent. He was saturated with the strong, musky odor of a woman's heavy perfume. Her hands hovered in spite of this, still aware of him. She was stymied for a few seconds by an atmosphere, a warmth, the nearness of his naked chest through the open placket.

Christina drew a deep breath and rested back on her heels. Her fists clenched of their own accord. Blood seemed to rush from her face to her palms. She was so annoyed. By him, by his actions, her own reactions; and by the damned reek of him. He stood there, a virtual hallmark of carnal knowledge.

"Give me my letter," she said. "That is my private correspondence."

But he turned, lifted his long arm—he held the letter easily out of her reach. He began to read.

At first, it was pure perverseness; a nasty aristocrat in him not about to be told what to do. Then his eyes jumped down the page and back up. He took it in.

"Oh dear." He laughed. "Poor Mr. Pinn. But you will need money for this." He looked at her over the edge of the paper. "Do you need a loan?" Then a look of distaste crossed his face. "What's this? Here, at the end?"

"The main body of the letter is an investigation I want done of Richard."

"And the postscript?"

"You can read it for yourself."

He looked a little alarmed. "And will these people"—he glanced back at the letter—"this Mycen and Weller, do this for you?"

"Without a doubt."

"Do you do this often, to have it outlined so thoroughly?" She had shocked him. His voice was edged with concern. Good, she thought. He had certainly shocked and upset her enough.

"No," she answered. "But my father was very particular where he invested his assets. He rejected three suitors before he settled on Richard. And by the time I married him, my father knew the date of origination of Richard's father's title and every shilling and square foot of property Richard would one day possess. He knew the condition of the property, the succession of title, the line of inheritance to the property and money—and he knew that no one could stand between Richard and all of it, except the baronet himself.

"I married Richard because I was rather taken with him. But my father allowed it because his grandchildren were to be titled, moneyed people. From his viewpoint, I was married off on the best of evidence, tied up neatly with a silk ribbon, just like a brief—" She drew a breath, as if to continue in the vein of this speech. Then she abandoned the stance with a hugh sigh. She had heard the belligerence rising in her own voice. This damned man, this earl, made her too defensive. Too middle-class. "It's all a little crass, isn't it? Still," she spoke directly, "I intend to stoop to it again, to find out why the little ribbon seems to be unraveling now on Richard's end. 'Know thy enemy'?" she offered. "Or at least where one's best interests lie."

"And myself. Am I being scrutinized as an enemy or a potential husband in the postscript?"

"Neither. You're just a matter of curiosity." But she had him; she could see it in his face. She had asked them to make inquiries about him, and he had something to hide.

"Little meetings in the woods?" she suggested. "Conducted mostly in French? Over my prostrate body, I might add. I think I have a right to know . . . ." She looked down. Where she got the nerve, she would never know; she added, "But if you were serious about the loan, to tell you the truth, I could certainly use it—"

"Not with that last sentence. Get a pen. Delete the last line."

She was stalled for a moment, not certain she had heard right. Did he really intend to lend her money? And did a few questions asked about him around London really matter so awfully much? What exactly was it, she wondered, that he was hiding? She fetched the quill and scratched through the postscript. "Now. Why did that upset you so badly?"

"It would upset anyone. It's damn well going to give Richard a seizure."

"You know Richard?"

"Only vaguely. He has gambling losses. I don't know how heavy, but I've seen him at the tables in London."

"And you?"

He squinted at her. "I have my gambling losses as well. You're turning out to be one of them."

"Did it ever occur I might want to help?"

"Me?" He stared at her.

"Are you in some sort of trouble?"

He stood there. Tight-lipped. Immovable. Pigheaded. Like a recalcitrant child confronted with a deed he would never own up to. "You can't help," he said. "Just don't create interest in me in your circle of barristers, solicitors, and—what?—inquirers? I'll lend you whatever you want."

"You make it sound like blackmail."

"It is."

"Then I don't want it."

He looked at her. "Where will you get the money, then?" he asked.

She shrugged. "My father."

"And what will he want in the way of interest?"

He did not mean money. She knew what he meant.

"And what would you?" she asked.

He let out a laugh. "Nothing. How much do you need?"

"At least a hundred pounds. To begin with."

"I'll sign a draft this afternoon. You can pay it back at your convenience."

She couldn't believe he was talking of lending her the money. And so easily.

He handed the letter back. "And you should stay," he said. He ran his hand back through his hair and looked about the room as if just realizing where he was. "Among other reasons, I'm leaving. That is the problem, isn't it?" He glanced at her. "My being here?"

"Where are you going?"

He sighed. His hands went out for an instant, a vague gesture of helplessness. "France, again. Bloody France." Then he dropped into a chair that faced her. "Do you mind if I stay here a while?"

She frowned. She didn't know how to deal with this. Now that she had stopped his tirade, was she going to have trouble getting him out of her room? "Why?"

"No one will bother me here."

He looked more than bothered. He looked exhausted. And very comfortable, settled there in her chair. Even a little intractable. She didn't want to tangle with him further.

"All right. I still have one or two things more to pack."

But she didn't budge. He was slouched down in the chair, his legs stretched out in front of him. They seemed to go for yards. And he was staring at her.

She was afraid to move. She settled back an inch, perched on the edge of her upended trunk. Everything she needed — her gloves, her hat, her nightclothes — were in the bedroom. But she was afraid to walk by him, afraid to walk near him; afraid he would follow. Or, perhaps more, afraid that even if he didn't, she would walk into that room thinking of him, this image of him: Loosened, stretched out, at rest in a private way that made her remember the unique grace of his body in even the most awkward of circumstances.

It was he who broke the silence.

"Your hair," he said, "I've never seen that color on a woman before." He was thoughtful for a moment. "You know I used to dream of a woman when I was ill. They gave me opium, and I thought it was the drug that induced her image. She used to taunt me a little. I would ask her name, but she wouldn't tell me. Every time. She would only smile." He left a little pause. "When the opium began to not be my friend, I began to use the little fantasy. It was the one thing I could do better without the drug than with it. I used to make love to her. I used to lie in my bed and summon her, let her occupy my mind. It rather got me through." He paused. Then he shook his head in wonder. "She looked exactly like you. I can't explain it, but she looked exactly like you. It's why, I suppose, you so take me aback every time I look at you. I have the eeriest feeling when I see you sometimes. As if I've imagined you into existence. I keep wanting to touch you to see if you're real."

The blood flowed into Christina's face. She bowed her head. The little revelation embarrassed her. But it also unaccountably, overwhelmingly flattered. She would have explained to him, tried to straighten out the funny trick his memory had played on him—

Only he was waving his hand, as if to dismiss the whole thing. "Sorry." He changed the subject. "Has your host provided you with any brandy? Sometimes there is some by the bed."

"I'll send for some."

"No. God." He rolled his eyes, then closed them. He leaned his head back. "I don't want to give a single clue where I am." Then he squinted up at her. "Would you mind

111

terribly if I went to sleep?"

Whether she minded or not, he had come to his feet again. She watched as he stoked the fire in the hearth until it flamed and crackled.

She glanced at the door. It stood ajar, her last bag perched a few feet in front of it. There was her letter on the desk. A nightdress and chemise, a book, her hat and gloves were only a few yards around the corner. Why didn't she fetch them? She could feel the heat, the imminent stuffiness of the sitting room if he continued with the fire. He was making it into a blaze. The carriage would be there soon. But she remained, fascinated. The earl, unkempt, undone, was hiding in his own house. And she was the retreat. She had been so before, in an opium dream, without ever knowing it. She wanted to put the feeling from her, but she couldn't. She felt sought out.

He threw his coat and waistcoat over the arm of a sofa. Then he disappeared behind it. He had stretched out on the stones of the hearth. Too close, she thought. Christina wavered.

"Well, I have to get my things, then," she said.

"Would you let the drapes down as you go by?"

She did so. And it gave the whole room a cavelike darkness. Only the fire for light.

She stood, playing with the drapery pull for a moment, watching him. Almost immediately, he was still. And as his features, his limbs relaxed, something about him changed. Suspicion, contrivance, convention all seemed to fall away from him. In sleep, he looked strangely innocent.

Christina turned quickly and went into her bedchamber.

The moment disconcerted her. Going to sleep in front of her had suddenly seemed more intimate — more forward — than anything he had yet done. Only a wife, a woman who loved a man, had a right to see such things. His ease in front of her inspired sympathy and concern. She couldn't be properly wary, properly angry. Lying on her floor, he didn't seem so much the highhanded earl, the man who knocked her down among trees and rosebushes or came pounding on her door. . . . No. In that moment, he had seemed more likely a lovely, benign stranger. A ship-wrecked sailor washed up on her shore. . . .

Chapter 10

When her carriage finally arrived, she had been waiting for it — gloves, hat, and baggage — by the front door for more than an hour. There had been trouble with the rear axle, the driver explained. He had had to fix it on the road.

"I'm sorry you had difficulty." Christina was more than polite. It was such a relief to simply get in the carriage and move away from the house — and the man who made her feel so helplessly caught in something too large for her to control.

The offer of a loan was nice, she reflected. She was intrigued. But still, she wanted to consider the whole prospect from a safer distance. She had decided not to go to her father's nor stay at the earl's. She would contemplate her options from a boarding house for women in London.

Then, two miles outside the Kewischester gates, her new plans dropped abruptly out from under her. With a sharp crack and a long groan of splitting wood, Christina's carriage seat took a plunge. Her stomach stayed in the air. Her head was thrown backward, with a bash, against the back of her seat. And the carriage, its rear portion dragging on the roadbed, came to a bumpy halt.

Christina scrambled to a window.

Outside, the driver was yelling, trying to calm the horses. They were rearing and whinnying their disapproval: Something, some strap of the harness, had given under the impact. The carriage traces pointed straight up to the sky. The horses were wild to be free of the straps that were trying to pull them into the air.

114

Christina pried open her door and stepped out. Into thick mud. This had apparently proved the final strain. She bent to look beneath the carriage. There, the axle, in two separate pieces, lay sinking into the ooze.

"Oh, Lord." She jerked her skirts up. But it was too late. She had stooped the front of her dress into the mess. Her shoes were bogged in the sludge. Her skirts and petticoats were caked. "Good Lord," she repeated.

And just as she thought things couldn't be worse, there was a violent lurch of the vehicle. The driver leaped back. He had been trying to release the poor horses from the disabled contraption that held them. But, alas, they had released themselves. The last strap that held the team to the carriage broke, and the spooked animals bolted.

"We've broken an axle," she told the butler who greeted her. "The driver is down the road about two miles trying to chase down his horses. My bags are sitting in the middle of the road unattended." She had decided to ask for the favor all her shrewder inclinations had advised her to avoid. "I need a carriage."

The servant looked at her more as if she needed a bath. "My sympathy, madam," he offered. "Of course. But one would have to speak to His Lordship about such a thing."

"Fine. Where is he?"

The butler's expression took on a mildly uncomfortable air. "No one knows, madam. He came home early this morning. No one has seen him since."

It didn't seem fair, she complained to herself. She'd gotten by this once. But now she either had to go upstairs and confront him again — she knew perfectly well where he was — or else risk not getting a carriage outfitted soon enough to still travel by daylight.

Christina left her damp shoes by the door, left her hat and gloves, and dusted her dress-front the best that she could. Then she made her way up to her old rooms. She had had one successful conversation with Adrien Hunt. And one debacle. As she went up the stairs, she was trying to ascertain what she had done differently in each of the two private meetings with him.

Yet, as soon as she entered the room, all rational analysis evaporated. No logic could take into account the full impact of his presence, what he could do to a room—and particularly what he had done to her own sitting room. She had opened the door onto a wall of stuffy heat. Hot, dark, it was like walking into a tomb. The fire had burned down a little. A more moderate blaze. Then she caught sight of him and stepped back against the door.

He lay on the stones of the hearth, one arm thrown over his eyes, a knee in the air. Shadows from the fire danced across his white shirt. It was eerie. In the hot, dark room, the macabre feeling of a tomb came to mind again. Then she realized there was something more that conspired to make this true. Under his right hand was something bright red. Christina went closer. It was a scarf. Crumpled under his fingers, spread under his wrist like blood.

She frowned. The smell, the atrocious fragrance that had been all over him this morning, was even stronger coming from the scarf. It was a woman's scarf.

Christina suddenly had a lot less sympathy for his exhaustion. She reached over, about to wake him.

Then she stopped. She grew warm, much warmer than from just the fire. His arm had risen. He peered at her from beneath it.

Everything scattered. She couldn't remember why she was there, what she was doing, or even that she disapproved of this man and everything he stood for. She could only stare at him. The heavy eyes, shadowed by the arm. The face, caught for a moment without defense, without

116

guise; the dazed expression of a man aroused from sleep, of a man aroused . . .

And, where first she had been held only by his gaze, suddenly she found herself in a more tangible grip. His hand wrapped itself around her upper arm. She was being pulled down on top of him.

Her first reaction was to laugh. "What in the—"

She caught herself on her palms. He had the devil's own temperature. He was hot to the touch. Everywhere, he was heat. His chest. His shirt. Both arms went around her—the skin of his wrist burned where it lay against her neck. His fingers spread into her hair.

All humor left. "What do you think you are—"

But it was obvious what he was doing. He was pulling her down. His hand held her head.

His mouth was hot, dry, as if he ran a fever. Then his tongue, not dry at all. So warm; a liquid heat shot through her. Christina began to shake. Every sensation from the greenhouse—every stupid reason why she should have been ten times more careful, slammed into her with one manifold rebuke. You idiot, her mind screamed at her.

You clever, clever creature, her senses murmured.

The dichotomy she wanted to deny opened its mouth and breathed like a dragon through her. As real as fire. As sharp as teeth. She detested this man, she told herself; she pushed at him. He was a horror—the smell of the vulgar perfume, engulfing her, attested blatantly to the fact. But she was also hopelessly attracted. His sheer carnal appeal raged against her, to the point of blurring her mind and melting all reason.

She made a weak gesture of complaint. "Let me go—" She struggled for breath, for control, for coherence itself. She could feel the beating of his heart, the movements of his body, and her own responses to these. "No!" There was a catch in her voice.

"Scream." His voice was husky from sleep. But alert. He

knew what he was doing.

"What?"

He made a line of kisses down her neck as he spoke. "Prove to me you'll really scream. Summon help."

"What? Ah!" She arched her back, rigid. His hand had slipped under her tumbled skirts and run up the back of her thigh.

"God," he said under his breath, "your skin is like silk."

Out the corner of her eye, she could see the red scarf. She shoved harder against him.

He only laughed. And tightened his grip at her back. "You honestly confuse me. I don't know if you'll scream or not. But let's find out."

"No!"

"Poor thing" — another low laugh — "you don't know either."

She tried to pull away with a jerk. But his arm tightened until no struggle was possible. Then, very slowly, he rubbed his free hand over her buttocks; just the thin fabric of her chemise . . . .

"Oh —" she groaned; pleasure, anguish. His touch was so damned appealing. She loved it. And she hated herself. What had she done? She should have opened the drapes, opened the windows, put air in the room. Or called to him from the doorway, asked to speak to him more publicly. But instead she had enjoyed being closeted for the moment alone with him. She had tiptoed around him, spied on him, run her eyes over him as if being there alone with him gave her some private right. And now, God, he was having his own private privileges . . . .

She twisted her hands, tried to free them. But they were trapped between his body and hers. He held firm. "No! Oh, God," she whimpered, "I came back for a carriage. Mine broke down. Please. I just want out of here —"

"You don't know what the hell you want."

"I do! I want out!"

118

"Then scream."

Her eyes welled. Her voice faltered. "No—"

He kissed her.

She tried to fight this, but nothing would stop the pleasure that came over her, wave upon wave, with increasing tenacity. Both his hands slid under her skirts. He cupped her buttocks, pulled her against him.

"Oh, please, don't do this to me. I can't." Her voice trembled, cracked. "I'm not this sort."

"You're very much this sort. You're beautiful. Don't be an idiot—"

"Don't laugh at me!"

"I'm not. Only I'm not awarding you sainthood either. Can you be such a fool?" He spoke directly into her face, "Scream, if you want to. That would stop me."

He seemed about to kiss her again, with a belligerence that bordered on violence. When, suddenly, he jerked, blinked. A tear had dropped smack onto his cheek. Then another one. He wiped at his face, then looked at his hand as if he didn't believe it.

And Christina let out a sob. Followed by a whole concatenation of sputtering, hiccoughing tears.

"Oh, splendid." There was apparently something else that would stop him. "All right, enough." He sat up and reached for his coat. "Here." He handed her a handkerchief. "You are really peculiar, do you know that?"

Reluctantly, she took the handkerchief he offered. She blew her nose.

"What frightens you so?"

"When I'm not being raped?"

"You know what I mean. The act itself? Are you frightened of the act itself?"

"No." She tried to avoid his eyes.

"What then?"

She was silent. She didn't know.

He took her jaw and shifted her face to look at him.

119

"Talk to me or let me put you on the other side of this foolishness—"

"You," she said bluntly.

He was taken aback. Then immediately recovered with one of his charming—rather self-aware—smiles. "I don't think so. I think if it were just you and I, we would have been to bed a week ago."

She raised her brows. "A week ago—" The absolute nerve of the man! But she refused to be distracted by such a preposterous suggestion. "It's you," she insisted. "It's who you are."

"It's who *you* are," he countered. "The prim, priggish Mrs. Pinn. Why don't you relax a little? Thomas says you used to be able to."

"You have no right to discuss me with Thomas!"

Again the confident, easy smile. "I might say the same thing—with Evangeline. Or the Earl of Martingate. Or Lily on her morning rounds. Or anyone else you happen to corner for ten minutes—which, luckily for me, is not too many, since you seem afraid to mix with people in even the most trivial of social circumstances. Why, Christina? You want to sleep with me so badly you can't see straight. And I'm keen to accommodate you—"

"Accommodate me!" She gave him a violent shove and tried to scramble to her feet. But her wet, stockinged feet slipped on the floor. Humiliation added to humiliation. She recovered herself on her knees and plunked back to sit on her heels. "You ass! You pompous, conceited ass! I have every right to protect myself—"

"From what?"

"From—" She couldn't find words miserable enough to fix him. "From—from what consorting with the likes of you would make me!"

"Happy, for just a short space of time?"

"No. From what you, what other people already suppose a divorced woman must become."

"Which is?"

"A pitiful, lonely woman or"—she spit it at him—"a whore."

She had done it. His face lost all expression; he was astonished. "Christina, no one would speak ill of you. I wouldn't allow it."

"You can't control what people think."

"I don't care what people think. You shouldn't either."

"But I do! I care what *I* think. *I* would think badly of myself, don't you understand? I don't want to feel pitiful. Or sluttish. There must be something else besides wife, spinster, or rich man's mistress."

"A nun," he offered drily. "A blessed nun."

He was getting up. Rather awkwardly. His one leg appeared to be difficult for him to move.

He stood over her. "Christina," he added, "sometimes you must come up with a few answers of your own. And be willing to live with other people's relative inability to comprehend. It's called growing up."

She didn't like that. It felt much too true. That he was older, more grown-up somehow than she was. And she resented his saying so, especially when she sat there crying like a child.

"What's wrong with your leg?" she asked.

"I should go." He moved. But she saw him flinch slightly as he put weight on his left leg.

"What's wrong with your leg?" she repeated. She had to twist around. He had walked out of her line of vision.

"I was injured." He made a dismissive wave of his hand. He was picking up his coat. "It only bothers me when I get very tired. Usually the fire helps. Where's my waistcoat?" It had slipped to the floor. "Would you be so kind as to hand it to me?"

She did. He took it and then her hand. He pulled her to her feet.

With the toe of his boot, he lifted the hem of her dress.

121

"What on God's earth happened to you?"

She looked down. "Oh, dear. It's the reason I came up here." She looked at him, helpless. How could she ask for his help now? "The carriage I hired broke down a few miles from here and—"

He laughed. "You came here to ask me for a carriage?" She nodded. "To leave?" Again, humor had asserted itself into the features of his face. "After trying to sneak off, first when I was gone, then when I was asleep?" He shook his head in mock impatience. "Honestly, Mrs. Pinn, you are the rudest guest—and least accommodating woman—I have met in a long time."

"Would you help me?" she asked meekly.

He laughed. "Yes, Mrs. Pinn. You may have a carriage, if that's what you want. Though I think you are a fool to go. I'm leaving, as I told you. And I'll lend you money without strings." He held up his hands. "Absolutely without strings. I don't know where you'll find a better offer—"

"Why? Why would you do this for me?"

He took a step. Again, his leg seemed to give a little. He winced, then smiled. "Jesus. Stupid thing," he muttered. "Because, my lovely young woman, I hate to see people I like backing themselves into destructive corners. Especially when I can easily provide relief. Now." He walked around to collect his coat and vest, then saw the scarf. He came back for it. "I ought to leave, I suppose. I hope my barber hasn't disappeared too far." He held his left leg out, rigid, as he stooped.

"Your leg. It was in France?"

As he stood, she received another of his long, contemplative looks. It was not the look of trust or confidence. She didn't know how to change this.

But she knew how to offer him something in the way of compensation. "You know your woman? The one from your opium dreams?" She had his attention. "I am the one." She couldn't help but laugh. "In a sense." She tried to jar

122

his memory. "Christina Bower," she said. "You sent me flowers. Don't you remember?"

But his face didn't. It remained blank. His eyes responded politely. "Vaguely, perhaps." Then he shook his head. "No, not really."

"We were at a dinner party. We met in the entrance way. You were very mean."

He nodded, sober, as if he now recognized something. But she could see he didn't. "I suppose it was something you did quite a lot. Tease the ladies, I mean. And your mind was elsewhere that night. But you did find out my name. And send me flowers. My father flew to pieces over it." She laughed, embarrassed now that she'd mentioned it. "It's quite all right, really. I don't think the incident itself meant much to you."

"No," he said. "Perhaps not the incident."

They had a very nice moment. He stared. She smiled. Then he shrugged and shook his head, smiling. "You are the strangest woman," he said. There was a pause. "And I do wish you'd consider staying. I won't touch you, if that's what you want—"

"Yes."

It was an instinctive response. Somehow, he'd made it possible for her to stay. Then she realized how. He had offered friendship. And honesty. He'd told her bluntly what she needed. Money. A secure roof over her head. And people. She needed to become part of things again. Then he'd shown her, just as bluntly, that all these things were right in front of her. Never mind that he'd told her she also needed to take a lover—him. That was his roguish self speaking. But there was a part of him that was genuinely wise and genuinely kind. And if there was one thing she could use right now, it was a wise, kind friend.

Chapter 11

Richard *did* have debts.

With money borrowed from the earl, Christina was able to buy up three of Richard's notes. She confronted him with these through her attorneys; he was made to understand. He would do whatever she asked, or his notes would be called in. Richard agreed; he couldn't cover his debts. He would go to prison if he didn't cooperate.

It was not a pretty scheme, Christina realized. But it was satisfying. She liked the sense of having turned the tables on conniving Richard. At this point, her lawyers awaited "whatever she wished." Christina felt like a child let out to play; a little in charge of her own destiny, at last. She decided to sit back and enjoy this feeling for a while. Richard, all the lawyers could wait. She announced it would take time for her to consider how she wished the final papers to read.

Meanwhile, as to the earl, it was exactly as he'd promised: He left, and she stayed.

This arrangement turned out to be a surprisingly fine one. With the earl away, the larger group tended to fragment into smaller ones. Christina was welcomed easily into a little batch of friends that included Evangeline, Charles, and Thomas. This group was made up mostly of married couples and other "serious people," as they called themselves. About a dozen or so of them would gather in the card room or front salon. They were a happy lot, homogeneous in age and tastes. All about thirty. And, one and all, enthusiastic for cards, talk, music, and dancing.

When Charles was in the mood, it was the last two—music and dancing—they liked best. Evengeline's husband played the piano quite well. Sometimes the little group just listened or chatted, with Charles' fortes and diminuendos trilling in the background. But usually, they moved all the chairs and furniture against the walls and danced. Christain had forgotten how much she liked this.

It was not a staid group. Everyone danced with everyone else—Evangeline would have pouted unbearably if they hadn't. After all, her partner, Charles, was at the piano. They laughed a great deal, were silly, then seriously intellectual by turns. Discussions could turn from metaphysics to the subject of women's ankles in an instant, with a vague and wonderful connection made between the two that would have confounded any philosopher.

These people made Christina smile. She looked forward to the afternoons and evenings she spent with them. They treated her well. Almost immediately, they seemed to let off expecting anything different from the young woman who had been so slow to join them. They accepted her. Christain felt herself well-liked—and quickly had the pleasure of becoming a favorite of several of the gentlemen as a dance partner.

Adrien had been gone five days when the larger group found cause to come together. Some traveling musicians had been found in the nearby town. They were good. They were many—nine of them traveling together. And a "ball" had been put together in a day.

The earl's recital salon was opened. It was a room where normally one sat and heard a duchess' nephew or "discovery" play endless pages of his own composition, imitation Bach or Handel. But the divans and little chairs with their footstools were moved to the side. The terrace doors were flung open. And the sound of a real orchestra drew those few who resisted in the upstairs rooms.

It grew dark. Wind from the terrace blew the curtains swirling against dancers as they promenaded past. It had begun to drizzle and bluster outside. But inside, it was bright and gay, lit by a thousand tiny-candled chandeliers, cooled by a perfect summer rain.

Food and wine appeared at one end of the room. The earl's guests lacked for nothing. Then, about ten o'clock, there was a stirring of servants toward the entrance way, a general movement like a swarm of lemmings out onto the portico and into the rain. It was obvious what was happening. The master of the house was returning.

Christina was drawn with several others to observe the arrival. The front door was already open. A handful of people stood just inside, shaking off rain. He was easy to spot. He was several inches taller than anyone else. A half dozen servants clustered about him. And a woman. He had brought a woman with him. Christina recognized her as Adrien took her wrap and folded it with his own over a servant's arm. It was the woman with the chignon, the one who had stayed so briefly just before the Chiswell girl had arrived.

This woman was older. Adrien's age, perhaps. She was tall, rich, elegant-looking. And composed — she looked not the least upset for having been rained on.

Someone called to them. "This way, old man. We have a jolly good impromptu ball going."

Adrien looked toward them. His eyes rested briefly on Christina. Then he declined. "Mlle. Deluc is very tired. She wishes to retire."

They disappeared.

And with them went much of Christina's former contentment. She resumed dancing, but a lump had settled in her throat, a tightness behind her eyes. He had barely looked at her.

126

Evangeline found her sitting in the crush of empty chairs pushed against the wall.

"Are you all right?"

"Who is she?"

"Who?"

"You know perfectly who I mean."

Her cousin made a sound, a sigh of impatience, worry. "I do. But I pray to God no one else does. You have no business minding, you know."

"Who is she?"

"Nadine Deluc. She sings with an opera company in Paris. She used to have a little soiree-following there as well. Artists, literary people, you know the sort. I don't know if she has it still. But, yes, for years now, though it is sporadic, if that's what you're wanting to know."

"I haven't the slightest idea—"

Evangeline bent and squeezed her hand. She whispered closely, almost with anger. "He sleeps with her. And you won't mind, do you understand me? At least not in public. Now get up and dance."

Christina got up, but thinking only to get away from a too perceptive cousin. Then she was yanked back by her skirts.

"Look! No, don't look," Evangeline whispered. Her voice was much lighter. She laughed, triumphant. "He's not with Nadine tonight. On the terrace. Watch. There is a cigar burning. Find a partner and dance, for heaven's sake."

Christina did so, mechanically. She moved through the steps, daring a glance now and then toward the terrace doors. But there was only the orange glow, the cigar outside in the dark. She began to doubt that the earl would materialize, or that he was even there. Until, suddenly, on a turn, she was staring right at him.

He had come to the edge of the doorway, the white recital-room curtains waving beside him. The rain, the wind and tossing curtains seemed to be in a conspiracy

127

with him to shed gloom. There, at the edge of the dance floor, in the penumbra of light and gaiety, music and chatter, he stood: dark, moody, brooding. He was not the least bit sociable. And there was no mistaking; his eyes found and followed Christina. Then, after a minute or two, he disappeared back out onto the wet terrace.

Twice more this happened. And each time, he retreated the moment she looked at him. She caught only glimpses. But they were enough. He was there. And his presence made her heart thump. Why? she thought. Things had been so pleasant without him. Why did there have to be this beating in her chest, this excitement down the veins of her arms, this tingling through her whole body? She was so aware of him. She laughed. She smiled. She danced. She created the gayest hour of her entire life. But she did it with a kind of perverse and strange pleasure. She knew she did it because he watched.

The next morning, Mlle Deluc came down for breakfast about fifteen minutes before Adrien did. She was the sort of woman, it occurred to Christina, that one expected to see with Adrien Hunt. Hers was a polished, regal beauty. She carried several more inches of height than Christina, and did so with such grace, it made Christina want to stand on her toes. The woman was stunning. Her skin was flawless. Her face was beautiful. And her thick hair, defying gravity with one effortless sweep, seemed held to her head, weightless in a mass. Undone, it would hang, Christina thought, as long and heavy, as shiny as an armful of shot silk.

Despite herself, Christina couldn't help but slide little looks at the woman. She was so lovely, free of all the awkwardness of youth without any of the physical drawbacks of aging. Nadine Deluc glided. She hardly spoke, yet seemed perfectly comfortable. She did as she pleased. Buttered her toast. Drank her tea. She pointed to the jam, *"s'il vois plâit."* It was as if the fifty people around her hardly existed, except as her audience. As if, Christina thought, she were the French queen: *let them eat cake.*

As it turned out, however, it was only that the woman did not speak English. Except for the cook, she couldn't even deal with the servants. This linked her in a peculiar way to Adrien. She possessed him. She depended on him completely. He spoke for her, while she spoke to no one but him — even sending him off on an errand. He fetched her a comb from upstairs, which she proceeded to casually affix in her hair, the heavy silken hair, as if she had just retrieved the comb privately, idly, from her own dresser.

She could have spoken to Thomas, a few others. But she didn't make the effort. I don't need English, I don't need anyone, she seemed to be saying; I have Adrien.

But the claim, this time at least, only lasted until the afternoon. Adrien lost patience with her at something. He answered her sharply, in the garden with several people listening. He lowered his voice quickly, but it was strange, Christina mused as she listened, how argument sounded so much the same in any language. The woman flounced into the house. Adrien went after her. It became almost ludicrous. What should have been private was echoed by the cavernous entryway's walls and floors.

Nadine yelled at him, a diatribe. People on the lawn became quiet, looked at one another.

One couldn't hear his response. But Christina could imagine. She had had hints of his quiet viciousness. And there was more substantial proof of it when he came back out: He returned bearing a faint hand-print along the side of his cheek.

When he marched from the house, out onto the lawn, Christina didn't know if he did it on purpose — if she somehow was drawn to it, or if it was just chance — but he marched straight at her. She stood between him and the path that led to the greenhouse.

He took her by the shoulders and pushed her aside. Though not without pausing. "Well, you seem to be every-where all at once," he said. "Come down out of your rooms, have you?" It is not a particularly nice thing to say, nor did he say it nicely. But there was no time to respond to it, either in substance or tone. He all but walked through her as he continued briskly down the path, toward the green-house.

It was like being run over by a coach and eight. He had pushed her right into the bushes.

She wanted to call after him. The miserable, inconsider-ate, highhanded. . . . She was going to go after him, going to give him a piece of her mind. But then, rather surpris-ingly, she was restrained.

Thomas drew her back by the arm. "Of all the crazy things I have known you to do, that would be the craziest."

The remark chastened her more than he would under-stand. No one knew better than she how foolish it would be to follow Adrien Hunt out there. Yet she had had that in her mind—

Wanting to hide any trace of guilt, she smiled, turned, took Thomas' arm. "Thomas Lillings," she said. "I am the sanest woman you know."

"Woman, yes. But not girl. You used to be full of the devil. 'A handful,' my father used to call you."

"I was not," she protested. "I was a perfectly well-behaved young lady."

They had begun to walk. There was a gravel path that extended around the house, making a neat border with the lawns and gardens.

"I could think of a dozen proofs to the contrary," he teased.

"Can't—"

"The day you sneaked off from your governess to see our new puppies?"

"That was excusable. Kneebob was a witch. She would

130

never have let me go off to see 'dirty old hounds.' " Christina laughed. "Don't forget who helped me climb out the study window."

"And calling her Kneebob, my God — to her face."

"She didn't mind that part. And she did bob at the knees, curtsying and kowtowing to my father — "

" 'Miss Nibitsky.' I heard her correct you on occasion myself."

"Well," Christina insisted with a laugh. "She didn't mind in private."

"Is that what you told her? 'Listen, Kneebob, I've been over to the Lillingses as to roll around with the new pups. That's why I smell like a kennel.' "

"I didn't smell like a kennel — "

He looked at her, as if remembering. Then he spoke more softly. "No, you smelled wonderful."

Christina glanced away. "It was a long time ago, Thomas."

"Yes," he admitted. "Only I wish I didn't remember it so vividly."

They continued to walk, around the far end of the house. As they turned, Christina could glimpse back down the path, see the long terrace that ran the length of the rear of the house, see the group, the others they had left behind picnicking in the garden on the grass. People, food, table-cloths, scattered about on the lawn. It was like a painting, a proper English country setting, everyone positioned by Gainsborough.

The side of the house rose steeply at her shoulder; pinkish-yellow bricks covered in thorny green sweetbrier. A small pond glimmered in the distance, clear water, bright fish. Farther off was the carriage house, the stables. And, coming from that direction, along the mews of servants quarters, was a crested coach, one of the earl's legion. Christina and Thomas came around to the front of the house just in time to see Nadine Deluc climb into the

131

vehicle.

The carriage shook from the weight of her bags as they were loaded aboard.

"Is she very nice, Thomas?"

"Who?"

"Miss — Mlle Deluc."

He made a low whistle. "Lord, no. She's a crocodile. I can't stand her."

"A crocodile?" Christina laughed.

"A man-eater. She goes through men the way the croc at the zoo goes through chickens."

"But not the earl."

"Well, no, of course not." Thomas thought a moment, as if trying to understand why this was true. Then he laughed. "Haven't you ever seen that Indian that wrestles crocodiles?"

"I think it's alligators."

"Same thing. But that's what it's like she and Adrien. A lot of snapping and tail-swinging and stirred dust. Then the croc on her back like a pet getting her belly stroked."

"That's not a very nice analogy."

"But it's true."

"The earl seems to like her."

"I don't know. She's spoiled and vain and an absolute despot when it comes to having her own way. I suspect he's just rather forgiving on these points — one loves to forgive in others what one imagines are one's own vices. And, of course, she's beautiful." He gave Christina a brief, sidelong look. "He does like beautiful women."

Christina ignored this. She smiled, instead, at her little victory, his admission: "And he is a bit of a crocodile himself."

"Oh no, Christina, he's not —"

"Come on, silly." She touched his arm and laughed. "I won't tell. It's nice to know you can find fault with him."

"I can't really. I find him a little arrogant at times. But it's an arrogance honestly come by; the first-born male of a

132

very consequential family. And he's brilliant; I can't explain it. It's not the sort of brilliance that sets itself apart on, for instance, verb conjugations. But he can beat the pants off anyone in chess. And he can talk philosophy, science, poetry in any one of several languages."

"French."

"Of course, French."

"Evangeline says he's fluent."

Thomas gave her a funny look. "He's fluent in English. He was born and raised in Normandy."

Christina was puzzled. "That would make him French."

"His mother was French. Heredity made him English. An English lord, like his father."

"Is that where he goes when he goes to France? Normandy?"

"There she goes." Thomas looked out onto the drive. The carriage there leapt into motion. The driver called, cracked his whip. Nadine Deluc was leaving in a fanfare of loud commands, charging horses, and creaking carriage springs.

Christina hated herself for looking, for caring, for having to ask, "Is he finished with her, do you think?"

"I doubt it," Thomas answered. "Ask Evangeline."

Christina did.

It was later that day that her cousin Evangeline answered the question, straight to the point.

"He is never finished with Nadine," she said. "She is a permanent fixture he keeps going back to. I will tell you a confidence. At the peak of my amorous liaison with the man, he saw Nadine. I was furious. That was the end of it."

"And the Chiswell girl?"

Evangeline would only shrug. "Her father's land abuts Adrien's to the south. She is sweet, young, adoring—"

"Fertile," Christina added.

"Well. One never knows. But she is an obvious choice as a wife."

Christina sighed. If Nadine Deluc embodied everything

she feared in Adrien's past—his love of beautiful women, his ability to woo and win them—then Cybil Chiswell was the threat of his future, the bride he would one day marry.

She didn't see how she could compete with these women. And she tried to convince herself: She must never, never try.

Chapter 12

Adrien Hunt seemed to be gone more, stay away longer; and, more often than not, when he did come home, he arrived very late. Christina took to waiting up for him. She didn't mean to. It was just a habit she fell into.

She would stay up, reading, writing letters, mending clothes; there seemed always some reason. She would be up sometimes until three and four in the morning. Often, she doused the light in the silence of predawn. These were the nights when no one came. But frequently enough, there was the *frisson*, the little excitement — she didn't know why it made her so. She would hear the sound of carriage wheels in the drive, then whiff the light out as if she were answerable somehow, as if she mustn't be caught up at such an hour.

Usually they came in quietly — for it was "they" now. There would be the sound of the carriage, hardly any talking, then the shuffle of soft leather shoes up the stairs to bed. Occasionally, she would hear his voice. Low, clear, limpid syllables. "Good night," he would speak to his companions. "No, no. You mustn't fret that," he said one night. He had come to the top of the landing, a dozen yards from her door. He reassured someone. "It went fine. I will see you in the morning." Then his tread retreated, faded back down the stairs toward his own rooms.

The days went on. Followed by the nights. Perhaps it was

the product of such irregular sleeping, but Christina began to have horrible yet fascinating dreams. They were dark, vague; sexual. Nightmares, she would tell herself. But secretly, she knew she half relished her game: Waiting for the real man to make real noises downstairs, then letting herself succumb to sleep—and the incubus that did everything but actually make love to her.

This was always left off. There was never the act of love itself. She would wake in the morning oddly relieved by this realization. No, she hadn't; not even in her sleep. Good. But she awoke also to a regular and distinct knot in her belly, an anxious, unsatisfied feeling.

Christina became fidgety as the days wore on. Her appetite slacked off. This general restlessness would last all day. Then back into the pattern, a sleepless night of waiting. And dreaming.

Until, one night, the pattern abruptly came to an end.

It was near three in the morning. Horses began coming up the drive. She was sure; she heard them. Then they turned off. A number of horsemen cut toward the stables before they got close enough to the house to disturb. A few at a time, men could be heard coming into the house. Shushing, trying to quiet the jingle of spurs and belts. There seemed to be a few more of them than usual. At first, Christina was alarmed. All the sounds were irregular, unfamiliar . . . . Were these strangers, intruders?

But they didn't behave like intruders. They made an orderly procession toward the sleeping quarters of the house. Then, as she recognized the voices, she realized it was just the newness of attire. No more silk stockings and soft shoes, but heavy boots. These men were dressed for hard riding, for work. She sat up in bed. Christina had realized something else. No Adrien. She was almost sure. She sat listening, pinning names to voices and the trudge of footsteps on the stairs. But no Adrien. And no Thomas. They were not with the rest.

Christina got out of bed. She found her dressing gown, slipped it onto her arms. She was lifting her hair from beneath the gown where it was caught, was halfway down the stairs, when she stopped. She could hear them. She couldn't see them, but they were not far away. All the terrace doors of the entrance room were open. Their voices carried up over the balustrade. Adrien and Thomas were in the garden. They were arguing.

"I wish you'd go to bed, Thomas. It's all right. Honestly."

"It's damn well not. You're no good to anyone when you do this."

"So maybe I need to be 'no good to anyone' for a time."

"It's not good for you."

"It does no harm."

"I can remember your shaking from it. Muscle spasms. Perspiring. Your nose and eyes running. Your eyes so dilated the whole house was like a vampire's cave—"

"That was from lack of it, after having much too much for way too long. I'm in control, Thomas. I know what I'm doing. I ought to. I ought to be a damned expert on the stuff. Now leave me alone."

"No." Then after a pause: "I hope this isn't your answer to Christina."

Christina's ears perked up at that. She went closer, moving through the dark on bare feet. She stopped at the inside edge of the terrace. They were just below. Benches, she knew, were ranged along the terrace wall. She was certain she could have looked over the railing and seen the tops of their heads.

"We're not on that again, are we? Look, Thomas. That woman—and now you—are both driving me absolutely mad. I just want to be left alone."

"And if someone needs you?"

"I'll be here."

"Catatonic."

"You can rouse me."

"Ha." But Thomas had no better answer than that. His tone became resigned. "Will you be safe out here?"

"Perfectly. Now run along."

"Adrien—." Thomas sighed. "France, the Old Man; it's going so well. Better than we've had any right to expect." A pause. "It is Christina, isn't it? It's at home you need it."

There was a laugh. Dry, a little cynical. "It feels, Thomas, just like the glow one gets in the pit of one's belly after having had a woman. It's that sort of languor, that sense of well-being. Only it is so much less complicated than a woman. And it is infinitely less complicated than Christina Pinn. Go to sleep, Thomas."

Thomas made a monosyllabic sound, a grumble. But he was moving; a slow crunch of gravel toward the terrace stairs.

At first, Christina thought to press against the wall, into the darkness. He would never see her. But as she heard Thomas shuffling up the steps, one, two, three . . . something in her just wouldn't do it. Something tired of hiding: Something that wanted to be recognized. She stood there, moved even a little more boldly into the moonlight.

Thomas came to the top of the stairs. "What the—" He couldn't comprehend. He was confounded, completely thrown into stammering bewilderment. "What—How—How long have you been here?"

Then she went past him, gliding on bare feet, the light fabric of her nightclothes following, fluttering in the breeze of her movement. A unique self-possession had taken hold.

"Who is it?" Adrien called from below.

She came down the stairs to find him already standing. He held a candle on a plate in front of him, pushing it forward as if to better see. But the candle was small, not meant for much light. Other bits of things were on the plate. The paraphernalia of his "medicine." The tiny light did nothing but illuminate the man who held it: Damp. Windswept. The features of his face flickered in sharp, preternatural definition. He seemed to be wearing thick, bulky wool. A seaman's jersey perhaps—they were not elegant clothes. But the man was more than elegant. He held one arm away from his body, poised. It was an aggressive stance. The outline of his shoulders was enormous, powerful. She seemed to be looking at some dark, secret side of him. All manner and politeness peeled away. As if, within the secret of the earl dressed as a sailor, was the secret of Adrien Hunt himself; his fears, his longings, his most basic, instinctive drives . . . .

She inched toward this, staring, her heart pounding. She was unsure of what she was doing until she came within ten feet of him. Until he recognized her. And she saw astonishment set him back.

The look made something leap inside her. It made her bold. She had power over him. She didn't understand its limits or its boundaries. She didn't know precisely where to grab hold of it. But she possessed something extraordinary. She had seen it in his face.

And she wanted him to admit it. She wanted to do something outrageous, something from which there was no retreat; not for him, not for her. She wanted to set the record straight. And Thomas, poor Thomas, was made witness to a statement made by a novice at such things: Impulse, instinct, or sheer insanity, she let her dressing gown fall open. With only the slightest movement of her shoulders, it slid to the ground. The moon was behind her. Its light came pouring through her chemise. So that, from where Adrien stood, she appeared iridescent. Silvery. An intentional simulation of drugged dreams. She held Adrien mesmerized.

From above, she was simply a woman caught in an act of enormous stupidity; caught in an overkill. "Christina, what can you be thinking?" Thomas called. He was on his way down.

On the ground, she ruled over the seconds. The wind

139

blew her shift against her body. Adrien stared. He wet his lips. He seemed about to say something, then couldn't. His extended arm began to tremble. The candle he held in front of him fell over in its dish. It rolled, spun out its meager little light as it toured the rim, then dropped. Darkness.

"Jesus Christ," Thomas spoke. She could hear his confusion as he came down the stairs.

But, for once, Christina didn't feel the least bit confused. She turned. And, following the instinct with an intensity that thrilled, intoxicated, she ran.

Past the muttering Thomas. Up the stairs. And into the house. She ran through the entrance way. Down its long run of marble. She shunned the staircase. There was suddenly something claustrophobic about corridors and bedrooms. She bolted through the front door.

Over the cobbles of the drive. Out onto the lawn. The grass was cold and wet under her feet. But she flew. She could hear boots clattering down the steps after her.

She darted a look over her shoulder. Her chest constricted. Triumph. Panic. Adrien. He was on a dead run after her and closing the distance. What was she doing? Was she mad? she wondered. She had to be, she thought, tearing through his front lawns in the dead of the night. But there was a sly voice inside her that didn't really doubt her sanity at all. It screamed, This is wonderful. It urged her. It felt in complete control. And she raised the hem of her chemise so that her legs could leap, could run as they had in her childhood. Like a gazelle, like a fairy. The fastest child in the valley, the fastest in the shire. . . .

But she wasn't the fastest in this shire. There was a moment's warning, the hiss of his breath as he came up on her. Then there was a jerk on her arm. He brought her up short. She lurched, lost her balance. He stumbled and tripped into her from sheer momentum. They both went tumbling to the ground. He turned her onto her back:

There was not the first moment's doubt, between either of them, what the prize was for catching her.

She resisted for a moment, balked against her own female ingenuity. But things were well beyond that now. He slid his hands up her thighs to her waist, lifting her chemise. He put her bottom in the grass — it was cold, prickly. He raised the chemise all the way and put her belly, her ribcage against his chest, against the scratchy warmth of his sweater. And without a moment's reservation, he pushed her legs apart and lay full length on top of her, between them. Her head swam from the feel of him. This was what she wanted. Waking, sleeping, her thoughts had returned a hundred times to the little glass house, to the episode in her rooms. She thought of him in this way, no matter how she had tried to remove herself from it. Let him. Let fact match fantasy. She wanted this. Join him. She wrapped her arms around him and clung to him. He raised his hips. She heard his breath rasping. From the run. From the knowledge of what he was about to do. His hand, his knuckles brushed the skin of her belly. He yanked at the buttons of his pants . . . .

"Ai—" She flinched as he pierced her. It was such a shock. The irreversibility of it penetrated as much as anything. She had never thought to feel this, another man's body within her. But she felt it, whole, entire. A sensation so strong.

He thrust deep into her, and let out a groan — followed by an urgent string of whispered words, "Be still my God don't move Christina." He was perfectly rigid for a moment, as if he were afraid to move. Only slowly, very slowly, did he set up a rhythm. And slowly, very slowly, sensation opened up to her.

It was all there. Everything his body had ever suggested before. The grace. The smooth, masculine solidity, wielded with an elegant animality. Lying beneath him, feeling his body enter hers brought a satisfaction nothing could describe. He thrust into her again, deep. She arched. Her fingers dug into his shoulders. Again. Then, slowly, again. Each time, consciousness itself moved away a little, *la petite mort,* and pleasure grew. Then grew stronger still. Until pleasure itself began to be a trial, something so sharp she almost couldn't endure it.

A slight easing would come only in gasps. He would draw out, and for moments she would partially recover. A ragged, hazy awareness where she searched from side to side for a guide mark, something to indicate these potent sensations wouldn't harm her—it was so unfamiliar, so unlike any act she had known with Richard. "What are you doing to me?" she murmured.

A kind of tantrum began to well up from the pit of her stomach. It was like having leapt into a void, then wanting to call oneself back; the victim suddenly of something as strong and relentless as gravity. Blind, senseless; only the sense of touch and feel. And another human being—who laced his fingers into hers and pinned her back, without a single defense, as her own pleasure rose in her throat like a scream. Never had she felt anything like this. The confusion. The hurtling compulsion.

She began to struggle again, though she didn't know against what. He accepted this with equanimity. He held her firmer; she wasn't going anywhere, he seemed to say. She pushed against him, with her hips and legs and arms, with her whole body. Her muscles strained, then seemed to revel in the sensation of his holding her tighter, harder. She pushed at him to the limits of her strength; it set up an amazing resistance. The opposition between them became sharp and savory. Male, female. It felt as though all of life breathed in the space of their bodies.

She called out. The words, animal sounds, escaped into his mouth. She couldn't be still. Until finally the violence contracted into one single convulsion. It tore through her, exploded, sent her quivering against him. Her arms about his neck, her fingers in his hair. Shivering. Holding him to her. While feeling every sense emptied, like a bottle up-ended. There was nothing left of her but this. Flesh entangled with flesh. And touch.

It took several minutes for both of them to catch their breath. She came to awareness slowly. Realization. The warm, embracing dark. The distant sound of night insects. A frog by the pond. Adrien was quiet except for the slight rasp of his breathing. He lay nestled on her body, his cheek against her breast. Hesitantly, she reached down and touched his face. She traced his eyes, his brow, his cheek-bone, the angle of his jaw. He answered by turning his mouth and taking her fingers, one at a time, sliding over them. Wet. Slippery. His tongue in the interstices. She spread her fingers. And another realization—he wasn't finished; he was beginning again. Through her chemise, he kissed the nipple of her breast with his open mouth.

He made love to her a second time there in the grass. She simply let her hands fall back into her hair; she let go. It was exquisite, incomparable. She shivered and trembled under the siege of his hands, his fingers, his tongue, never making the first move to stop his doing anything. All was permitted. She felt liquid.

She found it so much easier to flow with anything, everything he asked—so much easier to let him become her lover than to rebel against what now seemed always to have been ineluctable.

Sometime after, he scooped her up into his arms. She collapsed against him. Even as he carried her toward the house, he kissed and stroked and petted her. Christina had never felt such languid, heady contentment.

But as they came to the top of the front steps, a little breeze of reality wafted into their cozy situation. Thomas. He was leaning in the doorway, drinking a large measure of brandy.

"Here," he said. He put her dressing gown into the crook where her body curved against Adrien's. "She may need this. It's a cool night."

This didn't seem to trouble Adrien. He accepted the wad of nightclothes and went in. He turned and mounted the stairs.

But Christina couldn't take her eyes off the little bundle on her belly. "My rooms," she said. Adrien had turned on the first landing toward his.

"What?"

"I want to go to my rooms."

"Not without me."

She smiled. "No. With you."

This settled, he didn't question the wish further. He humored her up another flight of stairs.

And, likewise, in the bedroom, when she wanted distance—"Let me be for a minute"—he let her have it. He moved away. For perhaps fifteen minutes they demanded nothing of each other. No conversation. No contact. There was nothing between them but the solitary comfort of being able to be alone in each other's presence.

Christina sat on the sill of her window, looking out. Behind her was the noise, the splash of Adrien washing in the basin by her bed. She had a blanket wrapped around her shoulders. There was a fire going. She stared down onto the front lawn and drive. She almost knew, before she saw, what she would find. Out there, below, it was dark. But not that dark. The moon was out. She could see the shadows of trees. And she could see the shadow of Thomas lying out on the grass, drinking brandy and contemplating the stars.

144

Chapter 13

Civilization knocked. It was breakfast. The sound had startled Christina, but Adrien hadn't budged. Christina accepted the tray at the door. There was only one cup, but a larger than usual pot of tea. And there was milk — she didn't take milk — with the regular bread and jam. Discreet, she thought. There was knowledge downstairs. Not blatant. Not showy. But in evidence, there on the tray.

Presently, Christina sat in bed, wrapped in a blanket, drinking tea, eating bread and jam. She was naked except for the blanket, while the sleeping man beside her wore only a shirt, the cuffs and placket open. The woolen jersey was lost somewhere over the edge of the bed. His pants — she had empirical knowledge of the fact — were also somewhere on the floor. He slept in her bed, tangled among the covers, in just the rumpled shirt.

It was the earl who lay there, not the sailor. Beneath the jersey had been a heavy silk shirt. It was cut very full and long. It had lace at the cuffs, pleats down the front, and every edge was finished in a rolled hem with tiny hand-stitches. Christina smiled. Such details concerning his clothes, concerning anything that belonged to him, she realized, were a source of pleasure to her. Each fact, each recognition fascinated. She collected observations of him and piled them up like stored treasure. It was a kind of paradise to be able to study him, to take him in, at such close range, at such leisure. It was surely unwise, she thought, foolish, wrong, but all she could feel was joy in having him there in her bed. She felt like a child at

Christmas, staring at an impossible, extravagant gift put in front of her.

She leaned over on one elbow. Adrien's face was peaceful; unshaven, but serene. There were circles beneath his eyes, shadows across his face. He looked strangely dark nestled in the white of the bedding and loose shirt; the same sort of shock as catching glimpses of his dark nakedness against her white skin. His shirt was completely unbuttoned — he had a chest full of black hair. At the end of one sleeve, his wrist lay exposed, cradled in a mass of unconfined frills and cuff. His hands were neat. Clean, smooth fingers — on one, a heavy gold ring, an intaglio. The face of the ring would make a raised pattern in wax, a seal.

Then, at the lower edge of the shirt, a turned-up shirt tail, a break in the covers, a long stretch of naked abdomen. Last night, she had felt the dark, swirling hair as it fanned out across the muscles of his chest. But she had yet to be bold enough to touch the place where her eyes fell now. The pattern tapered over his abdomen, like the tail of a tornado, to run down his belly in a narrow line — a broken line; there was the scar. It was a lovely belly, taut, flat. Narrow hips. He was in incredible physical condition. Like a man half his age. The hunting and tennis and dancing, the coming and going of his life certainly seemed to agree with him physically. It might be partly luck that he had survived the brutal attack in France three years before. Yet it was also something unique to him that he had; most men would have succumbed to the loss of blood and inevitable fevers. Yet, even after such a trauma, his body positively exuded strength and robust health.

Christina reached out to run her finger along the scar. Her finger had barely touched him when his stomach suddenly contracted. He drew in his breath and grabbed her hand.

"What are you doing?"

"Looking at you."

"What?"

"I'm looking at you."

He laughed. "Looking at me?" he repeated. "Why?"

"Because you're beautiful."

Again he laughed. But he seemed uneasy, even a little embarrassed. "I'm supposed to say that to you." He made a face. "A man can't be beautiful."

She smiled. His unexpected abashment gave her courage. "But you are. Look." She took hold of the edge of his shirt and pushed it up.

He didn't seem to know how to take this. He laughed, protested, allowed it. He seemed sleepy, not completely alert, and — rather pleasantly — without his usual smooth response. She liked this discovery — that he could be disarmed, at least for moments, of his interminable self-possession.

"You're like a statue," she said. "Perfect." Then she sat back on her heels. She hadn't realized — The scar, in a single line, ran down and around his body. It was thin, neat as it went from his shoulder blade and under his arm. But as it came across his belly and onto his hip, the scar tissue became thick. He would have had a deep wound across his bowels and into his hip joint. "What an awful thing," she murmured. "That anyone could do this to you." She looked at him. "Tell me about it."

He shrugged. "There's not much to tell. A rather nasty mob. They brought everyone out of the house, made us lie down in the dust — there'd been no rain, massive crop failure — while they razed the house. They tormented us a little. I should have been quiet. Instead, I spit at one of them. Voilà. He cut me in two. It was a stupid thing to do."

"You spit at him?"

"It was about the only retaliation left to me, tied up with curtain cords, lying there on the ground in my nightshirt." He laughed at himself. "Silly, isn't it? But I had a great sense of myself then."

147

"Then," she repeated.

"Then." His fingers grazed her cheek. He pushed her hair back from her shoulder and drew her to him.

She smiled. "We should get up. We won't get another thing done all day —"

He lifted his eyebrows slightly and smiled, suggesting he saw nothing wrong with this. His fingers went farther into her hair, and he pulled her head down.

He kissed her with an easiness, an unhurried contentment. His hands smoothed down her spine. He pressed her buttocks to him. Then he rolled her over, brought his body onto hers. He became sidetracked, rose up a bit. He was trying to get rid of the sheets and covers between them. Christina held them. But his teasing mood persisted. They tussled. He pulled at the covers. "You're more beautiful without them."

"And more embarrassed." She'd won temporarily. "Richard once told me only whores make love with their clothes off. For an added price. Do you suppose that's true?"

"I don't much like this Richard, the more I hear."

She laughed. "No. I don't think I do either. But, do you think it's true? That whores charge extra?"

He sat back between her legs and took the covers with him, wrapping them about his shoulders. "I don't know." He was shaking his head at her, smiling. "I don't know any whores. Do you suppose Richard does?"

"Do you suppose?" She laughed. A jolly, real laugh such as she had not enjoyed in ages. "That prig. What an absolute, stuffy, old hypocritical prig!"

Her laugher faded. Adrien was watching her, running his eyes over her nakedness. Then his hands. It was odd, but after all her fears and worries, Christina realized she trusted him completely in this sense. It was a physical trust, having nothing to do with words or promises. Her body opened up to his. She could let him do anything; nothing shocked.

She brought his hands up to rest on her belly. "What now?" she murmured. Her eyes flicked to the door. "In here, it's all fine. I love your touching me. But a moment ago, when the tea came . . . Eventually, we have to open the door." He didn't seem to understand. "It's not so simple, you know."

"We're not going to discuss this again, are we? 'The complexities of being an earl's mistress—' "

"I'm not your mistress."

He grinned. "I think you are."

"I'm trying to tell you, I'm not."

"Fine." He made a mock solemn face. "And I am sure you are right. Now, turn over for a moment, will you?"

He took her by the hips. He knew about moving a woman's body; where to grab hold, where he wanted it to be.

"Don't," she murmured. "Oh—" she sighed, "Oh, God—" He kissed her mouth and neck as he rotated her. "Adrien— Ooh, don't—I can't think, ah—I can't think when you do this."

"Good," he murmured.

He pushed her all the way onto her stomach and slipped an arm under her hips. He lifted.

"God in heaven, what are you doing?" She struggled, laughing.

He made a guttural sort of sound; acknowledgment, preoccupation. His body curved against hers.

More earnestly, she cried out, "Stop!"

He did. Quite suddenly. He withdrew completely. She twisted around. And there he was. The wounded male. As if he'd been reprimanded for sexual perversion.

He wouldn't speak for a moment. Then he said very quietly, "I wouldn't hurt you."

"I know that." She touched his cheek. Then she shook her head and looked away. "No," she said, "we both know you will hurt me. Eventually."

149

He couldn't deny this. An earl. With no heir. For him, a barren lawyer's daughter could not be true love for all eternity — and that was why Christina had been so wary of beginning with him. She could so easily foresee the end.

"Christina—" he began, as if there were promises and explanations that could be made. Then he gave a huge sigh and rose from the bed. "Where's the tea?"

"Over here."

Bleakness had settled over the little bedchamber.

"Is there milk?"

She made a sniff at that. "Apparently. In the little pitcher. There's only one cup, though—here."

He poured and fixed his tea, then came back to bed. The bed sank, a deep depression where he sat and leaned back. It would allow nothing but a slow slide toward him.

Christina had to brace herself back. "Why aren't you married?" she asked quietly.

"There's no reason to be."

"An heir?"

"I can recognize any one of several children and have an heir."

She blinked. "You have children?"

"They do seem to crop up now and then, in the natural course of things."

"Bastards?"

"Not a very nice word for the little darlings, but yes. I have bastards."

"Many?"

"Five."

"Dear God." She was suddenly overwhelmed with the density of his life, the thirty-four years where she didn't exist, didn't fit in. Their one night together seemed all at once tenuous, fragile; even less significant than what she'd imagined. "Don't you want a wife? A real family?" she asked.

"I have a real family. Besides the children, I have a

grandfather in France. And some cousins abroad."

"That's not what I mean."

He heaved another long sigh. "I know. And if by not marrying you I would hurt you, then you're right. I would."

Had she been so obvious? She rolled away from him, or as far away as she could. The bed, his weight, wouldn't let her stay very far away. Slowly, she slid back in his direction. She turned and gave him her back. This seemed a particularly good decision, since she began to feel like she might cry.

"Christina," he said, "why marriage and marriage alone? Don't you care anything for romance, affection, loving?"

"I associate those things with marriage."

"Did your husband give you those things?"

"Don't box me into a corner with your crazy, specious logic."

"Is it? Just because it doesn't lead to the prescribed conclusion? The truth is, Christina, marriage didn't give you anything it was supposed to." He left a pause. "But I do."

He did not speak from arrogance. He was not asserting anything they didn't both already know. Whether it was love or not, whether it was affection or romance, he injected into her life what she needed, what she had heretofore always had to manufacture on her own. Friction, excitement, irritation, allure.

"I know," she said.

He rolled her over and laid her head in his lap. He adjusted a little, scooted to make them both comfortable. Then he sat back and drank his tea while he petted her hair.

There was an odd, little bright note that same day. An inkling of just how enamored Adrien was of her was demonstrated that afternoon when Cybil Chiswell and her

151

father called.

The lady and her father arrived without notice or warning just after tea. They were instantly closeted, apparently at their request, with the earl in his front study. Christina's heart sank. They were all behind the closed door for nearly an hour, only to come out and have the young woman lean on Adrien's arm and whisper to him. She and he walked back into the room for a conference between just the two of them.

Christina tried to behave casually, to not hover in the entrance room waiting for this episode to be over. Eventually, she went out with a group into the garden. When she returned, the room was empty. She couldn't find Adrien at all.

She discovered him out on the terrace all alone sometime later. "You are looking forlorn," she said.

He darted a surprised smile at her. He had been lost in his own thoughts. "It is always a little sad, I suppose, to see one's options narrow."

"Yours are narrowing?"

He nodded.

"Does this have to do with the Chiswell conference in the study?"

"Indeed. It was a sort of fish-or-cut-bait conference. Henry Chiswell wanted to know 'my intentions' and if I was 'trifling' with his daughter's affections. Good, old-fashioned words, to a good old-fashioned end." He looked at her. "I have never discussed marriage so much all in one day. And I'm not very good at it, apparently. Lord Chiswell was not pleased."

"So you told him you did not intend to marry his daughter."

"In so many words." He raised his hand to point. "Do you see where the woods end near the center of the horizon? The land begins to roll a little? Well, that's the edge of his land, her dowry. It's really fine land and would

152

fill mine out."

"Then why didn't you do it?"

He shrugged. "I was going to. That is, I had always more or less planned to. But all at once it seemed like an incredibly stupid reason to marry a woman. I think it was our discussion this morning. Love and affection, all that mess." He looked at her. "I suspect you have dulled a perfectly fine cynical edge I have been honing for almost ten years."

She smiled. "I'm flattered. And how did she take it?"

"Graciously. Too graciously. Though there was one awkward moment. After her father and I had already got through the worst of it, she insisted on raking it all up again. Privately. Do you know what she wanted to tell me?" Christina gave a shake of her head. "That she understood. That she knew a 'strong, virile man' might require 'outside interests.' And 'if that is the problem . . .'"

"Oh my—" Christina laughed quietly. "What did you say?"

He turned, leaned back on the balustrade. He looked at Christina. "I told her," he said with a grin, "that it wasn't so much a problem of a wife not tolerating my mistress but of my mistress not tolerating a wife."

"Did you really say that?"

"No." He laughed. "But I was thinking it." He grew more serious. "It would have been over, wouldn't it? If I had come out of that room engaged to that young woman?"

She bowed her head. "Such an understanding woman might have made you a good wife."

"So right." He flounced the bows at the back of her bustle. "And here I am, stuck with a perfect shrew of a woman, not the least bit understanding."

"No," she affirmed, "not the least."

Chapter 14

Living in proximity to Adrien Hunt was not quite so easy as Christina had first imagined. His life was a mass of social commitments and responsibilities combined with a long-standing commitment to his own needs and indulgences. Over the years, this life had acquired a momentum, an incredible energy dedicated to the fulfillment of these things. Trying to float along with this was a bit like trying to negotiate the course of a ship under full sail. Adrien Hunt moved swiftly. He seemed always sure of where he was going, what he was doing. It was flattering that he seemed also sure now that he wanted Christina there beside him. Still, on a day-to-day basis, she could find herself feeling less an object of affection and more a little pinnace dragged along in the wake of a looming flagship.

Dances. Parties. Tennis. Riding. He took her shooting; both target and for pheasant. They went to teas. They went on side trips; to a festival in the village, to a play in the town. Christina loved this life — though, for some reason, she found it a little more exhausting than she had at nineteen. It became an almost common sight, by midsummer, to see the young Mrs. Pinn dozing at a late-night dinner or over a midnight table of cards. Then, the earl excusing himself, gathering up her fans and feathers and pockets, her heavy satin skirts, and carrying her up the stairs to bed.

"I have never seen him so completely devoted, Christina," Evangeline told her as she was leaving. Her pregnancy was advancing and Charles was taking her home. "I think you will leave your mark."

Flattering. But also sad, Christina thought. Even Evangeline spoke of the love affair in terms that prefigured its end.

By August, most of the other guests had departed as well. The larger part of the group was traveling to Lyme.

"Usually, I would go with them," Adrien told Christina. "But I don't want to. I want you to stay as well. Here, with me. Will you?"

"Lyme?"

"Lyme Regis. It's a little town on the Channel coast. Pump rooms like Bath. A bathing beach like Brighton. But less crowded than either of these towns. I'll take you, if you want; it's very nice, really . . . But I'd rather get out from under all the social commitments. I'd rather be with you alone."

It was the right thing to say. "Yes. I'd like that."

So, with Christina by the hand, Adrien Hunt had waved good-bye to the carriages as they'd pulled away from his own door.

With fewer guests, the household calmed. Now and then, a batch of people would breeze in from London, or some personage with a retinue would upset the generally less frenetic pace. People seemed to appear in waves, one group drawing two or three others. But, mostly, the stays were short and the entertainments more independently organized.

Late summer brought beautiful weather. Adrien was, however, less available to enjoy it. He seemed to have to be away more frequently. He had, all summer long, dashed off periodically. He would be gone sometimes two or three days, return for a week, be gone again. Christina was sure he went to France, but he no longer admitted he was going there. He concocted various excuses. Business in London. Problems on an estate in far-off Cornwall.

For the last few days of August, Adrien made sure he was home. Christina's divorce decree would be entered on August 31st. Adrien had promised to accompany her to London, to support her through this last ordeal. Also, Adrien himself needed to go to London. He was to be gone the entire month of September, perhaps longer. He needed to "tidy up" some loose ends.

Christina wondered how she was going to be "tidied up." She couldn't live with him forever — she was sure Adrien didn't envision this. She wanted to spare them both the awkward embarrassment of having the former mistress still installed in the house when a new lady gained favor. Once the divorce was final, it seemed only logical Christina should find a place of her own.

Some major loose ends were apparently right there on the Kewischester estate. The afternoon before they were leaving for London Christina accompanied Adrien into the west wing — the offices — of his house.

He had disappeared into the west wing for an hour here, an hour there, on previous occasions. Yet, she had never gone with him before this.

He was presently at his ledgers.

"Adrien?" Christina called softly across the room.

He didn't look up, but kept reading, dipping the quill in ink, writing, sprinkling sand, blotting, reading. . . . He sat behind a huge desk nearly three times the size of the library desk in the east wing. This one housed a multitude of drawers and cubbyholes within his reach. On its giant marble surface stacks of items did battle for room. Papers and more papers, three quills, three inkwells, two ledgers, a heavily marked calendar, and a crystal dish with a lit cigar.

The room itself was not much to see. After only ten

minutes, Christina was as bored here as she had been in any of a dozen rooms in the west wing. The endless succession of rooms, offices, corridors, clerks, and lawyers, ad infinitum, was all too tedious for words. The only intriguing thing about the place was that one needed a key to get into these rooms.

"It would never do for people to realize how much like a bank clerk I can be," he had said with a laugh. He had turned the lock with a key that hung on his watch chain.

Indeed, as the morning wore on, Christina began to see that Adrien brought the same brand of energy to his business concerns as he did to his social obligations — though it was hardly on the scale of a bank clerk. He *owned* two bank charters, she discovered. And a shipping company, twenty-seven rental properties, and a dairy farm — not to mention the Kewischester estate, the hereditary seat of the earldom he managed. She was flattered that he had admitted her into this inner sanctum. And slightly amused. There he sat — the local "prince of darkness," the difficult, hunting, riding, drinking, dancing, womanizing, bastard-producing social horror and pet prodigal son of blooded society — overseeing it all, down to every last boring detail. He was right. There was a surprising side to him — serious, responsible — that would have shattered his reputation for self-indulgence.

Christina got up. She wandered into the next room.

There, a clerk sat over a table busily copying from a stack of sheets. He was lettering neat, beautiful script in a quick hand. He worked hard and carefully, giving the task his full attention. Each room, each worker seemed so industrious, so perfectly integrated into the whole of what the earl required. In fact, it was so well run, so organized, it was a little intimidating.

"Where are you going?"

Christina bolted around. Adrien stood in the doorway, the cigar in his teeth, a paper in his hand. She shrugged. "I thought I might explore."

"Bored?"

"A little."

He smiled. "Are you good at adding figures?"

"I'd rather move around."

"And I'd rather you didn't just wander. There are people working—"

She laughed. "Do you really expect me to just sit and watch you work all afternoon?"

He did. She could see it by the mild puzzlement this question caused him.

She threw him a look over her shoulder. "You can find me when you're done. I'll be off in this direction."

"Christina—"

Room opened into small room. A thoughtful clerk took note of her. A solicitor bobbed a surprised head up out of a book. But people knew her, who she was; she was not questioned. She walked briskly through eight or ten rooms, wanting to put the hub of activity behind her. Most of the rooms in the west wing opened on to each other without access corridors, somewhat like a maze.

Then, all at once, a corridor presented itself to her. Rooms opened off it. They looked cared for, clean. But they also looked unlived-in, vacant, and dated in décor. They had the still, sleeping quality of a museum. She walked along the hallway, peeking into each room. She noticed hardly any difference between these rooms and the ones Adrien had claimed as offices except that there were no clerks here, no more Adrien, no more of his vast reach into every corner. Then, one room was different. As Christina first peered in, she saw it was larger. But it was pictures on a wall that caught her eye and drew her in.

It was a dim room of majestic size and proportion. It had been perhaps a library. A few books. Large, comfortable chairs with footrests. Candelabras on tables positioned all about the apartment, as if for reading She wandered over to one table, fingered, then opened a large scroll of paper that lay on it. It was a map. Of France. It was heavily marked in various shades of ink. She looked again at the chairs. Suddenly they took on a new perspective. There were ten or twelve of them, and they all faced this particular table and the chair beside it. With a ripple of apprehension, knowledge flooded through her. The trips to France were planned here in this room. Somehow this made it worse, that they should germinate in the humming little mecca of the west wing. It made them more considered, more purposeful; more conspiratorial. The dimensions of Adrien's illicit activity, whatever it was, loomed suddenly larger.

Christina let the map curl up on itself. It made her feel like she shouldn't be there. It was the pictures she had been interested in, she reminded herself.

She went to a window and drew back the heavy drapes. The afternoon sun poured in, lighting the room with a dignity that surprised and pleased. This was such an improvement, she repeated the task, adding light from one huge window after the other, four in all. The room brightened and revealed itself. The pictures were hung in a formal pattern along the one wall.

Christina backed into the middle of the room. There were fifteen pictures. Dark, golden-hued paintings in various styles of portraiture. The last one she looked at made her heart leap.

"My goodness," she murmured. She went close to this last painting. A very young, but very recognizable man gazed challengingly out of the frame. She backed up a step to look again at the row of portraits. Indeed, the Earls of Kewischester, all seven of them, hung there on the wall with their various wives—one of them had gone through three. She had come across the House of Hunt.

Christina surveyed the canvas faces; one stern, one sublimely bored, each its own version of prescribed, lordly

159

expression. At the last picture, she paused again with great interest.

She judged it to be at least a dozen years old — Adrien at perhaps age twenty. He stood there in the perfect poise of aristocratic manhood, looking more pretty than handsome. His black hair was worn long and tied back with a stiff, blue satin bow. He wore no powder, even though twelve years ago that would have been very much the style; just as he now wore his hair decidedly shorter than noble fashion. She wondered if it was vanity that made him flout convention and current style. Or just an ever increasing desire to free himself from the care of his unusual hair.

The young Adrien was possibly not as personable as the present one. But something else in the canvas face mitigated this. It was in the eyes: Innocence. Asleep, the face of Adrien she knew held a measure of this. But here, the painter had captured a frank, uncorrupted naiveté she had yet to see in the face of the real man.

Christina's eyes caught sight of a mark, an irregular area on the wall to the right. She reached up to touch it with her finger.

"What are you doing?" a voice called from behind her.

Christina had to grab the last picture to keep from knocking it off the wall. She turned. "Heavens, Adrien, you scared the life out of me." She looked back to the spot on the wall, touched it again. He was behind her. She felt his lips brush her bare neck.

"Adrien, look at this. The wall plaster is discolored."

"So it is. I should have had the wall papered."

"And here, someone has filled in a hole; the plaster has shrunk." She ran her finger over the indentation. "Why, there was another picture here! Who was it?"

When he didn't answer, she turned to face him. He barely allowed her room — he had her backed against the wall. And, she realized, he wasn't going to answer. He was going to kiss her.

160

She put her hand up, covered his mouth. "Who was it?" she asked again.

His eyes frowned over the small, gagging hand. His mouth opened. He bit her hand, gently, and pressed himself against her. She leaned, let the wall take her weight. She had thought she might get used to this. But his nearness, his flirtations and advances still flustered her. "You're trying to avoid this. Why? You're . . . " she groaned, " . . . confusing me on purpose. . . ."

He laughed softly. "Mmm, so right," he said. "The second you left, I was wishing you hadn't. I didn't get another thing done. 'So,' I said to myself, 'I might as well go confuse Christina.'"

The only evidence of what had gone on were the muss of her skirts about her knees and the state of his shirt, untucked and hanging. Adrien was sitting, his back against the wall. His legs were bent, like a bridge over Christina's body. She lay in the shelter of his legs and body.

She looked up and over her head. Upside down, she could still make out the telltale marks on the blank wall where the mystery picture had hung. "Who was it?" she said.

"Who was who?"

"The picture."

He gave her a flick of his finger. "You are as tenacious as a flea, do you know that?" He laughed, leaned his head back. "My wife," he answered. "You must certainly realize it was a picture of my wife."

"Your wife!" Christina sat up on her arms. She would have gotten up all the way, but Adrien flattened his legs. One of his little games, he held her to the floor. "You never said you had a wife!"

"I don't have one. Not now."

"I don't understand. What—?Where—?" She tried to

161

calm herself. "What became of her? Is she dead?"

"Not that I know of."

"Lost then? At sea?" Christina wished she could take it back. It wasn't very nice, disposing aloud of Mrs. Hunt — Lady Hunt, she corrected, the Countess of Kewischester. "Let me up, Adrien. I have to go."

"Stop it," he chided softly. "We're divorced."

This should have relieved her, in light of her own failed marriage. But it didn't. The very fact that this was the first she had heard of this — when the subject must have stared them in the face a hundred times — was ominous.

"Why haven't you mentioned this before?"

"I don't know. It didn't seem important."

"It didn't seem important? While I am going through the process of becoming a social pariah, a one-in-a-thousand, to tell me you had gone through the same thing?"

"It wasn't the same thing. A divorce for an earl is — well — " He made a face. "The king and queen do not approve of such things."

"You are telling me yours was worse?"

"Infinitely. And I don't care to relive it. Christina, it didn't seem important. It happened so long ago."

"How long ago?"

"Nine years. A bit more."

"'A bit more,'" she mimicked. "How much more?"

"Months. It will be ten years next May."

"You keep track of it this carefully? 'Ten years next May'? This unimportant event?"

He swung his legs off her and stood up. "Christina, it was a long time ago. And it is nothing now. Like all other women you are afraid of."

"There are so many of them." She sat up. "And you married one, Adrien. You married one."

"When I was nineteen."

"You can't dismiss it like that — "

"Do you want to be held accountable for the marriage

162

you made at nineteen? Should I be jealous of Richard?" He offered his hand to her. "Come on. I want to leave."

A little meeker, she let him bring her to her feet. "Ex-wife," she said softly.

"What?"

"It's a new term I'm learning. You called her your wife, Adrien. When one is divorced, one becomes an ex-wife."

"I don't want to argue, Christina. Not when we have so few days left. By Thursday, I'll be in Cornwall, and you—"

"Cornwall, indeed," she muttered.

"And what is that supposed to mean?"

"You're not going to Cornwall."

"And whyever not?"

"Because you can't be there and in Normandy, too."

There was a pause. "Why Normandy?"

"Thomas said you were born there. I just assumed, when you went to France—"

"I'm not going to Normandy."

"Then Paris."

This time the hesitation was longer, the guilty space of a man reconnoitering. "And why do you think that?"

She didn't look at him. "Little conferences in French. Open trips over there. Then suddenly you are going to disappear for—how long? weeks? months?" She glanced up. "You have to be going to France. Have you forgotten you shot a horse out from under me? Other people may believe a sick grandfather and a few English friends who coincidentally all seem to speak French, but I have seen the little band of men all united in one place. I have heard the groups that come home in the middle of the night." She pointed. "And there is a bloody map of France over there—"

He retrieved her pointing hand. "Christina—"

She pulled away. She had worked herself up into a genuine state of distress.

"Don't stop me," she continued. "I'm worried. I think

163

you're in some terrible trouble. Oh, Adrien—" She threw herself against him, her arms around his neck. Her sudden emotion surprised even her. She cared about him. In a way she had never cared for anyone. This new, intense emotion felt wonderful. And frightening. Her body had begun to tremble.

"Shh—" He stroked her hair and cooed to her.

"Don't go," she murmured. "You're doing something dangerous, I can feel it. Don't go."

"But I have to go. And you have to stay." There was a long pause. Then he barely whispered the words, "Will you lie for me, Christina?"

She looked up into his face. She could feel his breath, the moist intimacy of the few inches between them. He waited. "How?" she asked.

"Tell anyone who asks that you know I am in Cornwall."

She made the smallest nod, and he pulled her head against his chest. She could no longer see his face. But she could hear the steady beat of his heart, and feel the gentle pressure of his hand as he played with the hair at the nape of her neck.

"Fine," he said. "That is just fine."

Chapter 15

Within an hour they would be on the road for London. Only a very small staff was coming with them. Adrien's valet. A cook. A maid for Christina. There were a house-keeper, two parlor maids, and a gardener already in residence at Adrien's London home. These few would easily see to their needs. They would be in London only a day.

One day, however, should be sufficient, they thought. The trip was a formality. Christina's divorce was settled in principle. It was simply a matter of signatures, of having the decree entered in fact.

That morning Adrien still had to see to some departing guests. Christina had to finish with her hair, and she had yet to eat breakfast. But they were moving leisurely toward these goals, expecting no complications, when a servant came and announced one.

"There is a gentleman to see you, Mrs. Pinn. A Mr. Winchell Bower."

She shot Adrien a look; shock, regret. And fright. All her peace of mind, the strength and confidence she had felt she possessed these last weeks quivered inside her as she rose from the table. Her father. The incarnation of her disobedience, of all the unfulfilled expectations of her life. If she could face him, then surely she could face anyone. She rose and followed the servant. Her father was waiting for her in the front library.

After she had answered his only letter, she and her father

had drifted into a limbo of silence. In that letter she had told him, perhaps too forcefully, she thought now, that she intended to follow her own way with regard to her divorce and her life. She regretted some of the stiffness of that letter. But she knew, too, that it had been necessary in a way; it was all part of the clumsiness of trying to stand on one's own feet after leaning so long on others. Like a child learning to walk. Unfortunately, she judged by his silence, her father had not been very forgiving of the lack of grace in these first steps.

It was with a great deal of trepidation that Christina approached the library.

She glanced at her bags, sitting alongside Adrien's at the front door. Her stomach turned. Her father would have had to have come by them. She steeled herself. No matter. There sat the truth. Indestructible truth. She had better make it her ally, for it would always be there. She would never have the life her father had wanted for her.

She drew herself up as tall as she could and turned the knob of the library door.

"Hello, Papa." She closed the door.

He turned. Winchell Bower was not a large man. Yet, when called upon to describe him, people frequently raised their hands, "like so," to give the impression of great size and strength. He was impressive. Like a fighter, a wrestler who had bought the arena in which he had been mauled and groomed. He was a successful man in a world that had never precisely meant for him to be.

His daughter waited by the door. She waited for the boom, the uproar. Grumpy, opinionated, he would burst out at her in a moment. He would be sure of what he wanted and where he thought she should be — home.

Yet, for once, Winchell Bower seemed to have nothing to say. He looked at her. Then his face rose to follow the height and length of the walls of books that surrounded them.

"Do you suppose he's read all these?" he asked. He was listless, quiet; subdued. "I will need a map to find my way to the front gate again." He made a gesture, a veering motion with his hand. "Someone had to meet me. The grounds. . . ." Then, as if this explained, "the staff—" He raised his brow and turned with an extended finger, the counselor making a point—"the reception room." He lowered his hand. This was not the point he wished to make at all.

He turned his back, began to run his hand along the spines of books. "I think—" He broke off. "I don't know what I think, Christina. All the way here I thought I knew. I did a slapdash job of things in London just to make time in my schedule to come here and give you a piece of my mind. But now—It seems I can hardly find a solid piece of it for myself. I've been stewing all summer, you know. Angry with you. Cursing you." There was a longish pause. "Worrying over you." That was all he would admit. He stopped, cast his eyes around the room once more, shook his head. "This house is nothing like what I expected. It is beautiful. Civilized. Proper. I don't know about the earl himself, but he keeps some very good company."

Winchell Bower had apparently run into people in the front reception room. A judge. "Lawrence Sinclair is as bald as a goose." He had never seen him without his wig and robe. And a member of the House of Lords. "I recognized him from a picture hanging in Merit Hall. I cannot believe who comes here to play. You are in very august company, Christina."

Her father remained puzzled, however, as to the earl himself. "Last September, he got flat-out drunk and had to be carried from the back room at Filby's. I know there is an actress in London who has a child by him." He looked over his shoulder to catch her reaction. "And I know he has a mean temper, like a spoiled child, if someone has a go at him. A few years ago he broke three ribs of Marmouth's

167

oldest son; just hauled off and bashed him. Not a very gentlemanly thing to do. Yet, I look around and see he is also this." He held his hand out to the room. "Do you know he has all the works of Ronsard? And of du Bellay. Here, *Defense and Glorification of the French Language*. In English, then another copy in French." He snorted. It was a familiar sound; disapproval, envy. "And look," he said, "the earl is a poet." He had his finger on the spine of a book. He took it down. "It's his." He handed it to her. Indeed. It was a collection of verse. Adrien was the author of a thin little book of French poetry, published in France in 1778.

"What does one make of such a man?" her father asked.

"I don't know. He's a dilettante in the sciences as well. He's doing something with flowers, genetics." And that wasn't even half of it, she thought.

"Busy, isn't he?"

"I suppose."

His voice dropped. "Not so busy that you don't see a good bit of him, I understand."

"I see him."

"You are his favorite companion, I am told."

She didn't answer this.

But the counselor let her know she had not got off scot-free: "I saw your bags were packed. Where are you going?"

"To London."

His face made a sharp frown before he could call it back. "Without telling me? You were coming to London without a word?"

"I was going to call on you, Papa."

"Call on me," he murmured in reply. He studied her for a few moments more, then seemed to dismiss the matter. He walked over to replace the book. Over his shoulder, he called, "I have been made a judge, appointed to the King's Bench." He announced this casually, without joy.

"Oh, Papa, that's marvelous. I'm so happy for you." Christina came forward. But it was not a moment of closeness for them.

Her father was vague. "Yes."

"When do you start?"

"Next month. I have to take a case to trial, then see who will cover some others pending. And I want to stay around long enough to push my own man for head of chambers." He looked around at her, pathetic. "There are yet one or two privileges I can pass down if I play my cards right."

This oblique reference seemed to be as close as they were going to get to the subjects of her barrenness and dissolving marriage. "Oh, Papa. I *am* sorry. From your point of view at least." She bent her head. "I have been a bitter disappointment to you—"

She was going to go on, defend herself if she had to. But the sound of her father's laughter—hollow, yet with a trace of the warmth she had so often known—stopped her.

"You haven't disappointed me," he said. His hand made a brief, tentative touch down her arm. "I am just angry at a world that can't see how valuable you are." He kissed the top of her head. "But you are valuable to me. Remember that."

The father-daughter tete-a-tete lasted only half an hour. It ended with Winchell Bower, in unprecedented humility, advising his daughter she must do what she thought best. It was on this note that a servant summoned them into the front salon. Adrien was waiting for them.

He wore formal, official dress that she had yet to see on him. The left side of his coat was cluttered with the colored ribbons and decorations of an earl. He was dressed to impress, and his explanation for this impressed even further. He had had to see to the departure of the Princess Anne, niece of the king, cousin to the Prince of Wales. She had been staying there in the state rooms for the past week.

This was given offhandedly as the earl fussed over Christina's father. She observed the two with a kind of removed and growing curiosity. Adrien Hunt displayed his

169

charm. He laid it all out like the ribbons and medals positioned carefully down his chest. The beautiful manners. The astute consideration. His peculiar brand of smiles and remote cordiality. Christina couldn't quite believe it — neither the scope nor the effect. With his deft and silky charm, Adrien Hunt took her father in. First, figuratively. Then, literally: He invited her father to share their coach to London.

"I would be delighted," was the response.

In the coach she watched them together. Their affability. Their nodding respect as they tested each other, as they found common interests, concerns. They got along well. And would only get along better. What a surprise, she thought. But then, as she rocked along, she realized, Of course, they got along. It was no surprise. It was for the same reason she herself had been so helpless against Adrien Hunt: He was everything her father had ever taught her to want.

The divorce was formalized quickly in a judge's chamber. Richard was present; snide, unhappy, and taciturn. Christina didn't blame him. She had gotten the better of him. Still, he seemed particularly gauche and ungracious — though perhaps it was sitting next to Adrien that made comparisons so unfavorable. Richard's pale beauty looked anemic. His words, his manners seemed priggish one moment, tactless the next. He sat there in an aura of vain self-indulgence. Without character. Without direction. Without poise.

The divorce decree read as Christina wished it to read. She was divorced because her husband found her sterility reason enough to dissolve their marriage: She had surprised everyone, in the end, by deciding in favor of the truth. It was over.

Everyone stood. Adrien pulled back Christina's chair as

she rose. Then, as she turned, Richard took her arm.

There was pain, bitterness in his voice. "You never looked so well, so glowing," he said, "married. Sin agrees with you."

"Richard—"

"I must have made you the wrong offer—"

Adrien's cane interceded with a thump across Richard's chest. The two men's eyes met. There was a moment of challenge. The judge cleared his throat. The two solicitors in the room each moved back a step.

Slowly, Richard let go of her arm. His mouth sneered as he spoke. "Fancy lord's tart—"

Adrien's cane snapped up. It struck Richard in the jaw. Christina could hear the awful sound of Richard's teeth clicking shut from the impact.

Richard cursed softly as he put his hand to his mouth. His tongue was bleeding.

"You shouldn't put your mouth where it can get in trouble," Adrien told him. He looked at Christina. "Are you ready, then?" He turned his back disdainfully on the other man.

And Richard, like an idiot, rose to the bait. He grabbed Adrien by his coat shoulders. From there, it all happened so quickly.

In one sweep, Adrien turned, brought his arms up, and knocked Richard's hands out flailing. Then an elbow, a fist, and a knee, and Richard was on the floor.

Adrien put his foot on Richard's heaving belly and bent over him. He hooked the gold ferrule of his cane into the other man's cravat and lifted him several inches off the ground. Richard's eyes bulged. His hands went to his throat, the taut fabric there.

"If you feel like a fight," Adrien told him, "consider me always at your disposal. I would like nothing better than to stuff your head down your neck till, to sit, you must squat on your face." He pulled the man an inch closer. "So long as you remember, the lady is off limits to you. Do you understand?"

Richard nodded.

"Good." Adrien let the knotted fabric slip off the end of the cane. Richard's head cracked on the floor.

Christina cringed as it did. For Richard, nothing could be worse than this. Adrien had leveled him. In every sense. In front of everyone. He deserved it perhaps. But Christina could not help but be a little appalled. The earl had—with perfect deliberation and thoroughness—put the baronet's son in his place.

No one went to Richard or tried to help him as he climbed, staggered to his feet. He spoke thickly, "Sodding bastard . . ." Like a bullied schoolboy, with only profanity for his defense.

Adrien watched him, waiting for him to make any sign of further challenge.

When none seemed forthcoming, Adrien picked up his hat, his gloves from the desk. "I am much worse than that," he said. He turned to look at Richard. "And, if you so much as come near her again, you'll find out how menacing I can truly become."

With a possessive caress at the small of her back, he guided Christina toward the door.

Richard called out to her. "Christina?"

She turned. He was bent over the desk, his face, his posture seething with anger and humiliation. "You won't always be off limits, you know," he said. He flicked a nervous glance at the man beside her. Christina grasped Adrien's arm. "In six months, I—anyone—will be able to hold conversation"—the word was lent its lewder meaning—"with you. Anywhere. Any time they choose. He's notorious, you know. . . ."

Christina had to step directly into Adrien's path. "It's just talk," she murmured. She herded Adrien out of the room.

As they came out into the street, he was fuming.

"It's nothing," she insisted. "*He's* nothing."

"He's dangerous. He intends to harm you."

"He doesn't. I lived with him, don't forget, for three years. He talks a nasty row, but he has never lifted a finger—"

"He lifted a finger toward me!"

"After you baited him!" She didn't keep the disapproval out of her voice. "Rather horribly, I might add."

"Oh fine. Now I am the villain for *making* your damned husband attack me."

"My *former* husband. Whom I don't give a damn about. Only I hate to see you be so highhanded—"

"Highhanded?" A light rain had begun to fall. He stopped and pulled her back under the overhang of the building. Their carriage stood waiting in the street.

"Yes, highhanded. You can be so unlikable—"

"You want Richard to like me?"

"No. *I* want to like you. And I don't, when you treat people as if—as if they were beneath your contempt."

"Richard *is* beneath my contempt. And *not* because of my social position. He's an ass."

"He felt your title—"

"Because of his own narrow, little mind."

"You used it."

Adrien turned her by the arm. "Christina, I am not a democrat. Not by birthright, credo, or temperament. And with people like Richard, one is either above them or below. It's better he sees me as above, is a little afraid, don't you think?"

"No. It's better for you to not indulge in such games."

He heaved an impatient breath. "Damn it, the game interests you as much as anyone. You like sleeping with an earl."

This caught her short. Her tone softened. "I used to," she admitted. "But recently, it's begun to annoy more than anything else." She looked at him, deadly earnest. "The man himself has turned out to be more interesting than any title. But he can hide behind his name, I've discovered. Draw himself up and wrap himself in it like a mantle. When he is the earl, that is when I can reach him least."

Adrien didn't like this. His face clouded. He stared at her, troubled—the look of someone who is mildly insulted but unwilling to pursue the offending subject.

"Come on," he murmured. "I still have the house to see to. And the bloody minister at Whitehall."

It was almost laughable: On cue—Adrien raised his head and looked at them—servants brought a small canopy. He and Christina, along with the mass of her great dress, were sheltered from the rain as they made their way out to the carriage. Adrien handed her in, then sat on the opposite side.

It was a very comfortable coach, a plush interior. Polished brass handles. Soft cushions. Leather curtains, lined in velvet on the inside where one could touch their lovely folds. And it was a very lonely coach. Christina sat back. On her side. She felt, that afternoon, more a prisoner than a passenger in the elegant world provided by the earl.

The remaining errands belonged to Adrien. He was closing up his London house for the winter, making arrangements for his long absence. He had to see to a number of things there: Draining the upstairs and downstairs plumbing—his London home was one of the first to acquire this innovative feature, so that the pipes wouldn't burst with the first freeze. Draping over the furniture. Then packing off the last of his London staff; they were being sent on to Cornwall.

There were papers to sign at his banker's. Also an appointment, which he seemed to find particularly disagreeable in prospect, with a king's minister at Whitehall. Growing more and more bleak, he went through with it all—throwing Christina sullen looks, hardly saying anything. Even the weather seemed to side with him. The sky grew darker and darker. The drizzle burst into a downpour.

Late in the afternoon, a last incident rounded out the already bad day—though it was less the incident than Adrien's reaction to it that annoyed Christina. Adrien was in one of the offices at Whitehall, talking to his "damned minister." The outer room where Christina had been deposited was dusty and poorly ventilated. She'd begun to feel a little nauseous. So she had gone outside. And there, on the open street, she was knocked down. A nimble, beggarly-looking fellow charged out of a carriage alley and grabbed for her pocket.

Adrien came out just in time. At the sight of him, the fellow ran off. "My goodness," Christina said as Adrien helped her to her feet, "am I glad to see you! Did you save my pocket?"

Adrien didn't return her grateful smile. "If he was after your damned pocket."

"What else—?"

"Perhaps Richard didn't feel like waiting till I was completely out of the way."

"Oh, honestly, Adrien." She brushed off her skirts. "You are being so silly about Richard. I was accosted by a smalltime ruffian after my purse, nothing more—"

Adrien had walked to the edge of the pavement and, with a kick, put the purse at her feet. "Not very effectual, was he?"

Christina picked up the bag. It was a soggy wreck. She held it out.

"He was out to do you harm," Adrien asserted.

She made a face. "I doubt it."

"I don't. Richard is angry, and ruffians like that can be hired for a tuppence."

The notion seemed so ridiculous. "This is really too much. In three years Richard never raised a finger—"

175

"But he thought nothing of sending others, lawyers, after you and after every cent you ever possessed."

"You are frightening me."

"Good. Perhaps I can frighten a little sense into you. You are going to have to be very cautious while I am gone, Christina."

She paused to consider this, then shook her head. "No, I lived in London a long time. It was an everyday pocket-thief. Richard would do me no physical harm."

But Adrien's expression insisted he would. "Fine." He drew an exasperated breath. "But it is such a pretty neck. And, in four days, I won't be here to protect it."

Chapter 16

The carriage bumped and joggled. That had been the primary sensation since sunset. Rolling, kidney-shaped movement. Christina looked forward to the moment when the motion would stop at the front door of the Kewischester house.

She rested her head back. Adrien's shoulder was there. After stewing for the first several miles out of London, he had shifted, finally, over to where she sat. At present, his arm lay around her, loose, relaxed. She suspected he was asleep. Then, as the carriage turned and followed the road, moonlight came through a crack in the window curtain. A slice of light swept across his face. She saw him close his eyes in response.

"What time is it?" she asked.

She felt him turn toward her. "It will be at least an hour more. Why don't you go back to sleep?"

"I wish we could stop. I wouldn't mind a few moments alone with a chamber pot."

"There's an inn not too far away." He paused. His voice was comforting. Low, smooth. Right by her ear. "In fact," he continued, "I was thinking of asking if you'd mind stopping. There's a card game there tonight."

"A card game?" She'd never met, she thought irritably, anyone with such a taste for social life. She shifted forward, away from him, to pull her wrap up around herself. "No, of course not, I don't mind."

He needed no further encouragement. He tapped sharply on the back of the carriage. The small window above slid open, and the face of John, the young footman, was lit by bouncing moonlight.

Adrien raised his voice slightly. "The Three Rose Inn."

There was a quick acknowledgment, and the window closed.

Half an hour later, Adrien was handing her out of the velvet interior of his coach, then carrying her over the mud: It was not exactly the sort of place Christina had been expecting.

They had stopped at a large wood-framed structure, well off the beaten path. It was an inn, but it seemed a mystery how it survived as one—except that it catered, rather royally, to the Earl of Kewischester.

As they entered, a stocky woman came bustling in from a back room, wiping her hands on an apron tied around her ample waist. "Ai!" She gave Adrien a strong hug. *"Mais tu es en avance, mon cher."* She called over her shoulder, *"André! André! Adrien est déjà là! Viens tout de suite!"*

Adrien had set Christina down in a bright, warm-looking foyer. She gave him a suspicious look as he took her wrap. The woman had just told him he was early. She'd been expecting him.

A small, wiry-looking man came out to them from the same far doorway. He and Adrien exchanged greetings, slaps on the back. Adrien introduced him as the owner of the inn.

"Enchanté, mademoiselle." The little man took her hand and kissed it. He, too, had on an apron, was covered in flour. Yet he held himself with great dignity.

"We'd have a late supper, if we could, André. In the room?"

The innkeeper smile. *"Bien sûr. Ce que tu voudras, mon ami. Ah, pardon, mademoiselle."* He turned to Christina; he had apparently noticed her discomfort. With an accent so bad it could only be real, he asked, "You speak ze French, yes?"

She shook her head. "No, not well. And it's *Madame.*"

"Ah la la." He shot Adrien a look as he led the way upstairs. "I hope I see no *furieux* husband here tonight."

"No, we left the furious husband back in London," Adrien answered. "No one else is here yet?"

"*Non.* You are the first."

The room into which they were shown was large and cheerful, furnished in roughhewn country furniture, with homemade curtains and bedcovers. It was friendly, welcoming. And, Christina noted, there was brandy — the Calvados Adrien preferred — by the bedstead.

The innkeeper left them. Christina took off her hat. "Do you come here often?" she asked Adrien.

"It's one of the two or three places nearby that has good food, good liquor." And good bedrooms, she thought. "And good tables," he continued. "It draws a peaceable crowd capable of paying their card debts. And then, André! and his wife are a nice sort."

"They certainly seem to like you."

"They like anyone with whom they can talk about France. The old days. He was once part of the king's staff there. Before the new regime. And," he added quietly, "I loaned him the money to buy this property. I think that has made me something of a hero in his eyes."

"Judging by the number of guests, that *was* a rather heroic gesture. It doesn't seem like a very good investment."

Adrien threw a mischievous look as he poured some Calvados. "I have made other loans, it seems to me, without very good collateral. Would you like some brandy?"

She had always refused the brandy on previous occasions, but she nodded, *yes,* this time. It was an act of rebellion; a bid to be less predictable. She was feeling just a little taken for granted. He hadn't stopped here for her. He had stopped for a bloody card game. And he had planned it.

He registered no surprise, but poured her a small glass of the liquor. Christina took it. She sat and cupped the brandy glass in her palms, staring into it. The fumes burned her eyes, but it did smell nice. It smelled like apples. She took a sip. Then opened her eyes wide and tried to clear her throat. This developed into a sputter and cough as the fumes were carried into her lungs.

"My God," she rasped, "I thought it would be sweet."

"No. It's quite like cognac." Adrien thumped her back, smiling, puzzled. "What's gotten into you?" he asked. "You don't seem the least bit pleased we've stopped."

"You stopped to play cards." She threw him an accusing look as she got up. She went behind the screen to find the chamber pot. And hide.

Her eyes watered. Her pride stung. It was foolish for her to be upset. She knew it. But he had been gloomy company in London. He had hardly spoken two words in the dismal ride out of the city. And now he took it for granted that she would stay in this room with him. So much for granted that he intended to have dinner, then play cards until God knew when, leaving her up here alone.

"I stopped because you asked it," he called to her over the privacy screen.

She wouldn't answer.

Supper came. The wine, the strange concoctions and confections from the kitchen which she knew to be delicacies of French cuisine. Yet, she couldn't eat. Adrien, on the other hand, ate well. He poured out the last of the wine, filling both their glasses, then leaned back as he pushed aside his clean plate.

"So what is it, Christina?" he asked. "Are you getting your menses? What? Or is it that you don't like my going down to the card game?"

"We're not married. You can do as you like."

"Oof—" He rolled his eyes and made a mock grimace, as if he'd received a blow. "Always very bad when the lady

180

mentions you're not married." He reached for her hand. She withdrew it.

"Actually," he said, "I could probably limit my interest downstairs to an hour or two. It's more business than pleasure. Christina," he spoke in a sincere tone, "they are expecting me. I was going to take you home, then come back. But it just seemed so much nicer to have you with me. It means"—he ran his finger along her arm—"I can make love to you now, take care of what I need to downstairs, then come back and sleep with you all night. It means I don't have to be away from you so much."

He pushed the small dinner table from between them and drew her—with some opposition—onto his lap. "Shall I," he whispered, "get you ready for bed? Tuck you in?" His hand had already begun with the tiny buttons down the front of her dress.

"Damn it, Adrien. Oh—" He leaned his face, his mouth against her bare bosom. "I wish I could be more sure of how you felt." She stopped him by taking his face into her hands, making him look at her. "You know you never give me more than bits and pieces of yourself. And you leave me alone a great deal of the time. For card games. For God knows what else. Why do you never tell me you love me?"

She felt his spine straighten. As if he might dump her on the ground in his haste to get up. But he restrained himself. Instead, he tried to kiss her mouth. She pulled back—it was so obvious what he was doing. She laughed.

Then he did push her off, gently. He stood. "Thank you very much."

"You were trying to divert the conversation."

"I was trying to kiss you." He looked around, his hand feeling the front of his vest, looking for something.

"They're in your coat."

He gave her a look; mild alarm. As if she had read his mind, trespassed. Then he picked up his coat and found his packet of cigars. "I hear people downstairs," he said. "Per-

181

haps I should go down."

"All right."

She was going to let him off without a fuss. For now. But when he came back up, there would be no excuses. No reprieve. This very nice room—not quite so much his territory as everywhere else she had spent the night with him—was the place where she would make her stand. If he was going to leave in four days—if she was going to wait for him—she was going to hear the word "love" from his lips. She was either going to be the avowed special woman in his life, or a woman at the beginning of a new life she would create on her own. She would not be left to watch and worry and wonder. . . .

It always worried Adrien when she became quiet and agreeable. It inevitably meant trouble was brewing beneath the pretty exterior of Christina Pinn.

She was, he lamented as he came down the stairs, such a miserably independent creature. In a way, he supposed, he counted on this. There would be no depression, no tantrum upstairs because he left. Just as she accepted his more lengthy and distant departures. She was a resourceful woman, capable of amusing herself. But, on the other hand, this independence could be a nuisance. He never knew exactly what she was thinking, exactly what to expect. Except that he could expect her ideas to be her own, not easily subject to his own views or wishes. Damn the woman, anyway.

Adrien was cursing her as he opened the door to the inn's back room. The familiar atmosphere greeted him. Smoky, warm—a generous fire crackled in the huge stone fireplace. His presence was noted; the jovial talk of the room quieted to a more serious tenor.

André. Thomas. Charles. He spotted Samuel Rolfeman among the other half dozen. Adrien grimaced. Damn her, he thought; damn Christina to hell and back. Why did she have to be in this particular mood tonight? When he knew already there was a rather difficult idea he wanted to sell her before the night was out? He wanted to leave Sam behind, to act as her bodyguard. He didn't expect her to love the notion. She would view it as an unnecessary encumbrance. But he wanted to talk protection, practical matters. And she wanted to talk love. He made a sour face.

"What's wrong with you?" Thomas moved a dish, already half-full of ashes, to the corner of the table by an empty chair. "I understand you brought Christina. Do you think that's wise?"

"It's fine. She's upstairs. She'll go to sleep."

"Couldn't be away from her for one night?"

"There's only four nights left."

Thomas made a grim tilt of his head. "Ah, love."

"Or lust." Adrien looked Thomas directly in the face. "She appeals to me in bed like no woman has in a long time." He smiled. "Her body is heaven, Thomas."

Thomas dropped his eyes.

It was, Adrien knew, a distinctly unkind thing to say to his friend.

It was becoming increasingly obvious that Thomas did not like Adrien's sleeping with Christina Pinn. He wouldn't admit it. In fact, he even spoke up for it when Adrien was criticized by the others: Better the woman they'd chased down in the woods had a lover among them—a stake in their secrecy and survival—than she retained her former hostility. Yet, on another level, Adrien knew Thomas did not like his fooling with Christina.

Yet, fool with her, he would. Adrien thought it best that Thomas understand this.

Adrien smiled as he reached into his inside vest pocket. "She's not suffering, you know, Thomas. She's exactly where she wants to be."

"Yes." Thomas remained glum.

183

Adrien dropped a folded sheet of paper on the table and sat down. He addressed the others as they gathered round. "The new man, Cabrel, got this for us. I think it's good, but of course someone has to go in and check it first." He unfolded the paper. It was a detailed map of an underground network of passages in the abbey at Limoigne.

There were no cards that night. Only a group of very intent players.

Adrien, with these men, was planning yet another rescue, of aristos being held in detention at Limoigne. In every respect, he knew he shouldn't have been doing so. This month, the French had doubled the amount offered for information leading to his capture. Claybourne, the English Minister of Foreign Affairs, still didn't know that Adrien was at the heart of the "unofficial English embarrassment over the French prison raids." Claybourne continued to send Adrien out chasing after his own shadow. But the voices, the plaintive cries for help from the relatives and friends of those incarcerated were increasing. Adrien found it difficult to turn his back on them. He already knew a dozen old friends or acquaintances in France, as well as a score of his grandfather's peers, who had made the trip from a prison to the guillotine. Adrien intended to keep his grandfather's name off that list by putting it on another: He wanted his grandfather to be among those brought from France this next trip. Adrien wanted Edward Claybourne's grip on him — via the threat against his grandfather's life — rendered useless, cut at the nerve.

Philippe de La Fontaine, Adrien's grandfather, believed he lived freely in Paris. He went about his business, bought his groceries, wrote his slightly dotty letters that somehow made it across the channel, complained of his failing memory, his health, his neglectful grandson. He harmed no one. And saw no reason why anyone should harm him. Adrien had tried to explain — without making the old gentleman too much a party to Adrien's own proscribed activi-

he reached and touched her cheek. His very blue eyes looked out of his dark face with a seriousness, a wistfulness that made something go limp inside her. Her resolve quivered, mewed to be let out of this, to put it all off just one more night. . . .

"Adrien," she began, "before you go, we must speak very clearly to each other. Very honestly."

He laughed. "Christina, I would be afraid to speak to you any other way."

"Good—"

"Do we really have to talk now? I'm so tired." He leaned forward, then shifted his weight. It always happened so easily—he pulled her under him and took a deep breath. As if he might hold it, submerged, for a hundred years.

He let it out in a groan. Her dressing gown had come open. He kissed her breasts, opening the gown further, kissing downward toward her waist.

"Adrien—" She tried to make her laughter light. "I thought you were tired."

"Not that tired." His hand reached over her to the oil lamp. He turned the valve. The light dimmed, guttered, then popped out. Darkness. Except for the brightness of a three-quarter moon coming through their window.

"Adrien." She put her hand directly over his mouth to stop the next onslaught. "I want to have a clear understanding before you go. I don't want to make you angry, and I don't want to make you feel cornered. But I have to know. We only have four days to wade our way through this. We have to start now."

There was a deep sigh in the dark. He rolled off her, then sat up on the edge of the bed, facing the window, silhouetted in the moonlight. There, by the bedstead, he poured brandy. A generous slosh, by the sound of it.

"You can't," she said, "evade the question I asked you this evening forever."

"And what question was that?"

187

"Do you love me?"

He laughed, then took a drink, tilting his head back and downing the entire glass. When he spoke, his voice was a murmur. "I am more involved with you than I'd like to be."

"That's not love."

He turned. His face was in shadow. Hers, she knew, would be in full light. "No, it's not," he said.

She bit her lip. "I see."

"No, you don't. I am very cautious with you, Christina. Because I like you. Do you imagine I've never said those words before? I've thrown them around rather liberally. And reaped all the benefits those words trade on—"

"But you didn't need to trade them with me?" she said. "Since 'all the benefits' came without them."

"Christina—" He leaned toward her. "I care about you. More than I want to—"

She gave him a shove. "Don't. How can you touch me so tenderly, then talk to me in such platitudes. 'I care about you.' Honest to God, Adrien. You make me feel like a visitor, and an unwelcome one at that. Someone you must carefully not offend—"

"You are, in a sense, Christina. I've not included a woman in my life, regularly, on a daily basis that is, in a very long time. Part of me comes to this, this closeness you want, kicking and screaming. It frightens me the way you look at me, the way you are curious about me. And it frightens me even more that I'm so fascinated with you, I put up with it."

He stood up. As if this settled the matter. He raised his arms, his shirt over his head. The rest of his clothes went. He poured another glass of brandy before he came to bed.

Christina sighed. She never got precisely what she wanted out of him. "I think," she said, "you have just told me that you won't say you love me because, quite possibly, you don't. And that I am supposed to feel flattered and singled out for this honor."

He laughed. "That's it. Approximately."

"Lovely." Only she wasn't quite so dissatisfied as she pretended. She recognized in his hesitancy, in his careful, circumscribing words that there was a genuine admission. Anyone this cautious was on unfamiliar ground; she was different from the others. The joy in this knowledge was odd, discordant. But she took what was available. . . .

She watched him in the moonlight. He was looking out the window, sipping the brandy; stark naked. She could not look even at this silhouette without being stirred. The wide shoulders, the long curve of back ending in the small, tight buttocks — almost nonexistent, less buttocks than taut, muscular extensions of his thighs . . . Christina lay back and waited. She anticipated his joining her in bed, his touching her. . . .

"Here. Try it again. It's better the second time." He had turned to offer her brandy. She shook her head. He brought it closer. "Go on. I think you might need it."

She smiled. "No. I'm fine."

"I have something else to tell you that might put your independent little nose out of joint. Take the brandy." She took the glass, held it for him as he slipped under the covers with her. "Besides," he said, "I might be in the mood for a little revenge for all the infernal talking you've subjected me to." She could feel his smile, its warmth; then, literally, his teeth. He bit her neck.

"Stop it." She laughed. "Here, you drink this."

He didn't take the brandy, but nudged forward to lay his cheek on her breast, his arm across her. "I have to tell you what I've just done. At the card game. One of the reasons I wanted to go. I had the opportunity there to ask a favor of a friend, a man I would trust with my life. His name is Sam, Samuel Rolfeman. I have asked him to look after you while I am gone, as a kind of bodyguard."

"I don't need a bodyguard."

"It's an extraordinarily lovely body, Christina. I think you do."

"Adrien. I love your being worried about me—" The stupid word, *love,* popping out of her own mouth, distracted her. She blinked, couldn't remember what she had wanted to say. She frowned. "That was very presumptuous of you."

"Christina. I am genuinely concerned—"

"And I am genuinely appalled—"

"Then be appalled. Better that, than mauled or dead. I don't trust that bloody idiot you married."

"Richard wouldn't hurt me!"

"A woman alone is vulnerable."

"For godssake." She shoved the brandy back toward him. "Set this down. I don't want it."

He took the glass, pulled back the covers, opened her nightdress and poured the Calvados directly over her.

"Ai!" She scrambled to wipe, to stem the flow. "That's cold! Are you insane—?"

He took her wrists, pulled them over her head, and continued pouring. Until only jarring, rude little droplets were all that was left to spatter from the upturned glass. The brandy ran. Her nightclothes caught what ran down her sides, over her ribcage and hips. It was wet, warm. Tingling.

"Are you quite satisfied?" she asked primly. "You can let go, now that you've had your fun—"

He didn't seem finished with his "fun." He held her firmly. Then, very leisurely, he leaned down to the neat indentation of her navel. He ran over it with his tongue. "You are strong-willed," he said between licks up her belly. "Resilient. Capable. And delicious—mmm—But you're not very strong."

She tried to pull in her belly, elude the touch of his mouth. But all struggles were in vain. She had never realized how physically powerful he was. He had her body easily pinioned, while he was relaxed, free to do as he pleased . . . . His tongue made a spiral around the tip of

190

her breast.

She jerked. "Ah! Adrien! I'm going to smash you with the first thing I can lay my hands on — Let go of me!"

He gave a throaty chuckle. "Not until you admit a woman can be a little vulnerable."

"What?"

"Say it." He lay full length on top of her, smoothing his body into the wetness of her skin until a kind of suction was formed between their bellies. "Mmm, you are heavenly," he laughed, "wiggling and wet."

The feel of him made her a little dizzy. "And you — you are making a thorough mess —"

"Which I'm going to clean up. Personally." He reached out and retrieved the entire bottle of brandy. "But I am going to make a bigger mess if you don't admit it."

She hedged. "Admit what?"

He laughed, rose up on one arm. And poured.

Christina screamed and squirmed. "Ah! Adrien. For goodness' sake!" The fumes rose into her eyes, her nose. She was getting a regular bath in the apple-fragrant liquor. "Oh, you filthy, wicked . . ."

"That's getting you nowhere." He reduced the flow from the bottle to a thin stream over her belly. She writhed. Then, slowly, the little stream moved lower. A thin rivulet ran between her legs.

"Ai!" It burned, but the alcohol evaporated quickly — leaving behind the warmest, most indecent sensation. "All right!"

"I'm vulnerable," he coached.

"I'm vulnerable."

"And I need a little protection."

She was put out at this addition, but gave in quickly rather than get another dousing. "And I need a little protection," she said. "From beasts like you, at least."

He let go, laughing as he sat up.

Christina flew at him, pounding, hitting him, pulling,

191

scraping her nails. "Oh, you beast! You miserable, smug—" Words failed her. "I could—I could—"

He withstood it, bracing his weight against the attack, then slowly pinning her back. Once more he lay on top of her. Except this time he seemed to have a more serious intent. He quieted her fulminations by kissing her. Hard. Deep. Letting the barrage of blows die of their own accord. Christina found her poor hands open, hovering above him in confusion. There was no playfulness now to his lovemaking. She could feel him, solid against her thigh; his whole body moving, preparing. . . . Sensation clouded everything. All reason. Reality. She could have sworn, distantly, there was noise, a pounding. . . . Or it was perhaps just her heart. She caressed him, groaned as he touched her breasts, as he drank from her skin the smell of flavor, the tang of apples. . . .

There was a rapping. It seemed almost as if at their door. But it was a sound from another world, so far off. Adrien's breath was right there in her ear. His hips lifted. And he pushed forward, the heat of him filling her; there seemed not a space anywhere he did not occupy. Not in her body, her mind . . . She let out a soft groan. And the pounding of her heart became a banging. A banging at the door. Not ten feet away.

A voice called. "Open this door! I know you're in there!"

"Who the blazes—" Adrien twisted toward the door.

Then it all happened so quickly. The door crashed open. Light, a lantern, swung huge shadows into the room. Adrien scrambled to put himself and Christina under the protection of covers. A heap of bedclothes hit her. But something else, a huge, hulking figure, hit Adrien.

There was cursing, the grunts and gasps of desperate effort. The bed shook from the struggle. Christina cringed—and her fingers brushed against the forgotten brandy bottle. The covers were thrashing, the mattress rocking; it was reflex. Her fingers closed around the neck of the bottle, then she brought it down hard over the head of the attacker. With a slump, the commotion in the bed grew still.

Yet, the room held another presence: The lantern moved. Footsteps tapped. Swinging light, chunks of dark shifted over the walls, around the furniture. Then, right at her shoulder, the oil lamp flared. And a small, wizened old man materialized out of the shadows.

He looked at Christina, frowned at her. His wrinkled, old face was pinched in an expression of disgust. His eyes jumped across the bed to where Adrien, arms extended, was looking down in bewilderment at his own chest. He was pinned to the bed by a giant motionless form.

"I have been," the old man spoke in a tight, disapproving tone, "halfway around England looking for you tonight." He followed this with a sniff of the air and a vocal shiver of repugnance. "By heaven, this place smells like a distillery!"

Adrien pushed his burden from him and turned to look at the speaker. He held up an arm to shield his eyes from the lantern light at the foot of the bed. "Claybourne?"

Then, with a double take out the corner of his eye, Adrien's gaze dropped fully to the bed. He picked up one rather large chunk of glass—the bed shimmered with broken bits of it. Very carefully, he turned the piece over in his fingers. He frowned, as if still trying to piece together what had happened. Then he looked at Christina. He reached and unfolded her small hand. A crooked smile began to play on his lips as he slipped his finger into the broken bottleneck. He gestured with the item to the other man. "This is not," he said, "a woman you want to trifle with, Edward."

Chapter 17

"I thought," the old man ground out between his teeth, "you were going to keep in close touch in case there were any rapid developments! I have traipsed all over London and half the countryside looking for you!"

The intruder was a short old man in a white wig. He didn't quite look real. His face was powdered to an even and unnatural monotone. His eyes shone out of it like little coals. His clothes, though neat and well-made, were outdated. As was the walking stick he carried — the sort that had been in in fashion twenty years before, as tall as a shepherd's crook. The effect was odd. Intense. Eccentric. Slightly out of touch. And somehow forbidding; in some way she couldn't name, Christina was instantly afraid of this little man.

Adrien moved some of the glass away by folding the blanket down. "Well, you found me," he said. "And there better be a damned good reason for you to come in here like this." He swung from the bed, then let out a breath. "Jesus. Be careful when you get out of the bed, Christina. There's glass everywhere, all over my clothes —"

"I've half a mind to haul you in" — the old intruder was on his own bent, seeing, hearing nothing but his own anger — "let you spend a night in goal. At least, then, I'd know where you were, when I wanted you . . . ."

Adrien padded across the room, not the least disturbed

194

by the old man's tirade. He undid the straps of one of their bags and began to dig through it, his nakedness almost an insult—of so little consequence before this intruder.

Yet it bothered Christina. The eerie lighting of the room drew sharp shadows across the ripples of muscle along Adrien's back. He bent, moved. His shoulders, buttocks, thighs alternately flexed, released. The peculiar old man grew quiet. He watched Adrien. Every movement. Every muscle. He became strangely docile—the way a poisonous snake is charmed, lost in the notes of sensuous music.

"I'd forgotten how nasty they'd sliced you," he said. "Does the scar hurt?"

"No."

"Nor limit you, apparently. I understand you blackened the eye of old Pinn's son this morning."

"He fell against a desk."

The old man laughed. "After you knocked him down."

"He was clumsy."

"He was undoubtedly a dolt to have provoked you. Though I doubt his fall had anything to do with physical clumsiness." Again, the old man laughed; nervous, prim.

It occurred to Christina that the old man was possibly disconcerted by any nakedness, not just Adrien's. And that Adrien already knew this. It seemed possible that Adrien— flagrant, casual—had set out to rattle the other man in precisely this way. Yet, all the while, making it seem the other man's shortcoming . . .

Adrien turned, stepped into a pair of silk breeches. The old man's stare froze. "What are you doing?"

"Getting dressed. I assume we are about to have one of our little talks. And I'm not about to do that naked in a bed of glass—"

"No, no— You have no smallclothes!"

Adrien threw an impatient look as he tucked in his shirt tail. He picked up his cravat, then went to stand before the mirror.

The old man wouldn't let go of the subject. "Is it true the French wear no smallclothes?"

"I don't inspect Frenchmen for underclothes."

"But you have put none on—"

Adrien looked at him in the mirror. "They rumple up, where one sits. They're uncomfortable."

The old face twisted up with pleasure. He dissolved into chuckling, rasping laughter. "And they ruin the line of a well-made figure. Ah, vanity." After some long seconds of this merry amusement, he spoke, wiping at his eyes. "My dear young man, you are so wonderfully transparent. Even the smallest surprise about you circles back on the same conclusion." He tried to calm himself with two or three fond sighs.

Adrien pulled the points of his stiff collar against his jaw and wrapped his neckcloth around. Then he flipped the cravat through on itself and turned the collar nubs down. All the while, he was watching in the mirror. Thank God, Christina thought. He wasn't quite so cavalier as he appeared. In his corner of the room, she could see his face—a glimmer that appeared now and then in the mirror—frowning, contemplating, observing their strange visitor with a fixed stare.

"We passed your friend, Mr. Lillings," the older man offered by way of conversation. "On his way to your house?"

"I presume. He's been staying there."

"Why don't you tell me a little about him? Is he a very old friend?"

"We met at boarding school. As boys."

"And how did Mr. Lillings acquire his French connections?"

"I don't know." Adrien shrugged. "He came with me once or twice to visit my grandfather. Then later, he studied art in Paris." Adrien twisted his neck once to adjust the fit of the neckcloth. "He's quite a good draftsman, actually."

"Would you say he was clever?"

Adrien turned, looked at the old man directly. "Yes. He has a good eye."

"I said, 'clever.' That's not the same thing." The old man cleared his throat. "Mr. Lillings must not be part of our plans."

Adrien shot a worrisome glance in Christina's direction. "Let's discuss this downstairs. There's a room in the back where we can talk."

"None of your evasions on this. No Mr. Lillings, do you understand? He has French upper-class allegiance."

"So do I."

The old man snorted. "As if that mattered in your case."

"I assure you, it doesn't in Thomas'."

"He's your friend."

"Which is why I want him with me."

"Which is why you are no person to judge in this matter." He drew in a reprimanding breath. "The man, my dear fellow, has been to France three times in the last month. That we know of—"

"Hand me my shoes," Adrien interrupted.

The old man was momentarily halted by this request. Mechanically, he reached down to the shoes in front of him.

Adrien was bent over the knee-buttons of his breeches, fastening them over his stockings. The old man came to the foot of the bed with the shoes.

As he handed them over, Adrien passed another quick glance, from the old man to Christina. Christina recognized this for what it was—a warning from one man to the other. The old man turned. She had the regard of both men for a moment. Then, the older one raised his brow. "This one speaks English?"

Adrien tapped a foot into a shoe as he drew on his waistcoat. "This one," he said, "speaks English and swings brandy bottles." Adrien winked at her and picked up his coat. He threw her an enormous smile—which did not, she decided, make up for the conspiracy of exchanged glances the moment before. "Now, if you'll help me with that lump lying there on the floor"—Adrien pointed to the unconscious man—"we'll all three go downstairs and leave the lady to modestly separate herself from the wet bedding and shards of glass."

Claybourne was reopening the subject of Thomas as they went through the door to the back room. Whereas Adrien could only think of Christina. How much had she gleaned this time? Honest to God, that woman seemed always in the wrong place at the wrong time. No matter how he tried, the whole business—from mistaken attacks in the woods, to conversations in the night, to stupid Claybourne on one of his rampages—seemed to be laying itself out in front of her.

As for Claybourne, Adrien was doubly angry with him. Not only was he a fool to discount Christina—luckily for Claybourne, his dealings seldom required any real astuteness with women—but he was exceeding himself tonight in being his usual damned pain-in-the-ass. What could the pompous old goat possibly want, when they had so carefully gone over everything just this past afternoon?

"No Lillings," Claybourne said, like the final word.

"Why?"

Claybourne sat while Adrien went to stoke the fire.

"At the very least," Claybourne said, "he would be sympathetic to the man we're looking for. Lillings lost his chief patron, an old artist-mentor, to the revolution. The man was guillotined about eighteen months ago. Did you know that?" Adrien made an acknowledgment. "Then you must realize that Lillings not only could be sympathetic, he could *be* the organizer of these prison raids himself—"

"Thomas! My God! He's no more your prison robber than I am!"

The Old Man chortled at this. "Now there's a good joke. You. To whom organization and initiative abroad means setting up a salon concert in Paris. Or a doxy." He laughed again. "Or brawl. No, my prime problem with you is keeping you off the cutting edge of a scythe long enough to find this fellow. Though, I must admit, I considered you briefly."

Adrien let a large log drop onto the old embers and new kindling. It fell heavily, collapsing the light structure of ashes and twigs in a puff of sparks. He jumped back, muttering, brushing at his breeches.

The Old Man was delighted with this. "You see? You are too impetuous, always in a hurry to get things done. The more I considered you, the more ludicrous it became. You are, my dear young man, the antithesis of our very calculating and disciplined Frenchman."

"I'm afraid you must add," Adrien said, dusting the grime from his pants, "that I am imprudent as well. I've already told Thomas about the venture."

The old man came up out of his seat. "What!"

"I've already included Thomas, discussed the whole project, and asked for his help."

"You had no right!"

"It's my neck we're risking."

"You will have to *untell* him," Claybourne sputtered at him. "Send him on his way—"

"I won't." Adrien came over to the little table and sat. "Edward, I have enough to worry about without trying to fool you." He made a smile. "I need Thomas. He is an honest fellow who still understands cunning enough to anticipate it. I can think of no man I would rather have watching my back."

The Old Man glowered at him.

Adrien smiled encouragement. "Come now, it's a *fait accompli*. You will think of a way to work it to your advantage. As you always do. And I'm sure this isn't what you came all the way out into the night for. Why are we here?"

Claybourne's face softened. Then spread slowly into a smile. "Ah, yes. I have some wonderful news. You leave tonight, not in a week's time. My Madman plans to open a hole in the wall of the abbey at Limoigne and relieve France of several dozen aristos in detention there. It is his biggest venture yet! We can't fail to snag him!"

Adrien's fingers went cold. He clenched them. He had planned to go over in four days—three days sooner than he and Claybourne had planned this afternoon—to do just that: They were cutting a hole in the abbey wall to gain entrance into the back passages. Now, to hear his own plans out of the Old Man's mouth— It was enough to stop the blood flowing in his veins.

"How do you know?" he asked.

The Old Man grinned. "I have my sources."

"I wouldn't trust just any source for such information. I've heard nothing of this, though I fancy I have worked my way into a trusted position within the man's outer circle."

"Exactly. You must see if you can do what Cabrel did. You must, in the next three days, work yourself in closer."

"Cabrel?" Their newest recruit. The very promising young Frenchman who had provided the map to the abbey.

"Bertrand Cabrel," Claybourne confirmed. "We sent him in from the French side. Which is how I want you to concentrate your approach. It seems that the little band is less suspicious of French introductions." The Old Man's joy grew. "I can't tell you what a breakthrough this is. To actually know in advance, instead of always guessing." He patted his vest and turned a smug look on Adrien. "But just rewards, I think. You know me. I like to come at everything from six different directions."

Adrien was staggered. "You have others?"

"Others what?"

"Besides me. And this Cabrel. Are there others?"

"Of course."

"I see." Adrien sat back.

"There, there, it is only a precaution. I still want you to do the delicate work. You are the best suited. It is your old stamping ground this madman is rummaging through. And I wouldn't trust Cabrel to sort out which man was which."

"Remember," Claybourne continued, "I not only wish to stop this operation. I would like to lay hands on the man responsible. It would be a great coup for me in the face of the French trying so hard, and so unsuccessfully, to draw him out. Plus, I must admit, I am developing a personal interest. This man is so fascinating. Did you know he impersonated me to get himself and three *émigrees* — dressed as my footmen and driver! — through the dock check we set up at Plymouth? Sat back in a little black carriage and talked through the window. He had my intonation, my favorite epithets, my ways, even down to the lavender lozenges I use to settle my stomach. The guard there didn't even question the authenticity, his words were so full of authority and lavender scent. I tell you, the fellow pays close attention to detail. And is audacious. Outrageously so."

The old minister gave an overall wistful sigh. "But alas," he continued, "the man is like smoke. No one seems to know where he is at any given time. It's as if he didn't exist in concrete form. There's a whole network of people drawn like a curtain in front of him. It's almost impossible to get in touch with him directly." Claybourne sighed. "Quite impossible." Then he chuckled, "But now we have this new attack. We shall shuffle you in as a friend of Cabrel's. With that, your present contacts, and your considerable charm with people, I expect you to have a wedge into the inner circle by the end of the week — with a clear sight on the ringleader."

Adrien had barely paid attention. "Who?"

"Their leader. I want the identity, English or French, of

201

the man organizing these raids."

"I will need to know who the others are first."

"Others?"

"The others, the decoys you have floating in the water with me. It will make elimination and identification of the man himself easier. You wouldn't have me waste time considering and examining your own agents, would you?"

"No, no, of course not—"

"I want a list."

The Old Man blinked. "Of my agents?"

"Every one."

The Old Man was hesitant. "All right," he conceded slowly. "But not on paper. We'll discuss it. I'll tell you their names so you can narrow the field. Also, you can have their cooperation if need be. But this is precisely why I must have you tonight. This is going to take some preparation. I want you to pack your things and leave with me now."

Christina. Adrien's mind blanked for a moment. He was going to have to leave her. With no further ado. The thought, oddly, made his throat constrict.

"I can't go," he told the Old Man. "Not tonight."

"You have to." The Old Man's mouth compressed. He wagged a finger. "So help me—" he threatened, "if you don't go voluntarily—"

"I need one more day. I have business. . . ."

The Old Man squinted and tilted his canny little face at the younger man. "It's the woman upstairs," he said quietly.

Adrien threw him a surly look. "Bug off, Edward. That's my personal life. Which you've invaded quite enough for one night."

Christina saw Adrien's outline through the common room window. A sigh of relief went through her. Then a little wave of foolishness. She had come downstairs, attired only in her dressing gown, her hair undone and wild about her shoulders. An unsettled, ominous feeling had made it impossible to stay waiting in the room any longer. She had to look for him. But there he stood. Alone, outside in the drive. Perfectly fine. She didn't know what she had expected—Adrien gone? Hauled away in chains? Or perhaps his inert body lying dead upon the floor? Their visitor of the wee hours, that peculiar, official-looking old man, had profoundly upset her.

Yet, there Adrien was. Fine. Standing. Tossing stones across the puddles in the driveway.

He seemed neither to hear the door open nor notice the little bit of light that came through as she stepped out. She came up behind him. "I expected you to come back upstairs," she said softly.

He'd turned with a start. Then, in a gesture of acknowledgment, threw his handful of pebbles across the road. They splashed noisily into a puddle, like a shower of raindrops shaken from a tree. "Will you look at that?" He motioned toward the horizon. "I came out here to be depressed and am thwarted even in that. Look." He turned her attention east.

The sun was rising. Sunlight, split, prismatic, was making a rainbow at the edge of the land.

She smiled and took his arm. "It's lovely."

"Not what I have to tell you isn't." He didn't hesitate, but plunged in. "I'm leaving. Tomorrow morning. It can't be helped, and it can't be delayed."

She stood there, trying to absorb this. She was glad for the demi-light. Her face, she knew, had gone ashen. Her hands felt clammy as dew. She dug into the firm flesh of his arm, as if to reassure herself that he was there, that the whole summer wasn't going to fade suddenly like the trick of light there on the horizon.

It was no trick, no phantom that drew her around to him. He traced her neck with the edge of his thumb, then the fine, chiseled detail of her mouth. Then his fingers ran lightly across her closed eyes and into her hair. He took her head and kissed her. Tender. Lingering. Thoroughly. This seemed to be all he wanted. He kissed her mouth for a long time, as if he might memorize it, hold its sensation in his mind. Afterward, he simply took her against his body and held her.

"He makes me nervous," she murmured against him.

"Who?"

"That old man."

He laughed. "That makes two of us."

"I don't want you to get involved with him."

"Too late."

"Then get uninvolved."

"That's impossible. At least for the present."

"Adrien?"

"Hmm." He stroked her hair.

"Thomas had a cousin once who—who preferred men. A male cousin. Do you know what I mean?"

"Yes." He backed away a little and laughed. "Only I am a little shocked you would talk to Thomas about such things."

"Everyone knew."

He shook his head at her, drew her against him again.

"That old man," she continued. "He watches you in a peculiar way."

Adrien laughed. "He is peculiar. But not in the way you're implying, I don't think. I do appreciate your concern though. I shall try not to be too naive." He made a low, ironic chuckle. "Lord, if Claybourne knew anyone had even suggested such a thing about him. . . ." He changed the subject. "Shall we go upstairs? See if we can get the glass out of the bed?"

"André has already been up. He and Marguerite changed the bed. He was quite worried—he's afraid of that man, too. Who is this Claybourne?"

"The King's minister I went to see today. The English Minister of Foreign Affairs."

204

Foreign affairs. This could only mean one thing. "France, again," she sighed.

"Shh. Cornwall. Remember what you promised. I'm going to France under an assumed identity; an English aristocrat can't travel where I need to go. While I'm there, it must appear that I am still in England. You will help me with this, won't you? I thought perhaps, if you moved into my house in Cornwall—"

"You want me to go to Cornwall, to live there alone?"

"Sam would take you. I would visit as often as I could."

Christina frowned. She still wasn't wild about this idea of his friend Sam. And living alone in Cornwall, for an indefinite period of time, did not sound very much like making a new life, becoming a happy and independent woman . . . .

"I'll have to think about it," she said.

In her arms, she felt his muscles tighten. He was disappointed she was so noncommittal.

It dawned on Christina that the trouble Adrien was in reached far—into the high echelons of British government—and wide—spilling over into a revolution on the European continent. This realization, in the light of Adrien's own uneasy concern, made Christina aware of another unpleasant reality: The smoothest, cleverest man couldn't control every situation. Under the right circumstances, even a smart man—especially a smart man—knew enough to be afraid.

Chapter 18

Adrien's barber and Mr. Dobbs, with his little black appointment book, could be seen pacing across the far opening, the archway, to the dining room of the Kewischester house. Both were being held off by dark forbidding scowls. Adrien and Christina were having breakfast and trying to maintain the illusion that time and circumstance were not pressing in upon them.

They had left the inn almost immediately, arriving home to wide-eyed stares. Christina, with just a simple dress clinging limply to her figure, no cushioned muslin or half-skirt to hold it out. Her hair was down. There had been no time to fix it; Adrien had been too impatient to go. He was unshaven, rumpled—though the household seemed accustomed to his unconventional habits of arrival and departure. He had received not one raised brow, but rather a quick response to his quiet requests. A large breakfast was served, almost before they could get their wraps off and themselves into the dining room.

Adrien pushed his plate away. "I'm going upstairs to start with Dobbs." He made a wan smile. "I'll see if I can't get through his list while I'm being shaved. Then I have to go into the west wing to see what can be done about the Cornish problem. Will you look for me, one place or another, when you're finished?"

Christina had to cover a yawn. "No, I think I'd rather

sleep while you arrange your estate matters. I'll see you this afternoon."

And see him, she did. Asleep. She found him, just past noon, soundly asleep on the divan in the library. He lay under a clutter of papers, his pen gone loose in his hand. He looked exhausted.

She checked on him periodically. But, just as she had slept all morning, he was out all afternoon, asleep like the dead. And thus their last day went. Lost in the out-of-step rhythm they had somehow fallen into.

It was almost dinner time when she returned to the library and found him gone. Only the papers, in an orderly stack, remained. It took another half hour to locate him, and then, only by luck, did she spot him in the greenhouse.

He turned as she entered.

"Are you avoiding me?" She smiled.

The guilty look that crossed his face changed her teasing tone to a more serious one.

"You are," she said with surprise.

He shook his head; no explanation. He put his pen down. He'd been writing. "Look." He reached for a long flower-stem and bent it forward. The end of the stem, where the rose petals had fallen off, was as fat as an acorn.

She didn't understand at first. "Is something wrong with it?"

He made a wry laugh. "It's set hips. They're all over." He held out his hand. "Bloody bush. I have no idea which crosses are which, or even if any are mine. The bloody thing has taken up with unknown pollen, with loose-living bees."

They both laughed. "Well, you should have some interesting crosses." She smiled at him.

"Without the time to work with them."

"But the seeds can be dried and saved."

"Yes." He let out a long breath. "They can." He held his hand out to her. She took it, and he brought her near. He

207

touched her face. "You are, I think, the only business I don't know how to tally up in neat columns. Can you be dried and saved?"

She laughed. "No."

"Will you being going to Cornwall?"

"No." She had decided against it; it didn't make sense for her. "Why should I go to the ends of the earth"—literally, Land's End was where his property lay—"for a man who won't even explain exactly why he should need this sacrifice?"

He accepted this as a statement, not a question. "All right," he said. "Then stay here. Not for me so much as for your own good. Let me protect you in the only way I can while I'm in France."

She hadn't thought of this. She hadn't thought of anything. "I can't promise—"

"You have plans to leave?"

"I have no plans. I've not been able to see anything beyond the day you're going."

"Well, I wish you would consider staying on the estate. Richard would have a devil of a time getting at you here. And Samuel—"

"Richard?" She looked at him sharply. "He's not going to bother me. And I've told you my feelings about your friend Samuel. I won't—"

"We're not going to get into this again. He'll be here in the morning. You can meet him. You'll see, he's a fine fellow. Pleasant, quiet, almost courtly in his politeness. He'll cause you no more inconvenience than your own shadow."

With that, he kissed her. The woman in his arms took his advice very much to heart: Why get into this again, indeed? She would do as she pleased. And he would be gone, with no say in the matter.

He murmured something. In French, she realized. When she looked at him, he apologized with a squeeze and a helpless shrug. "I was thinking of an old ballad. Though it sounds a little vulgar in English: 'I will go, but the taste of you will linger still full in my mouth.' "

He was up before dawn, packed, his few small bags loaded onto the carriage. There was a chill in the air, the first real hint that even nature considered the summer over. Christina went down with him in her dressing gown, then had to send up for a cloak.

They waited, the horses, the driver, Adrien himself anxious yet delaying. Christina didn't understand why until she saw the reason arrive. Charles—Evangeline's husband of all people—and another man rode up, dusty, dirty, as if they'd been riding all night.

Adrien made brief introductions. The much-talked-about Samuel Rolfeman had arrived in the flesh. He was a plain man, tall, heavy-boned. He had not a single feature one could call blatantly unattractive, yet Christina found the man exceptionally unappealing. The way a prisoner might find his jailer to be, on the whole, a rather gruesome-looking fellow.

She gritted her teeth, nodded politely while the man apologized for being so down-to-the-minute in arriving. "I had expected, you will remember, to not be needed for several days."

Adrien was solicitous, even grateful. Then Charles and Mr. Rolfeman went inside, and Adrien grabbed hold of the sides of the open portal of the carriage. He heaved himself in.

Christina could feel her hackles rising. Yet, she kept telling herself, Not here, not at this moment.

Adrien leaned out to her. "I'll try and get away within the month. For a quick visit. You'll be here?"

"You'll be able to find me, if you want to."

"I want you *here*. Where you are best protected from

209

Richard—don't discount him, Christina. Stay in my apartments. Make over the adjoining bedchamber. Do whatever you need to be comfortable; just talk to Dobbs or Lily. But stay where I can protect you most easily."

"You want me contained, shelved. That would be convenient for you—"

"I want you guarded. A woman roaming about on her own isn't safe. I want you close enough to Samuel that if Richard decided to do something foolish, he could stop it."

"Adrien." She looked at him. "You can't scare me or bully me into doing what I don't want to do."

He frowned. "Get in the carriage a moment, will you?" It was with resentment that he added, "Please."

Several moments later, Samuel Rolfeman came out and knocked on the side of the carriage. "You're supposed to be there by ten, Adrien. You're already going to be forty-five minutes late."

Christina reached for the door handle, then looked back. Adrien was sitting back in the farthest shadows of the carriage, stewing in his own unique brand of fury. She wasn't going to stay where he wanted her. She wasn't going to let Samuel tag along. And she had further turned on him:

"This is a fine note to leave on," he said.

"Well, you have slept with her, haven't you?"

"You know I have. What is the point?"

"She will be there. I will be a hundred miles away—"

"Nadine is in Vienna."

"Then someone else. I won't be pining away for you here, manipulated into a nice, convenient little waiting room while you are out doing God knows what."

"For godssake, Christina, what do you want?" He heaved a frustrated sigh. "Everything has been too rushed. I'd hoped we'd have some time alone together these last days, but that's been denied us. All I can promise now is that if I have only six or eight hours on English soil, I'd like to beat

210

a path straight back here and spend them with you. If you can't appreciate that, then by all means go. If you're not here, I will understand the message."

"Now you're making it out that if I leave, I'm putting an end to the whole thing. You're trying to bind me here. Why?"

"Oh, for godssake, leave." He gave the door a shove. It gaped open. "I don't give a damn. I want you to leave. Go on. Get out. Pack your things and leave. There, does that prove that I care for you better?"

"*Care*. The missing word left a space, a void into which Christina stepped out. She wrapped the cloak up tighter against herself and put her foot onto the gravel drive. She turned, still holding onto the door handle.

"Adrien."

"What?"

She didn't know how to tell him. "I could love you."

The door was grabbed away from her. "Lovely. Let me know if the conditional ever makes it into the present tense. Driver." The door slammed shut. The carriage sprang forward; it left with surprising swiftness and finality.

Christina stood there, riveted, telling herself, "He's gone." But she couldn't really believe it. It was one of those facts that had to be lived to be understood, she realized.

Then, as the dust settled, what she really couldn't believe was how she had sent him off.

Chapter 19

Christina had got down her trunks and thrown half her things in before she suddenly stopped. Not knowing why, she left her half-packed trunks and clothes in her room. She began to wander the house.

It was so empty and quiet. Everything so much the same. Yet so irrefutably different. On a hall stand, in an empty rose bowl, she found a stickpin. His. She'd seen it stuck through his cravat on several occasions. A tiny sword with a diamond hilt.

She carried the pin out onto the terrace, fiddling with it. The leaves of the large maple trees at the side of the house were beginning to turn. Autumn. Life went on. Adrien had been gone four or five hours, and already it felt like a lifetime ago. She felt like the autumn leaves. Cycling into a reddish, yellowing phase. Awaiting the wind to take her down, down to the earth; reality.

She unclenched her fist to look at the pin. It reminded her so of him. A dandy, she smiled. He was that. He groomed himself with a flourish, with an eye toward the ladies. Christina looked at the pin more closely. Yet she believed him when he said he had not been with another woman all summer. She was even inclined to believe him when he said he had not lived in such proximity to a woman in a dozen years. Her divorce was over. She had no better plans; no plans at all in fact. So why couldn't she stay?

"Mrs. Pinn?"

Christina turned. Sam Rolfeman. Her "bodyguard" was

proving to be something of a nuisance. He didn't let her long out of his sight.

"I haven't gone anywhere," she told him.

"I noticed your bags are down, your clothes are out." He took a deep breath. "Mrs. Pinn, I would appreciate it if you would not lead me a merry chase from here into London or wherever it is you are planning to go. Adrien asked me to look out for you. He's apparently worried about someone—Who? Is it your husband? Someone who might harm you. Why don't you make my life easy—?"

Christina turned and walked past him into the house. "My husband, Mr. Rolfeman, isn't going to hurt me. Adrien was overly alarmed by two trivial incidents a day ago. I'll be fine, and you don't need to follow me about to assure that."

"But I do. For one thing, I promised. And for another, if anything should happen to you, Adrien would turn me inside out for allowing it."

She turned to him at the foot of the stairs. "I don't want you to follow after me. Do you understand?"

He didn't answer immediately, but made a tight glum mouth and dropped his eyes. "I'd heard you were difficult," he murmured.

"Difficult? You haven't seen difficult yet, Mr. Rolfeman. Leave me alone. I don't want you hounding me."

With that, Christina took two fistfuls of skirt and turned her hoops and bustle around. She tossed the stickpin into its bowl as she headed toward the front door. Anywhere to get away from this—this irritating shadow that Adrien had set upon her.

She was almost to the stables when she noticed Adrien's coach had returned. She peered into the carriage house. "What's this," she asked the man unhitching the team. "I thought His Lordship had taken this carriage to the coast."

The man turned out to be no more than a boy of fifteen or sixteen. It was John Piper, Adrien's footman. "No, mum.

He sent it back once he got to the inn. There were horses waiting." The boy blushed and made a show of turning from her, hanging the riggings on the wall. Then he turned back. "Maybe I oughtn't to be saying this, mum, but I was on back of the coach this morning when you and His Lordship was arguin'. And someone oughta be telling you — you oughtn't to go so spare with His Lordship. He's hopeless gone on you. Ain't never raises his voice at you. Never loses his temper. And he's al'ays there. Ain't never seen 'im fancy so after one woman since I can remember — and I was born upstairs in the attic of that house —"

His eyes dropped from her face to her chin; a seeming shyness coupled with a determination not to look away. "And I wanna tell you," he added, "I don't hold with none of the gossip — it's nothing you c'n help, you know. It's just people don't see true square with someone's pure lovely as you." He took a breath. "But, for me, I can't believe you'd, well — you've the look of an angel."

Christina was taken aback. She had seldom heard a remark both so rude and so well-intentioned.

Then a further surprise. The young footman's eyes dropped a full six inches. His tongue wet his lower lip quickly as his eyes scanned Christina's white blouse at breast level. He eyed the cleft in the fabric that fell over high, round curves. Christina laughed.

"God in heaven," she said, "if you look at all angels like that . . ." She instantly regretted the remark.

The young man blushed a red so vivid it seemed as if all the blood in his body had rushed straight to his face. His eyes glassed to tears. He turned and began fumbling to put the last bridle on the wall.

Christina moved forward and touched his shoulder. "I'm so sorry. You see, I — Look!" She reached both hands out to his and smiled. She had to lean forward and peer up into the downcast face. "Flesh and blood." She squeezed his hands. "Human. Capable of saying just the wrong thing at

214

the wrong time. Truly." She was able to unbend at last and look straight into his eyes. "I am so flattered that you think I'm pretty. And that you think well of me—except, of course, that you think I am not kind enough to His Lordship." She laughed softly.

A slightly sly grin began to materialize on the face of her young confidant. "He's all hell with the ladies, isn't he?"

Christina made a disapproving face. "A bit, yes. I'm afraid so."

The grin vanished. "Oh, I'm very sorry—"

"No need to be," she said. "You're right. And everything you've heard, what people are saying about me, is probably true as well. Can you imagine the earl giving up two, almost three months of his company to a pure sweet angel, John?"

The young man smiled slightly. "I suppose not." His cold hands were warming in Christina's grip. She saw acceptance in his young face; there was no harsh judgment.

Christina drew herself up to her full height, a scant inch shorter than the boy. If John Piper could accept it, then so could she. She was the Earl of Kewischester's mistress. Which was not such a bad thing to be. In fact, it was a damn sight better than being Richard Pinn's wife. She felt wonderful, her morning's irritation forgotten. As she looked at the footman she realized a rather curious kind of social position lay there waiting for her to embrace it. A position of respect—of sorts—and power. Yes, she could love this— if she would only let herself. And she loved Adrien. She . . . .

"Oh, God." She put her hand to her mouth.

"What's wrong." Her new friend was immediately there.

"I never told him." Christina suddenly wanted to cry. She loved Adrien. She had loved the summer. She *was* happy living here. Yet she had let Adrien depart thinking she was deeply discontent. How could she have been so stupid? And so afraid! She had lost sight of how deliriously happy she had been in the present, because—practical, plotting little lawyer's daughter—she could not see how she could profit by it in the future! "What an absurd, scheming woman you are, Christina Pinn."

"Oh, no, mum, you're not—"

"Oh, yes, I am. But I am owning up to it and going to do something about it." But what? She didn't know.

Then John's half-smile froze as his eyes swung up and over Christina's shoulder. Samuel Rolfeman stood at the door.

"Where are you going, Mrs. Pinn? And if you're getting a horse for her, John, you had better get one ready for me as well."

Christina wheeled around.

Glaring silence.

John Piper broke it. "She was just fixin' to go to the inn. To surprise His Lordship. You know, he'll be at the inn all night, and he all but invited her—I heard him this morning. It's hardly a surprise he wouldn't welcome."

Christina threw a sideways glance in the direction of her gallant rescuer. He continued.

"He's at the Three Rose. Mrs. Pinn was just saying that on horseback she could be there in under an hour; it would make a gosh fine surprise."

Mr. Rolfeman looked at her. "You should know, madam, that Lord Kewischester is not much one for surprises. And he has business that would undoubtedly keep him—"

"Oh, a pox on his business!" Christina pushed by him. "And a double pox on your odious interference. You may forget the entire idea! I suddenly don't feel like going at all! John—" She turned a deliberate insult on the man in the doorway. "I've had enough of boring jailers." She nodded an affectionate good-bye to the footman and left Mr. Rolfeman without a word.

And by this exit, she finally succeeded in getting a rise out of the stoic Mr. Rolfeman. He called after her, shaking his fist. "I am not Adrien's servant! I'm his friend! The second son of a viscount, the owner of four hundred acres . . ." He went on, listing his assets, ad nauseam, until Christina had slammed the door and thereby drowned him out. Then, out of pure malice, she locked the front door. It was only ten minutes later, that he managed to get in at all — via the servants' entrance.

At seven, just before dinner, Christina went back to the stable. She had decided to at least explore the possibility of getting a horse that night without anyone's knowing.

At first, she was disappointed. John was gone. She had thought to ask for his help. Christina ventured into the tack room at the back of the stable, looking for him. All she found were saddles, bridles, rigs for large and small carriages; all manner of saddlery. But then she spotted the crowning prize; it made her realize the deed could be done: Sitting neatly folded on a drying saddle were a pile of clothes. John's regular work clothes. With the earl away, the proud young man had paraded home to supper in full livery.

Christina picked up a pair of breeches and held them to her. Oh, she laughed to herself, This is very, very wicked. Then she rolled up the clothes and tucked them under her arm. A horse was no problem. There was a stable full of them. The bridle and light saddle she could manage, given enough time. And now, the last obstacle while she did this — Mr. Rolfeman — had become negotiable; she could get around him.

He would never question John Piper out here brushing the horses and oiling the saddles. He would only be a little alarmed when he saw him take one of the horses for a ride.

Chapter 20

As she stepped out of the kitchen entrance, Christina felt suddenly giddy. The scheme was crazy and dangerous and not conceived with the best of sense. It was, however — as odd as it felt to consider this again — fun. As she climbed over the low garden wall and ran round the side of the house toward the stables, Christina was laughing in a way — silent, private, all for herself — she hadn't in years. Sheer joy.

Wait till Adrien saw her! She straightened John's snug cap, tucking in a stray piece of hair at her forehead. Adrien was going to have a fit! He was going to roar with laughter! How good this was going to be!

A half hour later, Christina climbed onto her horse and set off. Her father, she thought, had always sought to curb any unconventional rash behavior. Richard, the blighter, had fought from the very beginning to extinguish even the first thought of it. But Adrien — his way of looking at life accepted this sort of thing, she told herself, even encouraged it. And this adventure was going to outclass making love on the front lawn; it was going to make pale by comparison a few brandy-soaked sheets in a provincial little inn. With luck, it would equal any French escapade Adrien had ever dreamed up.

The reality of her adventure, though, was a little less jolly.

She made bad time. It was ten o'clock before she'd even gotten off the estate. Then, to add to her anxiety, she had not ridden five miles when she came across some fellow travelers who immediately saw her for a woman. They were pleasant enough. A few raucous comments were all she had to contend with. But the immediate recognition, in the dark at that, was unnerving. She stopped to remove her stockings, John's stockings actually, and she bound them around her breasts. At least that would reduce her profile and decrease some of the jiggle beneath the loose shirt. Then, as an afterthought, she untucked the shirt completely; this would veil her femininity even more. She remounted her horse, resolving to ride and move "more manly."

Nothing, however, could restore her blithe courage. The prank could have serious consequences, Christina realized, if she met the wrong sort of person on the road. Briefly, she considered going back, but that was out of the question. She couldn't face Sam Rolfeman. Besides, it was as far back to the house now as it was forward to the inn. The only thing to do was to push on. She pulled the brim of the little cap down over her face, and tried not to think of disappearing into raped, robbed, and murdered oblivion.

The signboard of the Three Rose Inn brought welcome relief.

When Christina took her own horse around to the inn's stable, she immediately recognized several horses, including the mud-colored stallion the earl himself frequently rode. Adrien was surely there.

Seeing Thomas in the courtyard boosted her sense of mischief again. This still could be amusing. She pulled the cap down and proceeded into the establishment.

"Hey! Boy!"

It took three calls for Christina to realize someone in the large common eating room was talking to her. Unlike it had been on her last visit, the Three Rose Inn was bustling with activity tonight. Virtually every table of the common room was filled. André could be seen, harried, in the far corner, serving spirits.

"Boy! Be ye deaf?" It was another man, wearing an apron

and also serving food and ale.

"No, sir," she answered, not knowing what else to say.

Thomas pushed past her and went up the stairs.

"Tek the wutter uptiz lor'ship's rum."

"Pardon?"

"Stupid lout! The wutter!" A bucket of water was thrust at her by the handle.

She took it.

"Rum thray, ye lout."

She stood still, unable to fully understand the man's vernacular.

"Rum thray." A foot on the buttocks started her, and the next remark—understood at last—sent her on her way. "Kewischester's rum."

Perfect. She'd have an excuse to walk right up to his door. Room three.

The water was heavy. While she tugged it up the stairs, she watched Thomas go into the room. A boy with an empty bucket came out. Then, two unfamiliar men went in and came out again.

At the door, she heard Thomas speaking—though if she hadn't seen him she might not have recognized his voice. She had never heard him sound so abrupt and out of sorts.

"Everyone's accounted for. But Rolfeman and Sloane. Charles, I know, was making a quick trip home. A message from his wife—her waters broke. But as to Rolfeman, I don't know where the son of a bitch is—"

There was a small splash, then the sound of a beautiful, deep voice that sent shivers through Christina. "I forgot to tell you," the voice said, "he won't be with us this time. Will you toss me that cigar?"

There was a plop.

Then Adrien's voice again. "Very funny. Now will you hand me a dry one and be as clever at making one burn as making one float. What's got into you tonight, Thomas?"

"Rolfeman has some nerve," Thomas answered in a

mutter, "backing out on this one. He's our best tracker. Here. Be careful where you drop your ashes."

"Thank you. I'll be most careful." There was a long groan of contentment, then a slosh of water. "Lord, I'm going to miss a frequent hot bath. Did I tell you that Claybourne has me going over as a coal loader? Coal! He loves to cast me grimy and poor. I can almost hear his glee over my heaving coal for a few days. I really think that man gets more peculiar by the day."

There was a pause. Then: "Well, I will tell the others we will have a quick go-over in half an hour. Since Rolfeman has gotten cold feet, we needn't wait—"

"I apologize. Don't think it's Sam. I asked him to stay."

Adrien was talking with something—the cigar?—in his mouth. Christina smiled in anticipation of hearing how precious her well-being was to him in that slightly muddled way he had of talking and smoking at the same time. He went on.

"He's keeping Christina Pinn from asking questions and giving answers."

Christina puckered her mouth and twisted it to one side in a frown. That didn't sound the least bit like his original definition of "bodyguard."

"Mmm. A good idea," Thomas said after a moment's contemplation. "I'm glad you haven't let your vanity make you less cautious."

"Vanity! Believe me, I have no delusions with regard to that woman. I'm just relieved to have a little respite from her. It takes the patience of Job to deal with her. It took me all summer to coach her into one little lie. And it took every spare moment to keep her out of things. She's as curious as a monkey. And about as polite. There is no part of my house or my life she hasn't stuck her little fingers into. There is simply no predicting what she'll get into next."

Monkey! That woman! Christina put the pail down and

folded her arms over her chest. She leaned against the doorjamb, preparing a list of his crimes to hit him over the head with as soon as Thomas left. Lying, deprecating, son-of-a—

"What are you doing, boy? Are you going to bring that water in or not?"

Christina stopped breathing. She was staring at the toes of Thomas' boots. He'd opened the door. The only logical move presented itself. Head down, she shoved the bucket at him. He took it and went out of sight around the door.

"Ah! That's cold! I asked for hot! Tell that idiot to get his ass downstairs and bring hot water!"

The bucket was thrust at her again, empty, with appropriate commands. The door closed. Christina breathed.

After ten seconds of battling her heart to a reasonable beat, she tossed the bucket over, planted her bottom on it and squatted, elbows on knees, to eavesdrop further, mumbling curses on Adrien Hunt's head and the heads of all his ancestors. She heard Thomas speak her own name again.

"Some of the men are still worried over the Christina Pinn problem. They're thinking perhaps to frighten her again might better insure her—"

"Frighten?" Adrien sounded amused.

"They think her silence that day after the woods had more to do with fear—"

Adrien laughed. "Who? Give me their names. I'll speak to them. Lord, you'd think full-grown men would have more respect for the vastness and density of female silences—what's wrong? Are you one of them?"

"No. No, I'll gather them up and send them in to you. I'm just a little concerned over—"

"Over what?"

"Why? Why are you protecting this 'little monkey' so personally?"

"You *are* one of them! You want to scare Christina? Hurt her to make her be quiet?"

222

"Don't be ridiculous. I would never hurt Christina. What I want to know, though, is why are *you* so adamant about protecting her?"

"I see." Adrien laughed. "I am allowed to save all the—how many are we up to? twenty or thirty now?—French aristocrats I like. But my wanting to protect one small woman, who just by chance got in our way—"

"I understand why you save aristos. You're part of them. You like the risk. I think, also, you feel guilty after messing in—confusing—their politics for so many years—"

"My dear fellow, I do not feel responsible for an entire French Revolution—"

"Not exactly—"

"Not at all. I'm getting out."

"What?"

"I think, after this one, we should shut down."

"Why?"

"It's getting too dangerous. England is hailing the damn revolution as 'great social reform.' The worse it gets in France, the better the English like it; serves Louis right, people say behind their hats, after supporting the insurrection in the colonies ten years ago. And the French authorities would like to catch us and take us apart, limb by limb. Claybourne is sending in more informers. France has Italian mercenaries trying to track us down. We can't go on like this forever. As soon as we gather up this last batch of aristos—with my grandfather among them—I think the Old Man's 'madman' should disappear into the wind."

Silence. Thomas clearly didn't know what to say to such a declaration.

Christina squirmed on her bucket. Her bottom was going to sleep on the tin rim. But Thomas' voice cut into her discomfort.

"Christina Pinn," he began, "We've got a long way from the topic. Why? To what extent is she influencing your thinking? Are you envisioning dreams of settling down with

223

her?"

Adrien let out a burst of laughter. "You are persistent, Lillings. Do you have designs on the woman yourself?"

"No. I just want to know if you have personal reasons for protecting her."

"Well, I'd rather like her to be there when I come back."

"Sweet man," Christina thought. She leaned closer, ready to perhaps alter her opinion of his motives.

"Look, Thomas, she's a nice woman," he continued. "Pretty. Bright. A little too curious, and a damn sight too honest. But I suppose I even like her a little for that."

"And that's all?"

There was some mischief in the reply. "Well, that's not quite all."

"You love her."

Adrien uttered a startled sound of objection. "Lord, you've been living in France too long. I like her, Thomas. She's a sly, grasping, argumentative little shrew. But she's so damned honest about the whole business, I like her anyway—"

Christina nearly fell off the bucket. If that wasn't the most condescending, degrading declaration of feeling she had ever—"

"You love her," Thomas repeated, sounding regretful over his own pronouncement.

Adrien rattled something at him in French, which concluded with, "so stop talking like some stupid Frenchman who thinks everything begins and ends with love." He harrumphed. "It's a wonder I've survived the summer. She seemed so sheltered, so pliable. But behind that sweet feminine diffidence, she hides a strength of purpose, a will of iron—No, Thomas. She's an impressive little baggage who's prim across the dinner table and exotic under the sheets. It's an interesting combination, but that's all. Besides, what are you complaining about? You yourself said that once we were faced with how her little mind worked,

224

my association with her could do nothing but help."

"You were trying to 'associate' yourself with her before we all came to the decision that you ought to."

"She's a very pretty woman."

"And you 'like' her."

"And I like her! Do you mind?"

"Adrien, you're very good at manipulating women. That's why we thought you should pursue her once she started in with her questions and letters—"

Very put out, Adrien interrupted. "So I did it! Much to my discredit. I have lived with a woman I would rather have run from just to assuage everyone's worry. I have cajoled her and humored her when, half the time, I would rather have turned her over my knee. But enough. Leave me some shred of self-respect. Allow me to have enjoyed the woman for a few moments of a grueling, teeth-gritting summer! And leave me in peace!"

Grueling, teeth-gritting summer! The bucket rocked under Christina, making a clack on the floor. She was livid. How big of him to have enjoyed a few moments!

"What was that?"

Christina felt her heart stop, then give a wild kick in her chest. She had a strong urge to throw open the door and confront the double-dealing bastard. But a stronger sense of caution, tinged with panic, shot through her. They had discussed "hurting" her. Dear God, let her sneak out and ruin him from a safe distance!

"Maybe it's that boy with the bucket of hot water. I'll see."

"Just send him away. I have to get out in a minute anyway."

The door opened. Christina scrambled in front of the bucket to hide its emptiness. A silver coin was tossed at her. It jangled to the floor. She used it as an excuse to bend down.

"That's all, boy. His Lordship doesn't want the water after all."

225

The door closed.

Christina thought she was going to faint from relief. She collapsed to her knees and waited for the strength to stand. Behind the door, Thomas pursued Adrien's feelings for her with a persistence she found unexplainable.

"Richard Pinn," he continued, "might disagree that you only 'liked' the woman. He's spread it around that you gave him a black eye and bloody lip for just touching her arm. Explain to me again how this was 'necessary.'"

"I will not—"

"A great 'show,' you said. And Maxwell, who knocked her down that afternoon, said you scared the pants off him. He said you actually gave chase for a few seconds."

Christina was aghast. Had that whole unnerving afternoon—Richard's near-beating, the purse thief, Adrien's show of concern—all been connivance?

The reply was low. "He was too rough."

"And it didn't even work—"

"It worked. It's how I left Rolfeman behind. He's with her now."

Thomas laughed. "Yes, Rolfeman. Who fights like the devil because they killed his lover. Rolfeman. Who likes men. You are really predictable on this, Adrien. You've not left our best tracker in change of a lively prisoner, as you're implying. You've left a eunuch in charge of your own one-woman harem."

There was a long silence in the room. A subtle tension seemed to ooze around the edges of the door. Then Adrien spoke.

"Thomas," he said gently, "perhaps you should not join us on this one. There's some bad feeling that—I can't put my finger on it, but—" Another long pause. "It's Christina, isn't it? You want to know when I'll be through with her. Or do you just want to know how strongly I'd mind if you intervened before I was through?"

"I make it a point never to become fond of women who

226

are fond of you. I don't compete well."

"Thomas."

"Yes."

"I would mind very much."

Thomas laughed uncomfortably. "I repeat, there has never been any competition between us. That's why we're such good friends. I don't bother your women."

"And I've never bothered yours."

"Not intentionally."

More silence.

It was Adrien who broke it. "Why don't you go for a walk or something," he said. "I could use a few moments to myself. Perhaps you could round up the men who are going over tonight."

There was another long pause, followed by a heavy sigh; like a man straining to move under an enormous burden of dead weight. "Right," Thomas said at length. "I'll be back shortly."

Water splashed, punctuating an awkward, deliberate change of subject. "A-a-ah! Where am I going to get a soak like this where we're going?"

Christina had risen. She forced herself from the door. That possessive, overbearing, domineering . . . Her mind blurred in anger. But she could think clearly enough to realize she wouldn't confront him here. No, she would go home—his home—and massacre him from a safe distance, with investigations and public revelations he never dreamed possible. That deceiving, treacherous actor! To use her like that, then stake her out like his own private—

Fate decided in favor of immediate confrontation. Four men came rushing at her up the stairs.

"Damn little snip! He's been eavesdropping! Get him!"

Hands and arms grabbed at her. The cap flopped to the floor. Gold-auburn hair came spilling down precisely at the

227

moment one of the men grabbed her under the arm and around her chest. He let go of the soft breast as if he'd been burned.

"It's a woman!"

The entire incident took perhaps five seconds, with hardly more noise than another clatter of the bucket. Christina was brought to her feet, hemmed in by four men. She turned around to find Thomas staring at them from the open doorway.

"What the—" Thomas couldn't say more for several seconds. Finally, all he could manage was to call over his shoulder, "Adrien?"

A noncommittal, guttural "mmm" came from within the room.

More desperately: "Adrien!"

Christina jerked her arms free and pushed past them all into the room. She rounded the door and stopped.

He was sitting in a tin tub of water, shoulders, neck, and arms exposed in every chiseled detail. His head lolled on the edge of the bath, eyes closed, hair damp and mussed. A short black cigar was clamped between his teeth. His face was relaxed, self-satisfied, almost euphoric; the portrait of a man in total control of his past, present, and future.

It gave Christina malicious satisfaction to watch his eyes laze open, then every bit of expression empty from his face. He went ashen, fumbled for words, found none. His cigar dropped to sizzle in his bath. Then, at last, like a raging Poseidon up from a hot steamy sea, he rose. Expression had finally found its way back onto his face: Blind, seething fury. It twisted, then reddened his features; then exploded into speech.

"Where the fuck is Rolfeman? And what the hell is *she* doing here?"

One elegantly muscled arm dripped water on the carpet as his finger slashed out in Christina's direction.

Christina found herself holding the empty bucket; she

pitched it at him as hard as she could.

His reflexes, annoyingly good, caught it at belly-level. He didn't even look at the woman who'd hurled it.

Christina opened her mouth, preparing to scream at him: *I'll ruin you! I'm going to tell everyone who'll bloody listen! I'll see you decapitated, hung, drawn and quartered!*

But she didn't say anything. She was disoriented. He was not reacting precisely as she would have expected. Oddly, she did not have his attention.

"By God, you get him here!" Adrien was roaring at his subordinates as he shoved a foot into his pants. He gave several more commands sprinkled liberally with curses. Two more men had appeared at the sound of his angry voice. People began running and leaping around, trying to please him. André, himself, turned up a moment later only to be told rudely to get out. Then, finally, Adrien turned to Christina.

"Just how long were you out there?"

She opened her mouth to speak.

Thomas cut her off. "God preserve us, Adrien. She brought the last bucket of water. I'm sure of it."

She'd lost his attention again. Adrien had turned and immersed himself in a flow of more orders to more people.

Then this was punctuated by a hiatus, as if everyone in the room had suddenly decided to hold his breath. Samuel Rolfeman walked in.

"Adrien, I've lost her—"

Adrien narrowed his eyes, then shifted them pointedly toward Christina. Sam grew quiet.

"You imbecile . . ." Adrien launched an unbridled stream of reprehension that made his previous cursing sound like a child's nursery rhyme. In three or four profane sentences he demeaned the man, dismantled his defenses, and reduced him to a limp rag without a shred of dignity.

Adrien was tugging on his boots as the room was jammed further. Eight more men entered.

Christina's brain seemed to be stagnated. Deeply troubling thoughts started seeping to the surface in disjointed bursts.

The colossal showdown she had mentally lived through a dozen times now — since Adrien's first deceitful word — was not going to take place.

Adrien's little band was assembling. There were twice as many as she'd imagined. And not all of them were English. More than half the voices were French.

Spies. Governments.

France. Politics. War.

Being knocked down in the woods.

The old Minister of Foreign Affairs. Adrien's own peculiar behavior with him.

The English minister's "madman." An outlaw of some sorts. It was Adrien. It was that stranger over there pulling on his boots, carrying on half a dozen conversations in a strange mixture of languages.

In English, he was discussing his earldom's affairs with Thomas. There was the business of straightening out some flooded tenants on Adrien's coastal estate. Thomas was to handle this and, while he did, establish his own presence there publicly by tomorrow night. This was supposed to appease the English minister's suspicions that he was involved in the French rescue operations: While Thomas was in Cornwall, the group would be breaking into an abbey on the outskirts of Paris.

In French, the most Christina could make out was that someone named Cabrel was going to join them in France tonight, then get "lost" into French hands tomorrow as part of the abbey rescue for some marquis.

There were other conversations. Even another language — German? Christina couldn't identify it precisely. People spoke to Adrien in all three languages, bombarding him with questions and comments while he got dressed — the dark sailor again — and answered. He shifted back and forth between the languages — between the conversations — as if they were one.

A madman, Christina bemoaned. He really was mad! But she couldn't quite make up her mind if the chaos about her was madness or a complicated engineering feat of incomprehensible proportions. Whatever it was, it made her feel small and insignificant beside it. And the man at the heart of the chaos made her feel imbecilic. She shook her head and bit her lip.

Adrien Hunt was either insane or a delicately balanced genius.

In either event, Christina didn't want to be where she was. She bit her lip harder to keep from crying. Her eyes flooded anyway. Nothing in her experience had ever intimidated her so completely.

Then one small hope arose in the muddle around her. So much was going on. Perhaps no one would notice. She began to creep toward the door. It stood slightly ajar.

She backed slowly to the wall, then inched along for what seemed like eternity, behind tall backs and intense conversation.

Less than a foot from the door, however, a hand — its long slender fingers in possession of a freshly lighted cigar — dropped down to the wall by Christina's shoulder; an arm barred her way. Then another arm dropped down on her other side to block her retreat. The room went quiet again. Christina looked up.

The madman himself, of course.

Adrien replaced the first barrier with a boot by her hip, as he drew on the cigar. He studied her for several moments. The end of the cigar glowed, then with a flick a shower of ashes dropped to the floor. His eyes met hers for a fraction of a second; then he frowned and dropped his eyes to his own knee.

"You can't go, Christina," he said.

She tried anyway to bolt through his leg out the door.

She yelled.

"Someone! Help me—"

Her head was rapped hard against the wall. The cigar singed a wisp of hair as his hand smashed over her mouth. She tried to wriggle free, but the heel of his other hand had shifted to her breast bone. The more she struggled, the more pressure he put on her jaw and chest. Tears began to run. Copious. Hot. Flooding down her cheeks, over the hand at her mouth. Her throat constricted horribly.

Their eyes met again. Hers—huge, wet. His—frowning, then quickly dropping behind the shelter of his long lashes. He let the pressure of his hands slowly ease as he spoke.

"I'm not proud of myself, Christina. But I'm not playing with you. I'll hurt you if I have to. Please understand that." There was a pause. "You may not yell. You may not leave." The tips of his fingers traced the impressions they had left on her cheek. His eyes flicked up to hers again. He seemed about to say something. Instead, he closed his eyes and expelled a long breath. Then he said with a softness close to regret, "There is no discussion this time. You go to France with us tonight. I don't dare trust you anywhere else."

He released her completely. She clutched her chest and put one hand over her mouth, more to stifle a hysterical sob than to hold her bruised mouth.

Adrien's face suddenly flashed into a smile. White teeth, deep creases, squinting ocean-blue eyes set off in the dark complexion. He exuded all the old magnetism. Christina wanted to retch.

"Don't look so woebegone, princess," he cajoled. "Surely there are worse things than the two of us sharing close quarters for a while." He turned his back to her and began snapping out something in French.

A stocky, muscular man at Christina's left said an encouraging word to her in English, then poked curiously at the lack of movement beneath her loose shirt.

"What have you done to yourself?"

A hand locked over the one about to probe under the loose garment. "Look if you like. But don't touch," Adrien spoke to the investigator.

"I was just—"

His teeth clenched, Adrien shoved the man against the door, slamming it closed with the man's weight. "No excuses," he snarled, "You don't touch her. Do you understand?"

"But I—"

Thomas interceded. He herded the stocky man quickly out the door. Then he shot a glare back, looking troubled and accusing.

The other men in the room looked baffled.

While Adrien stood there, looking angry—much angrier than he had any right to be.

His breathing was slightly ragged, agitated. Finally, he threw a hand back through his hair and rasped, "Get the hell out! All of you! Go on! Not you." He pointed to Christina.

Silently, they all did as he said. The door clicked shut, and Christina backed against it. Her hand closed over the knob convulsively. She couldn't catch her breath. The harder she tried, the more light-headed she became. Then she did something she'd never done in her entire life. She passed out cold.

Part II

Shadows in the Shade

Chapter 21

A group of men, seven or eight, scraped off a wagon and crunched into the snow at the outskirts of the city. It was dusk. In the distance, Paris was just starting to twinkle. By the time they had walked into the heart of the city, the snow and ice would be an eerie sparkle in the yellow glow of street lanterns.

Adrien Hunt pulled the collar of his coat up over the back of his neck and wrapped the wool muffler tighter.

A Frenchman called Le Saint, a good four inches taller than Adrien and, at least six stones heavier, thwacked him on the back. Le Saint was one of the newer recruits, four months new, and like many of the new men, not an aristocrat at all.

"Eh, La Chasse, a great run tonight? The Madman is one clever nugger, yes?" The man spoke in loud, scurrilous French. The mild copulatory reference was a genteel statement from Le Saint. The huge man was called Le Saint in the same way he was occasionally referred to as "Monsieur Petit."

"Great run, right," Adrien responded.

"Aaaugh! All night you've been wearing that face. You sit on a French bayonet?"

"No—ah—" Adrien sneezed. He wiped his face and sniffled. "No. It's just the weather. The wind was bitter on the water this morning. I haven't been warm since Thursday."

Le Saint swore by some reference to the Virgin Mother's anatomy, then slandered a stranger in Adrien's mind:

"Your mother's buttered ass, it's the cold! You were all smiles when the French boarded this morning. It was good. The Madman is one smart nugger to let you handle any problems like that. You got this long face after they left."

"They were suspicious."

"Pah! National guardsmen are suspicious of everyone these days! They eye one *another* with an evil eye." The man formed a V with his fingers over one eye and laughed loudly as the group walked on. "It worked!" he exclaimed. "The damn plan worked! As smoothly as the third man's cock in a whore! I love the Madman!" Le Saint shouted at the top of his lungs. He was shushed promptly by the rest of the group. "Whoever he is," he added more softly.

There was some general agreement among the group. One of the others elbowed Adrien in the ribs as they walked.

"You want things to go too well, La Chasse. You must make allowances for your own temperament. If you were not so conscious of every little detail, the Madman would not have put you in charge. But the truth is, you do well in getting what he wants from a scheme and the men. And there were no mistakes last night or this morning. It was magnifique! A work of art! Let's celebrate!"

There was loud approval from the group on that. The other men were all in their usual way after a run: floating in high-spirited exhilaration.

And Adrien was in his usual way: tightly coiled and looking for a way to unwind slowly before he snapped and rained loose parts all over everyone.

He sneezed again and acid from his stomach rose into his throat. His stomach growled from hunger. And burned. Lately it had an irritating habit of doing that from time to

237

time.

The men tramped into the streets of Paris in knockabout good humor. They pushed and shoved one another along, discussing the liquor they were going to consume and the women they were going to bed. Now and then, La Chasse caught a barb about his scoffed-at fidelity to his little "wife"—no one had ever asked if he were actually married to the woman, they just assumed—and his fondness for chocolate when the others drank rum. He tried to take it all in the good-humored way it was intended.

He succeeded, for the most part, because he hardly heard it. He was plunged deep into analyzing the bits of puzzlement that plagued him.

Edward Claybourne was hotter than ever for the Madman's capture, which made less and less sense. Over the last five months, the "great French reform" had soured on England's palate. It was coming to be seen for what it was, a wholesale aggression reaching out of France; while, within France, it had become a landmark example of gore and terror. Opinion in England had undergone a massive revision. The almost continual snap and hiss of the guillotine now—along with the memory of the past September when not only aristocrats were butchered but also clergy and ordinary citizens—had sharply jolted the happy English reformer.

The September massacres had jolted the French a little bit, too. People had suddenly become aware of what they said to whom. Paris was tightly controlled; no one came or went without papers, authorization. A tight, organized surveillance of French citizens had lent a hollow ring to the glorious revolutionary words on every French tongue: Many were swept up in a zealous patriotism. But those who weren't and wished to be let alone made the proper noise all the same.

The Madman had found himself on the scene last August when there were pandemic arrests. Prisons were crowded beyond capacity. Convents and hostelries were taken over to accommodate the overflow. The grapevine to the Madman had started to filter down a few more than the usual desperate pleas from aristos.

Then, on September 2nd, a horribly late message reached Adrien. One hundred and nineteen priests, who had refused to swear the oath to the Republic against Rome, were butchered in a monastery in the heart of a residential district in Paris. The screams had roused some frightened citizens behind their closed shutters. By the time a band of the Madman's men arrived for their first non-aristocratic "rescue"—a mere two hours after the message had first reached Adrien's ears—nothing was left but carnage and debris. Bodies and the remains of bonfires. Charred mockeries of pretended trials and releases, sending every last clergyman onto a saber in the hands of an assassin. Adrien had felt he would never get over the horror of that night.

But that was only the beginning. Over the next five days the French guillotine had chopped constantly. The lists of those condemned and killed ran pages long. During this period the Madman had rescued more people than he had over the last three years put together. He had managed the escapes of thirty-eight clergy, three nobles, fourteen merchants, sixteen laborers, some of their families, plus one tramp who had turned up at the last minute. The number included woman and several children—children!—who had been destined to be part of the continuing anathema.

At the time, it had seemed like a huge effort. Yet there was no containing the bloodlust that ruled those days. Mobs broke into the prisons. More than a thousand people were sabered, axed, shoveled, and spiked to death—never mind the ones lost on the guillotine. Adrien and his friends had witnessed some of the atrocities. Disembowelment. Decapitation. At La Force, the prison where the worst was rumored, acts of open cannibalism were reported.

It had been the worst week of the Madman's existence. It made the big event of this week — tomorrow — pale in comparison. Tomorrow, only one man was to be guillotined: Louis Capet, the former king of France. It was a final coup from the rising Paris Commune.

Since September, the Commune and the Jacobin political club had slowly drained away power from the moderate Girondists and the elected Assembly. The Assembly now was dissolved in all but name. Disorganization and a preoccupation with rhetoric had reduced this elected body to impotent dogma that was never coupled with praxis. A craving for action, any action for action's sake, had opened up civil control to the unelected, the self-declared. If, emerging, there was one man who epitomized this deification of mindless Doing, it was Jean Paul Marat, a diseased, rag-clad fanatic who energized the spirit of mob tyranny.

A street lantern, jutting out from its wall like a long-necked voyeur, spotlighted words that drew Adrien's attention. Crudely painted beneath the lantern were the words *Liberty, Equality, Fraternity.* What had become of these noble ideals? Adrien wondered. How could such lofty goals justify murder and mob rule?

Below these words, written in soft rock on the rough surface, Adrien noticed something more. It was the name, *Jeanette,* an address, and some obscene phrases describing what Jeanette might do for a few sous. He grimaced. Jeanette's message seemed to him the less insidious of the two; at least it was more open in its pandering. The revolutionary bywords he condemned, under his breath, as ideological feces, feeding maggots. He turned his head sharply from the wall.

An aloof cynicism toward all politics was becoming bitterly personal. He saw his grand acts to save the genteel nobility as nothing but desperate schemes now, sparing only some tiny proportion of innocent, ordinary men, women, and children. A hopelessness overcame him whenever he thought of a society letting this continue. There had been no great movement to stop this new turn of violence, though the outrages of September had yet to be repeated in the same spectacular manner. But Paris, indeed all of France, turned a deaf ear to her screaming unfortunates. The population, for the most part, were silent accomplices in the crimes of the minority.

It was going to be good to leave, Adrien thought. In a week he would be home in England. Long delayed, Adrien at last had concrete plans for putting an end to his own involvement in all this. He would put his mind to something more productive. Edward Claybourne would have to be satisfied with the Madman's sudden disappearance and with the Earl of Kewischester's refusal to take any new part in his crazy plots. He was getting everyone home. England intended to declare war on France within the month.

Adrien had to increase his pace. He had dropped behind the rest. Watching the others ahead, he had to hold back a silly smile that wanted to break through his depression. The Old Man's "Cabrels" had multiplied like the fabled sorcerer's brooms. Three of the seven men in front of him were infiltrators, forcing the Madman to take deep cover behind a cloud of only a few trusted men. The Old Man was delighted that Adrien had worked himself up so high and was sure that any day the Madman would include him in the "trusted." The smile broke into a grin. Adrien was quite certain that would never happen. But, on one count, he did find the leaving regrettable: Given another few months, he could have had the Claybourne financing providing manpower and carrying the entire operation without even knowing it.

"Ah! There she is!" Le Saint was saying. "Love of my life! Food to my soul! Soothing remedy to the savage beast! Le café!"

Far ahead, beyond a smattering of lifeless, winter-bare trees, a cluster of little lights flickered merrily. Le Café des

Petits Feux Blancs. The little group's frequent haven.

"Hey, sour face! Come with us tonight. It's a long walk home in the cold. Come have a man's drink and warm your pole for that little wife of yours."

Adrien bristled slightly. He liked Le Saint; the man had a kind of peasant-wise intelligence. But Le Saint also offended him at times. He didn't like his crudeness when it edged onto sacrosanct ground.

"That part of me never needs warming for her." Adrien managed to laugh. He hid his expression with a downward glance.

"Mention her name and watch his eyes." Someone made an attempt to do so. Adrien turned his head. "It's a goddamned crime for a man to be that enamored of his own wife!"

"Ah, but have you seen his wife?"

"Yes. Short and fat. Ugly as a pig!" someone else chaffed.

Adrien responded, half in keeping with the jocosity, half in warning, "I'll wrap your lying tongue about your neck, you nearsighted bugger."

"Chris-tin-a," the second syllable accent coming with difficulty to the French tongue. "Have you ever heard such a stuck-up name? And English, she is! Enemy of the people!"

"Oh, sweet enemy," Le Saint said with mock sobriety. "Let me screw England! Let me bring her to her knees. Preferably in front of my open pants!"

Adrien gave way to the urge and clubbed Le Saint on the neck hard enough for the man to yell out and stumble. "Uncivic words. I ought to report you," Adrien chided. "I ought to flatten you all!"

"I yield," Le Saint feigned fear, then repentance. "Oh, let us have another brief glimpse of her, and we'll kiss the ground she walks on!"

"You can kiss my ass."

The café came up on them.

A garland of small lanterns framed the door in a yellow glow. More lanterns and a host of candles flickered from within. Hence the name, Le Café des Petits Feux Blancs. The Tavern of the Little White Lights. Well, they weren't exactly white, thought Adrien. But then, it wasn't strictly a tavern either. Upstairs, above the holiday atmosphere of tables, food, and liquor, a troupe of working girls, in the true spirit of Fraternity, froze, in ribbons and garters and not much else.

Adrien wandered in with the group of men. Welcome heat and the smells of warm bodies, strong drink, and burning oil greeted them. Boisterous music was playing in the room beyond. A sudden surge of laughter nearly drowned that out. Adrien undid his seaman's coat and unwound the muffler as he followed the men into the café.

Three of the men immediately disappeared upstairs. The rest dragged chairs around one table.

"Colette!" Le Saint yelled. "We need five coffees. Put something in it to warm the bones, eh?" He glanced at La Chasse, then called back, "Make that four coffees and one chocolate for the youngster in the group."

Adrien made a sour face. A little put out with himself that he felt the need, he called back to Colette to bring the doctored coffee, not chocolate.

"Eh, La Chasse," Le Saint whispered over to him, "we're on you too much, *mon ami*. Have your chocolate. It's just that for every little light in this place, you've snapped at someone for not doing things to your satisfaction. We get even a little, yes? You drive very hard, and, no doubt, to the Madman's liking. But I tell you, if it weren't for the way you become peculiarly likable in the midst of coaxing a man's last ounce of blood from him, well — a different man would have mutiny on his hands at asking for so much. I think M. Lillings might lead it himself, after this morning. You nearly ordered him to be content with his lot. If he

243

wants to help in France . . . well, you ought to think twice. You have maybe less right to second-guess the Madman than you—ah, Colette," Le Saint's voice rose distractedly, "my little cabbage, you give me a toss tonight, huh?"

A buxom woman of about thirty, dark-complected, attractive in an overworked, unkempt way, had come up with a tray of mugs. Another burst of laughter made her call out her answer.

"You go upstairs if you want your sainthood recalled for the night." She slapped a hand away that tried to fondle a breast. Unfazed, she chatted and greeted the men in a friendly manner over the noise of the room.

"Eh, *mon poulet*." Colette ran a momentarily free finger under Adrien's chin. "Nice to see you. I haven't seen more than your empty breakfast plate in a month." Her dark eyes sparkled meaningfully as she set a cup down. "And I never see you like before."

"Like before? Balls!" Le Saint harrumphed in disgust. "What's this 'like before'?"

Colette cast a frowning glance at the giant, then jerked her eyes back to the last mug of coffee as she set it down. "Like before!" she asserted. "When your eyes turn that blue"—she gave a quick nod of her head—"we talk about 'like before,' too." She turned to clear the table next to the group.

Adrien had dropped his eyes to his mug, stealing a surreptitious look at Le Saint. The other man was scowling at him. Adrien grew uncomfortable. He reexperienced an old, groundless—and surely guilt-founded, he thought—anxiety: that, one day, after seeing him through all kinds of chicanery, his looks would be his nemesis; the petard by which he would be hoisted, so to speak. He gave a wan smile.

Then Colette called him back. "I don't suppose you'd be smiling at the remembrances of me?"

The smile turned sheepish. "No."

Colette stopped to eye him as she wiped her forehead

with the back of her hand. "How's that bit of a woman you're married with? She throw you out yet?"

His skin prickled at the word "married." He managed to grin over his mug. "No, not yet," he said, then shrugged. "Someday, maybe, but she suffers through me now."

"Some suffering," Colette commented as she tossed her tail-end and swished toward the kitchen.

Le Saint, recovered, grinned at the swinging skirt and got up. "Sassy bitch," he said with great appreciation of a woman worthy of such praise. He followed her into the kitchen.

Adrien was left with Charles Sloane and two of the Old Man's infiltrators. He had nothing to say to the "Cabrels," as they were called by the others privately, and nothing to say to Charles in their hearing.

He sipped the coffee. Cheap rum had been added. The combination offended his palate, then his belly. But it warmed. By sheer fire in his insides, if no way else.

Adrien glanced up at the two "Cabrels" again. Their presence nettled him. It was at odds with rational thinking that the English minister would have the time or the inclination to pursue the Madman's rescue operation so doggedly.

He grimaced into his coffee cup, then poured the liquid down his throat. For every *petit feu* in the café, Le Saint had said, Adrien had a complaint. It was true. For every *petit feu* there was a *petit chagrin* that glared out at him.

The Old Man.

The French.

Thomas: Adrien had asked him to stay in England; he was handling that side of it — taking the French aristos across the channel and setting them down safely and quietly in England. Yet, Thomas had accepted his new responsibilities with perfunctory coolness. He seemed to view them as some sort of a slight. In a way, perhaps, they were. Adrien had finally admitted to himself he was no longer comfortable with Thomas near Christina; it had become too apparent that Thomas was in love with her.

Then there were the "Cabrels," like the two eyeing him now. He winked collusion at them; they grinned conspiracy back, then looked away. What asses, he thought.

The original Cabrel had been left behind in a locked cell to be "captured" by the French. Word had it, he was still questioned from time to time. Of course, he knew next to nothing.

Adrien reviewed that night last August for the hundredth time in his mind. He'd been so preoccupied with Christina that he'd hardly remembered Cabrel until hours later, after he had calmed Christina down.

Christina. He'd been dumbfounded to watch her keel over like that at the inn. It was so unlike her. Then she'd been miserably ill crossing the Channel. He'd finally reasoned that he must have frightened her badly. He had meant to, of course, to insure her cooperation. But fear wasn't the word for what she had manifested for a few blissfully quiet hours. She had been petrified. He laughed to himself, still a little mystified as to how he'd managed to put her in such an extreme state. Occasionally, he wished he had that understanding to draw on.

An hour into France, though, she had evidently decided he was still the same man she had known so intimately in England. Once they'd crossed and settled down at a hostelry, her fear had dropped away with her seasickness. He'd heard her recovery from downstairs. She'd impaled the man he'd left with her, on a stickpin Adrien had thought he had left behind; stuck the pin right up to its diamond hilt into the man's shoulder. Much mutual railing and yelling had proceeded between the two, notifying everyone below that an Englishwoman was irate over something upstairs.

Cabrel had been with the group at the time. Adrien had made a special effort to blend into the twenty or so men who were all there for the next day's activities — and had continued to do so until they had successfully "lost" Cabrel into the hands of the enemy.

As he reviewed the details, he again assured himself that the only thing that would have set him apart from the rest is that he traveled with a crazy shrew.

His crazy shrew, he thought fondly. The one *petit feu* that glowed pleasantly in his life. He was looking forward to seeing her, talking to her tonight.

"Colette—" Adrien caught her by the hips as she came by. She stood in his arm a moment, a speculative smile making her weary features pretty. "Bring me a big wedge of cheese to take home," he requested. He reached to his belt for money as he released her.

"Just cheese?" She flipped a stray piece of hair from her face, then with her free hand—her other held two empty mugs by their handles—she reached up under his bulky sweater and wool shirt.

He stayed her hand with one of his while he dug with his other to produce a wad of assignats from the purse at his belt.

She shoved at him good-naturedly with the hand that he held, then saw the money.

"No worthless paper," Colette said firmly under her breath as she grabbed up Le Saint's abandoned mug. "Hard money. And you don't report me this time! Those searches are a pain in my backside."

Adrien chuckled and reached down into the leather pouch again.

The proprietor of Le Café des Petits Feux Blancs hoarded. Paris suffered, and Colette, certainly in the company of a great many other loyal citizens, profited. Food was short, but Colette always had some—for a price. And, periodically, "La Chasse" denounced her to the committee for it.

"How much?" Adrien asked.

She gave him an allover wistful look, then shrugged.

"Nothing. For you, nothing tonight."

"Then I most assuredly must report you. Trying to bribe a public official. Shame." Adrien was an official part of the local committee. He grinned in mischief.

She put her hands on her waist, the mugs clinking together on her hips. "Deux francs," she exhaled, "Why? Why do you denounce me for such a small offense when there are others—"

He dropped two coins into one of the mugs at her hip.

"Because, *cocotte,*" he explained, "I have to report *someone.* The section's revolutionary committee has its quota. We're expected to fill the register with enemies of the Republic— you wouldn't want me to look as though I wasn't doing my job, would you? Besides"—he smiled at her—"the national agent who comes to check on us is provided with certain . . . amenities here. He's not going to let them close you down or lock you up. Even if the guardsmen do one day find your store, the worst you will get is a verbal chastisement." He shrugged and grinned broadly. "The duty of a civic-minded committeeman, Colette."

Colette dropped her eyes away from his smile to the table. She made herself busy dabbing at a spill with the corner of her apron. "You have a strange sense of duty, La Chasse," she said, "And friendship. Someday we will be out of cheese when you ask."

"What? And leave me at the mercy of Christina's cooking? Now that would be cruelty beyond the crime."

Colette laughed. "Would that her bed were as English as her food." She bumped him with her hip, then was off.

Adrien sat back down and was confronted with the prying, shady faces of the Old Man's twosome.

Good God. He would have to talk to Christina about Claybourne's continued interest and see what she thought.

He enjoyed knowing what she thought on most subjects. Her views were perceptive and entertaining. He frequently profited by her fresh approach to a problem gone stale.

Then, of course, her underlying contrariness always made her willing to oppose him, to play devil's advocate.

He reflected on her contrariness for some moments. Last August and September he had not been so happy, or so understanding of it: Tempers had flared so easily, so frequently — and usually made for such blistering confrontations — that he'd been condemned to never really hear what she said. The situation had been impossible, quite nearly intolerable: Christina screaming, sometimes crying; Adrien shouting her down and shutting her up with his own volume and will. Weeks had gone by like this; weeks into months.

Then, one day, she had answered something he'd said — he couldn't even remember what — with a kind of stunning quiet. He'd yet to have figured it out. But, for some unaccountable reason, things had changed. A new reticence became more and more a part of her, more and more a part of the way she dealt with him; and, in it, he had begun to sense a new strength: He had bullied her into quiet, but not into conquered. In these silences, in her humble replies, he saw an ocean of determined and irrepressible "You don't make all the rules."

This adaption of hers he found intriguing, baffling, and more than a little unnerving. At times, he felt caught in his own game, but had forgotten the rules or mislaid his strategy. With the play still being too fascinating to leave alone. He would struggle in her killing little silences, trying to fathom the unspoken complexity that underlay a look, a pause. He unwound little pieces of her, but never the whole. A frustrating occupation, trying to know or predict this woman, but surprisingly absorbing.

There was only one bit of obstinacy which persisted with a lively, and thoroughly maddening, endurance. Ever since August and the fateful inn conversation, when it came to sexual matters, she put up a fuss. He was not to touch her. It didn't matter that a cease-fire had been declared, an amity established, that they'd come to prefer each other's company, or that they drew together with an extraordinary physical attraction. He was simply not to become intimate with her body.

His response, when confronted with this, was not profound, but it was direct: "Like hell I won't."

Over the months, he'd become a little more gracious. It had become obvious that her protests were purely token — though, in an obscure way, this galled him more than if they hadn't been.

"Don't.

"Let go.

"Leave me alone."

He hated the words, but his vanity could shake them off when she surrendered against him, her body stating strong emphatic retractions.

What he couldn't shake was another feeling, a feeling remotely related to indignation. He supposed he hadn't much claim to it, being Christine's abductor, a man not married to her and with the patently dishonorable intention to remain so. But as best as he could explain it in his own mind, whenever he knew he was going to have to hold her damn hands and pin her to the bed, if he wanted to make love to her, he felt as if *he* were being ravaged. What should have been ideal between them was flawed abominably by her protests. And, fair or not, he could have kicked her from France to Poland for fouling this private oasis with hypocritical statements like, "I don't want you to touch me."

Still, he'd yet to feel so put upon he couldn't grit his teeth and allow her her due.

"Adrien, you have no right."

He would laugh. *"Droit de prise.* It's worked for pirates for centuries."

"No."

"Mmm. Yes. But you're entitled to complain. Part of the rules." He would sigh. "Though I do wish you'd not."

"The reluctant rapist."

"It's not rape, and you know it." He never knew truly what to say though, how to counter; when, as sure as he'd not have her secure, she'd be up and off the bed, gone.

On more than one night he'd lost her that way and was just too tired, too surprised and unhappy to pursue her. On those nights, he would lie there alone, next to the warm sag in the mattress where she'd been, and he would want to weep, want to simply give way like a child. But she would inevitably be back; she couldn't go very far. And many nights, if his self-esteem could hold out long enough, if he could force her, coax her far enough past her line of resistance, he would win a degree of what he wanted: "Oh damn you," she'd finally say, or some variation on that theme, followed by complete and delicious capitulation.

He fiddled with his mug on the table, allowing his mind to wander. His fingers traced the curved handle, but his mind traced the naked curve of a woman's body. Diffuse daydreams of venery began pervading all thoughts of Christina Pinn, her continence just so much clothing on the floor.

Adrien laughed aloud at the images at the bottom of his mug.

"Now that's a dirty laugh if I ever heard one. Here's your cheese. And a man left these for you a couple of days ago."

Adrien looked up at Colette, then down at the things on the table. A quarter-wheel of cheese. Two books—he'd been waiting for the one book. And a cigar.

"What's this?" He picked up the cigar. A moment's longing crossed his face.

"A present. From me. For old times. Stay and smoke it. I'll sit. I have a few minutes."

He bussed her cheek as he rose. "Another time, *chéri*. And thank you. But I'm going home to the little woman by the hearth bed—er—fires—er—"

Colette pulled a sulking face that quickly broke into

laughter. "Take pity on her, *mignon!* Use a woman who's better fit—"

But her voice was already fading, caught in the swinging doors between the common room and the entrance way.

These doors flapped to and fro behind Adrien as he shoved his way through the outdoor exit. The night air met him abruptly. It was like walking into a cold wall. The wind had whipped up into a stronger, colder frenzy. It was snowing again. Adrien wrapped his wool scarf over his face to his eyes as he pushed into the winter night.

Chapter 22

New snow rose like powder, making small flurries about his boots as Adrien crunched down the street. He turned down the Rue de Valois, toward the apartment he shared with Christina in Paris. It was still a good walk, but his spirits lifted with each step. He began to hustle down the icy esplanade.

He stopped long enough to buy a newspaper to wrap about the cheese. Those not lucky enough to be able to afford the luxuries of life — food, for instance — did not deal very charitably with those who were when they met on the streets.

Adrien paid the vendor, then quickly disguised the cheese in a copy of *L'ami du Peuple.*

"Good God," he murmured as he realized what he'd purchased, "I may poison us."

He glimpsed a brief line of copy from the inflammatory sheet, there under the street light, as he wrapped the cheese.

"A man who is starving has the right to cut another man's throat and devour the palpitating flesh," the infamous editor wrote.

"Good Lord." He shook his head. "Adrien, my dear boy, I don't think this man would take kindly to your wrapping this cheese in his paper. Though, given the choice, I think his tastes would run more to your palpitating flesh than to the cheese. God preserve a nation that allows a man like this to come to power."

The editor, the same Marat of the Paris Commune, the same Marat of the Paris mobs, in August had become the self-proclaimed head of the newly formed Committee of Surveillance. Adrien shuddered again at how easily Marat was eclipsing the power of the hopelessly divided *Girondins* in the elected National Assembly. Marat controlled the Commune, the Committee, and the mobs—about three hundred hired assassins imported from Sicily and Genoa and all the Frenchmen he could incite to violence through his morbidly slanted journal. The combination effectively controlled Paris, and through Paris, France. Marat's position was precarious. There were others who wanted the uppermost spot. But, presently, he held power, tenuous or not; power he wielded with a capital P. The friends and relatives of those dead in September, and since, could attest to it.

Adrien had indirect contact with the maniac. When Adrien had first arrived back in Paris to set up a long term identity here, he had been lucky enough to be in on the formation of the revolutionary committees. Paris had been divided into forty-eight sections. Each section had its committee. Adrien was on the one for the district in which he lived—it was a marvelous means of ascertaining which neighbors liked to spy and tattle. "Uncivic attitudes" were reported to the small committees by local residents. It was an unholy arrangement of jealous neighbors denouncing each other over pettiness—vengeful lovers reporting one another on spiteful caprice. But registers were kept. A national agent from the parent committee, Marat's Committee of Surveillance, kept tabs with all the zeal of a *petit* commissioner. And repercussions for counterrevolutionary attitudes were often severe, sometimes fatal.

Occasionally, Adrien received a proclamation to "all brothers in the Department" signed by Marat himself. It always espoused justice in the name of the people and, once in particular, tried to justify the mass atrocities and murders in those noble terms, saying the butchery of men, women, and children in the prisons in September was "indispensable in order to terrorize the traitors" at large in the Republic. Who would possibly have the courage to speak out against this rising power if the people's justice was so swift, sure, and merciless? And so absolutely insane.

Adrien grumbled at himself. He'd let his worries and disillusion grab and twist at him again.

He tucked the sedition-wrapped cheese under one arm, stuck the cigar in a book, tucked both books under the other arm, then went off, shoving his hands deep into his pockets. He kept a brisk stride. He dodged a group of playgoers, a lady of the evening, then a seedy threesome all wearing red caps—Marat's mob's cachet—and singing the "Marseillaise" at the top of their drunken lungs.

Once safely past, he mumbled to himself, The song's overblown patriotic dignity suited its singers. He did not like the new anthem or the spirit it engendered.

His breath drifted white behind him as he stepped up his pace to something just short of a run. It was freezing. He wanted to get home to Christina, hear her voice, absorb some of her Spartan attitude. There was too much on the streets and in the cafés of Paris that depressed him.

Another sneeze. The cold shot through his clothes. Christina became another kind of beacon to him: physical contact. By the time he neared the house, images of sexual possession had begun to glow so sharply, they emitted their own tumescent warmth.

Adrien fairly bounded up the narrow driveway into the courtyard. Past the well, at the end of the courtyard, stood an amply lit two-story house. He and Christina shared one of the two ground floor apartments, a two-room affair suitable for an on-and-off coal worker and his wife. It was a dwelling significantly lacking in luxury and spaciousness, but it had come to be a place to which he looked forward to returning. For practical reasons, it had to be modest. The size of one's home was not easily hidden from curious neighbors under a few layers of sensationalistic journalism.

He acknowledged Sam Rolfeman at the front door, then began to readjust the books, cheese, and cigar to reach for the latch. Just as he'd balanced everything in one arm, he sneezed once more. Everything fell.

He was picking the cigar out of the snow when light angled out from the front door, spotlighting him. He glanced out. Christina's silhouette, arms folded, stood in the doorway.

His good mood curdled. He could tell by her posture, he would be dealing with her tart, priggish nature tonight. The partial erection that had accompanied him home suddenly became hesitant to accompany him inside.

"Four days," she said as he entered. "For four days I have had to contend with that man." It was Sam, again; she and Sam didn't get along at all.

Adrien closed the door and leaned against it. "Do you think," she continued, "that you could limit your censorship and tyranny over my life to at least only being a nuisance to me when you are around? Living in the shadow of your awesome control when you are fifty miles away is a bit aggravating. I'd like to live a little bit of my life on my own —" She stopped, then said only a slight bit more softly, "Your nose. It's all red. Are you drunk or sick?" Softer still: "Are you all right?"

He laughed at her quick reversal. "Yes." He stared at her as he unlooped the muffler and undid his coat.

She was lovely. It never ceased to amaze him how lovely he found her. Her hair was coming down in a dozen places—actually, she didn't do too well without a maid. Her face and fichu had something powdery on them; cornmeal, perhaps. Her dress was wrinkled. Her apron had a large, round wet spot where she'd leaned against something.

His eyes rose to her face. He smiled. Her reality was infinitely prettier than anything imaginable. His eyes dropped to the round wet ring on her apron. And infinitely more pregnant. God, but she was huge. It didn't help her disposition. But it didn't hurt her appeal.

Conception must have occurred sometime in June. He counted to himself: July, August, September, October, November, December. This was January. She must be at least seven months gone; and round as a ripe peach. He thought she looked magnificent like that: gloriously gravid with his child. Tender thoughts swept over him. Then she confused them with less wholesome thoughts as she plundered on into the territory known as his Innate Dishonesty.

"Must you lie about something as mundane as a bloody cold? Or are you afraid I can turn that against you? You are *not* all right. What have you been doing these past four days?"

The concern in her voice left him smiling again. He watched her fight a responding smile with a disapproving frown. He'd forgotten. She objected to his smiling at her when she was put out with him. This fell under Deceptive Manipulation. He frowned, putting all tenderness behind him.

He shook his coat off one arm. He had to set his packages on the table. "The wind on the water last night was fierce. My nose has been running ever since." The coat slipped off; he folded it in front of him. He picked up the top book from the table and offered it to her. "Here, I brought you this."

When she went to reach for it, he pulled it back a little. She stepped a little closer, reached—and stopped.

She puckered her lips and tilted her head back at him.

257

"You're not going to start that already, are you?" she asked irritably. She dropped her eyes to his pants. His coat, in front of him, covered the evidence. She turned and went to the fireplace.

There, she stooped to work with something—presumably dinner. He didn't want to think of that. Instead, he watched her bottom swing away from him, then settle on her heels. She didn't seem hinged in the normal way a woman was; he loved her loose, unjointed movement, the sway of her hips, the graceful way her body folded where it seemed to need to, even now with a belly so big she occasionally misjudged her balance.

He came near enough so that when she rose he could reach out and steady her: There was no help for it. His mind had already begun to plot how to corner her with a minimum risk of being too rough, of startling her, of toppling her. It was he who felt clumsy these days; clumsier and clumsier as she grew. How to approach her. How to be careful of her. How not to injure her and still get hold of her long enough to . . .

If only he knew how to not want her.

He stood, waiting; pretending to warm his hands at the fire. He was mentally salivating over her all-the-more-resplendent breasts when he realized she was looking at him. She flushed visibly, pulled herself up by the mantel, and moved away.

He stood with his back to her for some moments, his hands warming toward the fire and his temper heating just a little with them. Stupid woman. He hadn't seen her for four days. For the last hour he'd been able to think of little else but her. He could tell by the color of her cheeks, she wasn't as cool as she pretended. And she was playing this idiotic game again. The urge to give her a good firm kick implanted itself in his mind once more.

"What's this?" she asked.

He glanced over his shoulder. She was holding both

books he'd brought home.

"One is for me. A volume of Homer. The other's for you. The best I could do was a French translation. It's from the English *Treatise on Midwifery* by some doctor. Smellie is the author's unlikely name. It's supposed to be a fairly accurate account of the laboring and birthing process. You've expressed some fear over what lies ahead. I thought some knowledge might lessen your anxieties. I'll help you with the French if you like." He'd had considerable trouble in searching out and obtaining the one book. A printer had finally managed to locate the copy of Smellie. Homer had been thrown in for him as an act of love, he was sure. The printer was a good friend of his grandfather's.

"That was sweet of you. Yes, I should like you to help me with the words and phrases I don't understand. That's very thoughtful."

He turned, put his hands behind him to the fire; held in innocence for the moment. She was saying something about the baby and the book, but he didn't follow it. He was thankful she seemed intent on the gift. He couldn't keep his eyes from going over the line of her, all the curves of bosom and belly and buttocks. He wondered briefly if there was something wrong with a man who lusted so passionately after such a gravid little creature.

"Right here. What does this mean? 'To hold account'? 'to be held account for'?" She was pointing to something in the book.

He hesitated, then grimaced. He wanted very much to go over, see what she asked, answer it in patrician suavity as he wrapped his arms about her, then promenade her into the bedroom in mutual accord. It never worked that way. And how he detested being rebuffed by her. He went over to see what she wanted, nevertheless.

He peered into the book at the phrase she had marked with her finger. " 'If I were taking into account,' " he translated. "My word! That's the second sentence. You're

259

going to need a lot of help." He tried to sound casual. "Why don't you come read it in bed?"

"We haven't had dinner." She couldn't have said it any starchier.

"I don't want dinner!" he blurted. "I want you! Christina, let's not do this cat and mouse game tonight. Let's just go to bed together and enjoy it. I've missed you. I want—"

She snapped the book shut and dropped it on the table. She spoke in that soft, determined way she had lately. "Don't tell me what you want, Adrien. I'm here because you want it. I can't go anywhere unless you want it. Look at me! I'm fat, I think, because you wanted it! You couldn't be more pleased with this!" She gestured to her middle. She turned, about to put the width of the little room between them again.

He grabbed her arm. "You are such an idiot," he said. He pulled her back against him. Through the layers of clothes, he felt her delicate form twisting, moving, pulling to get away. Yet just the feel of her was such a relief; like truly coming in out of the cold. He rubbed his body against the squirming woman. He closed his eyes. His breathing immediately altered. He felt everything accelerate. He heard her in front of him make one of those funny sounds—like a child about to cry while being wrenched from the security of a nanny's arms.

"No, Adrien! Ask me, for godsake!"

"Will you come lie with me?" He kissed her neck. "God, woman, I ache for you. Come to bed with me, Christina."

"No."

A little put out, he stopped long enough to ask, "Why was I supposed to ask then?"

"If I'm only allowed one answer, then why bother asking? You're so damned presumptuous! Even when you're asking leave to—well, you expect things to be just your way all the time. You demand it! And what you can't just take you—oh—oh!"

He'd managed to slide his hands under the loose waist of her apron, skirts, and undergarments. This put his hands on her bare belly. He lifted the weight of the child.

"What a gorgeous melon you have here, madam. I think I should like a dozen. Do you deliver?"

"Oh, you fiend! You're doing it again. Oh! Ooo! Stop it! Answer me! Talk to me! You won't tease your way out of the conversation!"

He closed his eyes and shook his head. "You're beyond me, Christina. I don't *understand* this conversation. Not from the first word."

He scooped her up into his arms and started for the bedroom. He molested her affectionately, resigning himself to her protests once again.

"This isn't fair," she whimpered. "You know it isn't fair. Put me down." She struggled clumsily.

He snorted at the request and her struggle, then kissed her, holding her head to him with his hand. She made small sounds of complaint, but he could sense her ambivalence. Her mouth tried to pull away. She held her lips together. But there was a moment of doubt—which his mouth coaxed into something more relaxed. Then entrance. The kiss became full. She groaned, still trying to retreat. She tried to back her head away. He wouldn't let her; it took little to contain her. In fact, it was nothing to block and stop this small woman on virtually any physical front she chose to do battle. If only that were the problem.

She was working herself up into a genuine state of anger. Adrien nuzzled her neck. Her hair was slightly damp at the back. She must have just washed it; it smelled wonderful. Yet she kept trying to push away from him—like a cat trying to climb and scramble out of one's arms. As he placed her on the bed, he was praying she wouldn't get any more difficult than she had already become. The urge to lie with her had asserted itself strongly. From just carrying her to the bedroom, his pants had begun to pull.

He lay down beside her, then lost, for a second, his firm hold. A flurry of limbs and petticoats kicked up. He just managed to catch an ankle. Christina scooted backward and up, to a sitting position against the headboard.

Adrien sighed, stroked his hand down her leg—the only thing left to him. Then, with another sigh, he pulled himself up to sit beside her.

"Are you going to give me another miserable time with this tonight?" he asked.

"I don't give you a miserable time. You bring it on yourself. Just leave me alone."

"I can't leave you alone. I see you: I want to touch you." He tried to put his arm around her.

She shifted away, wrapping her arms about herself, over the top of her belly.

He pulled her backward into the crook of his arm. He lifted her hair, wanting to kiss her neck. Her hand came up, between his mouth and her skin. He kissed the back of her hand. Then he took possession of the hand and turned it over. He rubbed his thumb along the smooth skin, the delicate veins of her wrist . . . .

He felt the muscles in her arm flex, trying to make the arm hers again. She heaved a little breath when he wouldn't let her. "I don't want this, Adrien. Leave me alone."

He grimaced. Then he pulled her, backward, until the none-to-easily-balanced young woman fell across his lap. He looked down into her face. Some of his tension went out of him in a laugh. The face was so pretty. And so cross. But flushed. Even in the dim light of the room—just the fireplace was glowing—he could see the rise of color in her cheeks. He could see the heave of her breasts. And it wasn't all anger. Her eyes glowed. She watched him in a way he'd seen too often to mistake.

He touched one breast, let his fingers squeeze gently into the fullness of it. She put her hand up to stop him, but he caught her hand beneath his and pressed it to her own

262

breast. She closed her eyes and turned away. He could feel her heart beating hard beneath their hands.

"Doesn't it embarrass you," he murmured, "to make such a fuss? When you end by doing some of the things you do in bed with me? Honestly, Christina, what is the point?"

His only answer was a glance; a tight-lipped, peeved expression.

He breathed out an exasperated laugh and shoved her onto a pile of pillows and covers. He swung around and threw the weight of his leg across her. They lay, diagonally, across the mussed-up bedclothes. Adrien drew his thumb between her breasts, slowly tracing the deep valley that lay there. Downward, over her belly. With the heel of his hand, he put pressure on the soft pad of flesh over her pelvic bone—and she began her wriggling and scuffling again.

She was trying to heave herself up by her elbows, but the pillows and covers were too deep and soft. Her huge belly made it impossible to adjust her center of gravity. Adrien's leg over her hips made it impossible to roll to her side.

After perhaps a minute of these futile efforts, she let herself drop back with an "oof." Her hair spilled over Adrien's fingers. A generous, jiggling breast bounced against his arm.

"I hate you," Christina whispered. She was out of breath.

But he continued to battle with her affectionately, pushing for liberties he knew he wasn't going to get—while brushing up against all the pleasant possibilities of those he hoped for later. It was his most effective tactic. By wrestling with her gently—always hoping for compliance—he could let her spend herself, both her energy and anger. Then he would swoop in on a tired, teased, half-titillated young woman. . . .

He kissed her again. This time his hips followed his leg partially over her. His body fit neatly into the little depression below her pelvis where her legs pressed together. He rubbed himself against her. Then he lost himself in imagi-

263

nation. Her skirts had come up. He was aware of the nakedness of her legs. His hand found her hips and bare thigh. Something deep inside him groaned in satisfaction. His chest pressed more deeply into the softness of her breast. He could feel himself disappearing into her, into the act. . . . He not only wanted to bury his body inside her, but his mind, his total consciousness. . . .

Christina could apparently sense his more serious mood. Her hands flew at him. They attacked. Small, desperate, useless; the way birds will make a mad-dash effort to defend a nest, against even the largest of encroaching predators. He captured her small, flyaway fists. She made sounds; protest, more anger, frustration. He pinned her down with his weight.

It was always a little delicate here. He wanted to hold her down, but he didn't want to hurt her or the baby—it joined its mother in squirming. For a moment, Adrien let himself relish the feel of that. His child moving in her belly between them. Christina moving under him in a way that, if she only knew, would horrify her; the feel of her squirming body under him made him dizzy.

His fingers grazed her skin here and there as he began to open her clothes. He heard her catch her breath, make more muffled little sounds. Her breathing became irregular. She was struggling, but her struggles had taken on an erotic quality; a woman trying to stay afloat in the dark, sinking in a mire of pleasure. She groaned. He knew the sounds. . . .

"Please," she murmured. "Please—" But she had stopped shoving against him. The classically ambiguous plea. In the context of her hands dropping back into her hair, her chin lifting up, she was no longer asking him to stop . . . .

Adrien's mind spun. Wanting her became something frantic. All the blood in his body roiled up and shot to his groin. His pants were suddenly painful at the seam. He began to throb. . . . He was shaking when he rose up on his knees, unable to undo the buttons fast enough. He needed two hands. . . .

Then the consummate, nerve-rattling experience: As he was peeling down his pants, Christina bolted.

It was such a comeuppance, he couldn't compose himself for several seconds. He just sat there on his knees, breathing like a blacksmith's bellows.

But, before the fertile young woman could lumber from the bed, he caught a handful of copper-yellow hair.

"You're not exactly agile anymore, sweetheart." He pulled her unceremoniously back into the bed. "Lie down!" He shoved her onto her back.

Her head hit the pillows, and her face snapped around to him. Her chest was heaving, but there was a peppery defiance in her eyes.

Adrien exhaled, a semi-laugh; he closed his eyes. "Sorry. But you play with me on this, and I know it. When is enough, Christina? When do I get off?" Again he exhaled, trying to get rid of the anger, the hostility, the pure unspent passion. "My dear, I don't know what to do with you. Half the time you go to bed with me, I hear you coo in my ear. The rest of the time, you seem content to drive me mad. You anger me more with this than with any of the other nonsense I take from you." He nudged her neck with his nose, then cheek, then mouth. He pulled himself over her once again. "For godsake, let me make love to you, Christina," he whispered. "Let me do all the things we both enjoy so much without this stupid game—"

He had her pinned under him again. What could be more helpless, he thought, than a female spread under a man a foot taller, twice her weight; capable of doing whatever he would? The answer hit him forcefully: A man with his pants down and his ass in the air, desperately wanting that woman to accept him. Adrien wondered—not for the first time—who was really the weak and defenseless one here. For one moment, he almost gave up. My God, if she was really going to fight it this hard. . . .

Then something, instinct, or perhaps the persistent presence in his groin—his body there, like a disinterested third party, was oblivious to the fact that he was having to push her through this an inch at a time—made him lean down and taste her ear. It was the most beautiful ear. The most delicious neck. The smoothest, silkiest path to the fullest bosom. . . . Her breath went out in a burst from her mouth. The more she tried to catch it, the more she groaned in frustration.

"Adrien, you are impossible. Don't you ever give up?" Again, her breath rushed out. "Oh, for the love of God, rape me. But don't do this."

He was beyond listening. He curved his hips to rub against her. Her clothes were undone. Her skirts were up. With his pants open, the contact demolished every bit of self-control. The wanting hit him so hard . . . .

Christina gave him a shove. But a moment later, her arms came up around his neck. Her hands spread over the muscles of his shoulders and back. Perhaps the contact had undermined her purposes as neatly as it had his. Something had. Her pleas had ceased to make any sense. Her eyes closed and fluttered. Her lips parted slightly.

He accepted the invitation with grateful relief. He took her. Sensation turned over on itself in such a spin, he always wondered if he didn't hallucinate. And Christina was the drug. A powerful, unearthly drug. Worth every unpalatable moment of getting her down.

They made love for more than an hour, missed dinner entirely, and fell asleep intertwined.

It was their usual sort of reunion after he came off a run. Once she touched him, she embraced something more than pure physical sensation. She embraced his tensions, his needs. The anxiety of a run—the planning, the secret meetings, juggling "Cabrels," the actual implementation of getting the poor frightened people out of Paris and onto a

266

boat — dissolved in the close intimacy between them in the dark.

She loved him. Despite everything. He'd known it for some time. And Adrien was well aware that her love was worth having. It was pulling him through a terrible time. He was dependent on it — a little bothered by how much. But he was elated, too. How perfect to have such a fine woman in such a beautifully ill-defined giving relationship.

Chapter 23

Adrien pulled at the blanket to cover his thigh. Then he expelled a soft curse into the darkness.

The chill of the room and the pain in his stomach had wakened him. The fire had died down in the bedroom hearth. But what fire was missing in the fireplace was burning in his stomach. The small irritation that had been with him off and on for the last few months was on again, and worse than usual tonight.

Christina shifted in the bed. She'd gotten up and put on her nightgown in the last hours. She slept now, but he could see she was having trouble finding a comfortable position. Perhaps, she was cold, too.

He sniffled as he swung from the bed and began rummaging about the room. He found a sweater and climbed into it, shuffled into his pants. He looked about for some more warmth. No more blankets. No more wood. He went into the front room and broke off the legs and the back of one of the chairs. What did it matter? It was just for a few more days. Next week at this time he would have roaring fires in every one of the dozen fireplaces in his London home.

Wistfully, he let the comforts of his London house steal up on him, then shooed them away with a shake of his head. It served no one's best interests to remember he didn't need to be here, that just a short distance away a comfortable house—a comfortable life—waited for him.

In the bedroom, he blew on the embers of the nearly dead fire. He sniffled again. The chair pieces caught, bringing some promise of heat to the room.

At the sight of the flames, he turned and went out to the front room again, then started rooting through things on the cluttered table. He found what he was looking for: a tiny bit of indulgence. He sniffed at the cigar. A bit stale, but tobacco.

He had returned to the bed and puffed on the cigar for no more than two or three minutes when the burning in his stomach gave him a violent twist—acid rose in his throat, his eyes watered.

The stale cigar went into the fireplace. "Goddamned bellyache."

He'd seldom been able to enjoy even a decent cigar for several months. He'd all but given up trying.

He went out to the main room and scrounged a piece of cheese. Empty, his stomach was always more cantankerous. He walked back to the bedroom filling the irritable void with the cheese.

"Is something wrong, Adrien?"

"My stomach again. Or maybe just the damned weather. My nose is running off my face."

"Your nightshirt is clean. In that pile of laundry over there." Faint light from the street illuminated Christina's hand pointing to a stack of folded clothes on the chest of drawers.

He found the heavy flannel and exchanged his trousers and sweater for the warmer, more comfortable item. Then he crawled back into bed.

"Why are you awake?" he asked. "You didn't look too comfortable a while ago." He gave her a pat on her belly. "It's hard to sleep with that load, isn't it? Just a bit longer, though."

"A few weeks at most."

"What?" He tried to look at her, but he could see only the vaguest outline in the dark. "I'd rather thought late March. That's more than a few weeks."

She laughed. "We will test your true authority, your lordship. You see if you can command him to stay in there ten months. Now, give me a shove. I need up."

With help, she got up from the bed. Her silhouette disappeared behind the screen in the corner. A strong stream hit the chamber pot.

He called to her. "It's just, counting from June—"

"Mid-May." Christina came into view. He imagined she smiled as she sat on the bed. "My last flow was mid-May. Three years with Richard, and not a whisper. With you, I'm so fertile, just moving into the same house and I never see blood again."

He blinked at the crudeness. She had become a lot less prim in the last five months. A lot less worried about what anyone—including him—thought. Then he relaxed back into the pillows. Christina ran her hand over his chest. He loved her touch. And her attitude: He remembered other women, less accepting, trying to wring marriage from less-wronged circumstances. Christina never mentioned it; bless her. He felt safe. He closed his eyes.

She groaned as she lay back in the bed.

"What's wrong?"

"My back. It's been killing me all night. If I could only get some relief for—ah! Oh, that's lovely. Oh, thank you."

He pushed at the muscles of her back through her shift. He moved and kneaded the areas he remembered could get the stiffest. It had been a long time. Elizabeth in London, five, no, six years ago. And much longer ago, Celeste.

"Oh, you do that just right," Christina groaned. "Ah, yes, right there. Oh, that feels wonderful, Adrien." She gave a low giggle. "You have such a flair for this." A sigh. "How did it go yesterday?"

"Dreadfully."

"You had trouble?"

"No, I just wrung myself into a limp rag worrying that we would. God, I'm so glad to be getting out of here."

"When?"

"Next week. The 27th. We're leaving by boat in broad daylight with a group of English dignitaries hightailing it out of here while they still can do so agreeably. We sign on as part of the house staff of a Mr. and Mrs. Wimberly in a day or two. This time next week we will be tucked into a large canopied bed in high comfort in the best district in London."

No comment.

It was purposeful silence, he suspected. It made him uneasy. He very much wanted her to stay with him, just as things were, once they reached London. But he was virtually certain that the lawyer's daughter would want to renegotiate the terms.

As if to have something to say, she sighed and remarked again at how marvelous he was at doing her back. "Experience, no doubt," she added.

He winced.

She continued. "You're probably more of an expert on pregnancy than I am. Do you stay with all the mothers of your bastards when they get this fat? I don't know how you can stand it."

He planted a smacking kiss on her cheek. "I admit, pregnant women have an erotic appeal all their own."

"And pregnancy results in screaming, squalling brats. How does that appeal to you?"

"Fine." He laughed.

"I don't believe it."

"It's fine. Really. I like children. My own, anyway."

"How many did you say you had?"

He snuggled to nest his body against hers. He smoothed

his hands around to the wondrous growth of her waist. "This will make six."

There was a long pause before she spoke again. "Your others? How old are they?"

"Let's see. There's a set of twins in Cornwall. They would be almost four. I have a daughter, born in Paris, transplanted to Scotland last spring, who is sixteen." He laughed. "I have a cocky little stinker of a son in London. He's eight, no, nine now; precocious, swaggering. He imitates me down to every detestable detail. I love it. He has a sister, five, very quiet — probably overly shy from living with the beast. She's also mine."

Silence. Then, weakly: "I had envisioned them all by different women, for some reason. And all about two years old. Crying. Messing in their pants. And if you ever did see them — which I thought was unlikely — I envisioned them snotting on your breeches and chocolating your lace. I certainly never saw them bouncing on your knee. You do that, don't you? You visit them. And love them."

"Well, of course, I love them." He turned and pushed himself up on one arm. To his surprise, she was crying.

"What a lovely big family we all are," her small voice said. She tried to brusquely turn her back to him. But his baby conspired with its father to keep her from it. Adrien had reached out and settled his hand over her midsection to hold her. Dutifully, the baby kicked his hand.

"Did you feel that?" he asked with sudden pleasure. "He's a strong little devil. And he sides with his father. Caring for one's children is better than not." He added most seriously, "You should cry if I didn't care, Christina. But to love them, that should be cause to rejoice. I'll love yours. Especially well. I'm sure."

All she said was "Oh, Adrien." As if he were an idiot of the worst sort.

"Christina" — he frowned, trying to see her expression in the dim light — "what have I done now?"

"You have two!" she accused softly. "Two by one woman, three years apart."

"Elizabeth. She's a lovely woman. An actress in London. She'd been—"

"Oh, stop it!" She finally succeeded in hoisting herself to her side. "Don't tell me any more. I'm sorry I asked." A sob. "Dreadfully sorry."

"Christina," he whispered in her ear, "if numbers matter, I'd love to foist a dozen off on you." He reached around and caressed her belly tenderly. "You're so lovely fat. You're so lovely any way, slender or fat. I should like the opportunity to keep you fluctuating back and forth indefinitely." He was startled by how much his last sentence sounded like marriage. He grimaced and hoped it sounded more like living together for an indeterminate period under ill-defined rules. It apparently did.

"You are amoral, Adrien Hunt." She sniffled. "You could live with a harem and a hodgepodge of children and never see anything wrong with it! Like it, in fact. Love it. You love them! You love them all, don't you? Every one of those little bastards. And all the mothers, too!"

"No." He frowned in surprise. "No, I don't. I don't love the little snip with the twins. I don't love the French governess, the mother of my sixteen-year-old. And Elizabeth, well, we have an understanding that could only be called respect; it's certainly not—"

"Oh, I think I'm going to be sick." She started clambering from the bed.

He yanked her back, rolled her, and kissed her; deep and hard, in flagrant contradiction to the fact that he was not supposed to—this was undoubtedly where he was supposed to let her be moral and angry.

"You silly gamine." He lay half on top of her. "You haven't asked me what's on your mind even once. But I will tell you, *mon petit chagrin:* In all due modesty, you love me. You have, for I don't know how long. Before France, I

273

think. And you want to know how you stand with all the other women in my life. I will tell you. At the top. Above them all. Above and beyond the reach of any dozen, with or without brats to snot on my breeches."

"I notice how you phrase the love relationship," she said. "Do you love me, Adrien? What am I dealing with?"

He sighed, mentally debating for a few moments. "You're dealing with a man who's quite confused," he admitted.

"Who would go through any contortion to avoid declaring his feelings one way or another."

He stroked down the side of her hair. "Who is scared, Christina. Who is scared that besides having to cope with the French authorities in a double blind, with large batches of people who wish to God they weren't French, and with a crazy old English minister — not to mention a runny nose and a plaguing stomachache — he's going to have to start coping with love again."

She didn't say anything for a time. Then: "Did you just tell me you loved me?"

"I believe I did."

"What a romantic way to put it. Classed with a runny nose and a stomachache." She laughed suddenly and kissed him. "Tell me again."

His stomach churned. He wondered if his admission was for the best. He pushed her away as he rose from the bed again. "Don't make a fuss over it, Christina. It doesn't make a terrible lot of difference if I love you or not."

"Doesn't make a difference? Why, it — where are you going?"

"To find something else to eat. My stomach feels like it's going to burn a hole right through my bowels."

"There's milk in the window box. And your loving me, Adrien, it makes all the difference in the world."

At the pronouncement of that sentence, he heard his narrow platform of safety collapse with a bang in his ears.

He knew what was coming next as instinctively as the fox knows what follows the bark of the hounds. His stomach rolled over on the cheese. If she still had the urge, they could be sick together.

She was still sniffling in a wave of tears as he walked into the front room. But she sounded so happy. So bloody happy.

He lifted the lid to the cold box of food in the window, wondering how he was going to get out of this gracefully. He could hear her in the bedroom saying precisely what he didn't want to hear.

" . . . we should be married before we leave, really. The baby's not due for another four or five weeks, but I'd feel more secure not waiting too long. Why did you let it go so long?" He heard her laugh as he poured the milk into a glass. She went on with a giggle. "We may well have to rush from the church straight to get the midwife. What glorious gossip . . . "

She droned on. He could have shot himself. What had ever possessed him to admit such a thing to her?

He padded back into the bedroom, aware, in the twenty-degree weather, that he had begun to sweat; a twitchy feeling, cold, clammy. He wiped his mouth on his sleeve and started rummaging around for a handkerchief for his nose.

"You haven't said a thing, Adrien."

"No. Are there clean handkerchiefs in this pile of laundry?"

"Somewhere. Here, let me help you."

It took her a good minute to navigate out of bed. She was hunting through the pile when he blurted it out.

"I don't want to marry you."

She stopped her search, straightened and stepped back. "Why, for godssake? Do you like having bastards?"

"No. I don't like having wives."

"You stupid—" She dumped the pile of clean clothes on

top of him and shuffled off to sit on the edge of the bed. "That doesn't make any sense. You support three sets of wives, in essence. You said you don't love the others, and you love *me*. Besides, you and I are already married in every sense but the legal one. If you love me, then—"

"Don't drag that into it. As I said, it doesn't matter. I'm quite content to love an unmarried woman." She let out an angry sound. He tried to soften his statement. "It's not rational, Christina. It's just—it's so hard to explain."

"You're damn right it's hard to explain. Your other marriage was ten years ago."

He was stopped. How miserable of her to have hit it on the mark, just like that. "I won't talk about it," he said at length.

"I know." All the fight had gone out of her. She wasn't going to push it. "You hinted once," she said, "that the divorce was bad. Was it that awful?"

He made a wan laugh and came to sit beside her on the bed. "It was horrendous. My wife divorced me under the most damaging, most sensational circumstances she could manage."

"For infidelity?"

He laughed again. It was a good guess, a logical guess. And true; but only in a technical sense, not in spirit. "I wanted a divorce," he explained. "And it seemed to me, being stupid and twenty-three at the time, that the gentlemanly thing to do was to go out and have a discreet affair to give my wife grounds. Only Madeleine was a little pigheaded about the whole thing. So I had a slightly less discreet affair. Then another." He took in a breath, let it out noisily. "It turned into a kind of rampage. The miracle, I suppose, was that I didn't end up with some social disease. Though, from one point of view, I contracted something of that ilk: I became infected with infamy. Anything I've ever done since has always been tinged with the impressions I made then. I've never been able to shake it."

276

He leaned back, put his arms under his head. He was suddenly comfortable talking about this. "The papers had a field day," he said. "An earl, not just divorcing, but divorcing in scandal. You can't imagine. Madeleine began legal proceedings. I continued; a lot of drinking, craziness, a *lot* of women—and nearly all of it public. I had gotten on rather a roll, you see. She was so angry, and I was so happy she was. Eventually, I was cited for debauchery—some of which was actually true—that would make your hair stand on end. However, much of it wasn't true—if you can believe me. I lost control somewhere. It all got out of hand. I was so covered in mud and slander after that year, I had to go abroad.

"Legally, though, it didn't do her much good. English law is blissfully unfair on some points. She had two strikes against her. She was French, and she was a woman. This left my property and wealth virtually still under my control, no matter what she said I'd done. She won the divorce, but nothing more. She retreated to France. I haven't seen her since the day the papers were signed."

Was there no more to it, he wondered? Could it be summed up so easily as that?

He heard Christina sigh, very softly. She whispered, "Was it an arranged marriage?"

"No."

"You were in love with her?"

"Yes."

"Are you still?"

It didn't take even a moment to think about. "No. I'm in love with you. And, for the first time in a dozen years, it seems all right to be in love again." He added softly, "More than all right."

"Then marry me, Adrien."

He'd thought surely this little history would have daunted her. "I can't—"

"You can—"

The trump card. "It was an English divorce, Christina. My wife was a French Catholic. In France, I am still married to her."

He felt her roll onto her side in the dark. Away from him. "Oh God," she groaned. But, other than that, he couldn't fathom what in the world was going on in her mind.

He reached for her. "Christina," he tried to tell her, "being my mistress is no disgrace in London society. My children have a good life. Marriage is an unnecessary complication—"

She rolled back toward him, onto her shoulders, and hit him. Right in the nose with the flat of her hand. It hurt, then made him sneeze. "Damn you, Adrien Hunt," she whispered, "My father didn't polish my speech and educate my sensibilities so I might decorate your own private brothel! I wasn't bred to produce bastards!"

"And exactly how did you plan on getting around that before tonight? Now that you've wrenched some leverage from me, I suppose—"

"You pompous ass!" she hissed. "Did you honestly think I'd planned on going back to London with you and setting up house without another word said?"

"No, I expected—"

"I planned on leaving you, you idiot! At the first opportunity! I planned on going where no one would know any differently, making up a suitable lie, scraping together what dignity you'd left me and making a decent life for myself and my child—"

"Leaving me?" he broke in hoarsely.

"Leaving you! Is that so hard to imagine? That a woman might prefer some peace of mind and a little honor to your blithely bestowed favors?"

"Leaving me?" It was as if he couldn't quite translate this foreign notion. He couldn't grasp it. "You were perfectly willing to accept my blithely bestowed favors last summer

278

in Hampshire."

"Oh, you stupid man—"

"I'm stupid? You were, quite happily—and quite publicly, my mistress last August. You were looking for a way to extend things, not end them. Will you kindly explain to me the difference between now and then?"

"Six months. And a baby in my belly." But she wouldn't let him off there. "I tried last August, Adrien. I wanted you. I wanted to be able to be what Evangeline told me once I could be: a woman who took her happiness from what fate offered. But I can't. I've tried, and I'm miserable! I feel like a slut when you touch me. I feel like a peasant when you order me about. I want to be good enough to share your name, to be your equal, do you understand? I'd be miserable with *just* your name, without your love. But your loving me—well, the choice is clear. I have a chance at happiness. Marry me. The other choice, starting again somewhere else without you, is awful, but a damned sight better than hating myself and you, too."

There was a catch in her voice. "Oh, Adrien," she continued, "can't you see the difference? There would be too much notoriety beside you in London. I could never dust myself off if you threw me over. And there would be this little reminder for everyone to look at—who, bless his soul, deserves at least a bit of what my father wanted for his grandchildren: a chance to look any man in the eye. There'll be no doing that unless I leave to make that kind of life for him. And for myself—" She stopped, sighed noisily. "Oh dear, you're absolutely silent again. This all sounds like some hopelessly concocted ultimatum, doesn't it? It's not. Honestly."

"No. It sounds like extortion. Damn it, Christina. You can't leave me! I won't let you!"

"Only a husband can say that. Or a kidnapper. Are you prepared to be one of those, once in England?"

He smiled grimly, "Oh, a kidnapper by all means. I've

279

really taken to that." He rolled toward her, to pull her under him.

There was frustration in her voice. "You're hopeless," she said, "Do you know that? You're beyond help." She threw her arms around him. "And I love you. I don't want to go from you."

He slid his arms about her, feeling reassured by this admission. "Then that settles it. You won't. Now, no more of this foolish talk, and brace yourself"—he laughed in what he hoped was a convincingly light manner—"I'm about to rape you again."

"No."

The smile left his face. Damned woman. He gnashed his teeth.

"No," she repeated, "no more rape. I have a week before I must be strong; I'm going to enjoy being weak. Make love to me, Adrien. I want it." He realized she had begun to cry silently. "I want it desperately."

She pulled him down on her, until he had to resist to keep from lying heavily on the child. He frowned as she hiked up her gown and began pulling on his nightshirt. He caught her hands. "Damn it, Christina. Are you going to badger me all week with this? And add the sweet morsel of, finally, being a little more agreeable. This threat is—"

She put her fingers to his lips. "Is nonexistent," she finished for him. "Come kiss me. There's no threat, honestly. I love you, and I want you."

"And you won't leave me. Say it."

"Adrien, don't bully me."

"Now," he said more sternly. "I want to hear this crazy notion of yours put to rest."

"Adrien," she pleaded with some emphasis.

He lay over her, silent, motionless; scowling.

She heaved a huge sigh. "Put away your lordly manner, my dear earl. Rest easy. I have no intention of badgering you into doing something you don't want to do. As if I could. O-oh. Oh! Get up! The baby's moved. I want off my back."

He hesitated. He was relieved at her reformed attitude, and then immediately befuddled by her command to get up. He didn't want to get off her. But the only play he'd never felt good about ignoring was the one he'd just had pitched at him. He was suspicious that despite previous intimations, he was being maneuvered away from the physical comfort he now wanted. Added guilt piled up on him when he remembered how much closer she was to term than he'd realized.

"Come on, now," she said impatiently, "I can't breathe properly with both of you on me this way. Move."

He did. Grudgingly. She followed him, turning onto her side. She began to pull at his nightshirt again. He jerked to grab her cold fingers as they grazed over his warm belly.

"You're not going to fight me now, are you?" she giggled. She rolled, pushing his hands up and out; she straddled him, settling on top of him. He laughed when she spoke. "I'm going to have my way with you, young man. And you may as well know, I'm merciless. I've been known to kiss a man in unspeakable ways in unspeakable places. Are you man enough to take it?"

He broke her hold and hugged her. "I am man enough for you, Madame La Chasse. And man enough to tell you I love you. I love you with a passion, woman."

It ended oddly. Just at the end, she began to cry again. He would never understand her, he thought; never. But the tears were brief and silent, and he let her think she'd hidden them — since that appeared to be the point of the mad wiping jerk to her eyes with her sleeve. Then she'd fallen asleep against him.

As the sun rose, he held her in his arms, feeling a deep contentment.

He had forgotten how pleasant it could be to have her cooperation. What pure sweetness it was to have her yield to him from the first. This physical satisfaction, the strong healthy movement of his child between them, the fact that Christina had given up on the idea of marriage, the sure feel of having everything his way — all should have made him perfectly happy. But there was a flaw somewhere. Some horrible flaw he couldn't put his finger to.

He frowned at the sleeping face, the damp, tawny lashes, the great tummy, the yards of messy golden-red hair all over the pillows. There was a tightening in his chest at the sight of her. He truly loved her, he thought. What a blow. That must be what robbed him of complete contentment. He felt hopelessly vulnerable.

He gently wiped at the dampness, still there in traces, about her eyes. Those silly tears.

It hit him.

With growing excitement, Adrien knew he'd hit on the flaw: Her unhappiness. Her attempt to conceal it was at once sweetly generous and bleakly ominous. This sadness in her must run deep, be very frustrating. And he was the cause. He'd selfishly put his own fears and reservations between her and all the things that would make her happy. And he'd done so like a bloody despot, worse than the poor dethroned king of France. No wonder she was up in arms!

Adrien stroked the hair of his *petite révolutionnaire*. He was distraught at the strange feelings in him. She was right. So much for the past, he thought. It was time to make a future. He loved Christina. He'd marry her. He'd tell her, no, ask her — he'd do it right and please every romantic notion in her pragmatic little head. He'd find the right moment and ask, "please."

On impulse, he slid from the bed and tore through some bottom drawers of the bureau. He found what he was looking for — the stickpin that had somehow made it across the Channel, the one he'd taken from her after she had used it as a weapon. By the early morning light, he scribbled a note, stuck the tiny sword through it, then affixed its foil-clasp. Its diamond hilt glittered. It would make a wonderful surprise. He tucked it into the pocket of his coat. He would send it today. It would be ready and waiting when they got to England.

Unable to sleep any longer, Adrien got up and got dressed; exuberantly happy.

He had dozens of things to coordinate before their departure. He turned his attention to these details, anticipating with high spirits the rewards of this final plan.

Adrien was so transported with energy and elation, he could have shouted by the time he reached the streets. He bumped into a puppeteer, scattering papier mâché faces into the snow. He danced around the man, tossing heads at him with enthusiastic apology. He smiled an old lady into a swoon. Then jogged off toward the café and breakfast. He felt wonderful. In love with the world. By God, he pronounced to himself, Christina Pinn was good for him! He wanted to yell it out. And he'd be good for her! He'd make the goddamndest effort a man ever made for a woman. He'd be a damned good husband to her. And a good father to their child. No, children! The idea of legitimate heirs pleased him all at once. He rounded the corner.

And froze.

The café was surrounded by a good dozen national guardsmen and a complement of another dozen or so *gendarmerie*. Too many for a search or sealing of the place. And, considering that Louis was supposed to be having his head basketed at nine o'clock this morning, there shouldn't have been a single one, either guardsmen or police. Something important had to be calling them from the crowds and sights of La Place de la Révolution.

Adrien frowned and stepped back into the shadows of the building. A woman's voice—Colette's—screamed coarsely from within the building.

"The Earl of what? Well, you can turn the whole place upside down, if you want," the voice screeched. "There's no filthy Englishman here. And there never has been! A bunch of fucking bureaucrats you all are! No, your description reminds me of no one. Do you know how many men come in and out of this place in a day? What the hell would the mad Englishman be doing here? No, I know no one named La Chasse. . . ."

Pressed against the cold stone wall, out of view, Adrien started making adjustments — major adjustments — to his plans.

Chapter 24

Christina awoke late. She lay there, slowly becoming aware of the silent snow beyond the window, the coziness of her bed — Adrien seemed to have found wood; the fire was lit — then the emptiness of the room. A vague reluctance to pull from bed held her a moment longer. Then, like a huge, unwelcome shadow, the memory of last night's conversation fell over all this. It ruined the small pleasure of her winter bed, like some omnipresent beast that had crawled in beside her to nestle in the indention of the mattress where Adrien had slept. His words, "I love you but. . . . " These dampened and chilled the snug warmth of the room; then also dampened and chilled the comfortable satisfaction she had taken so much pain to make for herself.

All those determined months of knowing precisely what she was going to do, seeing just how she could see herself through this. So much had hinged on his not caring too deeply, on her ending sensibly what was going to end eventually, anyhow. Christina sighed. It seemed the end now was unfairly complicated.

She rose sluggishly. The child was low, heavy. Christina moved with effort, each step measured. Her robe was on the floor with all the clean laundry — what a mess. She bit her lip, shook her head, then moved back to the bed for her shoes. She picked up Adrien's discarded pants and sweater and tossed them into a basket in the corner. Then plodded out to the front room.

She felt none of the lightness or energy she had experienced the evening before. Christina felt an aging without Adrien's presence. And a responsibility that weighed heavier than the two stones of pregnancy that had added physically to her weight.

In recent months this responsibility had become a ballast. It had given her a kind of calm. The calm of decision and resignation. As her belly had expanded, she had seen her options shrink. No matter how many tantrums she threw, there were miserably few choices left her. There was only one consolation: As she had embraced the obvious wise choices for her own, she knew the woman in her was finally outdistancing the little girl.

The baby moved. When it did so now, it did so with less of a flutter, more the push and shove of a good-sized animal in tight quarters. They would meet soon, she and this stranger who seemed so much to have a mind of his own; deciding when to churn and thump at her, deciding when to sleep like a rock, deciding indeed to begin within her without so much as fair warning. With perfect presumption, this child decided everything. So much like its father. She smiled a wan smile, then patted her midsection. She would have Adrien's child; it was still a wonder to her. The idea, still, as it had from the beginning, both pleased and appalled.

She hadn't even considered the possibility when she'd come up out of her dead faint last August. There was Adrien, looking into her face, seeming a little perplexed, a little worried — then looking a good bit more concerned as she threw up over the railing of the ship, which had not even cast off yet. She had continued, all the way across; heaving herself hollow, folding in on herself, unable to control it. Adrien had found he had her quite literally on his hands; she couldn't stand. And still she hadn't thought of pregnancy. For goodness' sakes, she was barren; a doctor

286

had told her so — doctors!

It was not till Adrien had carried her in from the deck (only to have her throw up in his berth), that the conclusion had been unavoidable.

As she lay there, he placed one hand firmly on her breast. She recoiled. "You pig! Don't touch me!" She tried to pull away.

Then he moved her hand further down, to where his own went. He pushed hard and low on her abdomen, "Here. You can feel it." He took her hand under his and pushed again. "Your womb is coming up out of your pelvis." He cocked his head to one side to look at her. "You're really not pretending? You didn't realize?"

She stared at him, trying to swallow the urge to be sick again. "Realize what?"

He shook his head, even had the nerve to smile a little. "You're bloody pregnant, Christina. How could you not know?"

She was bewildered and, suddenly, very nauseous. "I can't be," she moaned.

"But you bloody well are." He made an incredulous laugh, then threw his head back and laughed harder. "Barren, indeed. It had to be the middle of the summer, almost right away."

"You're happy!" She made a shove at him.

"No. Honestly." Yet he continued to laugh. "I'm stunned," then — the scoundrel! — "I thought you were safe."

Safe indeed! She had never been safe with him. Not from the first moment. And not till the last: The only way was to leave him.

And to this end, Christina needed very much to remember the scoundrel in Adrien, to remember the anger, the resentment she felt. Yet, after last night, it all seemed so hopelessly tangled. That he loved her — this seemed impossible, horrible, wonderful; the worst thing to be true. And the child, he would furious to be deprived of it. Christina had just realized that aspect last night. He had spoken of his children with great fondness. He would feel the loss of this child. In his own unorthodox way, he actually wanted it.

She was not pleased to deprive him of his child, nor was she proud of the deception she would practice in doing so. Months ago she would have relished such a strike against him. But now it was simply an unhappy by-product of self-defense. Being totally honest with Adrien — as she had seen last night — would mean countless rounds of bullying and charm and reasoning and persuasion and. . . . He would be undefeatable in his persistence; too clever, too attractive, too relentless by miles.

A sound outside, brisk steps in front, made Christina's turn. It must be Adrien. Then the steps halted as the front door began to rattle and bang under someone's excited fist.

"Madame La Chasse! Madame La Chasse! Where is your husband? Did he come here last night?" A voice bellowed at her in French from the other side of the door.

She opened the door. "Monsieur Le Saint, what is the urgency?" She'd only seen the man once or twice before, but one did not easily forget the man or the name associated with him. "Oui, Monsieur was here, but he has left early this—"

Le Saint rushed past her into the room, darting searching looks about. He charged into the bedroom as if expecting to find someone. He tore back out and grabbed Christina by the arms, breathing stale garlic and rum into her face.

"He *is* the Madman! Do you believe? He *is,* I tell you! I know it for a fact. But—oh—sweet Mother of Jesus—the committee knows it. The *big* committee!"

"What?"

"It's true! They've issued a warrant with names and titles—Did you know he was an English lord? Mon Dieu! And a description of him accurate down to his"—Le Saint caught his breath, halted and amended his vocabulary in the face of Christina's Madonna-like presence — "down to his toenails," he finished. "They turned the café upside down this morning. It is only a matter of hours, maybe minutes, before they trace him here. No one was saying anything when I left, but — well — there is great pressure. The guardsmen were destroying chairs, tables, bottles, windows; looting and knocking people about damned freely. People will — well, if he doesn't come back here in a short time, you should leave, pack up —"

They both froze. There were people, steps, voices, sounds of running coming toward the house. The door burst open.

A moment's panic. Then Adrien. Looking concerned, immersed, involved, but whole and very clearly not under arrest. He was unstoppable, she told herself; he would handle this.

She got her instructions. Three brief phrases in English amid a torrent of mixed-language directives to the half-dozen men who quickly crowded in after him.

"Grab what you need. You're going. This minute." He turned to Sam Rolfeman behind him. "You get her away from me for the time being. Take her to the cottage. That should still be safe. Then stay with her."

Christina frowned as she looked from Adrien to Sam, from face to face as the men all seemed to talk at once. "No —" she began. Anxiety overflowed into selfish channels. Not yet. They still had a week.

"Adrien," she tried to break in. His French signaled and directed, pointing at this man, a break of his wrist to another, then a distance drawn with the side of his hand. "Adrien, I want to wait, go with —"

He held her off with a gesture and finished in rapid French to the others. Then he threw her a smile; it was a labored lightness even he couldn't quite carry off. "I'm going to have one hell of a day. And you can't run as fast as

I can, my dear." He tapped her belly.

"Don't joke. We'll hide. Then sneak out tonight."

"Sam will take you to a very nice place to wait for me. Of course, we'll hide. We'll have a cozy day or so together at the cottage Sam will take you to. Then we'll slip out through Spain. It's all preplanned, Christina. Don't worry." Again the smile. "It's safe. Now go."

He'd turned his back. His very broad, beautiful back. Christina suddenly remembered the scar that embraced him, that encircled his body; a reminder of the last time he'd misjudged the French. It was no time to think of his fallibility. She cringed, then put her hand on his back, smoothed his coat. A coldness washed over her; it settled in the pit of her stomach. Suddenly, Adrien seemed the only warm thing in the room. She hated what was here, these other men, their demands, France itself. It was an irrational sort of loathing; people who had been kind, a country that was essentially beautiful. But nothing felt beautiful now. She felt only an empty cold fear.

Adrien's hand reached back to take her and draw it around. She leaned against him. He brought his other arm over her head to her back, pulled her nearer. All the while, he babbled on. They stayed like that for some time. He, talking, stroking her hair occasionally, brushing her shoulder with his thumb; giving no other acknowledgement. Christina, holding on to him with an icy premonition; it was all happening too fast, going all wrong.

She left him to go the bedroom. There, she gathered up visaed passports, citizens' cards, declarations, documents of French birth. No one traveled without such things. She grabbed up a few articles of clothes, some personal items, a few things for Adrien. Mysteriously, he had dumped out a bottom drawer; everything on the floor. From this, she picked out a fresh shirt and pants—then found herself staring at something that had been at the bottom of the drawer: A scarf. The red scarf. Why on God's earth had he kept that? She grimaced and kicked it under the bed. When she returned to the front room, Adrien was speaking in English.

". . . then relieve them of their papers and get to my grandfather's house, on the Rue du Honneur. Arrest him with the papers. Wave your sabers about like any good guardsman, then loot the house of anything you think he might need to take with him. Don't let him become suspicious that you are packing for him. And *don't*, under any circumstances, let him know my hand is in this. For an arrest, he'll come quietly. For me, he would singe your ears with his cursing and put up such a fight you would be lucky to get him away without breaking his bones. Oh, and watch his cane; he'll have no compunctions about breaking your bones."

"Adrien—" Christina was trying to gain his attention again. "What is happening? Why aren't you coming with us?" He seemed annoyed as he glanced down at her. "Why aren't you coming with me now?" she asked.

He kissed the top of her head. "I wish I had time to explain. You have to go with me on this. We'll talk tonight."

There seemed a signal among the men. Their feet began to stir; they were moving.

As Christina started to move through the door, however, Adrien grabbed her arm. He pulled her back into the doorway. There, just out of view, he took her into his arms and kissed her properly. Precious seconds. Delicious seconds. His body was frenetic, charged. She could feel the thrill coming off him, catching it—even against her will, against her better judgment—as he backed her against the doorjamb. She let it come.

She knew that what he was doing brought him alive; each time, each crisis, each impossible obstacle—as he climbed over, it brought an essential, vital renewal. Yet she knew this process was also killing him. If it didn't do so directly today, then it would by inches, starting with his stomach. He was truly mad. And it was so easy to be mad along with him, when she could feel the muscles of his body reaching, straining for her, his tongue entering her mouth like he owned it. Her knees felt weak, her body flushed and warm. All logic and rational thinking rushed straight to her core and melted.

His mouth went down her neck to her bosom. His hands pressed her breasts as his mouth kissed what he exposed. His breathing became heavy. "Oh, Lord," he murmured. He sighed noisily and raised his mouth to her temple. "Tonight," he said. "Nothing on earth could keep me from you, Christina. You must know that."

She made a wan laugh. "That's precisely what I'm afraid of. Nothing on earth: If you end up under it, rather than on it—" She sighed. "Keep your earthly self together, please."

"Yes. I shall try."

Sam was leading her away. She was dazed. The last she saw of him, that day, was his standing on the porch, huddled in on himself, his hands in his pockets. With everyone moving away. He looked so harmless. So cold and alone.

Chapter 25

Samuel Rolfeman was a calm man. Gentle, quiet, and absolutely loyal to Adrien down to the last syllable of any instructions. He liked Adrien unusually well, respected his intellect with something like awe, and saw nobility of character where others saw characterless nobility.

He annoyed Christina immensely. He agreed with Adrien on virtually everything. Which meant that Christina, on principle, disagreed with anything he said. As a result, Sam had come to be rather silent with the young woman; he was not one for altercations. And, try as she might to be sensibly quiet herself, Christina usually baited the man at any opportunity.

Regularly, Sam separated himself from her. He went outside in the snow for instance, rather than stay in the same room and have to answer what were seldom more than rhetorical questions. However, on the seat of an open wagon, there was not much room for separation.

They had gotten through the most worrisome details of leaving Paris and had presented their visaed passports at the city limits half an hour ago. It had been an uncertain, anxious affair. They had both been checked and rechecked, searched, even Christina's belly examined for its authenticity. Christina was only now breathing easy enough to start giving her companion annoyed, sidelong looks.

The wagon moved slowly, jouncing unexpectedly, off and

on, over rocks hidden in the snow. The two in the wagon were sitting huddled together out of necessity, neither one pleased with the arrangement, but neither one willing to be several degrees colder away from the other's body heat.

"All right," Christina asked. "You said that once we were out of Paris, I could have my answers. So where are we going and why were they so interested in me?"

Sam glanced at her, seemingly reluctant to begin. "The French are looking for an Englishman. They know he went by the name of La Chasse."

"That much I had reasoned for myself. They know he has a woman, don't they?"

"They have a decent enough description of you."

"So why did they let us through?"

He shrugged. "Their information has some amazing blank spots, along with its accuracies. For instance, the description of Adrien is remarkably complete. His physical description — the small scar on his upper lip, educational background — right down to what he read at university, personal habits. . . . We were all flabbergasted when we saw the broadsheet released this morning."

"My God. It has to be someone close."

"Except there are some important omissions. You, for instance. The description of you, while relatively good, misses one rather large fact." He glanced at her midsection. "They're looking for a slight, very slender Englishwoman."

"They don't know I'm pregnant?"

"That variation doesn't seem to have occurred to them."

"But I'm English. That will surely fix me."

"Not now, we hope. Your passport says you're a Breton. You'd speak a patois, bad French, funny accent." She made a face at that. "And there are a hundred different dialects in Brittany. Judging by our exit from Paris, you've passed."

"So where are we going? And why? And who? Who are the best candidates for traitor? It has to be someone who knows him."

Samuel didn't speak for a time, but looked straight ahead. "Someone suggested you."

"Adrien," she stated flatly.

"No."

"But he didn't defend me either, did he?"

"In a way. He said it didn't matter if you would betray him or not. I had the impression he half believed you did somehow get word to the authorities. Did you?"

Christina's heart sank. "No." Never had she felt so alone, so misunderstood. "And I wouldn't," she added.

The wagon lurched left, then right. As Christina clutched Samuel's arm, he said, "Some people wanted to leave you behind." He let that sink in. "Adrien wouldn't hear of it. He said something about love giving license. Would you understand that?" She shook her head. "He didn't say it meanly. Only a little sadly. And imperiously; as if no one better challenge your right to slaughter him if that's what you choose to do. It seemed quite daft to me. But he seemed to think it made sense."

"He thinks a great many things make sense that totally elude me. When did all this start?"

"This morning. At the café where Adrien usually eats breakfast—"

"He doesn't eat breakfast."

Sam looked at her. She could tell that his aversion to contradicting her was in conflict with his passion for truth. "He eats breakfast while we talk every morning. We meet him at the café."

"He doesn't like eggs."

"Oh," Sam nodded. Perhaps this let him out. "No. Bread and cheese, I think. Sometimes ham. Or fruit. The proprietor saves what she knows he likes."

"I should have known."

"What?"

"She."

Samuel said nothing, though Christina could feel his

unease. Then he added, "She's a friend. She undoubtedly saved him from being taken this morning. At no small expense or risk to herself."

"I'm sure she's had her compensations."

He blurted, "It was your cooking." Sam shook the reins, made a sharp click with his tongue in his cheek. "It was not the woman. He never made it out to be more than a personal preference. You cook English; he has a French tongue."

"And don't so many of us know it. So he takes his French tongue over to this woman every morning—"

In frustration: "Madam, he merely wanted to avoid hurting your feelings unnecessarily. He is—"

"A liar and an actor. He has it down to a virtual science. Why else do you think he can do what he does here so successfully? He pretends to be whatever is needed; like a bloody chameleon. Sam, how long have you known him?"

"Twenty years perhaps."

"Certainly long enough to know his weaker points."

"And how long have you known him?" It was an accusation.

Christina heaved a sigh and put her hand to her middle. "Long enough. But a truce, Sam. All right? I have known him differently than you."

"A difference some might say would make you take his part more often."

Again the wagon jolted; it kept her from having to defend herself against this. After a time, she asked, "Where is His Lordship anyway? And where is he sending us?"

"His *Lordship*," Samuel said emphatically, "has sent all but a handful of men home to England. You and I are going to a secret retreat in Normandy he had secured for just such a purpose. He has arranged for the departure of thirty-five men, including the thirteen "Cabrels." And, to insure the others are not bothered in their leaving, *he* is leading the National Guard, the *gendarmerie,* and half a dozen mercenary agents a merry, very visible chase through the streets of Paris."

"He's what?" She turned to look at him.

"He's alone. He's intentionally letting them chase him—close enough so he doesn't lose them and close enough so they might anticipate having him, if only they can get enough streets secured—but far enough, one hopes, that he can slip through once the ship sails."

The wagon jerked, made a series of creaks as it righted itself on the pitted road. Though it had snowed the night before, the sky was clear now. The promise of sun.

"Are the others in danger?" she asked.

"The French have an incomplete list. But not one man has been arrested. They followed us around all morning, hoping we would lead them to Adrien. It appears they want him above everyone else. No doubt the only reason they want you or his grandfather is to attract him."

"Oh, Sam, how did all this get started? Yesterday it was coming to such a nice, quiet end. Who? Who would have done this?"

"We've only had the most hectic moments to speculate. Nothing fits completely."

"What does Adrien think?"

"He suggested a spy from a while ago. Back in May or June, a Frenchwoman pretended to have relatives in need of help. She found out a great deal before she disappeared."

"Ah, yes. I remember vividly."

He cleared his throat. "Oh, yes. At any rate, there is the possibility she has resurfaced. But that doesn't explain how they know about you."

"What do you think, Sam?"

He hesitated. "Adrien's a little angry with me for the suggestion. But there are others who share my opinion."

"Which is?"

Silence.

"Come now—"

297

"Thomas Lillings."

Shocked, "Thomas!" Christina laughed. "Adrien's right. It's ludicrous. It makes the spy notion sound almost plausible. Do you know how long Adrien and Thomas have been friends? Since boy—"

"Yes."

"Why, we haven't even seen Thomas in—"

"You haven't seen him. Adrien sees him regularly. He turns refugees over to him at the borders and at sea. Thomas heads that end of the operation. Adrien gets them out and pointed in the right direction. Thomas sets them down. But the two of them have had words. Thomas wants the operation to work like it did before. Adrien insists it's too big to work like it did. This way saves them both from being in the vicinity of the Madman at the same time: When the prisoners are rescued, Thomas is highly visible in London or somewhere else. When the outcasts turn up in their new location, Adrien is carousing with a good dozen witnesses. It is a practical plan. Thomas has difficulty arguing it is not. And when he says someone else could do his end, Adrien praises him into silence. But there's no mistaking the feelings in the air."

"Sam, this is so silly—"

"But so true. Adrien says Lillings would not carry their differences so far as to arrange for his decapitation. And, he says, Lillings certainly would not include you in turning him in, if he did. M. Lillings is most protective of you. He inquires after you every trip."

This left another gap in the conversation. Christina filled it lamely, "Thomas and I are friends."

"Better friends than you think perhaps."

"I don't understand."

Again Sam hesitated, then leaped his reservation. "M. Lillings gave his hand away about three months ago. By chance, Thomas learned you were pregnant. Apparently, Adrien hadn't told him. One understands why: When the

298

father of your child came on aboard an hour late, Lillings fisted him in the face. No warning. No explanation. Just a solid punch in the mouth that sent him flat on his back. Topped off with some florid language on Lillings' opinion of the situation. Lillings was in a villainously foul mood. I didn't know he could be so ugly. And Adrien, I think, still hasn't reconciled himself to the attack, on his person or character."

"He never said anything—"

"But came home with a nasty mouth, I'd bet."

"Yes. That." She sighed. "He said the boom had hit him."

Sam sniffed. "It was a boom, all right." There were several seconds of uncomfortable silence. Then Sam said, "But as I said, Adrien argues in favor of his friend's honor. Actor, liar, overlord that he is."

"Don't."

"He's no fool though. Lillings has been ordered back to England to stay and hold tight. Much to his displeasure." He clicked to the horse again. "There are blankets in the back," he told her, "and it's a long way. Why don't you go in the back of the wagon and sleep? There are some apples back there, too. Colette sent them."

"Colette?"

"The café owner."

"Hmm. That was very kind of her."

Chapter 26

Though small in size, "cottage" did not precisely describe the Madman's retreat. Its plain Norman exterior, its isolation in the remote countryside were at odds with its rather elegant interior. Christina was not in the house thirty seconds when she saw unmistakable signs of the English earl's personal touch.

One entered the house through a narrow antechamber, nothing more than a long corridor of empty brass hooks. At present, the first two were occupied by Sam's hat, greatcoat, and woolen scarf, the third by Christina's heavy cloak and shawl. Off this entrance way, in one direction there were bedrooms; in the other direction, a large, comfortable parlor, then kitchen. The parlor was a particularly attractive room, with its large fireplace, its old-fashioned iron implements for stirring the fire, and its enormous woven trug for carrying wood. The fireplace seemed central to the room. Everything faced it. And two lovely, tall rockers — dark, carved mahogany — sat at its very edge, inviting patience and calm.

The room particularly pleased Christina. Near the fire, a dense, dark rug, obviously country-made, lay over the room's larger Persian carpet to protect it. Marks showed where sparks and ashes had declared the little rug's usefulness. A cabinet held colorful china. Plates and teacups. Meticulously hand-painted, peopled scenes; the russet colors preferred by old Dutch masters. Several little tables were scattered about. One could have tea by the window or by the fire or in a dark little nook beneath a pass-through to the kitchen. The room didn't look lived in; it lacked Adrien's newspapers, his stray sheets of paper with doodles in French verse, her own books and bits of sewing. Yet it lacked nothing else. It was very livable. The size of the room, the furnishings, the very walls themselves seemed to create, not only the feeling of convenience, but a sense of comfort — to the eye and soul.

At least, this was how it struck Christina. She liked the house in the same way she liked a certain part of Adrien; a part that knew how to live well, a part he carried with him even into the most unlikely circumstances.

She missed him.

She needed surroundings that didn't seem to have his fingerprints on everything from floor to ceiling.

At present, Christina sat in the far dark-wood rocker by the fire. She had settled there several hours before. It faced the front window and had seemed a good place to take up her vigil. She had taken her dinner there, in her lap. She rocked there now, waiting.

The movement soothed. Yet, it was less soothing than it had been the hour before. Or the hour before that. Adrien was late. Sam hadn't said so. And, of course, Adrien hadn't told her a specific time. But less than one hour remained to the day in which he said he would see her.

She and Sam had gone quiet. Silence had become the most comfortable arrangement between them. The room was warm. It gave off a belying cheerful glow. Only the front window remained honest. It was a dark, uneasy square in the midst of the pleasant, printed wallpaper. Periodically, snow flung itself against the glass of the window. These flurries had become little jokes in poor taste: Each movement of snow outside the glass seemed to be the possibility of Adrien's return — when, in fact, it only heralded yet another complication to his safe arrival. Heavy snow. Even knowing this, Christina's heart had leaped at least a dozen times in the last hour, thinking she'd seen him — a flicker of movement in the glass — and then the image would blow away or lie finally in little crescents against the mullions.

"Why don't you go to bed?" Sam had come out of one of the bedrooms. "I'm sure he'll wake you when he comes."

"He should have been here."

"Not necessarily —" Sam came over to the fire, threw on another log. "I've put your things in the front bedchamber. It's small, but he will want, I think, to have a view of the front and side." He paused, as if trying to think of more words; as if words might somehow bridge the limbo in which they found themselves. "I'm only second-guessing, of course. He'll think nothing of shifting everyone around to suit himself." He laughed at this. "You know, he never made any claim on any of the rooms. He was very careful in picking the house. Location. Suitability. All that. And then very careful in its appointments, its maintenance. But he never made a move as if he'd ever live in it."

Christina knew Sam himself could use reassurance at this point. Yet she couldn't muster any. None, but the typical English response to crisis:

"Tea?" She heaved herself out of the chair. "I'll put some on."

The kitchen, already a marvel for just existing in such a small house, boasted several innovations. It had been adapted for eating as well as cooking, allowing people to cook and serve themselves with minimum energy. It had running water which flowed directly into a sink for laundry. The room even boasted the novel idea of a cookstove.

On the modern stove stood a very unmodern iron teakettle. One of Adrien's absurd combinations. The kettle longed for a hook over a fire, the stove for a kettle with a perfect, flat bottom, nothing so black as the old hammered kettle.

Christina went about the ritual with the kettle and teapot and cups. There was sugar, even milk in the window box.

From the parlor, Sam called her. "Someone's coming, I think."

She came into the doorway, the tray of hot tea in her hands. The cups rattled.

"Just act normally," Sam cautioned. "With the light, remember people can see inside easier than we can see out."

She set the tea down on a table by her rocker, then went to look over Sam's shoulder. It had stopped snowing.

The house was set in a shallow valley. From any angle of approach, there were miles of gentle slope. Space in all directions. And sound. It carried well.

If one looked closely one could see a gray silhouette in the distance; a wagon, on straining wheels. It carried perhaps half a dozen men, half a dozen voices.

"Go find something to do," Sam told her. He turned. He was right up against her. He touched her arm for a moment, a kind of affection. "Something ordinary. It could be anyone."

"Adrien—"

"No."

She glanced at him; at the certainty in which he'd uttered this.

"Unless he's bound hand and foot on the floor of the wagon: It's the sort of cart they use for prisoners."

A chill ran down her back.

Christina tried to busy herself, but had trouble concentrating. She and Sam had worked out a husband-wife charade in the event of passing strangers, a game similar to the one they had played that morning. But she could think of nothing save looking past Sam through the window.

The wagon came closer; close enough to hear that the voices argued.

Within the room, "It's not he," Sam said again.

Christina threw him an angry glare. "You're so cer-

303

tain—"

"He won't come by wagon. Couldn't get by the checks on the roads. Couldn't risk the occasional traffic. And certainly couldn't come over this snow without the benefit of a roadbed."

"How *will* he come?"

"I don't know. A horse would be nice. If they allow him the opportunity of one. Otherwise, on foot."

"On foot!" She turned around. "Across country through a snowstorm? Oh, that's jolly smart! No wonder we haven't seen him. He's probably out there under three feet of snow. Does he think he's immortal?"

She bolted from the window into the entranceway, yanking cloak and scarves as she went, throwing them over herself. "I'll see who's in the wagon, then, if he's not among them, I'm going after him."

Sam was beside her on the front porch, silent, but with a grip on her elbow. They could see better outside. It was a clear night; their eyes were better adjusted. The wagon that approached looked little better than a vegetable cart. It was open at the back. Its passengers held firm to its sideboards as it negotiated the bumps in the road. The wagon still had a long way to come, and the going was rough. Snow all but obliterated the roadbed. The wheels churned soft wings of snow.

Sam murmured to her. "Come inside. I couldn't let you go, anyway. My responsibility is to get you safely to England." His fingers tightened on her elbow.

She resisted. Her eyes narrowed at him. "When?"

"Pardon?"

"How long did he tell you to wait? When are you to take me, if he doesn't come?"

"Tomorrow."

She expelled a sharp breath and jerked her arm away. "Tomorrow? Not much bloody leeway, is there?"

"No, there's not." He said it calmly, patiently; as if she'd at last understood.

The voices from the wagon were becoming more distinct. Words could not be distinguished, but tones could. Anger. A great deal of French. Though none of it his. It was not Adrien who came.

Behind her, she heard the front door close. Sam had gone in.

Across the snow, French syllables began to stand out — cut off crisply at their ends — like stars coming out on a clear night. Christina couldn't make out the people, but she could hear these bright little pinpoints of sound with an unnatural vividness. They danced across the snowy expanse. And they gave a kind of illimination: It became evident whom the wagon brought. Cursing, declamatory bursts. Followed by an antiphony of murmured reassurance. Adrien's confreres tried to sooth Adrien's grandfather as they carried him along.

"Mon Dieu! Ca sens mon petit-fils! Qu'il est énervant! Qu'il aille se faire fiche!" And more. Adrien's grandfather promised, rather colorfully, to knock the teeth from his head if this was another of his grandson's pranks.

It was not reassuring, not cute, not clever. Christina turned abruptly. She shoved the front door so hard it swung on its hinge to bash the wall. She aimed at the hooks with her cloak, but then another hard blow: She was brought up short. She smelled cigar smoke. A specific variety she hadn't smelled in several months. . . .

Her things fell to the floor. She followed the smell. In the doorway to the parlor, she stood searching the room. Sam turned. The group outside clattered up to the front of the house. They began to unload. Feet scraped on the front stoop. But, in the room, no one. Only Sam. Holding a cigar.

She stared at the tobacco, at Sam; as if he had committed murder. Her throat tightened to where she couldn't swallow, or even draw air. A great floodtide seemed to suddenly overrun her mind. Memory mixed uneasily with apprehension. Remembered angry words, love words, misunderstood phrases, clear and unpleasant sentences, emotions, trivial details, monumental decisions; no distinction. As if something, a great dam, had let loose. So much chattered into her mind, she couldn't separate it to make any sense.

Sam came toward her. "Are you all right?"

She shook her head, *no*. Then reached out. "The cigar—"

"Does it offend you?" He didn't understand. With a gesture, the stick of tobacco made a sweet-acrid trail through the air, a kind of incense. He could see her eyes fixed on it. "There is a surplus of these. He asked me to help him get rid of them. He says they bother his stomach. I can take it outside—Are you all right?"

Her eyes were hot. They were suddenly dry, prickly. Her legs wouldn't move. Sounds blurred in her ears. Her eyes wouldn't focus. The smoke filled her senses. "It smells like his skin," she murmured.

It smelled like his hair, his sheets, his clothes. His mouth had tasted of it. There was such an ache in her chest, like a steel axe had buried itself in her.

Sam guided her to the rocker. She felt ghostlike; outside of herself. Part of her watched the poor woman sit in the chair. "I feel so—"

"I think you better sit down."

The front door opened. Loud confusion, cold came in through the entrance way. Voices called. "Sam! Sam! Where the hell are you?" But Sam didn't move. He stood over Christina, frowning down at her.

"Are you going to be sick?" he asked. "What's wrong with you?" He made a slight laugh. "Listen, he's going to be here, I'm sure." More laughter, though a bit forced, "And he's going to bloody-well murder me if anything happens to

306

. . . you know . . . you or the baby. Are you—Is it?"

"Yes." She shook her head. "No." She closed her eyes, trying to grasp hold of something. Then something absolute materialized: "Yes. I am going to be sick."

Half a dozen men had entered. Everyone talked at once. It doubled the cacophony in her head. A small old man was yelling in heavily accented English. He brandished a cane. Sam raised his hand, a threat to take the cane away. As he made the gesture, his coat rose. Christina saw he had a pistol. Her blood ran cold. The noisy anxieties in her head seemed to crystallize around the sight, the hilt above his belt. The room moved. Everything else stood still, mute against the loud mental alarm of the gun. The old Frenchman grated the air with his voice. "Where is he? I demand to settle this now! Who's that?"

A long bony finger had swung on her. "Never mind," the old man continued, "I can tell by the look of her my grandson is around. My God"—a sigh of vicious disgust— "when I said 'He who bulls the cow feeds the calf,' I meant it as an admonishment to more responsible behavior, not license to start his own herd. Where is he!"

Christina felt the tea tray in her lap, the best Sam could do on such short notice. She couldn't imagine what had become of the teacups and spoons, the pitcher of milk, the sugar. But it was a relief they weren't there. The tray was lacquered papier-mâché, hand-painted.

Though later she discovered she was absolutely wrong— it was actually flowers or some such—at the time, the tray seemed painted after a picture she'd seen by Hogarth. Dark edges, a bright focus. Two about-to-be lovers in the woods. The man had hold of the woman's fingers, his leg planted firmly in her skirts, between her legs. The woman was resisting, but one knew that she wouldn't for long—for one thing, there was Hogarth's second picture of the same two people, sitting on the ground, the woman with her skirts above her knees, the man with his breeches open, the two

307

of them looking disheveled and distraught. But it was more something in the woman's face in the first picture, the sly look with which she watched the man even as she denied him. . . .

Christina was declared the only one who could silence Philippe de La Fontaine. He murmured profuse apologies. *"Excusez-moi! madame. Je manque d'égards, de prévenances.* I am a thoughtless, old fool. You must forgive me." He, with the rest of the men, bore witness: If she had managed to keep a shred of dignity to her, it was vitiated by the paroxysms of nausea that followed. It put an end to all argument. It seemed to express aptly — too aptly — what everyone felt. She was sick for half an hour.

Chapter 27

At three in the morning, Christina lay awake in bed. The house was still. If she listened, there remained a thin drone of conversation in the front room. But this registered only peripherally now and then, like the noise of an insect, a mosquito.

Vaguely, Christina was aware that she was hungry, but she was too disinterested in her own hunger to do anything about it. Sleep wouldn't come. She had been waiting for that for more than an hour.

Bored with staring into the dark, she sat up and lit the lamp by her bed. A book had been placed on the table beside her. Absently, she picked this up, paged through it. Childbirth. In French. She wanted to laugh. She missed the table as she set it back. The book fell on the floor, where she left it. A moment or so later, there was a knock on her half-open door.

Adrien's grandfather appeared just inside. "I may come in?" He held a tray with soup and tea. "For you." He held it out, meekly awaiting permission to give it to her.

She accepted it. He smiled broadly. He grabbed hold of a chair by its back and dragged it toward the bed: As if her nod had included this, his company. The chair gave him trouble. It was heavy, high-backed. When he finally sat, the large piece of furniture dwarfed him. He looked like a little old monkey, a grotesque macaque; or a gargoyle.

The tea and soup Christina had set on the bedside table. Philippe de La Fontaine leaned forward and nudged the food a bit closer to her; translating, in any language, that she should eat. Then, again like a circus monkey, he disappeared, head over knees. He came back up holding the book from the floor. This he proferred, in a palsied reach toward her. By contrast, his eyes were very steady, direct. They were a clear lake-blue.

Christina was not up to even cursory politeness.

When she didn't take the book, he pushed it onto the bed beside her, nudging it until it lay against her thigh. Then, he leaned back in the chair, as if all this had all been enormous activity for him.

"Since circumstances did not permit an introduction. . . ." His teeth clicked in his mouth. "I am Jean-Charles Joseph François Philippe de La Fontaine." He had a heavy accent, but seemed willing and capable of English.

"I know who you are."

He smiled, a curve of closed lips, then tilted his head. His eyes were full of unmasked curiosity. As if she were truly another species from him. "You are his Christina?"

"My name is Christina, yes." She sat back into her pillows, "Someone has drawn all the curtains. Would you open them? On your way out?"

He made a short, abrupt laugh, then a moue of disappointment. "I am to leave then?"

She slid a look at him: That was precisely what he was to do.

Again, he laughed. "And I thought he cowed them all into simpering little toadies." He stood up. But he hesitated. He opened his palms. "I am bored out there." He made a shrugging plea for sympathy. "And I do not like those men. Englishmen meddling where they haven't the first notion . . . In what is none of their business in any event . . . Besides, I am feeling a little overwhelmed. I wish"—he

310

hesitated, looking for something, the right word, the right sentiment — "for Adrien." *Ah-dree-ehn*. Christina almost didn't recognize the sound. It was a French name, she realized; a French spelling. "I would rather be with someone," her visitor continued, "someone with whom I had at least one thing in common."

When she didn't invite him to sit down again, he tilted his head to one side. "Are you really not going to be friendly? My acquaintance lends a certain — what? — authenticity, don't you realize? Adrien doesn't" — he was looking for a word — "mix," he selected, "he doesn't mix me in with many of his ladies. I've only met a few. All of whom have been most willing to be kind to me. . . . "

He took her silence for acquiescence. He sat. He made no further attempt at conversation, seeming to content himself with moving his false teeth around in his mouth. Christina ate the soup, drank the tea, then settled back into her pillows again. For a time, there was the soft, sporadic click of M. La Fontaine playing with his teeth. Then quiet; he went to sleep in the chair.

Somewhere near dawn, the outer room became more noisy. Shuffling feet. Jingling belts. Voices taking on a murmuring intent. Christina awoke to these sounds. She had apparently dozed.

Philippe de La Fontaine was already awake. His eyebrows lifted toward her, offering speculation. He got halfway through a few words in French, then changed to, "Something in the wind?"

Christina rubbed sleep from her eyes, arched her back. She'd lain in a bad position. She threw her legs over the side of the bed and braced her belly. She lumbered to a sitting position.

"Did you think he would marry you?"

She looked at Adrien's grandfather, surprised.

The little man was studying her again. "Did you get pregnant," he clarified, "thinking he would marry you?"

"No." She frowned as she bent to hunt her shoes. "I believed I wouldn't get pregnant."

"Ah. A surprise then. Have you accommodated yourself to the notion of a child?"

"More or less."

"Adrien seems very pleased." He nodded to the book on the bed. "I helped him get that book for you."

"Thank you." She didn't know what else to say.

He smiled. "He tried to bribe me with that child of yours. He said I could visit it whenever I wished, watch it grow. . . ." His tone was once more asking permission; would she approve?

She frowned, then averted her eyes for fear he could read her intentions—that neither he nor Adrien should watch the child grow.

He sighed. "You really don't like me?"

"I like you well enough."

Silence. With slow dawning, *"Ah, ce n'est pas moi, alors."* He wanted it confirmed. "It's Adrien?"

The noise in the parlor moved to the entrance way, the sound of coats and hats and scarves being put on. Christina started past M. La Fontaine, but he took her arm; a surprisingly firm hold. "Don't be too hard on him. Or on the child. He does not make a bad father. And he is delighted by this child; one can see this in his face when he speaks of it. He really does have some right, you know. And obligation."

" 'He who bulls the cow' ?"

He made a face. "I am sorry for that. But still—"

She shook her head. Then Sam Rolfeman, wrapped in his greatcoat and scarf, was at the door. The sound in the entrance way began to travel outside. On the other side of her window, was the rattle and crunch of men, heavy boots and gear, moving in the snow. To this, was added now the approach of horses being brought from the rear of the house.

"He should have been here by now," Sam said to her. It was a parting phrase. He was carrying his hat. "Le Saint will stay with you. The rest of us are going back after him."

Christina felt a sinking in her belly. Sam, the last optimist, looked tired and sleepless. "Perhaps you should wait just a little longer—"

He shook his head. "It's been long enough." He tried to be light—with the awful result being the sort of tone and demeanor one used at a wake; he forced a laugh. "If he comes while we are gone, he'll be furious we've broken from his plan. Tell him to make it a good lecture; it's one I will enjoy. Oh, and someone will check back in a day or so just to see if we miss him coming or going." He paused. An impatient voice called to him from outside. He looked at Christina. "Take care. We'll let you know—" He waited for better words, then gave up.

Christina followed him to the front door, then stood there leaning against it after they'd gone.

"He has always been in trouble. He thrives on it." M. La Fontaine was in the hallway. "He was born when I was fifty. Fifty years of quiet organized sanity. Then chaos. I've lived the last thirty-five years in perpetual terror of what he'd do next. Shall we go into the salon? We could share the fire."

"Will you tell me about his wife?"

This jarred him. "No." He reconsidered. "Perhaps," he said more gently.

Le Saint could be heard in the kitchen as she followed the small Frenchman into the parlor. "There is not much to tell," M. La Fontaine said. He sat in a chair by the fire. Christina sat opposite him. "Adrien married his cousin. He was nineteen. She was seventeen. By the time he was twenty-four they were separated."

"Divorced," she said.

His smile corrected her politely. "An English divorce. I mean you no injury, my dear, but here you associate with a married man."

313

Christina looked into the fire. "Why did they separate?"

He made a face; he wasn't going to discuss this. "Who knows? I raised him. Did you know that?" he offered. Again he allowed her quietness to mean he should proceed. He settled back. "His father sent him to me after his mother died. So I had him when he was very young." He looked down at his hands. He made folds in his trousers. "Very sweet. Precocious. My wife had just died. We were two." He held up two fingers pressed together. "And he, *très cher*, how do you say?, *comme la prunelle* — not *prunelle* to you — *de mes yeux?*"

"Apple."

"*Oui.*" He smiled, a fond satisfaction. "The apple of my eyes. Then when his father died — Adrien was eleven — I lost him. For a time. His uncle put him in an English boarding school." He sighed, "One must allow: an English education for an English lord. I couldn't contradict. Besides, the uncle was his legal guardian, and I was but a foreign grandparent. But I missed him." He frowned. "And I did not like where he went." There was a pause, as if he were not going to explain any further. Then he added, "A very severe place. From which he eventually escaped by being equally, severely bad; they threw him out."

"Why?"

"Disruptive," he said, "and 'resistant' to correction." He gave a small burst of laughter. "That, I already knew. I rarely hit him." He made a dubious look. "Perhaps this is his trouble." He reconsidered this with an affectionate nod — "But I think not. When I did hit him, he was always so outraged, extraordinarily so. It used to amuse me, the amount of dignity he had, even when he was very young. His father and I used to joke about it. The only child in England and France who escaped a whipping for simply being above such things. Though his father, I suspect, always worried he was secretly weak for not beating him." He sighed. He shook his head; what could one do? "The

314

uncle made up for it, though. But that is the English way, *n'est-ce pas?*" There was a brief look of disapproval. "An English education is accomplished at the end of a cane." He snorted. Then he brought a finger up, in a single knowing wag. "There is where he learned about power — and what it meant to be wretchedly without it. An English upper-class education. The schoolmasters chastising the boys, the boys growing up to be little schoolmasters practicing on each other. He has never been quite the same boy since. Though who is to say . . ." One could sense that the old man was trying to make strong feelings less strident, more conventionally acceptable.

He frowned. "This is not what I started to say," he said. "*Ah, oui.* I was telling you. I raised him. I lost him." He grinned. "Then I got him back: They threw him out of that school; then another, then a third. His English uncle threw up his hands.

"He was seventeen when he arrived this time — and I took one look at him and could see part of the problem immediately. He had shot up more than a head taller than myself, and was filling out alarmingly unlike the men of my family. He reminded me of his English uncle. . . .

"And *this* Adrien," he continued, "*Mon Dieu,* he turned the house upside-down. Willful. Self-centered. Difficult. And entirely too clever, including too clever in getting around adults. He did precisely as he pleased. And Marie-Madeleine" — he shook his head — "his cousin, took one look at him and thought she had met the handsomest, wisest, most courageous fellow on earth. . . ." His voice trailed off.

He got up slowly to drop a log on the fire. He squatted there, playing with the fire, stirring it like memory, staring.

It was just after this that they heard the sound. Soft, with seeming intentional quiet, something — someone — was stealing up on them outside in the snow.

Where was Le Saint? Christina wondered. She no longer heard him. She looked at her only other ally, the slight, eighty-five-year-old Frenchman. Then she heaved herself up, belly first, and reached for the iron poker.

Coming up over the ridge, Adrien had seen the light. Like a beacon. A mirage. As he came up to the house, though, it didn't feel so much warm or comforting as . . . unreal, impossible. He had been so long out in the dark, out in the snow. He was so cold. The light coming from the little house seemed more like rays coming from a tiny alien sun; life on another planet. Adrien came up to the door. It opened. He stepped in. Then stopped cold.

He was greeted by a woman brandishing a poker. He laughed. Her feet were so tiny, her belly so large. Yet she held that poker with a resolve that made the veins on her slender wrists stand out. There was very real danger in her intent. She menaced him with surprising mobility, despite the obstacle of her enormous and perfectly round belly.

She stared at his eyes — there was little other hope of recognition since he was wrapped from head to foot in woolen rags. Then she came a step closer. She scrutinized and frowned. Then closer still. An uncertain recognition flickered in her face. The poker came down a degree.

And he was attacked by a wave of vanity. Numb from cold, the threat of being bashed in the head with an iron poker yet a possibility, suddenly all Adrien could think of was how awful he must look and smell. He was muddy and soiled. Smelling of garbage and worse. Completely covered in scraps of rags, all but for his eyes. A mummified derelict, perfumed by the back passages of Paris.

"Easy, Christine." He raised his hands slowly, lest she hit him out of sheer uncertainty. "It would be too ironic to have you succeed after eluding this end all day."

The poker clanged on the floor. "Adrien!"

Her arms were around him, her hands pulling the rags at his face.

316

"Don't. You'll get yourself filthy."

He was ambivalent, wanting to hold her, pushing her back; preoccupied with how much worse the filth was going to smell in the heat of this room. He felt compelled to keep this from her.

She ignored him, went on unintelligibly about worry and fear and "they've gone out after you" and "everyone thought" and "where have you been?" Her hands were shaking.

"Oh, you fool." She was crying. "What a bloody stupid thing to do. We were worried to death."

He adored her fuss, her concern. She ripped away the last rags covering his face, and made a lovely groan as she verified his identity. She touched his cheeks — in need of a shave; she caressed him with both palms. As if this too were a way to check who he was. She clutched him.

He took her by the elbows and set her from him. "You'll get filthy, I tell you." Suddenly, he couldn't look at her; seeing her was so sharp a sensation. He retreated into the territory of their shared domesticity. "Do I have more clothes?"

"In the front bedroom."

"I don't suppose you would find them for me? I want to wash." He indicated the kitchen. Only he couldn't resist another glance at her, "Are you all right?"

She laughed, slightly giddy. "Only about to collapse with relief. I'll get you your things."

It was then he noticed the small, motionless figure in the rocking chair. His grandfather; watching, overly interested.

"*Tu es vivant, Grand-père?*"

"I should be asking you that, young man."

"It's just I never thought to see you so quiet, except in your grave."

He received one of his grandfather's arch looks. "There is doubt, *mon petit*, as to who will see whom in the grave." The rheumy eyes bore into him. Adrien had to look away. He sighed. He was not quite ready for this. If he could have avoided just one of them, the old man or the woman . . .

But, foremost, he wanted these clothes, these tatters burned. He began tearing them off and tossing them into the fire. And a bath . . . Then a meal . . . There was a bottle of wine somewhere. . . .

The fire began to crackle and smoke; it made an offensive smell. There was nothing for it. The strips of wrapping that he wore about him seemed to take forever to unravel. He had been adding to them all day, each time he could find a bit of cloth, trying to seal out the cold a little better. Then, of special difficulty, he sat to unknot the rags that covered the lack of warm boots.

"She's very nice. I like her."

"What?"

"This woman. Christina. Or did I hear, just now, Christine?"

Adrien shrugged. He kept himself looking busy. "I call her both, I suppose."

"Not your usual sort."

"No."

"Why?"

He applied strength and broke the frozen strap; the knot was hopeless. When he risked a glance up, his grandfather's eyes were waiting.

The question was repeated, *"Pourquoi est-ce qu'elle n'est . . . pas ton type?"*

In irritation, "How should I know why she's not my usual sort?"

This didn't seem to disconcert the old man. He began to clack his teeth.

"The man said you shouldn't do that," Adrien said irritably. "You'll make blisters."

The old relative stopped. He began to hum to himself. His good humor was annoying.

Christina came in with a basin of water. "The fire is out

in the kitchen. Le Saint has gone to bed. I think you'll be warmer here." She held out some fresh clothes.

Adrien felt strangely shy of undressing in front of both of them; nowhere to hide. But of course she was right. The fire felt wonderful. He sat on the edge of the little table to strip off the last layer of shirt; then he lathered his chest. She did his back.

"Where is everyone else?"

"You've just missed them by an hour or so. They went out to look for you."

He frowned. "When are they coming back?"

"In a day or two."

He wasn't pleased. "Splendid. So we are delayed again. The idiots."

"It's just you were so late—"

"They had every damn road blocked, either gendarmerie or National Guard. I never counted on so many of them." Then, catching her worried expression— "so nice of them, actually, to make me feel so important."

"Oh, don't. If you make light of this—" She raised her arms. She ran the water over his head, into his face.

He grabbed blindly for the towel. "Christine—" Water sloshed into his lap. His trousers, the last reserve of modesty, were soaked. Christina was laughing.

"I needed to get fresh water anyway."

Adrien looked up from the towel directly into his grandfather's face. "What are you grinning about so smugly? I'd expected, by now, a small avalanche of abuse from you."

The old man shrugged. "I bide my time." He smiled again. "And I watch. Perhaps I think I might learn something from this woman of yours."

Adrien had taken Christina onto his lap, where she'd fallen asleep against him. He'd rocked, talked to Philippe de La Fontaine over her head. Now and then, he'd indulged himself in the feel of her hair, her skin against his mouth or chin. She smelled so good. The intimacy of her body was palpable. He played in it, off and on—that inch of space just above her body where there was heat and moist scent, but no contact. Periodically, he would brush his lips against her cheek, or against the smooth place where her hairline met her temple. He petted her with half-attention; he dropped these quasi-kisses on her half a dozen times, hardly aware of it as he talked. The conversation was an old worn-out one anyway. His grandfather didn't wish to leave France.

Later, he carried her into their room and went back out; a more comprehensive war was waged against the old relative. When he came to bed it was daylight again. He hadn't had a proper night's sleep in days; just the feel of the bed at his back brought a wave of unconsciousness. Christina roused him, however. How did it go with his grandfather?

"Good and bad, I suppose. I sank to new lows, but got what I wanted."

"Which was?"

"He's coming with us. Willingly. To live in the house in Hampshire. Do you mind?"

There was a pause. "It's your house."

"But you do like him?"

"Yes. Why did he change his mind?"

"He thinks he is bailing me out of trouble once more. It's his favorite thing. Loves untangling my messes."

"Which mess is this?"

"The estate in Hampshire. My affairs in London."

"Oh, those messes." She sniffed. "You outright lied to him."

Adrien blinked awake; she was accusing him of lying again. He was lying, of course, but he felt he could defend it.

"Not at first. I gave him my best speeches on home being

320

people, not places, and the rest of his family being either dead, fled, or out of touch. He was moved, but he needed something more concrete. So I admitted that things in London had gotten a bit out of hand, and I was behind on my correspondence in Hampshire, and some of the land was lying vacant when it should be rented. You know. All so large . . . and I'm gone so much of the time. One minute on that track and I knew I had him. I polished it and embellished it for fifteen minutes, then said good night to a traveling companion. It's much easier on him than tying him up and crating him across."

All she said was, "Your own grandfather."

He sat up on an elbow. "Do you know how important it is that he comes with me? Life or death. To have involved him in something that would kill him . . ."

"Why didn't you tell him that?"

"I told him he would die if he stayed."

"No, the other part. About its killing you if you were to become responsible for his dying."

He was dazed. Christina had put into words a truth that might have influenced the old man. What a novel idea. Telling someone you love the truth of how you feel.

Chapter 28

Breakfast found Christina once again alone with Philippe de La Fontaine. Le Saint had been sent on some sort of errand. Adrien was asleep. Over dark coffee and bread, Philippe seemed eager not only for Christina's company, but to speak of what she wished:

"She and her father," he was saying, "had moved in with me by then." Christina and Philippe sat opposite each other at a table in the kitchen. "Their house in Paris had been part of a large fire in their *quartier*, so they had lived with me for perhaps six months when Adrien arrived. She and Adrien knew each other since—I don't know—since they were very little." He made a characteristic shrug and dipped his bread into his coffee. This seemed his custom, just as he seemed to prefer his coffee exceedingly sweet and strong with lots of hot milk.

"*Ah, la, la,* I was so slow," he continued. "It took me several weeks to realize. I had, I suppose, expected them to behave as they always had to each other. Polite, slightly antagonistic strangers; competitors for my affection. They had always seemed rather wary of each other; not likely to become lovers. But then, I hadn't taken into account adolescence, all the confusion of urges that flood—"

"I found them together, in the pantry that led to the

servants' quarters.

"He had, you must understand, already a kind of presence with the ladies. He was very handsome. Something of a dandy. He had acquired a habit of dress, I think, at school. It was not quite English; enough French to pass in England for very stylish, enough English, I think, to intrigue the French girls. And he had acquired a . . . a kind of polite tenacity: I can still remember seeing him at the end of that dark corridor, wondering, Who was that? That man who so courteously was talking, kissing our little cook's helper, or so I thought, toward the pile of dry clothes in the laundry. *Ah, dommage,* then of course I realized . . .

"I separated them, trembling myself. What was I to do? If Geoffrey, her father, ever learned. And there Adrien was, silent . . . euh—*frémissant de colère,* ah, seething, boiling. And not just from resentment for me. He had, how you say, the arousal of a man; a demi-child with the breathing, the flush of a man for a woman.

"I think I was a little offended. My own Normandy upbringing protested. In *La Normandie,* this is something for a man and wife, not for two children at play.

"So. I explode. Most at Adrien. He is the oldest. He is of her family; her cousin, her protector. I lecture them in the hall, holding each by the arm like naughty children. But I can see. Madeleine reacts like a child in my grip. Adrien, he does not. He takes it, but he is silent in a way that frightens me. Too independent. Too much he keeps his own counsel. If I ever had had any control over him, I see, in that pantry, it is gone forever. So, I do what I can. I move Madeleine down the street to friends. I explain she must live there. 'A girl needs the company of women,' I tell her father—though it is not too long before he is figuring it out: It is impossible not to.

"It was a miserable year or so of the two of them staring at each other across populated rooms and chaperoned parlors. When they are in the same room together, they see

323

no one else. And the looks! Madeleine is blushing every time she catches his glance, and he is bold beyond belief in how he looks at her.

"Then the crisis. They disappear on her fifteenth birthday. Geoffrey makes a large celebration, a ball, in hopes of attracting competition for her annoying cousin. But, of course, he may as well have invited only the one young man, for she will dance with only Adrien. And then, as if we made it happen by dreading and protecting and fretting over precisely that, they disappear.

"When they come back—*ah, mon Dieu,* what a *dispute!* Geoffrey confronts them; Adrien stands up to him, like no young man should to his elder. Madeleine's father is outraged. First, he says, Adrien must marry her. Then, as the argument heats, he says, no; he would rather see his daughter in a convent than married with the likes of Adrien.

"But, alas, it turned out Adrien really did want to marry the girl. For what must be surely the most dangerous of all reasons: youthful passion. But there were good reasons for the match as well. Geoffrey had spent an enormous amount on Madeleine's birthday celebration. He had hoped to show her off, to announce by inviting all his friends, everyone eligible, that she was now available for reciprocal invitations. He had dreams of a rich marriage for her. Though not as he'd expected, he got what he wanted. In Adrien's interests I put the proper amount of incentive before Geoffrey. Namely, Adrien's English title, land, and wealth, which his uncle controlled for the time being, but which Adrien would come into at his majority. So the wedding was set for the next year, with a generous allotment bestowed on the bride's father and no dowry whatsoever. Adrien was sent off on his Grand Tour to keep him off Madeleine until the marriage.

"It seemed the perfect solution to the entire mess. Adrien stopped his carousing, settling all his interests on his cousin. Madeleine thought she had married the king of England and France, both. She had two pregnancies so fast it was cause for gossip — they lost a set of twins, then miraculously had another set that lived, at least for a time; they were not healthy children. Still, everything seemed to be going rather well for them. Adrien came into his holdings; his uncle had been wise and good to him in that regard. Madeleine miscarried another single birth. Her letters seemed unhappy after this. I visited. She appeared a little depressed to me then. And though they didn't argue exactly, I sensed a tension between them. Still, nothing I thought they would not get over. Then, voilà, I get a letter. Adrien has moved to London. Nothing is too low for describing his behavior there. Then, so much disaster, I couldn't absorb it all. All at once, Madeleine is brandishing the notion of divorce. I visit. They are, every one of them, sick. The twins die within three days of each other. And Madeleine is in Paris before I am, triumphant with English divorce papers in her hand. Then, at wits' end; her life a shambles.

"Her father was next to no help. In no manner on earth, he told her, could an English divorce nullify a marriage made in the eyes of France and God.

"I think, secretly, Madeleine had harbored such notions. I don't think she ever credited Adrien with being truly English. She went to England on a lark. But everything in the house was French. The food, their furniture, their clothes; even their holiday celebrations. The wallpaper on their wall, everything; and especially the language. Madeleine knew no other language but French. She seemed almost frightened to learn another."

"In fact, she did not learn English until after the divorce, and it is relatively bad" — Philippe grinned across the table at Christina; self-mocking — "Not nearly so elegant as mine." He reached forward and tapped her hand. "And, you know," he said, "I give you these details because you seem to want them. Also, partly for revenge: Adrien has been devilish with my life in recent months. But mostly, I deal you cards he would keep from you, because you are the first, I think, who holds a trump or so of your own with him."

Trump, indeed, Christina thought. As if anyone could trump this. Adrien had flouted everyone to marry a cousin he had known — and probably loved — all his life. How did one overcome that? It was a good thing she was leaving him and this affair.

Chapter 29

Adrien slept most of the day. Then, just before dinner, just before they were about to wake him, they were all roused from the peaceful lull that had settled into the house. Adrien was the first to hear it: The sound of people traveling toward them across the snow.

He came tearing out of his room, shoving his arms into his coat, muttering curses. "A wagon and riders. Did they take a wagon when they left?"

"No."

The travelers were recognized almost at once. It was, despite the addition of a wagon, the others returning. There was also something — someone — they were bringing back whom they hadn't taken with them.

"Lillings!" Adrien called out into the crisp evening air. He had stepped out onto the porch. His voice, his stance were both angry. *"Qu'est-ce que tu fous ici?"*

Christina watched from the window.

Thomas didn't answer the crudely phrased question. But cheers had gone up from the other men as they recognized Adrien. They would have descended on him, but Thomas quelled them; inaudible words. He sent the others, with a gesture, toward the barn. A vague tension managed to insinuate itself across the hundred yards of snow.

Thomas descended from his horse and handed it over to Sam Rolfeman. He walked toward the house alone.

Adrien stood, hands in his pockets, hunkered down in his coat, his breath visible under the porch light. Christina watched as he and Thomas spoke across the expanse of snow. They had lowered their voices. But she could see Adrien's breath clouding the air; cold, forceful little puffs of anger. Then, the argument came inside.

"Because I was bloody well sent here," Thomas said as he entered. "Claybourne grabbed me yesterday afternoon. Scared the crap out of me—he had some brute with him about eight feet tall. I honestly thought, for a time, I was going to be sent over as a corpse, as a present to you."

Thomas stopped, confronted by the sight of Christina. He stared at her. "Hallo, Christina," he said finally. His eyes stayed on her face for a few moments, then dropped to her belly. "Christ," he muttered, then looked away.

Adrien was taking his coat off in the hallway. "Christina, can you find something to do? I want to talk to Thomas alone."

She didn't move.

Thomas sagged into a far chair. "You're the one that has something else to do," he told Adrien. "Out in the barn, in the wagon. We have the Frenchwoman. The mystery *émigré* who needed our help last summer? You are going to be fascinated by her story." He paused. "Incidentally, she is the one who turned you in two days ago—"

Adrien crunched through the snow toward the barn. He nodded at the rest of the men; they were returning to the house.

"We've trussed her up for you; she wants to speak to you alone," Sam murmured.

Adrien looked over his shoulder at them. He was vaguely irritated that this was becoming his duty and his alone. Then, another feeling stirred a little inside him; a feeling of a very different hue. Scarlet red. Perhaps it wasn't so bad that he was going out here alone. He could remember the scarf, its strange attraction. Adrien admitted to himself, as he got closer to the barn, that he had a certain lurid curiosity — a curiosity he especially wouldn't have wanted Christina to notice — for what tangible form the scarf might take. He laughed to himself. What a peculiar, perverted sensation to know that an enemy, a female enemy, would be tied up in the barn.

Adrien let himself in, then spent a few wasted seconds trying to set the latch. He got it hooked at last, but he could see that a stiff wind would knock the loose bar out of its catch again. He turned. Around one stall he could see a rumpled skirt peeking out. A pair of hands, limp, graceful, were lashed to the post above. The woman couldn't see him. But she knew he was there. She called out. A frightened French voice.

"Qui est-ce?"

He came around the edge of the partition. Expecting anything but what he found.

He was speechless for some seconds. All he could think was that he wanted to turn around and run. "Madeleine?" he whispered.

He had seen her the day she was born. But the day he had first *seen* her, really seen her, was actually about eighteen years ago, when she was fourteen and he was seventeen.

His grandfather, uncle, and cousin Madeleine had come from Paris to meet his boat. It was a cold reunion. Adrien had been sent down from yet a third school in England. In disgrace again. His English relatives had given up — and begged for help. His French relatives had complied. He was greeted at the dock in Le Havre with no less leery a welcome than if they'd been shipped an axe murderer.

His grandfather thrust him into the carriage by taking his arm and pushing him in headfirst. One wrong look, one foul word, he was warned . . . "You are to behave yourself." And the young Adrien proved he could. All the way to Paris.

He looked out the window, offering no communication. It was assumed he was uncomfortable with French. So his Uncle Geoffrey lectured in a mangled version of the language he called English.

It was here, in a dim carriage, that Adrien got his first look, in sly glimpses, of the cousin he had not seen in six years.

Madeleine sat far back in one corner, her eyes fixed on him; as if indeed he might carry an axe in the folds of his cloak. Then slowly, as they joggled toward Paris, she relaxed. By the city's edge, she was throwing odd, conspiratorial little smiles at him, punctuating her father's litany of injunctions and ultimatums with nonsequitur looks that Adrien found wholly unbelievable. Try as he might, he found himself unable to ignore her.

It was not that his cousin was beautiful. Even at fourteen, she was promising to be a bit thick through the hips. It was more that she had a kind of singular appeal. Like the long braids that came over her shoulders, she could be—as she was for the most part that day in the carriage—demure and childish. But there was something else lurking; Adrien noticed, that very first day, that the braids didn't lie very flat over her chest.

He watched her with curiosity that first week. She had long fingers that fluttered and poked. They seemed perpetually into everything. Into Cook's mixing bowls. Wrapping round her own pigtails, sticking them into her mouth. And, as animated as her hands were, her eyes were the opposite. Solid, dead serious. They pinned you and stared without a waver. They missed nothing.

Especially when Adrien entered a room. Then another change would come over the girl. At the sight of her older cousin, she would put on a womanliness, the earnest way some girls can put on their mother's clothes. It had to do with her expression. A way to her walk, her laugh. And, like a child dressing up, she usually got it horribly wrong, very overdone. But even at fourteen, there was every indication that a kind of brazen flirtatiousness would one day suit her quite well.

Yet she never made an overture. And Adrien wasn't about to. He had seen, despite the sly looks, that she was eager to please her elders. He remembered she had been a first-class tattle when they were both little. He also remembered vaguely he had never much liked her then.

So the safest thing was to avoid her.

When Adrien wasn't at school — they'd put him at the university there — he was restricted to the house. For something to do, he'd begun to help in the back garden. The gardener and his son were pegging down the roses *à l'anglaise*. Adrien was awarded some authority simply by virtue of the fact that he had seen such gardens.

This garden became more and more the place Adrien preferred to be. It was a very unaristocratic preference. But it was accepted by staff and relatives alike, with a shake of the head and the oblique explanation that he was, after all, English.

Adrien himself labeled it botany rather than gardening and threw himself into it. Half the time he was supposed to be studying at the university library he was actually there foraging for books on botany. He became far more absorbed in French soil than French people. Though it was in the garden that his involvement with the French cousin began.

He was sitting on the ground, bent over a flat stone on

which he was cutting flowers open very methodically.

"You don't look like a blight."

His eyes jerked up. His cousin Madeleine was not ten feet away, staring at him. Instantly, he was looking for his uncle, Grand-père, someone. He had been there four and a half weeks, and he and his cousin had never once been alone. She had never even spoken to him directly.

He blinked. "Pardon?"

"A blight. On the family. My father says you are. But you don't look like one. I think you look . . ." she hesitated the longest time. Then found the word, "sweet."

"Sweet," he repeated.

"Are you really so wild as they say?"

"Oh, much wilder." He put down the razor he'd been using to dissect the flowers and gave her his complete attention.

"How much?" she asked. Rather bravely, she narrowed her safe distance. The axe murderer in easy reach of a razor. It surprised him she would come near him at all.

Her skirts brushed the edge of his elbow. Perfume swam over him. He looked up. Her young face had been dusted and rouged with face paint. It was not awkwardly applied. Yet, despite its owner's attempt to make it so, it was not a womanly countenance. Adrien's eyes dropped to her mouth, its unnatural color. Her father would have been furious: In fact, her red lips were an almost sure announcement that neither her father nor their grandfather was anywhere around.

Adrien stared at her, this strange-pretty, overly sophisticated cousin. She looked and smelled like a forsaken child-cum-whore. Some poor creature forced into compromising circumstances.

"What are you doing, Madeleine? Your father's going to kill you if he sees your face like that."

She gave a half-confused, half-peeved little pout, but

didn't back down an inch. She cocked her head. "Papa's gone to see his banker. Pepe" — their grandfather — "went with him. Mlle Durand" — her governess — "has a headache and is lying down —"

"You're not supposed to be here."

"I'm not."

"What —" He frowned.

"I'm not here," she said shyly. "I'm up in my room studying." Her smile lit for a moment. Then she looked away.

He considered her, then stood and dusted his hands. Again he found her staring at him.

"Where did you learn your French?" she asked.

"Here. Then in school."

"Papa says you have never been in school long enough to learn anything."

He made a dry face. Then one of mild, surprised discomfiture. His unruly masculine nature was creating a snugness at the front of his breeches. Could he possibly be attracted to this . . . this child? No. But that damned part of him had a mind of its own. God knew it came alive at unpredictable moments — it could be roused over nothing more erotic than a tub of warm water.

"Well," he said, turning and deftly shielding the front of himself. He stooped and began to carefully scrape and fold up his project; his scattered flower-genitalia. "I think you'd better go wash your face."

He heard a little catch of breath. "You're not very friendly, I can tell you that much."

He was trying too hard to think only of gathering his specimens, his tools, of gathering his thoughts; neither of them knowing he was mounting the assault. "I think your father would want you to be more careful in picking your friends."

She bent beside him. Her perfume rose up and around

333

him, this time with an insidious allure. He stood up. She too. Very close now. She was much shorter than he. She handed him a forgotten tool. A trowel.

He took her wrist instead.

No amount of painted-on sophistication could hide the little shock that ran over her face. As if she had never imagined her little game could go further than just the moment before.

He took her other wrist. The trowel dropped. He kissed her. Their mouths touched hesitantly. He could feel — in a tension down her arms, in the way she seemed poised to flee at any second — that she was genuinely frightened by this boldness. He waited to see if this might outweigh a curiosity he could also sense in her.

But she allowed the touching of lips.

"Close your eyes, Madeleine."

"Why?"

"It's how it's done."

"Are you instructing me to any purpose?"

"I'm going to kiss you again. If you sin, you may as well do it right."

"Is it a sin?"

"It will be when I'm finished."

She backed at that. Yet the wrists were still in surrender.

"I shall scream if you do more than kiss me," she said with a sudden sureness, "but I have decided that a kiss is not a sin, no matter what my father says. You may do it again."

License. He pulled her up against him and touched her mouth again with his own. He kissed her for some minutes in a full, heart-pounding embrace.

"Here," he murmured. "Put your arms here." He drew them up around his neck. "And don't hold your mouth so tight."

"I can't help it," she whispered. "This frightens me."

334

"It will be all right. Just relax and open your mouth a little."

"Open my mouth?" Her eyes widened. "Why? That sounds dreadful —"

He shushed her and kissed her again.

The truth was, despite how much his elders bemoaned and complained, this "difficult and wicked" young man's experience had never included either an open garden or a curious young girl. In fact, at seventeen Adrien had lain with exactly two women — and on both occasions the situation had been somewhat reversed. Brisk, well-orchestrated encounters manipulated by women considerably his senior.

So there was a certain amount of fumbling on his part. Fidgeting on hers. In the crush of one embrace, he pushed his tongue into her mouth. For a few seconds, there was an ethereal warmth, a surrender. Then squirming. She broke away, wiping her mouth with the back of her hand as if he had played some absurd practical joke.

Cowed, he asked a little crossly, "Don't you like this at all? You're not very good at it."

She frowned. Her eyes showed a hint of glassing over. "Well, I don't know if I like it. It makes me feel funny. And my stomach — here —" She started to lower her hand to show him the location of this funny feeling.

He jerked her hand upward and away.

"Well, I don't know," she said belligerently. "My stomach feels funny: Either I like it or I'm going to be sick, I can't tell —"

"Good Lord."

Her mouth opened at this blasphemy. He took his opportunity. A rich one, as it turned out.

After an instant of struggle, she allowed the penetration of her mouth. His senses reeled. He kissed her for some time — certainly a long time by his "adult" standards. They stood. They embraced. He shifted from one foot to the

335

other. Adrien was never particularly aware of its being by design, but he eventually moved her around and over a few steps, putting them in a more sheltered position, behind some tall bushes.

Then, with a sudden brainstorm, he became aware — in a very conscious way — that if they lay down there, among the vegetation and statuary, they would not be visible at all.

She accommodated. In only minutes, he was on top of her. And in serious distress. The jaws of a paradox set themselves around him like a trap. Holding back. Pushing forward. It was making him dizzy. He was desperate to avoid any messy, humiliating finale. Yet with equal desperation, they were heading in a direction that offered almost no other end. He suddenly realized he had never intended to deflower his cousin, but meant sincerely to stop somewhere along the line. But where?

The springs of the trap tightened. The more he kissed her, the more wrong it felt. Which, in turn, God help him, fevered the act further. She was so completely forbidden — like a sister, it occurred to him — that no one had even mentioned he shouldn't touch her.

"Madeleine, I—" He swallowed, trying not to breathe so heavily.

She attempted to pull his head back down to her.

He resisted.

"Oh, kiss me, please," she whispered. "I didn't know . . . . It's not at all like being sick—"

"It is. There's a relief to the feeling. And I would show you that relief, only I think I should not."

"I've displeased you." Her eyes began to mist over again.

"No. The contrary." He pushed himself from her, groaning at the frustration and discomfort of it.

"I have. I'm ugly."

She was not outrageously pretty. Just outrageously attractive. Like a field of grass. Just so much green, like what

336

one saw along the walks every day. Yet a whole field of green grass called one to lie down in it. And once down, the smell, the coolness, even the taste of a blade of it in one's mouth . . .

"You're not ugly." He had to tense his muscles to keep from showing her instead of telling her.

"As ugly as Medusa. You've turned to stone."

A little brutal to herself, he thought. He laughed at her. "Only part of me."

She didn't understand.

He didn't mean to offend her. He pulled her hand to show what he meant. It seemed so natural.

She jerked violently away. Gasped. Then picked herself up and ran.

He was left rolled over on his elbow, feeling stupid. And somehow tricked—cozened, as it were: The imprint of her hand translated easily through his breeches. That small, light touch was to burn on his flesh all week; all year.

A mistake, he thought. A multiple mistake. He should have taken her deeper into the garden, spoken less, kissed her more, drawn her further into more liberties, then had her. It could have been done. He was sure.

Yet it was wrong; he knew that. She was his cousin, a woman of his family. He owed her his protection. From exactly this sort of thing. Still, this was a protection he was loath to bestow.

All week he wrestled with this dilemma and the awful knowledge of how he wanted it resolved. Then a brilliant idea occurred to him. He could marry her. That would make it all right. And, thus, the seed was planted in his mind—an impregnation of a thorny, strangling idea, sown by his own contrivance to relieve guilt.

But watered and nurtured by circumstance.

A few days later, he had her cornered in the maid's pantry, when Fate—in the form of Grand-père—stepped in.

Adrien was handled none too gently by the scruff of the neck, then browbeaten, in a long painful session in his grandfather's library, about his duty to women in general and to his cousin in particular. But worst of all, Madeleine was sent from the house and from him.

And worse still, he saw her frequently. With a minimum of half a dozen chaperones. It turned the fever into a true sickness with real physical pain for which there was no relief, try as he might.

Adrien cultivated the friendship of Madeleine's governess in the hope of paving a circuitous route around the obstacles springing up between him and his cousin. Only this became awkward when the governess proved to be a lonely young woman with romantic notions of her own. And more trouble. Adrien impregnated the governess.

He was humble, contrite. Yes, he knew it led to children. Only it never had before. Of course, he would see to the child. For God's sake, no, he didn't want to marry a French governess. John, his English uncle, had some duke's daughter mapped out—a small fact Adrien had hidden in the back of his mind until called to bring it forth for Grandpère.

It was a year of frustration, foolish mistakes; adolescence at its most painful. He was plagued with feelings of guilt and of impotence at the hands of others around him. There was only one truly beautiful night, a few hours that lit his life before he was plunged even deeper into self-pity and disaster.

Madeleine's fifteenth birthday. There was a huge ball, her first. They danced every dance together. She would have no one else. He felt like a king.

"Come out of here with me. We can get away, I'm sure."

She gave him a shy look, just a slide of eyes to his face from beneath her dark lashes. "You know I want to."

"But?"

"But Papa. He would be so disappointed. Already he's displeased. I'm supposed to be finding a husband, not flirting with my cousin."

"Perhaps you can do both."

Her eyes came up more directly. Her gaze held on his face until she blushed in the realization of how long she'd stared. She looked down. "Don't tease."

"You would be a good match. My uncle could not disagree; he would only grumble at having to change plans."

"He has someone else for you?"

"I don't even know her name." But he did. Georgina Kent, only daughter to the Duke of Wilsbury. Filthy rich. Pretty. But totally uninspiring. He'd met her twice.

"You'd flout your uncle and marry me?"

"Will you go against your father in favor of me?"

Her eyes slid up to him again. "I would. I mean I want to. I've thought of it so often. You can't imagine—"

"But I can. I'm roasting in my own hell from imagination."

"A nice place for you. Celeste"—her governess—"had a girl, I'm told."

No comment. He didn't know quite how to handle this area. He'd become a father the month before. An experience he hadn't been able to categorize yet. He'd held the child, felt very strange at doing so, but wanted to do so again. That part was unexpected, the wanting to visit a tiny baby. And that part was also private. For now at least.

"You have no defense?" Madeleine was being coy.

"What can I say that will sound right?"

"Repentance. Blind devotion. Sworn love." Her efforts to be cavalier fell flat. She looked up again, in all seriousness. Then unwittingly said what would keep him flying—all the way to the altar—for the entire next year. "It doesn't matter," she spoke. "None of it matters. I love you, Adrien.

339

I'd go to ruin — and may, it appears — for just a moment of your love."

They slipped off to the carriage house, one at a time. They met, and there, between heated declarations of love and marriage, they consummated a year-and-a-half-long romance — in which they had been alone together scarcely more than a few hours all told.

It was, as deflowerings go, rather uneventful. Any pleasure she might have had was overshadowed by fright; just as his was overshadowed by an inept eagerness that simply couldn't be stemmed. It was approached by both of them almost as something to be got through.

Darkness descended quickly on their sweet sin. She was taken from him again. He was, like a naughty child, sent to his room — on the other side of the world. He was sent on Grand Tour, dragooned out of the house. It seemed, then, he was perpetually being thrown out of places. And his one possession became worse than none:

Images of his cousin, the feel and look of her in the hay in the carriage house, haunted him across two continents. When he returned a month before the wedding, he longed to put an end to his torment and just take Madeleine off for an elopement.

But she was guarded like a relic of the cross. Everywhere, sober faces stopped him from even a private word with his bride-to-be. He was stiffly put in his place: on the outside, a dark relative admitted only through convention. He felt not like the groom but a guest of the bride. The bride's criminal cousin.

He saw his daughter again that month and was very much charmed by her. She walked. Celeste had shyly encouraged the child to speak one of the few words she knew — "Papa." Insipid cuteness. He detested himself for being so pleased with the nonsense syllables. So pleased with a bastard daughter; two counts against her.

Looking back, he remembered feeling almost over-indulgent toward himself then — and it was true; in many ways, he had denied himself nothing. But he did deny himself one thing, he decided as he stood there in the barn stall. Forgiveness. He never forgave himself for even the slightest error. A mistake was a mistake.

And he was looking at one right now. God, Madeleine looked so much like he remembered. And it felt so much the same: With Christina in the house, it felt devilishly wrong to be out here, alone, with Madeleine . . . .

Chapter 30

The woman before him was babbling happily in heavily accented English. "Adrien! I wuss so afraid you wairn't here. Or woo-dunt agree to see me. And Thomas wuss so nasty and *secret*. . . ." Her words seemed to open up and come at him, like a torrent. The English seemed doubly strange. He had never heard her speak it, and what he heard now was awful; the accent held as if for beguiling effect.

"Adrien?" Her voice held a quiver in it. *"Tu vas m'aider, n'est-ce pas?"* When he didn't answer, she repeated the question in English, "You are going to 'elp me, aren' you?"

No, he thought, he was going to turn his back on her exactly as he should. But he couldn't. He came forward and began letting her free.

She smelled sour; a mixture of too much perfume and the cold sweat of fear. Why, he wondered, hadn't he recognized this before? The red scarf. The perfume itself had been unfamiliar, but the smell of the woman mingled with it, along with the tendency to use too much, had been well known to him. He should have known. . . .

Her face was an inch off his chest as he reached over her head to untie her. It was a warm sensation feeling her breath there. And her breath had that peculiar, sweet quality; always so, like a young child's. Despite everything, he realized she was not repulsive to him. Adrien found

342

himself looking to the door. Like a guilty man.

Pure foolishness, he told himself. He jerked his eyes back to the knot that was proving so difficult. Even if Christina walked in—which she had no reason to do—what did it matter? Being caught in the same room with Madeleine was no crime.

He closed his eyes, yanked at the stubborn rope. No, it only felt like a sin. It always had; that had been part of the fascination.

He heard her slightly wicked laugh. "Nervous, *chéri?* You used to be much faster at getting things undone."

"What are you doing here?" he asked gruffly.

She purred a laugh. The last binding gave. And she engulfed him. Arms, hands, mouth went at him in an attack he didn't want, yet seemed to have no defense against. His memory played havoc with him. Her touch, the feel of her, her smell, taste, the movements of her body, these all seemed so familiar, yet experiencing them remained bizarre.

Over her shoulder, his eyes flicked toward the door again. Guilt. Lord, he must be steeped in it. Could he honestly imagine poor, pregnant Christina traipsing a hundred yards in the cold snow. . . .

He freed his mouth from the onslaught of affection. He tried to set Madeleine away from him. But she drew his hand to her breast and pressed it there. A little charge went through him. God help him, he remembered what her bosom looked like naked. Small, perfect, high. With dark pink nipples that stared like blank eyes . . .

"Madeleine, don't you find this just a little—fast?"

"But I understand you play very fast these days."

He gave an uncomprehending blink.

"I've kept track of you a little," she explained. "And though you were devious and hard to discover in France, in England over the past year you have been quite visible." She paused to look at him, smiling. "And 'fast' is kind. I have never seen such a long or ever-changing parade of partners, *chéri*. What's wrong? Can't you hold one woman's interest longer than a few months?" Her laughter purred again. So appealing. So unnerving in its easy, teasing quality.

Before he could disengage himself, she'd kissed him again. And again he allowed it. Only for a moment. But she recognized the victory before she suffered the setback of having her arms removed from him completely.

He took a step backward, feeling truly out of his depth. Some perversity in him was perfectly willing to be kissed by her. Some piece of the old, eerie attraction to her was still very much intact.

He heaved a labored sigh. "Thomas said I was to find a woman here that has caused me a great deal of trouble. And I find you."

She cocked her head and smiled mischievously. "And you find the woman, I'm afraid. As if I hadn't already caused you enough." She giggled, full of girlish charm. Her blue eyes challenged. "Can you laugh at it all yet?"

"No."

She lowered her eyes and grew serious for an instant. "Nor I. But I can make a good show of it." Eyes bright again, "And I rather backed into causing you more trouble." Her face flashed into a charming smile. "And did an *excellent* job of it. *De première classe!* You are, how they say, in the soup, dear. Very much thanks to me."

"You were in England last May?"

"March, April, and May. I took on a silly task of trying to locate some Englishman there." Her eyes teased. Her lips smiled as if this were some wonderful game. "So I could more easily spy on my husband, you see. You might know him. Tall. Dreadfully handsome. Hair about this long." She reached out and gently tugged at the hair curling over the back of his neck. "About this black." Her nails combed through his hair at the side. "A long, straight nose"

Fingers lightly down his nose to his mouth. She whispered softly, "Lips, warm, smooth, a very handsome mouth that gives kisses—"

She had worked herself up against him again. He stood immobile. "I'm not your husband," he contradicted.

She pulled a pouting face. "I keep forgetting." She smiled, rolled her wide eyes at him. "Let me see," she continued, looking down at her hands now resting on his chest. "Where was I? *Ah, oui.* I was very patriotically researching for my country—I had a friend of some influence here; he and I, well, it was a favor to him—while I was very surreptitiously checking on one Earl of Kewischester when, *tiens! Devine!* The paths started crossing and falling into a pattern. You must know the rest. You knew there was someone onto your game. I realized who I'd discovered and buttoned my mouth. I told my friend it was a blind alley. Really, dear, I was so touched in those three months. There you were, unable—in ten years—to form any sort of bond with a woman, then off to the rescue of aristos, *my* relatives. It was a touching tribute."

"They were mine as well."

"Yes."

He frowned, confused again. She had lent the word a kind of open, incestuous implication. . . .

She squeezed his arm. "Mmm. More muscled at thirty-four than at twenty-four. No, thirty-five; you had a birthday in December." She was opening the buttons of his coat, sliding her hands into it, taking his shirt from his pants.

Her hands moved lightly and deftly. Some part of him hung on the depravity of allowing her one moment at a time. Like allowing one's murderer certain liberties.

Her hands slipped beneath his layers of clothes, under his shirt. He went to stop her, but succeeded only in having his hands caught, then led around to rest on her buttocks. He swallowed and shot another look at the door.

"If you look at that door one more time, I shall slap your

345

handsome face. That door is getting more attention than I am. Don't worry, dear. Thomas promised me. . ."

She went on, but Adrien's mind froze on those last words. Thomas. Reason, not guilt, kept the image of Christina coming through that door. One person had a great deal to gain by sending Christina across a hundred yards of snow. If she didn't barge in, and soon, he would eat his . . .

"Adrien." Madeleine's voice was a little breathy, a little irritated. "I am asking you to make love to me." There was a pause. "Now, don't pretend you don't want to. Let's bury the past." Her voice rose slightly; more irritated. "Well? Will you?"

He flashed a smile at her, felt her relax. "Not this instant, no. We have a few points to settle first. For instance, Thomas seems to feel that I have you to thank for my current dilemma."

"I told you, you do."

"Would you be so kind as to explain? Why, if you didn't turn me in last summer, would you turn me in now?"

"Well." She put on a coy shyness as she cuddled up to him again. "It's so embarrassing now. Now that I see the full effect I have on you." A sly look up. "Tell me you don't want me right now? Just as always."

"I can barely think of anything else." This wasn't entirely true, but it would suffice.

She cackled quietly. "And that you don't love me."

That, he could have told her. With amazing ease. He felt light and buoyant in that knowledge. But he was silent. He put on a sulking face. He didn't hate her, he realized. Because he didn't know her. She was a composite, the oddest juxtaposition of strange and familiar. Everything about her—her movements, her stance, her voice, her expressions—all seemed familiar. Yet the final impression she left was that of a stranger.

She laughed once again in solicitous confidence, touching his face endearingly. She puckered her mouth and spoke in his least favorite mannerism of hers, a sort of affected baby talk. *"Mon minou.* Do I tease you too hard? What is my penance to be before the way is clear?"

He had to stifle a nastier reply. Instead: "Just tell me what happened. What do they know? And, for curiosity, why, for God's sake?"

"All right. But don't be angry now. Promise. I'll stop the moment I see your temper."

"I won't be angry."

"Well, this morning—no, I suppose it was yesterday morning now—I went with my, ah, friend to do his boring morning routine. Which has included, from time to time, the questioning of a man of yours. A M. Cabrel, I believe. I had been through the whole silly business a dozen times. Heard the monotonous story. But yesterday morning, M. Cabrel added one phrase more: As he described again each man he could remember, he ended the list with 'and a black-haired man with the clinging wife.' Wife, mind you! I asked a few pointed questions and assured myself he was talking about you. But he would not yield on the point that you had brought some sultry young doxy over with you. And cared for her most lovingly—carrying her to a room you shared with her, stroking her hair, cooing at her. Ick! Well I'm afraid I saw red. An hour later, I suggested that— though I should never want to appear vindictive, the horrible divorce and all—my ex-husband might just possibly be the Madman everyone was looking for. God help me for sounding like a woman scorned, I told him, but so many of the pieces fit—I had only held my tongue because it sounded so preposterous and jealous, but I could be silent no longer. It didn't take my friend too long to lap it up, and, voilà, sweet revenge. Poor dear, how I wish I had thought it out more. They found the scarf, you know."

"What?"

"My red scarf. It was in your apartment in Paris. You

kept it, you dear. But how in the world did you get it? It's caused me terrible trouble. My friend is convinced now I was seeing you."

"You're not working for the committee any more?"

She laughed. "Decidedly not. They'e ready to wring my neck." A pause. "They know I protected you, Adrien. And I'm glad I did." Lower. "There's no other woman, is there?"

"No." Adrien found he could smile at her, fully, eye to eye. "Only one."

She smiled back broadly. Her mouth was made for smiling. Wide, feminine, appealing. At thirty-two, she was still at her peak of attraction with that smile. She would be attractive at forty because of it. And survive; she and he were both survivors, he thought. He would help get her away, then be done with her. Forever. Adrien sighed at this wonderful realization.

A movement beyond caught Adrien's eye. The barn door opened. A wide-eyed Christina came hesitantly in, stopped cold, then seemed about to speak.

Adrien pulled Madeleine into his arms, turning her back fully to the door. Over Madeleine's shoulder he looked directly at Christina, motioning with his eyes for her to leave.

Christina at least had the decency to be speechless, but she stood staring at him.

"And that was all?" he asked, determined to keep Madeleine occupied and Christina unseen by her.

"Almost. M. Cabrel gave a good description of your— companion. I gave a brilliant description of you, right down to this" —she touched the thin scar at his lip— "where I bit you. Do you remember?"

"Yes."

"We used to fight at very close range." She whispered. Yet her voice carried on the crisp air. It carried too well. "It was dangerous," she added.

"Yes." He sighed.

"Where is she?"

"Who?"

"Your woman. There were rumors that La Chasse kept a woman somewhere—"

"Oh, she's gone." Adrien looked pointedly at Christina, making a small hand gesture signifying that she comply with his words.

Christina stood saucer-eyed, glued to the spot.

"Adrien? Is something—?" Madeleine was alarmed by his sudden movement behind her back. She was about to turn.

He could think of no other way out. He kissed the woman in his arms. She groaned, then wrapped herself into it.

Adrien stared hard at Christina, all the time that he kissed Madeleine. Then, slowly but very definitively, he bent his wrist and pointed his finger to the door. Leave, by God, Christina, he wanted to scream at her. She doesn't know; no one has a better picture of you than the one Bertrand Cabrel was able to give six months ago when you were nothing but scared and seasick. My God, they think you're pale, sickly, subdued—and *thin!*

From across the barn, he could see the robust, pregnant young woman's eyes mist. Her lower lip quivered. Christina turned and slipped away, quickly and quietly. The opening, where she had stood, was a void, a slice of pitch-black night. As if there was nothing, less than nothing, beyond the dimly lit barn. Then a flurry of snowflakes contradicted this, blowing in on a gust of wind. It had begun to snow again.

Chapter 31

Only Thomas was in the parlor when Adrien came in.

"You, I'll deal with later," he said. "Where is Christina?"

"She went for a walk. Out that way." He pointed toward the back of the house. "I don't think she wants to see you."

Adrien left Thomas to gloat. He darted a look around as he passed through the kitchen. She wasn't there. But as he bolted through the back door, he nearly tripped over her. She was sitting on the stoop, huddled in the same coat she had been wearing on her little trip to the barn — it was Thomas', he realized.

He squatted beside her. She jerked around to look — glare — at him.

"Well, that was quick," she said.

"Christina." He forced her to look at him. Shiny paths showed down her cheeks, but her eyes were dry now. He slid down to huddle next to her. "It's cold out here. Let's go inside."

"It was warm enough in the barn a few minutes ago. Why don't you go back there? Or is she in your bedroom?"

"She's gone. That is, she's about to be. Sam will take her to the Belgium border."

She queried him with a tentative look.

"I didn't want her to see you," he explained. "She doesn't know exactly what you look like or about this." He was allowed to touch her taut belly. Then he parlayed this touch

350

into a full-scale wrapping of himself about her. "She'll protect me again. She doesn't dare do otherwise, actually. We had a bittersweet parting, with every assurance that she'll say nothing."

Christina didn't seem able to believe this. "You're just letting her go? But Thomas says she's the one who turned you in."

"What more can she do to me?"

"What she's already done is enough." There was a pause. She seemed to look at him, evaluate. Then she said, "No matter how angry I got at Richard, I wouldn't try to get him killed."

"Madeleine doesn't think things out. You would have to know her to understand that. In her mind, she was just trying to get me in trouble, like a child tattling. She doesn't think about consequences."

"Maybe she ought to feel some."

"I don't want revenge, if that's what you're suggesting." He made a dry laugh. "If you only knew all that Madeleine and I put each other through a dozen years ago . . . . Or how sour revenge can become when you're glutted with it . . . No, I don't want to hurt her. I just want to get rid of her. Madeleine's finished business; reporting me to the French was the last thing she can ever do to hurt me." He made a huge, happy sigh.

"My dear woman," he continued, "I wasn't angry with her. I didn't hate her. And I don't love her. I barely even *know* her, it occurred to me. I didn't want to have to keep her here, for the obvious tensions that would produce. So I took precautions to secure her cooperation. That was all. She's gone. And my honor is intact. So help me God." He raised a hand as in the swearing of an oath, then added a quick sign of the cross. Forehead, chest, shoulder to shoulder.

"Are you Catholic?" Christina asked.

"Church of England." He made another sober swearing of

351

oaths, hand raised.

He thought he detected a faint smile on her face. He felt his own smile grow so wide it hurt . . . .

"Excuse me." A voice behind them interrupted. "You're going to be even more angry with me if you don't see this fairly soon."

Thomas stood in the doorway, blocking the light from the kitchen. He stepped out onto the porch, offering what looked like a letter.

Adrien rose, helped Christina to her feet. As they came up the steps Thomas flinched, took a step back.

Adrien made a dry laugh. "I'm not going to hit you, Thomas. Though you deserve it. That was a malicious thing to do; to set me up, then send Christina out to the barn."

"We, all three of us, had a right to know how you'd respond to seeing Madeleine again."

"Did we?" Adrien pushed Christina past them. "Perhaps you and I need to discuss exactly what rights we, all three, have."

Christina took hold of Adrien's arm.

"There's nothing to discuss." From the shadows, Thomas' face came around into the light. He looked at Christina. The sadness in his expression was so large, there was no place to hide it. Christina had to turn from him.

"The Old Man said he knew I could locate you. He sends you this." Thomas held out the letter.

Adrien took it. He broke the seal without taking his eyes off the other man; as if this, too, might be another deceit. Then he dropped his eyes to the page.

He stepped, as he read, toward the open kitchen doorway. So that he stood in the wash of yellow light coming from inside, his face in sharp relief. Christina watched the chiseled features compress into a bitter look.

"Splendid," he said, handing the note to Christina. "Just splendid. Isn't that a work of art?"

352

As she began reading, he pushed his way into the house:

"My dear Mad Friend,

Congratulations. You fooled the schoolmaster, the mark of a most excellent student. But, alas, your wonderful joke has come to an end. And I find I cannot laugh.

Still, in the interest of the mixed affection and admiration I have for you—imagine my two most intriguing enigmas in the same person!—I would like to give you this much warning. And, of course, deal you some pain in the bargain. Here is how it stands:

As your friend and mentor, I advise that you not return home.

I have just spent the bulk of my evening having the arrest papers drawn up for the Earl of Kewischester. They are most complex for I have succeeded in pressing the matter of interference in Anglo-French relations into full-scale treason. Difficult. And I hang by the thread of my position intertwined with the imminent threat of war. But done. Which, I am sure, you realize means that even as you stand there (Are you still standing, my friend? There's more!) reading this, a great deal of damage has been done to you, and will continue to be done to you, *in absentia.*

A lack of legal heirs makes the actual legalities of confiscating your properties relatively simple—traitors are not very well protected, I'm afraid. But, I had no idea there was so much! Or that you dabbled so freely in so many diverse enterprises. We will be opening up your ledgers at the Kewischester estate, I believe, by next week. I'm hoping to have dispersed everything and made you a property-less, penniless outlaw by mid-March. You are well on your way now.

Of course, if you return to fight this (I do love the incentive. Aren't you tempted?), you will be hanged.

353

Quickly. Quietly. And—even though I yearn for a long, drawn-out internment—quite finally. You are too slippery, too ingenious for me to take chances.

As for your men. I mean them no offense. They have been abominably good at their parts of this game. But I simply can't be bothered—the French war draws heavily on me. No arrests, unless yours of course, will be made. I must say, this gives me a certain perverse satisfaction. You can watch your friends return to their pleasant, natural lives, while you must run headlong into uncertainty.

Running. Yes, I do like that almost as much as destroying your earldom. I won't let you come to rest here, and I won't let you land comfortably anywhere else. As you are so well acquainted, I have international contacts. They are all alerted to you. You will have, no doubt, moments to catch your breath. But it will be, by and large, a life of constant flight. A life in the air.

Until I finally lay hands on you.

I do have such mixed feelings for you, I can hardly describe the total. I can only tell you that I desire to see you a broken man, completely bowed before me. To deprive you of ever again knowing life as you have previously known it is as close as I can come to bending you down. I only wish there were more.

In deepest affection,
E. Claybourne, Minister of Foreign Affairs"

Christina entered the parlor half expecting to find Adrien distraught, dazed by the blow that had befallen him. But he was not.

". . . then you will all leave tomorrow. M. La Fontaine will not be pleased by his state, eh, Grand-père?" Adrien was joking. He was actually joking. And making plans to return to England! "But better a sweet old woman sailing with her sons than a dead old man killed for his grandson's sins. Christina will lend you some clothes. You won't mind, will you, dear?" He called to her from across the room, but didn't wait for an answer. He continued speaking to Philippe de La Fontaine. "I will hope to see you at the docks, that you will be able to meet Christina and me there in five days. We will have a grand reunion then. But you are safer split off from me."

He walked over behind Christina, behind the chair where she'd more or less collapsed. Absently, he began massaging her neck and shoulders. "I would not split off my dear wife from me," he was saying to the others, "unless Satan himself held a gun at my temple." He kissed the top of her head.

Philippe was staring at her in a peculiar manner. Wife? Had Adrien said wife?

"Now, Le Saint. You are to go to Le Havre and find an English captain for the trip across. I want the marriage to be legally binding, so a French magistrate won't do. Try Fenton on the *Silver Jack*. He'd know how to get the right papers in order, as well as how to keep his mouth shut. And I want duplicates made up. A set for me. A set you can carry separately to the registry. Oh yes, and let's send Claybourne his own personal copy, to arrive, say, the same afternoon we do. Attach a note. Tell him to stuff them up his ass with my compliments.

"Then the rest will be up to Sam and the men. You have five days to spread everything into every tavern, every club, every public hall. The simple facts. Everything we've done. There are people in England who should be grateful enough to come forward and corroborate. But it is up to you all to set the tone. Political opinion, since all these massacres — especially since Louis' today — should run in my favor. The Madman must be such a public wonder that the Old Man won't dare do much else but applaud when I arrive. He will, no doubt, stir up some trouble. But with

355

war looking so likely, now should be as good a time as any to become a hero.

"Oh, and see if you can rally a small crowd at the docks on Thursday. Claybourne might meet me there personally with some mischief. We want everything public. If I am arrested, I want the newspaper there to cover it. Get the *Times*—see Mr. Tallying there—to editorialize on the subject of the Earl of Kewischester's secret occupation this summer. Give Tallying any information he wants. He'll be sympathetic; he's a Burkite. Just make sure this doesn't come out too quickly.

"The delicate part, of course, will be building the whole thing without tipping Claybourne off that I'm going home almost immediately. The less time he has to think of a countermeasure, the better—he might find one.

"Let's see now. Oh, there's my attorneys. They'll need to be prepared. I want to spend as little time in jail as possible, if that's the way Claybourne decides to handle it . . . ."

He was in fine form. Making plans. Allowing contingencies for his contingencies.

Christina stood up, moving out from under his hands. She went back into the kitchen. She should have been happy, she thought. He was going to marry her. He hadn't formally asked, but then he didn't need to.

She scuffed about the table aimlessly while the men talked on. She made some tea and sat down with it.

But she wasn't happy.

She would have to tell him.

Balancing her tea in her hand, she went back to stand in the doorway to watch him. His eyes were steady on a man standing in front of him, intent in conversation. Then they flicked up a second, over the man's head. He threw her a moment's recognition, a look of perfect, glancing intimacy. Like a small, weighted dart. Lobbed in her direction; easily hitting home. She stood, mesmerized by the zing of blue; shot through.

Then the baby inside her, oblivious to this moment, began to counterpoint it with a funny hiccoughing motion. The whole front of her jerked once, twice. The third hiccough was so violent as to rattle the teacup she had more or less balanced on the shelf of her belly. Christina patted her middle and turned away. Her offspring was right. No lovesick delusions.

Yes. She would marry Adrien. She knew that. For the baby. For Adrien himself — he needed her most desperately now. She wouldn't abandon that need. Then she laughed. She would even marry him a little bit for her father; no matter what mess ensued, he could not help but be pleased.

But not for herself. Not like this. And she had to tell him.

Chapter 32

It was a little after three in the morning when Christina caught Adrien's attention. Le Saint was just being packed off to Le Havre.

It had been decided that Christina and Adrien would travel to the Normandy coast in a day's time. There, they would meet Le Saint and, hopefully, a willing, close-mouthed captain. They would be married on board an English ship. Then it would just be a matter of waiting — while everyone else, having returned to England, would try to link Adrien's name to the rising English public outrage against the "reign of terror" in France.

"I need to speak with you, Adrien. Before he leaves," Christina called from the doorway of the kitchen.

He looked her way, one brow arched over a sudden, questioning awareness of her. But as he came toward her, his face changed; from questioning to irritatingly arrogant: The smile he wore said he knew the answer to the question before he asked it.

"You were hoping for a formal proposal?" She had retreated into the kitchen. He had followed. He stood smiling, leaning against the doorjamb. "Will you marry me, Christina? I meant to ask you differently. But, well, circumstances being what they are —"

She shot him a contradicting look, then put on the kettle and got down another cup and saucer.

"I thought you'd be pleased—"said the man behind her.

"Do you want some?" She gestured to the teapot.

"No. Christina, have I done something wrong?" When she didn't answer immediately, "Tell me. What?"

He was going to correct for it. A man who had been analyzing, categorizing, and solving problems all night. Christina wanted to laugh.

More a lament than a censure, she said softly, "If you had been listening for the last half-year, you would know."

His smile became unsure, the half-smile of a man who hates to call the next shot.

Christina poured herself a cup of tea. Then she emptied her lungs with a deep breath and turned toward him. "I don't want to be your captive for the rest of my life."

"Oh, Christina, really—"

She sat down at the table with her tea. He walked behind her.

He spoke as he poured more water into the pot. "You've hardly been a captive," he said. "Why are you so up in arms? Honestly, I'm sorry I didn't have the opportunity to ask you on bended knee. But it's not as if we've never discussed marriage. Or as if we didn't both know you'd marry me—"

Their eyes met as he came around the table. He did a kind of double take, a blink. Then he asked, "You will, won't you?"

"Yes, but—"

"Good." His moment of doubt was over. He sat down and put two huge spoonfuls of sugar into his tea. He was looking for the milk.

"I'll marry you," she continued. "I wouldn't deny you what help I can be when you need it as badly as you do. But I won't live with you. I want to set up my own household. With my money. Something I can afford; a nice country existence. I want to know what it feels like to be on my own, no one to order me about. Or sabotage my will

359

with their sometimes-very-appealing, but very overbearing personality. I want out from under you, both figuratively and literally."

All humor, any pleasure in the situation left his face. "Christina, things will be different in England. This has been such an unusual situation—"

"No." She flicked her eyes up to him a moment, then back down to her untouched cup of tea. "I've been in England with you and—"

"And it *was* different, damn it!"

"And you hated it. I remember the conversation in the inn, Adrien."

"You remember stupid things—I said stupid things. But I'm telling you now, I want to live with you. As your husband. I have wanted that for—"

"Oh, please, Adrien. At least spare me that!"

He had the good grace to stammer for an instant. "Wh-what—"

"Not two days ago you were beside yourself with joy when I abandoned the subject of marriage."

He made a broad gesture of denial with one hand. "Well, yes. But that was before—"

"Before you needed an heir. Adrien, I understand your wanting to marry me now. And I don't fault you for it. I would do exactly as you in your place. I'd grit my teeth and marry."

"Is that what you think?" He pushed away from the table and stood. As he rose, his leg caught on the leg of the table. "Well, it's just not true!" His teacup overturned. The table banged down.

Hot tea steamed, poured off the table edge onto his empty chair. Then ran to the floor. A pathetic, drizzling sound that dominated the room for some seconds.

"Adrien," she said softly, "this isn't necessary. I said I would marry you."

"But we will live together! If I'm your husband, you'll

have to. It's the law."

"And that's the condition. I set up my house. And you don't bother me or make demands that I live with you, as would be your right as my husband. You must promise. You must give me your solemn oath you will never take this favor I do you and turn it against me."

"I won't—"

"Then I won't marry you."

The look on his face changed. It became mildly incredulous; wounded. "But why?" he asked softly.

Christina sighed. "Your life is so complicated, Adrien. Your women. Your children. Your plots—I am sure this one will no sooner be over than you will devise another; you can't live without the stimulation, the intrigue—"

"That's not true—"

"Of course it is. But I find this all not very conducive to peace of mind. At least not to my peace of mind. In my whole life I have never been churned so, emotionally, as I have in the last eight or nine months."

He turned his back. He went to the corner cabinet, and then returned to the table with a bottle of hard cider. He righted his cup and filled it to the brim. But he turned from her, taking just the cup in his hand. He took a small drink.

After a moment, he laughed; a quick, soft sound. "So the lawyer's daughter would take the title and run." He glanced over his shoulder. "And I'm not even to see the child?"

"You could visit whenever you wished. But you would have to send advance word. I would never be there when you came."

"This is ugly. Do you know that?"

"It's the way it has to be for me to be free of you."

"What's so wrong with being free in the same house with me? You could do as you liked. We could sleep together—when it pleased us both. You could have your—" His voice caught; a moment of tight frustration. He was looking for a word. "Fling"—he found—"with someone else, if that's what you want."

"That's not what I want, and you know it."

He turned and leaned on the chair-back toward her across the table. "I don't know anything anymore." She could see the anger just below the surface, the sharp concentration of his blue eyes. And while part of her cowered at the sight of this, part of her bristled. "I thought I knew you," he said. "A gentle young woman whom I had every intention of asking to marry me for no other reason—"

She stood up with a scrape of her chair. "Adrien, if you throw that meretricious, self-pitying argument at me one more time, I shall walk out on this discussion altogether. You want to use me in this marriage. And, if I weren't usable, I don't doubt for one moment I'd also be unmarriageable."

"You're telling me I'm lying—"

"It's no secret you're a liar! You lie to your grandfather to get him across the Channel. You lie to your ex-wife, to get her quickly out of the way. And this isn't the first time you've tried to lie to me—"

He eased back from across the table. If she had slapped him across the face, he could have been no more incensed.

"I see," he said finally. He looked down at the cup in his hand, then drained it. He made a face into the bottom; a wince. His eyes teared for a second. He squeezed them. "God, this stuff is awful," he murmured, lowering his teacup.

He turned, setting his cup down with a clatter on the sinkboard. He ran his hand back through his hair. Christina felt a twinge of longing at the familiar gesture, at the careless grace that underlay even this simple movement. He stood in that position for some seconds, his hand holding the back of his neck. As if he were lost in some vast and uncharted wilderness; looking for a way out of hostile terrain.

Apparently, he found one. He turned back toward her, composed, his face calm. Cooled, in fact; distant. What the scheming sailor couldn't fix, the earl would put from him, relegating it to a pigeonhole of unpleasant business.

"All right, Christina," he said. "I have ruined your life long enough, haven't I?" A mocking smile worked its way onto his lips. "So you shall have what you ask, except"—he exhaled, determined—"for two conditions of my own— presumptuous as it may be of me to bring any into this discussion.

"First, you must stay with me till the child is born. I want a London doctor to deliver it, not some country midwife." He paced a step away, then turned toward her again. His face had grown harder, colder. "And, two: You're getting a full-fledged title; I want a full-fledged heir. When the child comes, he lives the life he will inherit: He lives with me. *You* may visit."

"Adrien, I can't possibly—"

"If you're going to raise an earl, madam, you can't do it from some country squire's roost. An eagle is raised in an eagle's nest. It can't learn to hunt and fly by pecking at the ground with chickens."

With that pompous, superior comment, he exited out the back door.

He stayed out there a long time, not coming in till long after Christina had gone to bed.

The ceremony took place at nine o'clock the following evening on board the English clipper, the *Silver Jack*. It took only ten quick minutes to make a lawyer's daughter into a countess. Lady Christina Bower Hunt. Papers were signed. Then signed again as duplicates were prepared. Afterward, the ship went out to sea, taking Adrien's grandfather, Thomas, and the last of Adrien's band. Only Le Saint remained in France. And, of course, the bride and groom.

Le Saint remained in Le Havre, to keep a watch on that port. It was from there they hoped to leave. While Adrien and Christina retreated to a little house—only two rooms actually—in the town of Honfleur. They arrived there late, knowing they would have at least three days—and nights—in confined quarters, alone together. With very little to do but wait.

And argue, Christina worried.

But she couldn't have been more wrong.

Adrien put down their bag of food in the front room of their new residence, then followed her into the bedroom. There, he took off his coat, then undid his cravat. As he began to take his shirt from his pants, she asked, "Are you sleeping here, then?"

He looked at her over his shoulder. "Would you rather I didn't?"

The neutral option this question seemed to offer left Christina in the air for a moment. But, in the end, she sighed and answered honestly, "No."

He resumed undressing.

Christina walked to the window, wrapping her shawl more closely around her shoulders.

From her window view, high on the hillside, she could see the sea; the Seine emptying into the Channel. And she could see, across the wide mouth of the river, Le Havre, a boat ride away. There, in the distance, masts of tall ships and the high pulleys and riggings of the docks pierced the horizon. The commercial port from which they would leave stood, like an ugly big sister, on the far bank of the river. While Honfleur, below, was picturesque.

Christina looked down over rooftops to the man-made basin below. It was nothing but sand and a motley collection of marooned small fishing boats now. Little boats, of all colors and shapes, tilted on their sides. The tide would rise in a few hours and right them. Christina only wished she could count on something like that; she felt like one of the little keeled boats. Stuck and waiting. Vulnerable.

Adrien came up behind her at the window. "Don't jump," he said. He began rubbing her back.

She made a surprised laugh and turned in his arms. "I wasn't going to."

His face was sober in the morning light. She realized this was their first opportunity alone, relaxed, without confusion all around them since Paris. Something tightened in the pit of her stomach. She realized, by her answer a moment ago, she had given him permission to make love to her. And that, all disagreements notwithstanding, he intended to.

"Adrien," she asked with despair, "what can you possibly expect of me these next three days? This next month?" She had agreed to stay till the baby came. And agreed, reluctantly, that he should have the child for at least six months out of every year. With or without marriage, the earl had made his point; he had rights and would insist on them.

Adrien pushed his palm gently across her breast, massaging. It was here that his eyes remained as he spoke to her. "What I expect," he said, "is for you to let me show you how wonderful it could be: the two of us, alone together, together in a life in London."

"Oh, God," she groaned. He pulled her to him, bent his head to kiss the hollow of her neck. She accused him softly in his ear. "You *have* started hatching your next plot, you wretch." Her voice caught a second. "Against me."

Chapter 33

The wind coming off the Channel whipped at everything. Immediately, as they had arrived at the docks, it had taken down a long strand of Christina's hair. Now, it alternately blew this wisp, and others, arbitrarily straight back or directly into her face. She had given up trying to keep it out of her eyes—both hands were required to manage her cloak.

Many people stood around her in similar fashion, holding down wayward, billowing clothing, trying to combat the chill in the air. Passengers on the dock fidgeted; they stomped, milled, huddled together as they waited for the ship to allow boarding. While longshoremen worked pulleys or paraded by, carrying crates of cargo, like slow and endless trails of ants.

For over three hours, belongings and cargo had been hauled into the belly of the ship. It rode low in the water; as laden as Christina. She closed her eyes and let out a long breath. The baby felt, this morning, like a tone of carpenters' nails, assorted boxes, this end up. She was tired of standing, tired of carrying her own load on her own feet. Why didn't they board? Why didn't they go?

The man at her elbow was as anxious to leave as she, Christina knew, though in a different sense. Whereas Christina viewed the coming day as a nerve-racking, depressing ordeal, Adrien entered his next adventure as if it were a song. It was a relief to him to at last be able to go and confront Edward Claybourne directly.

The gangplank at last cleared. A sailor waved. And Christina, along with everyone else, began to converge on the small ship. Behind her, she felt the pressure of a masculine hand drop against her spine. Adrien. Possessive to the last. She had been unreasonably cross with him all morning. Every charming gesture, meant to reassure, somehow had just irritated her more.

A pretty young woman pushed by them on the gangplank, then apologized shyly. Christina could tell, by the blush and lowered eyes, that the girl had received one of Adrien's more devastating smiles.

This didn't add to her good humor. Christina glared over her shoulder.

Adrien made an innocent face.

Christina threw an accusing glance at the young woman. The girl was no longer in a rush but was moving with them. She was doing a remarkably poor job of concealing her girlish interest in the man at Christina's back.

Realizing where she looked, Adrien made a face. "Did I accidentally smile? Sorry, I was only being polite." He continued as they came onto the deck of the ship, "Honestly, Christina, I don't know whether to applaud or hide under this onslaught of sudden jealousy." This was not the first time he'd been censured this morning for looking at other women.

He found himself a place at the ship's railing. There he leaned, looked down into the chopping waves, pulling his coat collar up. It was clearly a tactic to try and ignore the girl next to him. But Christina couldn't help but scowl at her. The little idiot kept sliding looks from beneath her fluttering lashes.

After a minute, Adrien risked a glance at Christina. She shot back a black glare at him.

"Well, damn it! I can't help the way she looks at me!"

"You encourage it," Christina hissed as she herself turned to look into the water. "Your damned smile—"

"Is a gift from my parents! When something pleases me, that's the way my face looks. Jesus." He turned around, putting his back—elbows against the rail—to Christina.

"Well, I wish someone would rearrange it for you."

Her voice lost some of its petulance. She began to feel foolish. It was her fault, not his, she thought. She'd been short-tempered all morning. Uncomfortable, impatient, nasty. Frightened.

She was about to tender an apology, when Adrien suddenly grew alert. She turned and followed his gaze—somewhere on the docks. But she could see nothing of interest. Then a sudden shriek from the young woman beside them started a chain of events that left Christina speechless.

The girl had squealed, as if someone had pinched her. When Christina looked, she was confounded to see Adrien smiling at the woman again. Only this time, the girl looked distressed, uncertain whether to return the smile or not.

Noise came from the dock. It began to draw everyone's attention. A half-dozen National Guardsmen, armed with guns with long bayonets, were running, shoving their way up the gangplank. Christina turned to Adrien, alarmed, her mouth half-open in warning. Then her jaw dropped completely. The guardsmen literally had to pull her husband from the young girl beside them. He had been kissing her! He had her wedged against the ship's rail in an incredibly loving embrace!

The baffled young woman who had received this kiss sputtered angrily in English. The guardsmen issued orders; terse, guttural French. Adrien, in a mixture of the two languages, began to explain.

One guard pointed his gleaming bayonet toward the poor girl. "That must be the woman." Christina had never seen a bayonet up close. Polished steel. With a razor's edge, a sharp point. How lethal it looked. "You." He gestured to one of his companions. "Take her. And you" — pointing the dagger's end at Adrien now — "are under arrest in the name of the Republic of France."

They grabbed the young girl's arms. She leaned her weight backward in resistance. She clamored: A gross error was being made. They tugged at her, not understanding her English. A battle ensued.

Adrien joined in with vigorous denials, neither the girl nor he willing to go along peacefully. Both swore, in French and English, that they didn't know each other. Coarse laughter erupted. One armed man poked the tip of his bayonet into the belly of Adrien's wool coat. "You were certainly well-acquainted a few moments ago." The other men joined in. While the other passengers — in respectful homage to the cruel reputation of these nationalized police — slowly pulled back from the scene. Someone, the captain of the ship, she realized, took hold of Christina's arm, and pulled her with them, joining her to the retreating crowd; separating her from Adrien.

Meanwhile, the innocent girl began to cry uncontrollably. As she was pulled forward. The more insistently Adrien and the woman protested, the more crudely the men implied a lie. Then they escalated their fun. A guard pushed. Adrien pushed back. Voices grew louder. Adrien's French grew coarser. And the butt of a gun, coming from nowhere, slammed into his belly.

He doubled over for a moment. Everyone grew quiet. Slowly, in the eerie silence, Adrien straightened up. There was fury on his face. "I was only trying to tell you —"

With a harsh laugh, his assailant plunged the gun butt into his belly once more.

"Son of a bitch." The phrase hissed out along with Adrien's breath. And, head down, he charged into them.

His shoulders took three of the six men. Guns clattered.

Profanity oofed out. Two of the guards were knocked backward and together, toppling over some kegs. The third one fell close enough for Adrien to knee him in the face. The man's nose spurted blood. Then, a second, more organized clattering: The three remaining bayonets leveled. A fourth came up. A retrieved fifth. They pointed, like spokes in a wheel, with Adrien at their hub. He stood bent, eye-level with them.

A new kind of silence. Nasty. Menacing. The guardsman with the bloody nose rose, his face lit with anger. And retribution. He turned his head sideways and spit blood, then without further notice his weapon flashed up. Adrien jerked sideways, narrowly avoiding a malicious stab at his eye. But it caught his cheek. The blade sliced him from temple to chin.

Christina grabbed the railing. She put her hand to her mouth. Adrien's cheek lay open to the bone. Blood poured down his face and neck, running into the collar of his coat. He looked unsteady as he was shoved into formation.

It didn't seem real. The stomp of boots on the planks of the ship. The guards. The woman — stunned speechless by the sudden violence. With Adrien in their midst, marching, stumbling away.

As they started down the gangplank, Christina fought an urge to undo everything her husband had just arranged at the cost of his cheek. There she stood, left safely on the ship, while he and another woman were being carted away. She wanted to yell for them to let him go, to scream that she belonged beside him, or to simply scream his name over and over. Then, as the baby twisted violently inside her, her mind fixed on another alternative.

She let out a long, agonizing scream, and grabbed her swollen belly. Heads whirled to a new diversion. Christina fell to her knees. "Ah! The baby!" she called.

Two women rushed forward. Then another diversion quickly took everyone's attention.

Adrien had shoved the woman in front of him into two of the guards, then folded himself over and smashed backward into the men behind. In an instant, he was over the edge of the gangplank and into the icy January water of the Channel.

Diversion gave way to pandemonium. The guards in quick succession cocked their hammers and fired into the water. One round. Two. Then, whether by design or accident, a shot discharged into the crowd. The shot went wild. But the passengers and crew of the boat scattered, running, screaming; berserk at the threat. People on the docks scattered, riotous.

It took fifteen minutes for the six irate guards to organize themselves through the panic and commotion. One went ashore with the wild and fretful woman prisoner. Two paced the dock, guarding against the escaped man rising from the water in that direction. While the other three came back onto the ship, stalking its edges over the rail, waiting for their lost prisoner to resurface.

But he didn't. Adrien had disappeared completely, after the first crazy seconds of his escape.

The ship pulled out. The captain agreed to send the three guardsmen back to shore in a small boat after they were a half an hour out. The plan was to separate Adrien from the ship, to look for a swimmer trying to follow it. And meanwhile, they would search the ship from stem to stern to see if he had managed to get back on it somehow. If he wasn't on ship or on shore after half an hour, he would be presumed dead. No one could survive the Channel water this time of year for very long.

Christina had been taken to the captain's cabin. She lay there, in his berth, trying to decide how long was enough of this feigned labor. She was impatient to be up. Everyone had been so kind to her, she was feeling strange and uncomfortable about her ruse. She was eager to put it behind her.

But not that eager. The guardsmen were still on the boat. She heaved up awkwardly. It was impossible in such narrow quarters, and with such a large belly, to rise straight up from the bed. As she struggled up, one of the women who had come to her aid peered in at the cabin door.

"Just checking on you, dear. How are you feeling?"

"All right. The pains have stopped—"

"Well, they could start again if you don't rest, you know. If I were you, I'd keep myself in bed until it was the proper time for that babe."

Christina couldn't explain. There was no reason to be concerned for the baby. But the relief she had felt at seeing Adrien escape was gradually turning into anxiety. She didn't want to cause suspicion, but she wanted to get to the deck. "I'm all right, now," she reaffirmed. "I just need some fresh air."

The woman came all the way into the cabin. "Looking for the babe's father, you are," she accused gently. "Don't look so shocked. I saw you come on board with him. Everyone did. No one would have let him get away with what he did to that girl if you hadn't been so rounded." The woman paused. "He must love you very much to try such a thing. If they would slice him up for telling the truth, God preserve him if they caught him in such a large fraud."

"He loves to win," Christina snapped much too quickly.

The woman laughed at her response. It was a warm, friendly laugh. "Don't we all. Well, go then. Look out for the papa of your babe. The guards have just been put onto the small boat." Then more seriously, "They never saw him, you know. I don't mean to be unkind, but you may be looking for someone who is not there."

Christina had walked the full circumference of the ship

372

more than twice. She pulled her cloak around more snugly and resumed a similarly circular monologue she had been having with herself. Adrien was the most resourceful person she knew. He was safe. He was fine. He'd turn up, right there on the boat, at any moment. She must have really believed this, for she kept staring out to sea.

The boat with the French guard disappeared in the distance. The small ship sailed on. Faster than any swimmer could have gone. Christina's cheeks began to sting, the cold whipping against their wetness. When had she begun to cry? She didn't know. But tears were running down her otherwise stoic face. He'd swum back to France, she was telling herself, in a very stealthy manner—

"You're not going to make me chase you halfway round the boat again, are you? I'm going to freeze to death if I can't go inside somewhere."

She turned. And there he stood. Soaking wet, minus his boots and heavy coat. But alive.

She ran into his arms, clasping him, laughing, crying. He was freezing cold and salty wet. But she hugged him and squeezed him over and over just to know he was there.

"Where have you been?" she was saying. "You need a doctor!" She touched the gash down the side of his face. It had stopped bleeding, perhaps from the extreme cold. He was ice. "We have to get you warm."

He smiled, despite the cold, the wound, his lack of dry clothes on a winter day. "I'm much warmer already." He tried to pull her back up against him.

But instead, she tugged at him. "You come with me."

She led him back to the captain's cabin, not knowing what the captain would think of her extending his hospitality. But there was no other place to take him. There was a small stove in the cabin. There were blankets. Perhaps she could even requisition some of the captain's clothes.

Adrien sneezed as they came in. A shiver ran over him. His body twitched from it. He seemed to have to consciously make himself relax. He sat on the berth, lifting her little bundle of clothes there. "These are the captain's quarters, aren't they?" Then another chill hit, running through him so severely it made his teeth chatter.

"Come on. Let's get these off you." She began to pull at his shirt. "Have you been in the water all this time?"

"No. God, no." He lifted his arms. "I managed to get hold of the anchor rope—someone extended it for me. We have a friend on board, I think. Anyway, I climbed up the rope and stayed in the anchor-hold until they came there to look. I hung outside on the anchor itself while they searched that area."

"Ah—" His pants gave, as they came over his knees, nearly toppling Christina. "Here." She shoved him over, piling blankets on him, then crawling under them with him. She nestled against him to lend him her heat. "The captain," she said.

"What?"

"The friend. He pulled me back into the crowd. Then saw that I was taken here. He seems to know you."

Adrien shrugged. "I've never met him." He shivered again. "God, that water was cold—by the way, thank you for your lovely scream. It was helpful. Though I did intend to shove the girl into the guardsmen and take to the water anyway."

"That girl. Oh, Adrien, what you did to her—"

"They'll let her go, once they realize they have the wrong one." There was a pause. "You realize whom they would have if they didn't have her?"

"They would have eventually let me go as well."

He laughed at this. "Perhaps. I could have thrown you in the water, too. By the way, can you swim?"

"No."

"Lucky I didn't then." He laughed again, refusing to take this too seriously.

She sat up to look at him. Color was coming back to the

374

surface of his skin. But he still felt chilly, clammy. His body did not have the normal temperature. Yet she could tell he was going to be all right. She shook her head at him. "You have been too lucky, too often, Adrien. You have come to count on it. And, you can't, you know."

"I don't." His look became more sober. "I don't seem to have much luck with you, for instance."

She looked away, shifting her gaze to the gash down his face. "Here. Let me get something for that."

He took hold of her arm. "How can I convince you I want you? That I want to live with you, love you, be your husband?"

This was not a conversation she wanted. She had avoided it for four days and hoped to continue to do so for another month. She was not up to a mounted assault of Adrien's reasoning and coaxing and logical conciliations. She jerked away. "Not by foolish acts of bravado, certainly. Not by getting yourself half-killed."

She ripped a length of muslin from one of her chemises, tearing it with frustration and fear and anger. Then, none too gently, she pressed it to his face. He flinched, but his face quickly resumed a faint, crooked smile. He continued to stare at her, unabashed. Then he took her ministering hand and kissed the palm.

She took her hand, her eyes away. "And not by being charming with me either, Adrien Hunt—"

The door of the cabin opened. The captain of the ship entered his own quarters, barely glancing at them. He went to a chest, foraged, and produced a pipe.

"You're the English earl, aren't you?" he said matter-of-factly as he turned to pack the pipe. "The one that London's making such a to-do over." He smiled up a second, then puffed as he held a piece of kindling to the bowl of his pipe.

Adrien drew up on an elbow. "Do I know you?"

"Nah. But there's nary a soul what don't wish 'e knowed

you. Right proud o' what you been doing—keeping Madame Guillotine from kissing a whole lot of French necks."

Adrien couldn't respond. It seemed he knew how to deal with a bad reputation. But notoriety for good deeds—public praise—was going to put him a little off-center.

The captain continued. "Ain't been no one so popular since Saint George after the dragon. A real hero, you are." He smacked his lips, blew smoke. "And me a little, now. I figured, soon as those Frenchies came after you, who I had on my ship. It's me what put down the anchor a ways. Figured a fella as smart as you could swim and find it."

"Well . . . I'm grateful. . . ."

The captain waved his hand. "Nah. S'pleasure." He laughed. "I'll be having stories now awhile o'er my ale." He gave the chest on the floor a kick as he walked toward the door. "And if I was you, I'd put me on some decent clothes. You're apt to get quite a welcome on the English side. Man a the hour, all that . . ."

They had come up onto the deck to watch the coast come into view. It was still distant. But England lay on the horizon.

Adrien, dressed warmly if a little snuggly in the captain's clothes, was once more leaning on his elbows, looking out over the ship's wood rail. His hair blew. His skin was flushed a healthier color against a gentler wind. His cheek, seen to by a doctor on board, was held from bleeding by a line of fine stitches. The muscle twitched there periodically, partly from the ordeal of having it sewn, but partly also, Christina thought, because it was a painful wound. Still, he was coming home in better condition—and under better circumstances—than they had had any right to expect.

"You will do all right. You always do all right," she told him.

He furrowed his brow but made no answer. He had been

lost, the last half hour, in the sort of silence Christina had come to dread. It inevitably meant warfare. On his ground. The verbal, the logical.

She glanced at him.

He looked formidably handsome, vaguely sinister. The slice down his cheek, she could see already, was going to work to his advantage. It brought one's eye down the line of his bone, the chiseled cheek, to his broad jaw. It underscored his dark, perfect features, then gave a macabre, mysterious flourish.

The wind blew his hair back from his face. His hair shone, fluttering in the late afternoon sun. Like a flag—a black pirate's flag that waved with bold good health, irrevocable, innate good looks.

Then he sighed, a huge breath; a surrender. "Christina, every time I try to image a future without you, my mind goes blank." After a moment more, "I don't think I have a future without you."

The harbor was gliding up quickly. Like the future itself. Yet Christina, too, found herself not able to see it. Not able to imagine . . . She touched his hand.

The touch held in it the possibility of a reprieve. And Adrien knew it for such. He smiled up at her a moment, just a fleeting thing on his face. Then his face frowned; it paled sheet-white. He shoved her violently away. Christina spun, landing on the slippery deck hard; shocked, hurt, confused.

She heard explosions, three of them. She looked up only to see three red blotches appear along Adrien's body as he was thrown backward against the rigging of the ship. Odd; she remembered the scarf in that instant. It was as if he wore one now; at his head, his chest, his groin.

It dawned on her. Christina screamed. Noise, more screams from the ship, from the dock, right beside them, made a riotous counterpoint to her own heartbeat suddenly clamoring in her chest. She began toward Adrien. Toward

377

where he hung, stunned, by one hand from the ropes of the mast.

On the dock, Christina was horrified to see, three men were standing high on a parapet, with long-barreled guns. Repriming their barrels!

Her progress seemed incredibly slow. She was a foot from him, when the gunmen unloaded their second volley. Three more red stains burst on Adrien's body. His arm, the side of his neck, his belly. His belly!

Someone was screaming so loud and continuously that all her confusion blurred into that sound in her ears. As she reached Adrien's body — now slumped on the deck — she realized the screaming was coming from her own throat. And that Adrien didn't hear it. His body looked lifeless. Eyes closed, he didn't react at all when she slipped in the sea water and blood and fell right on top of him.

She ran her hands over him, her palms turning red, the front of her dress, her cloak covered in his blood. Yet she kept touching him, assessing him. The wound at his head just grazed his temple. The same at his neck, a near miss. His shoulder had caught a ball, but he could live through that. And the chest wound was high, several inches from his heart or lungs; not a fatal shot.

Not fatal, not fatal, she kept saying to herself. The blood at his groin was coming from a wound high on the inside of his thigh. A ball was lodged in the muscle. Then his belly. She stared at this. Then forced herself to open his coat.

"Dear God," she murmured. The ball had entered his coat neatly. There had been just a bubble, a little jewel of blood. But underneath — "Dear God," she murmured again. A bright red stain was spreading across into his shirt. Blood was all over pants. He had been hit squarely in the bowels.

Christina gagged. Her own belly tightened in a heart-rending, sympathetic spasm.

"Adrien!" she screamed. As if she could wake him. "Adrien!"

Someone took hold of her shoulders. She was being pulled from him. She fought this, tried to cling. But Adrien was being lifted away from her. Onto a stretcher.

"Adrien!" she cried out again. His breathing was so shallow. It seemed there one moment, then undetectable the next. Her eyes were fixed to his chest.

"Easy mistress," someone was saying to her. "We'll get him to a surgeon. Move. You can't do him any good lying on top of him."

Her stomach wrenched again. Hard and painful. She looked down. Her huge belly was soaked scarlet. "God!" she cried out loudly. A blur of tears had begun to make her blind as well as bloody and helpless.

On the dock, the gunmen had disappeared. An enclosed wagon had been pulled up to the ship to receive the injured man.

"Who?" Christina asked in confusion. "What happened?" Her mind was blank. He had been there. He loved her. He was dying at her feet. Then being taken away.

"French marksmen is the best anyone can make of it, mum."

"No." Christina's mind could make no sense of it. "They thought they had him dead back in France. And why would they send gunmen ahead? When they could have simply shot him from the docks in Le Havre? Why? Why?" But she was sobbing so badly no one seemed to understand her.

She lurched along, struggling to stay with the litter that carried Adrien's still body. Then she was denied the right to climb inside the wagon; denied the right by a stern presence already there. A small old man—dark, steady eyes that seemed to burn from the shadows of the enclosure. Recognition gripped her. And panic.

"I'll see to him, Lady Hunt," said Edward Claybourne. "You go home. I'll send word."

"No!" She tried to enter the wagon, but two men behind her stopped her. Then another pain in her belly took her breath away. The men had to hold her to keep from doubling over onto the ground.

The wagon started to pull away. Only half-recovered, Christina began to run after it. "Adrien!" she screamed. "No! No!"

She ran fifty yards, breathless, when her eyes widened. The next spasm sent her to her knees. She grabbed herself around the middle.

"Oh, my God—" It was real. The baby was coming.

Sobbing and feeling wretchedly helpless, she pleaded to anyone, to everyone, "Go after them! They're taking him!"

Someone mumbled for her to be calm, that her alarm was out of proportion. They were taking him to a good surgeon.

"They're going to kill him!" she insisted.

But gentle hands were picking her up. "Christina, it's all right." It was Thomas.

Another contraction made her dig her fingers into his neck and shoulders. She let out a guttural exclamation, shocked by the force of the spasm. "The baby's coming," she got out in a whisper.

By the time the pain subsided this time, she was in the carriage. Grand-père was waiting there.

"Don't let them take him away," she murmured to every face she saw, to anyone who would listen. Yet even she knew she was becoming incoherent. "They shot him. They shot him over and over . . . over and over . . . ."

"It's all right, Christina," Thomas was saying. "Everything is being done that can be. They've taken him to St. Catherine's Hospital. They'll save him." Philippe de la Fontaine's wizened, gentle hands reached for her. She leaned into his arms, collapsing, sobbing. To Adrien's grandfather, Thomas said, "It's the baby. I could feel her whole body contracting in my arms as I carried her."

"I saw an inn at the top of this street," Philippe suggested. "We'll take her there and send for a midwife."

"A doctor," Christina protested weakly. "Adrien wants a doctor."

"All right, a doctor."

"And Thomas—" Christina gripped his forearm as hard as she could. She focused her eyes on him. "You go to the hospital. See that he gets there. Stay with him. Then come tell me how he—aiy!"

Another contraction interrupted. How could anything be so strong?

"All right." Thomas gently smoothed his hand over her belly. A strange emotion played for a moment over his face. "I'll go to him. If that's what you want." Then to Philippe, "You take care of her. I'll come as soon as I know something."

Thomas closed the door, and the carriage lumbered off, up the steep cobbled street that sloped away from the sea.

Part III

Shadows in the Dark

Chapter 34

"You're doing fine," the doctor told her cheerfully.

Christina fell back. The all-encompassing pressure retreated once more to just a dull ache low in her back. She sank — damp, rumpled — into a mound of humid covers, twisted sheets. She felt limp, not fine.

Her waters had broken. The baby had descended. And the opening in her body, like a magic door, was materializing. These facts had been murmured to her over the hours, along with other encouraging words. Yet, to Christina, everything that happened in the tiny room at the inn seemed to be happening in some distant reality. As if she had indeed slipped through some strange doorway into another dimension. Where was Adrien? she asked periodically. How was he? Where was Thomas? Yet, no one told her anything. She was given no information that really mattered to her.

She stared up at the canopy, waiting for the next pain.

Over the last six hours she had memorized her little corner of this room. It was dim, gray, colorless. She lay in the shadows — the main window was blocked by a large screen that had been erected for the sake of her modesty: Friends and relatives had gathered on the other side of the partition. Her father. Evangeline and Charles. Adrien's grandfather. Sam. Others. Several people she didn't even know. Two members of Parliament. As well as — she realized only vaguely how rude she had been, not fully able to comprehend — the Prince of Wales and his cousin the Princess Anne. Christina knew that the general feeling in the little inn was one of honored excitement. Pleasure. Joy. Nobility was being born. In the presence of royalty. Yet on her side of the screen, she could have screamed at them all. It was Adrien's child . . . . Where was Adrien?

The doctor came around the screen again, and Christina quickly rose up on an elbow. "Mr. Lillings has to have returned by n — ah! Ah!" A new swell of pain cut her off. It demanded all her attention.

Christina grasped her belly, crying out. The force, the incredible pressure still amazed her. All she could do was race for her breath. And look for the other side of the contraction.

"You're doing very well, Lady Hunt," the doctor reaffirmed as he unceremoniously lifted the sheet that covered her legs.

She didn't care what he did to her. She counted to herself. At sixty-seven seconds, the last contraction had peaked; she had been able to see the end of it.

She tried not to rush the count now: sixty-eight, sixty-nine, seventy . . . seventy-three, seventy-four, seventy-five . . . . She gasped another breath. Where was it? God, they were getting long. She clutched the covers.

"Easy, my dear lady. Gentle. Ah, yes. I think we shall see a crown very soon — "

Christina was oddly disinterested in this news. She drew a deep breath as the pain leveled off and forced herself to submit quietly to the medical hands. Is this really what Adrien had wanted? Another man to move so freely there?

"Mr. Lillings," she gasped out. "He has to have returned by now."

"My dear countess, I can't let a gentleman in — "

"He's here?"

"He's downstairs."

385

"I want to see him."

"Now, now—" He patted her knee solicitously.

She rose up on her elbows and directed an emphatic stare at him between her legs. "I want to see him now. Get him up here."

Standing at the foot of her bed, Thomas looked tired and haggard. His coat revealed traces of unsympathetic elements; mist or light rain. His face, the pallor, revealed that this was the least of his worries. He was a man who had been through an ordeal. Christina's heart dropped. In the dim light he looked a hundred years old. And this could only mean one thing—

"He's very bad off," she said.

Thomas looked down at his wet hat, wiped at its brim. When he spoke, his words were hardly audible.

"He took a ball in the abdomen. Another through a lung. And one directly through his brain. He was hit other places, but any of these three would have killed him. He never even regained consciousness, Christina."

She raised herself up, almost sitting. "You're wrong," she said flatly. "The chest wound was high, near his shoulder. His head was hardly grazed."

Thomas only shook his head. "I stayed," he said. "I saw the body, Christina—"

"So did I. Only the wound in his belly was serious."

He shrugged. "Whatever. The end result is the same. I'm sorry."

"No."

His eyes lifted to her. They held impatience; an accumulation of small annoyances, unspoken grievances.. "Christina," he said. "I know you were in love with him. But love can't make someone alive when they're not." There was both cruelty and pain in the way he pronounced the words: "He's dead," he said emphatically.

"Thomas, I saw—"

"So did I. So did Claybourne. And so did Sam, if you don't trust us. Anyone could have seen him who wanted to. There was no question—"

"I want to! Ah, wait—" She put a hand on her abdomen. Another contraction.

She drew her breath up and away from it, wishing she could withdraw her body and continue this conversation. But the pressure rose, gripped, compressed her around the middle. She bit her lip.

"Thomas—" She held her hand out.

His face panicked as he took her hand. "Doctor!" he called. Thomas came around the bed, trying to support her. The doctor hurried in.

Christina raised herself up farther, pushing back on Thomas, gripping, pushing back against the bed. And pushing down with the muscles of her abdomen.

"Don't push!" the doctor said sharply.

And Christina was left bewildered, her body telling her to do one thing, the doctor demanding she do another.

He was frowning over the sheet. "It's not the crown," he murmured. "It's the buttocks. The baby didn't turn in the womb." He was rolling his sleeves up farther, then extracting instruments from his bag. His attitude had changed to one of intense concentration; worry.

She watched him, tight-lipped, anxious, as he came around to her. Something cold, a doctor's instrument, touched her. There was a mild burning.

"Now. Push," the doctor said.

And it was like being set free. She bore down, the contraction working with her. All the pain seemed magically transformed into supernatural energy. It was going to be all right. The doctor, the surgeon Adrien had wanted there, knew how to cope with upside-down births, upside-down lives . . . .

She thought of Adrien. She longed for him to be there.

387

To hold on to. To squeeze and push against. To hold her and touch her.

But there was only Thomas.

"Ah—Oh, God—" She gasped three quick breaths and pushed again. Then a slight smile appeared on her face; the light of achievement, of discovery. Breech or not, she could feel the child coming into the world. She puffed and panted, laughed and cried. Then a tiny mew of noise, soft sounds she had never heard before—And a healthy male child was held up for her to see.

"Adrien!" she cried out.

The sight of the child so affected her. The long proportions. The full head of black hair. The fair little eyes.

Behind her, Thomas put her weight down gently. He kissed the top of her head. Then she heard him go over to the basin in the corner and be violently sick.

Three days later found Christina still in bed. But it was a different bed. And under very different conditions.

Against the advice of everyone, she had transported herself and her infant son into London. There, from Adrien's huge mahogany bed, in his house on Hanover Square, she dealt with his agents, bankers, and lawyers. She was trying to hold his estate together, yet prevent it from going into probate.

"Good day, Lady Hunt." A solicitor nodded to her as he left the bedchamber. His footsteps could be heard to echo on the landing, then down the stairs.

Thomas, standing by one of the French windows, turned. "You're being so foolish, Christina. And not just from a legal point of view. Adrien's not coming back. To build yourself up, counting on—"

Quieter footsteps entered. The nursemaid. "He's awake again, madam. Shall I bring him?"

"Yes." Christina turned her attention back to Thomas.

"I'm not building anything up. I'm merely doing what I must. The estate is not going through the courts until a few questions are answered to my satisfaction. And now—" she pushed a pile of papers from her lap, "that you have expressed it, I will thank you to keep your wishful opinion to yourself."

"Wishful?" he chafed.

"This reminds me, dear Thomas, of when your brother went away to school. And you told me he had gone away for good, so I had to play with you—"

"Goddamn it, I saw the body—"

"With the face blown off."

"He was hit in the face."

"He wasn't." A little quieter, "How *did* Claybourne know he was coming in that morning and on what boat?"

This threw him. Thomas stuttered a reply. "I—I don't know what you're talking—"

"You do, I'm afraid. Everyone else might believe it was French assassins, but I don't. Those marksmen were Edward Claybourne's. I don't have a doubt in the world that is true."

Thomas turned to look out the window again.

"Did you?" Christina asked gently. "Did you tell Claybourne?"

There was a long pause before he answered. His voice was flat and distant. "I never thought he would kill him, Christina. You must believe that."

"Why?" she said. "You were friends. *We* were friends."

"Are," he corrected. "I did it so you could get free of him. I thought Claybourne would arrest him, hold him. Then you could be off. That is what you wanted, isn't it? Back in France when I last saw you there?" He sat in the chair by the window and bent his head into his hand. "God," he said. "How did this ever get so complicated?"

The nursemaid arrived with the baby. Little Xavier, pronounced as the French—as Adrien—would say it: *Zav-*

yay. Christina's little savior. She smiled as she took the bundle.

Thomas frowned, then came forward. Again, he was standing at the foot of her bed. He reached to lean on the canopy frame overhead. "Do you want me to pack up and get out?" he asked. He had spent the night in the house.

"No." She threw a small blanket over her shoulder for modesty, then drew the baby to her breast. Much to everyone's horror, she was nursing her infant herself. "I have made some terrible mistakes myself. Out of stupidity and jealousy. I'm not going to make things so easy on you as to simply cast you out. Instead, I thought I'd offer you a way to redeem yourself."

"How?"

"Help me."

"Do what?"

"Find him."

He made a skeptical laugh. "You're as insane as he was."

She gave him a dry look. "Will you or not?"

He let out a huge sigh. "Of course."

"Good." She looked down. There, beside her, among a host of other papers, was a death certificate. Adrien Phillippe Charles Xavier Hunt, aged thirty-five. "Now, it seems to me, if Adrien is not dead, two things have to be true. One: That is not his body in the casket in the Hunt tomb at St. Mary's. And, two: Some doctor somewhere has to have treated a man with a very bad stomach wound —"

Chapter 35

"This way, doctor."

The doctor followed Edward Claybourne down a narrow, steep run of stairs. At places, as he descended, the stone walls all but touched his shoulders. He was broader than Claybourne, heavier. And younger, though not by many years.

Light closed off slowly from above. The walls rose higher and higher. Dutifully, Angus Townsend followed Claybourne's swinging lantern, though he could probably have found his own way down these stairs in the dark. He had been down them several dozen times, most recently just three days ago. Usually, he came to this prison to sign death certificates. But occasionally, as now, Claybourne relied on him for his actual medical ability. And always, Claybourne relied on him for his silence. That was understood, part of the happy little bundle of coins at the end of each visit. You do what you're told and say nothing. Angus was good at saying nothing and was relatively good at appearing to do what he was told: These were the cardinal rules by which he survived a difficult marriage to a woman he no longer even liked. He did what he was told. He said nothing. And he took on extra work, including prison work, if it would keep him away from home.

"How is the wife?" Claybourne chatted.

"The same. And your man? How's he?" Three days ago,

391

Townsend had removed a steel ball from the belly of one of Claybourne's "special prisoners."

"Well. Too well, probably. You'll see. He's got the constitution of an ox."

Keys clanked and jangled at the cell door. Then the light of their lantern opened up the little room to them in a flood. The prisoner, on a cot, raised his arms against the glare. His wrists were bound together.

"Well, at least he's conscious. That's an improvement." The doctor set his bag on a little table. He looked about the room. It was as he'd remembered it. Cleaner than the usual cells of this prison. Austere. One table. One cot. One blanket. No windows. No light.

"If I weren't so interested in moving him, I wouldn't bother you again," Claybourne began. "But he's developed a slight fever."

"I don't mind."

"Here, help me move him onto his back. Careful!" The prisoner struck out with his bounds hands at the English minister.

Claybourne leaped back. Then laughed. "Not quite so quick as usual, eh, La Chasse? Can't even reach an old man. But you are lucky. You are going to live. The one ball that might have killed you just pushed your intestines aside—like a marble dropped into a bowl of spaghetti." He chuckled. "So—" the old man was very cheerful about the whole thing, "since you're awake, we'll summon a little extra protection, hm?" He yelled over his shoulder toward the cell door, "Guards!" To the doctor, "Please be a little wary. He can be a lamb, or he can be a regular handful. You never know quite what he's going to do."

A regular handful. Townsend contemplated this as he laid out his instruments. The man on the cot, he noted, was already perspiring heavily. The muscles of his arms jerked; involuntary spasms. And all this from the effort of one swing. The doctor shook his head. Only a man dead and cold could have been less dangerous.

Nonetheless, three guards tromped into the room. They brought two more lanterns. The cell virtually blazed with light and long shadows. The prisoner turned his face against the wall.

Claybourne spoke to the guards. "We'll get these bandages off. You hold his arms. You, his legs."

There was no resistance. The man's arms were pulled up and back and held firm by one man. A guard at the other end leaned on his legs. Ridiculous precautions. The prisoner's trousers were already ripped up one leg to his waist, allowing access to the dressings on his thigh and belly. And the old hands of his chief tormentor began to yank and fumble with the bandages.

The doctor brought a lantern closer to the prisoner's face. The man flinched. And the doctor let out a surprised exclamation. The prisoner was gagged! Tightly, into the bite of his mouth! It was absurd, but more and more, Townsend was beginning to feel party to torture, not healing. What man could possibly merit such treatment as this — wounded as he was, then bound and gagged in a dark cell?

The doctor reached down to turn the man's face. "Let me see your eyes, son." But the man jerked his head away.

"Hold his head." Claybourne gestured to the third guard standing by the door.

He came forward and grabbed the man by the hair, pulling his head straight back until the veins and cartilage in his throat were in sharp relief.

"He's not cooperative, Angus," remarked the old minister.

"He might be more so if he were treated less like a wild beast."

The old minister stopped fumbling with the bandages long enough to look at the doctor. "I can see you disapprove. But let me make the situation clear. This man has caused me more trouble than any dozen have in my last

393

thirty years. *No* precaution I've taken has not been worth the trouble."

"But the gag. Is that really —"

"Necessary? Yes. I didn't order it until yesterday. Hopefully, my last mistake with him. He talks a smooth story. And one very foolish guard believed his promises of money and protection. Pah! Fool. The guard has paid for his stupidity. He is in a similar cell at this very moment." The minister gave Townsend a meaningful look. "There is no excuse anyone could offer me to explain the escape of this man. Do you understand what I'm saying?"

Yes, Angus Townsend was beginning to understand quite well. The minister's usual businesslike detachment was missing in the case of this prisoner. Terribly missing. And the old minister was a terrible enemy to have — especially at such close range and liberty.

Townsend took off his glasses and cleaned them on the tail of his coat. "I need to examine his eyes," he said.

Room was made for him to come closer. The man's rough-bearded face was forced around.

It was not a face Townsend had been prepared for. He had seen it while the man had been unconscious, of course. But awake, the man's face took Townsend aback. It was intelligent. Full of knowledge of the situation. And full of unconcealed hostility. What normally made men meek, made this man angry. A shame, Townsend thought. This was probably not the best attitude under the circumstances.

The doctor touched the long red wound that ran down one bearded cheek. Someone else had seen to some stitches there. It was healing all right. But it would mar an otherwise strikingly handsome face. Fine bones. Unusual coloring. Townsend had been too busy trying to keep the man alive to notice such details the night they had brought him in. Who was this man? he wondered

The doctor contented himself with examining the man's eyes, the nodes of his neck — trying to ignore the fact that

Claybourne was simultaneously carrying on a sadistically joyous and one-sided conversation with a man held down for him by three guards.

"We take no chances with you, eh, La Chasse?" He gave a cheerful pat to the wound on the man's thigh as he took the last of the bandages off. "My marksmen were so good at making it appear a fatal shooting, it almost was. But then, we had to have it close. Needless to say, I am delighted you've lived." The old fingers started to undo the heavy bandages at the man's gut. "Unfortunately for you no one else is too delighted. You're dead, you know, to the rest of the world." The prisoner wasn't paying attention. The doctor could tell that the area of the second injury was very tender. The prisoner had begun to sweat again. A tenseness pervaded his body that said he fully expected an intentionally painful time of it.

The old man made no attempt to disappoint him. The prisoner flinched through the minister's words, hardly aware of them. "A lovely hero's burial. Very touching. I myself spoke movingly at the funeral. You became too dangerous for conventional charges and trial, my dear man. Even if I could find a law you'd broken, you were above the law in most people's eyes. But not beyond my reach."

As Claybourne began opening the prisoner's shirt, the doctor was reminded of one of the reasons this man had survived. He was a sturdy, strongly built man, in what would have been excellent condition before this disaster befell him.

"A superb creature." The old man's voice reaffirmed the doctors thoughts. His old hands ran over the man's chest. "I'm so glad I've been able to preserve you—in a sense. By the way, did I tell you? You have a son. I'm told he looks just like you. Not that you'll ever see him."

The prisoner closed his eyes. As if he might will himself away from all the pain Claybourne kept heaping on him.

"Has he been getting any sleep?" the doctor interrupted. He moved Claybourne aside and opened the last sticky bandage at the main wound.

"I don't know. I don't think—"

The doctor looked at Claybourne. "Haven't you been giving him the sedative I left?"

"No."

"Why not?"

"I am out to save his life, not make it comfortable for him."

"You have to give him the sedative. If he doesn't sleep, he'll get weaker."

"As it is, I can hardly contain him, he's so damn strong. He's bound, you know, because he knocked a guard unconscious the first night after his surgery."

"Well, if he were sedated, he couldn't do that, could he?" Townsend finished with wiping the wound and went over to his bag to get clean bandages. "He's in considerable pain."

"Good—"

"It's not for your gratification I mention it." He brought the bandages over. "Look. The muscles of his belly twitch involuntarily at the merest touch. He is in a sweat from just what little we are doing to him now. You're going to have to listen to me, Claybourne. He can't sleep like this. You have to give him a sedative, or he won't last thirty-six hours. And the fever will take him into unconsciousness long before that—"

Claybourne didn't like this. He frowned.

"Remove the gag," the doctor instructed. "I want to hear him breathe. Also, if you are really interested in his living, he needs a cup of water down him, one way or another, every hour or so—to help his body cope with the fever. His limbs should be free to move. This would improve his circulation. And he needs extra blankets and clean, warm clothes—"

Claybourne laughed. "You know, he is a prisoner of the

Crown, not visiting royalty. A prisoner, Townsend."

The doctor shrugged. "You will have to decide whether he is more your prisoner or my patient."

Townsend waited to be stopped as he took his scissors and cut the gag off the man's face. He didn't know how much good his boldness would do the man—or himself for that matter—but something bold needed to be done.

The prisoner's eyes had opened to watch him. They shifted to Claybourne, then back to him. Again, the doctor had the impression of intelligence.

"I speak some French. Would you prefer that?" Townsend asked the man.

Claybourne intervened quickly. "He would be a fairly poor spy if he didn't speak good English, wouldn't he? I want to know exactly what is said between you."

"Here, does it hurt here?" The doctor pushed and released his abdomen, checking for loose blood in the cavity. The man wet his lips, tried to speak, then shook his head *no*. "Would someone get him some water?" Back to the man on the cot, "Have you moved your bowels since the surgery?"

The prisoner's mouth almost seemed to smile. Again he shook his head to indicate *no*.

"Well, you will. There is rumbling in your belly, which is a very good sign. Your organs have decided, despite the insult, to resume. I want to know when. All right?"

The smile materialized fully for a moment. The man had a very fine set of teeth. Straight. Very white. They reflected a lifetime of good food, good health. He nodded.

"Now—" water arrived; the man took a drink, "tell me about your head. Does it ache?"

He indicated it did.

"Where? How? Is your vision all right?"

And another small shock. The raspy voice that answered was educated. One didn't miss the accent; very upper-class, very English. "It's fine." He closed his eyes, opened them.

"But I can't tell you where—" he swallowed, "where my head aches. My belly feels—feels like there's an axe in it—"

"I know. I'm going to leave you some laudanum."

The man shook his head. He didn't want it. "It would take a quart—Get me opium. A pure finger." His voice went lower, to a tone that alarmed for its sincerity: "Or hemlock. I don't care which. I want out of here," he said hoarsely. "Get me something that will take me away—"

The room swam. But Claybourne was a bloody genius at keeping a man conscious, Adrien had discovered. The cot was set at a slight angle. Adrien's head was an inch or two lower than his feet. It gave him a headache, but it kept the blood flowing to his brain. Claybourne wanted him in pain, and he wanted him awake to feel it.

The pain was not the worst thing, however. Adrien had never known such a sense of isolation as he felt in this place. To be one against a multitude of guards, examiners, doctors, tormentors . . . To be struck, poked at, moved about, talked over like a dumb animal . . . No friends, not an ally in sight. Never had he been so utterly alone.

And now, if Claybourne's taunt was true, even Adrien's outside world, his outside hope, had been closed off to him. Did everyone really believe him dead? No lawyers trying to free him? No friends complaining of his treatment? Was there no one even looking for him?

Adrien closed his eyes and turned his face toward the wall. He didn't doubt that this was true. And the knowledge registered like a blow; another loss. It was getting hard to keep score, there were so many now.

The ungodly pain. The narrow cell. The dark, damp silences—broken only by the sounds of his imprisonment. The rattle of keys. Boots that stomped in and out of his cell. Loud, manhandling confrontations—always so profoundly one-sided . . .

But at the top of any list of losses was the one Adrien tried not to think about too much. It was too painful. Still, in his dreams, he sometimes heard the sound of Christina's voice. And, if he wasn't careful, he would find himself remembering her softness and warmth, which would only serve to make his present circumstances all the more harsh and unbearable. How he missed her. How often he turned in his sleep, in his pain, feeling for her in the dark. Part of him was dazed by her absence; she had become so much a part of his life, he could barely comprehend being on this hard, cold cot without her.

No Christina. No one here for him at all. No one but Claybourne. Adrien couldn't even count on himself.

He had already proven he had the strength to hit one guard, and the wits to bribe another. And he had already proven that this was nothing. Pathetically inadequate.

Just outside his cell door, Adrien could hear his last ally, drifting off, pronouncing his doom.

"Frankly, I don't think he's doing as well as you're leading yourself to believe." The doctor's voice echoed along the stone walls. "He is slow to respond. He seems a little disoriented. Don't judge everything, Edward, by how lucky you've been so far. That man shouldn't even be alive."

"Lucky, faugh. I planned—"

"Yes, you planned. On advice gleaned from a theoretical chat over a tankard of ale. We spoke of lead balls to the center of the body, not of a bloody massacre—"

"Come now, Angus—"

"Don't 'come-now-Angus' me. The only reason that man is alive is that his body was so damn mysteriously cold. He hardly bled, all things considered. I am furious that my casual discussion blew a hole in that man's gut—"

"Not so furious, I trust though, that you would like to see your wife stand trial—"

Townsend heaved a loud sigh. "That is always the most bizarre threat, Edward. You know I can barely tolerate the sight of Mildred—"

"Yes. And I know you will protect her to your grave—you have already jeopardized your career, your own life, in trying to keep her 'little mistake' from coming to light . . . ." Their steps grew faint. Though Claybourne could be heard, continuing in confident solicitude: "We go through this every time, Angus. You want your delicate sensibilities to be on record. I understand. No one likes this sort of work. But it's necessary. France does this to ours, I assure you—it's hardly more than a game. We'll get the information we need from him, then trade him for one of ours. . . ."

Adrien had no idea how much later it was when he was nudged in the ribs. Claybourne's face materialized through the smoky light of a lantern.

"Wake up." The old minister reached over him. The sour smell of his body, the pit of his arm, crossed Adrien's face. Adrien's hands were untied. Blood rushed into them. He worked his fingers, then his arms. The shoulder that had taken a ball would not move at first. He massaged it as Claybourne spoke to him.

"Don't get any sudden notions," Claybourne cautioned. "Gregory is at your head." He indicated with a nod.

Adrien could see only the shadow on the wall. Huge, shifting. But this was evidence enough. He remembered Gregory, the giant from the abandoned manor house.

"And don't get too excited about the doctor's concern. You and every trace of you will be gone from here by tomorrow." Claybourne smiled.

Adrien's feet were untied, and a tin mug was thrust toward him.

"Here. Sit up and drink this."

Adrien groaned as he moved his legs over the side of the bed. Any movement that involved his abdominal muscles took considerable patience. He could hold the pain elsewhere to a minimum. But there was no avoiding the ache

400

that cut to the center of his body. Then, the most exasperating effect of any movement: As he pushed himself up on his arms, the room went black in splotches. He had to stop, hold for a moment. . . .

The next he knew, he was back on the cot, stretched out, and Claybourne was no longer smiling.

"Here." Adrien's head was lifted. "It's only water. Drink it."

Adrien closed his eyes, turned his head away; half-reaching for the unconsciousness that had held him for just a few seconds.

"Come on." His head was jostled. "I'll tell you about your son."

Some blankets were bunched up, propped under his neck for a pillow. The tin mug was placed in his hand. Adrien took a draught of water. "My wife?" he asked hoarsely.

Claybourne smiled and pulled a chair over. "She's never been better. She looks wonderful in black." He crossed his legs thoughtfully. "What a striking woman she is." He leaned a hand on the cot and lowered his voice in mock-frank assurance. "And, I'm not the only one who thinks so. Your friend, Mr. Lillings, is stumbling all over himself to console the pretty widow. He has even moved into your house." Claybourne waved a hand. "But, of course, your grandfather is there to chaperone. A perfectly fine arrangement, despite gossip."

Adrien stared at him over the mug. This was more information than he'd wanted.

"Oh. I almost forgot." The old minister reached into a pocket. "I have something for you." He took out a thin little package, rolled in paper, twisted at both ends. He opened it then held it out on the bony surface of his hands.

"Christ—" Adrien spilled the water as he recognized what was being offered. Though he didn't dare reach for it. "And what," his voice whispered, "am I supposed to do to get that?"

401

It was a finger of opium. Glossy black. With an odor, remembered, like the taste of a woman. He could already sense the bitter fumes in his mouth. Adrien closed his eyes, and let his head drop back. God, did he want that.

Claybourne laughed. "You don't have to do anything. Here."

The drug was put — tacky, slightly warm — into his hand. Adrien stared at this unexpected development, looking for the catch. Then it occurred to him. "I can't swallow it. It would make me throw up." He wet his lips, wondering how much energy to waste on this. He was certain Claybourne was not here to improve his circumstances. "I need a piece of metal —" he began. "Something that heats quickly. A candle. And a reed. Or something else I can roll into a tube —"

"No." Claybourne smiled, then made a face. " 'Hemlock.' Honestly. Did you really want that poor man to think you were suicidal?" he asked.

With a swipe of his hand, Adrien shoved the tin cup, the water, the drug —

And giant hands from above latched onto his arm. A grip like a bulldog's jaws. Adrien was yanked backward by the offending arm. His whole abdomen arched. It was pulled taut.

"A-ah!" With his other hand, Adrien tried to grab his belly; as if he could somehow hold himself together. While stars shot before his eyes. White pain. Edged in and out with blackness —

He could hear Claybourne chastising the hulking shadow. "Give me that water over there. . . . That was much too rough; I don't want him to pass out . . . ."

Half a pitcher of water came down into Adrien's face. All he could do was sputter and try, in great gasps, to catch his breath.

Claybourne was standing over him again. "No tantrums," he said, looking down. The opium was retrieved and laid

402

on Adrien's heaving chest.

"You can—" Adrien hissed, "stuff it—up your ass—"

The Old Man laughed. "There you go. I knew you would be clever enough to figure a way."

Adrien turned slowly to his side, curling toward the wall. Claybourne leaned over him. There was a change of tone in his voice. He whispered, "Is she a very nice woman?"

Adrien didn't answer. He was nudged, and the question was repeated, closer in his ear.

Adrien knew who he was speaking of. Christina. And this made him go weak himself. Adrien could detect Claybourne's interest, his curiosity. And he agonized over it. If he hadn't married her, he told himself, Claybourne wouldn't have bothered. The marriage had protected him—so Adrien had thought—and exposed her. It declared her importance to him. Adrien was beside himself as he realized that Claybourne, almost certainly, was watching her now, inquiring . . . . And there was no way to warn her, no way to protect her at all—

"Your wife," Claybourne whispered. "Is she a kind sort? Compassionate?"

Adrien still wouldn't answer.

"What I'm getting at," the old voice said, "is that I think she likes him. And he's in great pain."

Adrien glanced up, looking into the face that overshadowed his. "I don't know what you're talking about."

"Mr. Lillings, of course. Shall I tell you what I've observed?"

"No."

Claybourne smiled. "Mr. Lillings. If she's there, he doesn't see anyone else in the room. His mouth goes dry; he keeps wetting his lips. And when she's not looking"—Claybourne gave his low, gravelly laugh—"my God, it's indecent! His eyes drop all over her." Softly, "He wants to sleep with her." A pause. "Like a man in bad pain wants opium. Do you think she'll let him?"

403

Adrien rolled his face back toward the wall. "I don't know."

"Shall I find out? Your new gardener in London—"

"No."

Claybourne's dry laughter reverberated through the cell. It was a sound of satisfaction.

Then a wrinkled, spotted hand reached over Adrien to the bed where the opium had rolled. Claybourne's fingers retrieved it delicately from against Adrien's chest. The drug was laid on his cheek. Adrien closed his eyes.

While old fingers stroked his hair. "I'm going to leave you alone with this and your imagination," the Old Man said. "If you can't think of something to do with it, I assure you, we will. And, my dear boy, remember it relieves all sorts of pain, not just the physical." There was a short laugh. "Oh, and please be aware of another thing. An insensitivity to pain is an easy enough thing to verify—we will know whether you have been a good boy and taken your medicine or not."

Chapter 36

The weather was bright and clear. Everything was still; snow-covered. Like a scene on a museum wall; a translucent watercolor, washed from sunny blue to perfect, undisturbed white.

Christina Hunt marched into this picturesque landscape, leading seven reluctant men.

The high iron gates creaked as they pushed their way past. Once inside, all eight of them paused. Involuntarily, in unison. It was reverence that made them stop, perhaps. Or sheer awe. St. Mary's Cemetery, just outside of London, held the dead of a great many families. More than a hundred graves. As well as a large structure, a tomb, at the rear.

Fresh snow crunched underfoot as they began to thread their way around tombstones and the mounded earth of graves. Their breaths trailed behind and mingled in low conversation. Slowly, they made their way across the frozen ground. They walked toward the distant tomb.

Built in the classic style, it stood two hundred yards off, at the back of the cemetery. Marble block, Ionic pillars, classic Greek arches; peering through the bare branches of winter-dry trees. It belonged to the Hunt family. It sat there on a small hill, slightly higher than everything else around it, proclaiming that family's privilege and position, even here among the dead.

Christina, Thomas, and Winchell Bower walked along silently, moving gradually in front of the others. Edward Claybourne was part of the group left behind; a clutch of necessary officials. He spoke to the other public men by first name. As they walked along, Christina realized he knew each one—knew their interests, the names of their children, their wives, their personal circumstances. They formed a cohesive group. Five government officials, colleagues, on a public errand, sent out into a cold winter day by a legal system and a magistrate in London who didn't know any better . . .

"It's an interesting structure," Claybourne could be heard saying. "Built originally in about 1200. Though the present façade is much newer . . ." As if he were giving a tour; trying to make this trip somehow worthwhile.

This graveyard trip had been fought for more than two months. Every sort of paper obstruction had been put before it. "Truly," Claybourne had told Christina to her face just the day before, "had you less influence—or a less capable ally somewhere in the legal system, I would never indulge such pure female hysteria."

And even her "capable ally" had his reservations. "Christina," her father murmured as they walked. "Are you still sure you want to do this?"

"Yes."

"It's not going to be pleasant. No matter what we find—"

At the entrance to the tomb, Thomas held out his arm to guide Christina down the steps. The structure was half in the earth, half out. One descended between two embankments of dirt—

They stopped. There was a man sitting on the bottom step, in front of the high arched door.

He stood up quickly, turning, dusting his hands off on

his coattails. "Dr. Billings is ill," he began.

Then Claybourne spoke from above. "What are you doing here, Townsend?"

"Billings is . . . indisposed again. His wife called me."

"That idiot—" Abruptly, Claybourne cut himself off and put on a more businesslike tone. "Very well. You will have to do." Claybourne came down into the earth foyer, jangling a set of keys out of his pocket.

Another official came forward and broke the state seal. The burial place had been declared, two and a half months before, a national monument. The Crown had taken over its maintenance. And its security.

Claybourne darted a frowning glance at the newly arrived doctor, then opened the door.

It was pitch-black. Dank. A hole in the earth. It reeked of mold and damp stone. Christina reached out to the pillar by the entrance—the only thing she could see—as the others went past. She stood there trying to orient herself. The cold of the stone pillar came through her glove with a jolt. She withdrew her hand abruptly.

A torch flared. Then another. And another. Claybourne himself carried the fire from one to the next, igniting flames along the wall. The tomb, with its vaulted ceilings and grey-white columns of marble, materialized from the darkness.

The room was shaped like a cross. The torches displayed it like some wavering nightmare of overlapping shadows: an arrangement of walls and arches and stone sarcophagi, radiating from a marble tablelike structure in the center.

The group congregated there. The table, Christina thought, looked more like some pagan sacrificial altar than a suitable place for its apparent Christian use: Candle wax covered its surface. A stand of iron spokes held the remains of candles, offerings long since melted into an amalgam of dirty tallow and burnt wicks.

"Townsend," Claybourne said, "come with me. We'll let

407

you do the honors of primary identification." Claybourne knew exactly which sarcophagus held what they had come for. One, inscribed and elaborately ornamented, was recently sealed. As the rest of them followed, he spoke to Christina. "Perhaps you will reconsider, my lady. This is not a healthy thing for a young woman to pursue—"

"I want it opened."

"As you wish."

She knew, from his tone, he would spare her nothing, then, after this.

He motioned to one of the men, the gravekeeper who had met them at the gates. This man came forward and, with a huge crooked bar, wedged the heavy lid. The stone lid was well sealed. It took four such attempts, then all the men present to lift off what showed itself to be an eight-inch slab. Christina shivered. No man would ever be able to push such a sheet of rock off alone. She thought of Adrien. And the huge weight . . .

Inside the sarcophagus was another box. Dark hardwood. Elaborately carved and polished. The fittings made of gold. There was inlaid ivory. Jade. At either end, belts made of leather were slipped down and worked underneath this coffin. And, slowly, it was raised. High enough to allow the hinged lid to open. The belts were secured.

Thomas squeezed Christina's hand. Her father touched her shoulder. Claybourne brought the doctor in front of her.

"The death certificate?" Claybourne asked.

She withdrew it from her reticule and handed it over the doctor's shoulder.

With no more preamble than that, the lid was unlatched and raised.

It was very heavy. In the end, Thomas had to step forward and help the other four men lifting it. Christina, involuntarily, stepped back. She closed her eyes for a moment.

"Well?" Claybourne asked the doctor.

The doctor consulted the paper in his hand. "Male, black hair, blue eyes, six feet two inches. That is the general description of the deceased here."

Claybourne took the death certificate from his hand. " 'Distinguishing features,' " he read. " 'Has all his own teeth.' " He looked up.

"What's left of them are his own," the doctor replied.

"Many?"

"Half the upper arch at the right back of the mouth. Some on the same side, lower arch."

Claybourne turned, smiling. "Were there any other features you wished to confirm, madam?"

He was so confident. And Christina was shaking; she couldn't help it. Her voice broke as she spoke. "There was a scar that ran from here"—she indicated under her arm—"to here." She showed where the old French injury cut downward across Adrien's body. Then she bowed her head. It felt horrid discussing this; such a personal sight—she could see it so clearly cutting across the muscles of Adrien's chest and abdomen—with these staring, disinterested men.

"Well, Townsend?" Claybourne had to prompt the doctor.

Nothing happened for several seconds. When Christina looked up, she found Doctor Townsend staring at her. There was a strange look on his face.

"Townsend," Claybourne said with a little more irritation, "check for the scar."

He did. Then looked toward Christina, as if speaking just to her. He announced almost sadly—and certainly without any surprise in his tone—"The scar is there. Poor devil," he added.

Christina stood fascinated. The doctor, with all his years of experience with death and bodies, was as shaken as she was. He fumbled with the corpse's clothes, trying to put them aright, then had to have help. Claybourne and another man stepped in as Townsend turned abruptly from the coffin, wiping his hands down his coat front.

"I am going to button his coat," Claybourne said over his shoulder to her, "assuming you don't want to examine the naked body yourself."

Christina allowed him to finish. Then stepped forward and looked down. The mild odor of decay rose up to her. But this was nothing compared to the sight. She let out a cry and leaped back.

It was Adrien. A grisly, unrecognizable face, but the rest, the clothes, the build, the posture of the body—She had been ready for anything but this.

"No—" she gasped. Her face went cold. Her knees gave out. She felt her father's arm go around her, Thomas' hand catch her elbow.

A vision of Adrien ran before her eyes. In the same dark blue coat and gold-thread waistcoat. These rings. This watch chain. Moving. Smiling. Running his hand back over his beautiful hair—

She blinked. And stood a little more erect. There was something wrong with the hair.

"Wait—" She pushed at the people trying to help her. "Let me see again."

"Christina." Her father tried to hold her back.

"Lady Hunt." Claybourne would have joined him.

But Christina suddenly found enormous strength and resolve. She pushed through them. "I want to see—" She stared down into the coffin. Stared down into what remained of a face, the face of some poor man killed for his resemblance to the Earl of Kewischester. "It's not he," she said distinctly.

"Now, my dear woman—"

She turned on Claybourne. "It's not."

"How can you possibly be so sure?"

She didn't know. She turned back again to confront the gruesome corpse. What was it about this very clever impersonation that made it wrong?

410

"The hair," she began. Except that it really looked all right. It was just a little longer perhaps than Adrien usually wore it — That was it! "Look," she said, pointing to the hairline. "The roots are brown. The hair is dyed."

"It's true," Angus Townsend had told them, "that the hair on a dead man will continue to grow. Just as will the toenails, the fingernails. . ."

The doctor had been more than willing to add his voice to what seemed an imminent investigation. But Claybourne had moved the group, and excluded Dr. Townsend, after obtaining "only the objective medical information needed."

"Angus can sometimes get too emotional over this sort of thing," Claybourne explained as they boarded the two carriages that had brought them to the cemetery. "I was reluctant from the start — I hate to see him have to deal with a corpse. His son, you see. The boy died a year and a half ago. Angus was the doctor on call that night, was called to his own house by his own wife. Very sad. The boy was always a little feeble in the head. Some fool thing with a kitchen knife, an accident . . ." He paused. "Did Mr. Lillings decide to go in the other carriage?"

"No," Christina answered, "he stayed so Dr. Townsend wouldn't have to travel back alone."

"Well, that was a useless thing to do!" Claybourne sat forward abruptly in his seat, as if he meant to go back after Thomas.

For an instant, Christina thought, the doctor knows something; his reaction . . . he's our link. . . .

Then Claybourne smiled and leaned back against the leather headrest. "I suppose Angus could use some comfort though, under the circumstances." The carriage moved off.

Christina pondered this remark, half the way back to London. Such a humane response. Where she had been sure, just the moment before, she had detected worry, concern. Perhaps Claybourne had decided he could have confidence in the doctor. Or—the thought was a little uncomfortable—in Thomas. Claybourne might still believe that Thomas was in collusion with him. He had helped put Adrien wherever he was, so, Claybourne might assume he would continue to help. A foolish mistake—

Yet, Christina frowned. Claybourne was an astute man. He couldn't have missed, over the last two months, that Thomas had shown nothing but distaste and hostility toward him: There was no mistaking that Thomas hated Edward Claybourne—the man had played him for a fool, then all but made him into a murderer. The question was, Why didn't this attitude matter to Claybourne? How could he smile and settle back, knowing he was leaving Thomas with the doctor who, a moment ago it seemed, might have something to say . . . ?

For the rest of the trip, Christina was left with an uneasy feeling.

At Whitehall, Claybourne's office was set out with tea. Christina's father had to return to his own offices to keep appointments. But Christina stayed. She sat herself down in the midst of five men who were finally officially mulling the problem of the wrong body in the wrong grave.

And watched. Claybourne was meticulous. He didn't miss a beat. If he knew or had any part in this grisly hoax, he gave no indication.

By the end of the meeting, Claybourne had delegated various aspects of the investigation to the other three men, chastised them politely—making them somehow responsible for the whole fiasco—and put himself firmly at the helm of the search for a man who, just four hours before, he had denied was even lost. He had alienated no one. Convinced everyone. He controlled every aspect of the search.

Like another man she knew, Christina realized, Claybourne was a man of the moment. A man who knew how to harness the tide. Some organizational part of his mind, a

412

gamesmanship, reminded her very much of Adrien.

They should have been friends, she found herself thinking.

Christina was staring down into her teacup.

"Excuse me, my lady"—Claybourne interrupted her thoughts—"but just one thing before we are off on this. Is it at all possible that the earl might have dyed his own hair? Without your knowing?" He said this with a show of great politeness and deference.

Christina looked at him sharply. "Adrien didn't dye his hair. I thought we had settled that is not his corpse."

"But how do you explain the scar?"

Again, Christina felt taken unawares. "I—ah—I don't know—"

"Wethers." Claybourne gestured to one of the men. "Make a note of that. The earl could possibly have dyed his own hair."

Christina stood, clinking her cup down on the table beside her. "I said he couldn't have," she asserted. "Or if he did, he dyed every hair on his entire body."

"What a bizarre thing for a wife to know," Claybourne suggested. He raised a brow and turned a look on her. "Surely, he didn't completely undress in front of you in broad daylight."

"Surely, Mr. Claybourne, you can keep your lascivious curiosity to yourself."

But he was undaunted. He shrugged and picked up a quill. He began playing with it. "It was merely professional interest. To help with the investigation." He turned to one of the other men standing, staring. "Wethers—" the man's eyes shifted to him—"you will begin with the undertaker, then? See if you can trace the body directly back to the earl's arrival that day. Or, if the body we have leads you elsewhere, start at the docks. We need to know what became of the more proper corpse. . . ."

A cold dread began to seep into Christina's veins. What

413

had she accomplished with all this, with her ten weeks of nearly ceaseless effort? Claybourne was now in charge of the search for Adrien. And never had he had better reason to produce Adrien's corpse.

Dear God, she thought. Pray there is something — besides her inept help — standing between Adrien and death. . . .

Chapter 37

Adrien didn't know exactly where he was. He knew only that he was locked in a cellar of some old, dilapidated estate; a place where Claybourne could come and go with impunity and where no one else cared to go at all. He hadn't seen a soul, but Claybourne and Gregory, since the prison.

The cellar was not much of an improvement over that first place he'd been kept. It was dirty. It had a low ceiling, an earth floor. This, and the presence of huge columns, structural support for the house above, every five feet or so, made what would have been a fairly large underground room into a claustrophobic den. And a dark one at that. Except for what daylight came through one high window, the place was lightless.

Adrien was not wild for grubbing around in someone's dark cellar, but he had dutifully explored. The place held nothing. No cast-off junk, no implements that might lend themselves to a new use; no covered-over windows or doors. There was one small opening on the far dark wall he couldn't explain. It looked as though it might have been used for the delivery of something. Coal, perhaps. Though that wasn't a very good explanation, since the coal furnace was across the room, on the same side as the window. It didn't matter anyway. Once, he had moved the rocks that were stacked against it; beyond these was a bolted closure, padlocked with a key.

A knock came. Dinner was slid, on a tray, through a small opening at the bottom of the locked cellar door. Sounds from the recesses and dark corners of his room indicated other creatures were more interested in this meal than he. They could have it, Adrien thought. Weak tea. Rather unpleasant looking food. Then, as he bent down, he saw another finger of opium. God, he wondered, what was he going to do with it all?

He had stopped taking it after the first three days. This was something he made himself do. He had continued to pretend, for Claybourne's sake—and, thus far, there had been no "tests": His acting was good; it drew on experience. But in reality, he wasn't about to get entangled with Madam Opium again. Not if he could help it. He needed his wits about him.

He picked up the stick of opium and looked around. He was afraid to hide it in too obvious a place. Claybourne spent too much time down here in this hole with him—and the man paced, wandered, poked. Thus far, Adrien had gotten away with climbing onto the headboard of the cot in the room—the only furnishing—and digging his fingers into the flower bed at the window. That window bed had possibly the happiest little batch of scraggly weeds in Hampshire.

Adrien was almost sure he was in Hampshire. Something about the weeds, the little patch of sky he could see, the air itself; there was spring in the air. He knew the smell of home.

Out of his window, there was little else to see. The

416

window faced onto a carriage entrance, a drive with an overhang and pillars that blocked out almost any other view.

Adrien began quietly to move his bed under the window again. But he had no sooner gotten it in the right position and climbed onto the headboard, when a carriage, traveling full speed, turned down the drive. It charged into his carriage entrance, spraying gravel in through the window. He quickly got out of the way.

"Gregory!"

It was Claybourne. What was he doing here so soon? Adrien wondered. He never came till after midnight.

"Is he awake?" Claybourne asked.

Adrien didn't hear the response, but he heard the man get down out of his carriage and stride into the house. His footsteps marched across the floorboards overhead.

"I hope he's not too stupefied to appreciate this," Claybourne's muffled voice said. "We've got to have our fun, then be done with it tonight. Tomorrow, I need his corpse."

Christina arrived home from Whitehall late in the evening. She had had dinner with Evangeline and Charles. But she had not been very good company, she knew.

In the hallway, she took off her bonnet and looked around. There was no sign of Thomas. But the housekeeper came running down the stairs.

"Sorry, mum. We didn't hear your carriage arrive."

"No matter." Christina shrugged out of her coat. She handed over her gloves. "Please tell Cook I won't require dinner. I'm going straight to bed. Do keep something on for Mr. Lillings though." She paused. "How is Xavier?"

"Asleep, mum."

Christina sighed. Her breasts ached with fullness.

417

"And M. La Fontaine?" Rather than let Adrien's grandfather go to Hampshire as planned, she had invited him to stay with her at the London house. He was a consoling presence and seemed happy for her company as well.

"He's fallen asleep in the library."

"Will you see that he gets upstairs?"

Christina went to her apartments.

She had her bath and crawled into bed. She tried to read. Yet, she couldn't concentrate. Without wanting to, she kept listening for Thomas, hoping he was so late because he had come across some information worth following —

Yet, he didn't come and he didn't come. Eventually she fell into a heavy, restless sleep.

She didn't hear him when he finally did arrive. Not until he was at her door.

"Christina?"

He had come through her sitting room and peered into her bedchamber. He had carried up a lamp from downstairs. Her own oil lantern still burned dimly on the night stand beside her.

She raised herself up on one elbow and pushed her hair back, away from her face. She squinted at him, trying to awaken, to understand why he was here in her room.

"Did the doctor tell you anything?" she asked. Her voice was foggy with sleep.

"No." Thomas came fully into the room and leaned his back against the door. It closed. He stared at her for what became a long period of silence.

"What is it?" Christina asked finally.

He didn't seem to know for a moment. He looked down. Then he said, "I've come to tell you I can't help you anymore."

"What?" Christina pushed herself up to a sitting position.

Again, she had to push the drape of loose hair from her face. She had come to sleep with it loose. A preference of Adrien's. "What are you talking about?"

"I can't help you find him."

There seemed to be something in the way he said this. . . . "You know where he is?"

Thomas seemed taken aback. She had somehow divined something she shouldn't have; she could tell by his reaction. He sighed and bent his head. "I think I might."

"Where?"

He didn't say anything.

She sat up all the way. "Did the doctor tell you?"

"No." He came forward, holding the light out before him. The arm's length of light hid him. He moved in the shadow of it. But the light would illuminate her, Christina knew. She pulled the covers up a little. Then, as he came close, she didn't need to see him. At least not to ascertain one fact about him. The stale sour smell of ale—strong ale—was on him. He'd been drinking.

"Not in words," he explained further. He set his oil lamp down on the tea table by the bed and sat on the bed's edge. His shin touched her knee. "Whatever hold Claybourne has on the good doctor, it's firm."

Again, Christina waited for further comment. But it didn't come. She realized something was bothering Thomas. Something that would make him drink, that would not allow him to sleep. Something that would make him come knocking on her door in the middle of the night to talk, in need of a friend. She was fully awake now; beside herself to elicit the information he had. But she resolved to try not to rush him.

He sat, staring. When finally he did speak, it was hardly the sort of conversation she wanted.

"I haven't seen your hair down like that since we were

419

children," he murmured. He looked down. "Except, of course, for that other time."

She remembered, too. That night on the lawn with Adrien. With Thomas watching from the house. Christina bent her head, as if this memory could wash over them both and be gone.

Something dropped, small and hard, into the covers between her legs. Her hand automatically searched and retrieved the object. A small, heavy metal ball.

"What is it?"

"A musket ball."

"Where did you get it?"

"From the basket of candles in the Hunt family tomb."

"What—"

"Townsend put it there." Thomas let out a breath, an exhaustion. Then began. "After everyone left, Townsend said he would stay for a few more moments. I was to wait. The idiot took a candle and lit it—it took him a long time to find one he liked. Then he knelt. He left me standing there while he knelt and prayed for a man I set up to be killed."

Thomas' face made a kind of involuntary, anguished flinch. Just a momentary spasm. He looked down. Christina reached over and touched his hand.

He withdrew his hand instantly. As if she had pinched him. "I couldn't figure it," he went on. "The candle had half burned before I got so bored and irritated I started to rummage through the candles myself. And there it was. As soon as I picked it up, the bastard stood up and said, 'let's go.' Didn't offer another word all the way to London."

"Are you sure the doctor put it there?" Christina marveled at the small piece of steel in her hand. It was tangible. She clenched it. Something in her gave a little cheer of joy—

420

"I know he did. It was put there for me to find. And for him to deny if I said anything."

"Didn't you press him for an explanation?"

"Yes. But, as I said, he was as silent as a damn grave all the way back. He wouldn't explain a jot."

Christina leaned backward toward the light, rolling the steel ball between her fingers. It was a musket ball. There was no mistake. Her heart leaped again. Then she looked at Thomas.

Only to see his eyes jerk to her face.

Guilt. It was all over him. But for more reasons than just being caught staring at her nightdress, her bosom. He wore it in the slant of his mouth, in the creases at his eyes. And in the liquid, rheumy look of pain she saw in the brown irises. A deep, self-accusatory culpability.

"They don't take steel balls out of dead men," he said. Again, he looked away. "The implication, I'm sure, is that Townsend saw him days after he was already supposed to be dead. Townsend removed the musket balls from him and left him alive."

"And you know where he is," Christina added too hopefully. She was finding it difficult to go slowly, to care too much about any suffering Thomas might be going through at this particular moment.

He didn't answer. Instead, he frowned up at her, a flash of an irritable look. "I might," he said. "I'm not sure." He paused. "But I won't tell you." With more pain than maliciousness, he added, "I can't."

"I don't understand, Thomas. If you—"

"I don't want to find him."

He said it clearly enough. But Christina refused to hear its meaning. "If you're thinking he'd be angry over your telling Claybourne—"

"You know perfectly well what it is. I couldn't bear

421

having things return to as they were."

"But, Thomas—" Again, she reached out.

He shook her hand off. "You, making calf eyes at him. And him, touching you, absorbing you"—he made a small sound, as if physically in pain—"knowing your naked body whenever the urge comes upon him."

Christina tried to ignore the overly familiar way this seemed to come out. "He's my husband, Thomas—"

He groaned-growled at her. "I don't give a damn." No longer shunning the touch of her, he took her by the shoulders. "Don't you see? I don't care that he's your husband. I don't care that he's my friend. It's not that I feel remorse at what I did to him." His face came close to hers, hissing the hot smell of stale ale in her face. "What is killing me," he breathed, "is the sudden knowledge that I would do it again." With a soft kind of menace she had never heard from Thomas, he told her, "I covet his wife, Christina. You think he'd allow me to stand around, good friend to both, while I mentally undressed and slept with you every time I looked at you? Why do you suppose he sent me from France to begin with?"

"No—" His hold bit into the flesh of her upper arms. She strained, concave, as she tried to resist the grip of his fingers.

He whispered close to her face. "I thought I could make it all up to you, up to him, all the wrong I had done. When I honestly believed he was dead. But realizing today that Adrien is probably alive . . . Well, it makes being repentant a damned sight more difficult—"

"Thomas—" Christina tried to push him back. She realized suddenly he had much the same strength, the same build as Adrien. It was a mystery to her as well, she thought, why he didn't appeal to her and Adrien did. "Listen, Thomas," she said, "you've been drinking, and you're not thinking very clear—"

Without further notice, his mouth took hers. He leaned his weight upward, onto his knees and pushed her back.

She went into the bedclothes. "Thomas—" She turned her face from his mouth, more angry than frightened by what he was doing. "For God's sake. You have no right—"

Beyond any discussion of rights, he began pulling at the covers.

"So help me, Thomas Lillings," Christina warned. She tried to keep her voice down. "People are going to find us like this. Get off me!" She squirmed. She shoved. First in token resistance, then sincerely with all her might.

Her nightgown was coming up. He was trying to wedge himself between her legs. She whispered vehemently at him, resisting, reprehending. . . . "Thomas—"

But he wouldn't quit. He was undoing his breeches.

She braced her knees together and caught him on the chin as he came down on her. She flung a pillow in his face.

He growled, panted, "Let me love—love you—Christina—" He was trying to circumvent her legs, get her arms, pin them down. . . .

She smashed the heel of her hand into his eye, digging her other hand into his hair; she pulled, kicked. Covers churned.

He let out a short burst of pain, then a slower groan as her kicks and blows rained down on him. Slowly, he seemed to be getting off the bed. Christina followed to the foot of it, throwing pillows, then finding and throwing the iron bed-warmer.

It almost hit him; he didn't even try to avoid it. He seemed to be in a daze. "Oh, Christina—I'm so sor—"

"Get out of here!" She had found the vocal chords, the volume at last, to scream at him. "I never want to see you again!"

423

"Christina—" He held his hands out in supplication.

She hit him squarely with a book, followed by a water pitcher. "Get out!"

Even as he backed down the stairs, she followed, continuing to sail whatever was available at him. A vase of flowers. The small table that had held them. "You filthy, dirty—Get out of this house!"

He stopped at the front door, staring at her; his face full of shame, defiance, anger. His hair had come out of its queue. His shirt was out, his pants unbuttoned. He conveyed a dumb, confounded confusion; a man undone. Without any hope of repair. He frowned deeply at her, then turned and fled.

Christina crumpled on the last stair. She put her head on her knees. Why couldn't she trust him? He was her friend. . . .

The housekeeper and butler found her murmuring this over and over. "He was my friend." They found her crying there softly at the foot of the stairs. Barefoot, freezing. Sobbing into her knees, muffling the sounds of her grief in her folded arms.

Samuel Rolfeman came down the stairs of his London house wearing a nightshirt and a blanket he had jerked from the foot of the bed.

"Who in damnation," he muttered, "can be banging on a man's door at this hour?"

The answer to this question stunned him. Christina Hunt stood before him, wrapped against the night winds and misting rain.

"Sam—" Her voice broke.

Her face was white as a sheet. Her eyes were red and swollen. Sam had seen enough grieving women in the course of his last years in France to know the signs. The first thing he thought was that, at last, there had been definite confirmation. Adrien was dead. And the woman who had given all of herself into loving him, into finding him alive, would now go to pieces.

"Won't you come in?"

She hesitated, turned. In the street was her coach. Her driver and footman were hunched at their posts, damp and cold. Sam motioned them to go down into the kitchen. "Wake them up downstairs," he called. "They'll get you something to drink."

Sam drew Adrien's widow inside.

But she wouldn't be taken any farther than the inside hallway. She spoke again, in a strained voice he had never heard before. "Sam—I need your help." She looked around her. As if she had no idea where she was. "Desperately," she added.

From above, a voice called. "Samuel?"

They both looked up. Didier, Sam's new "companion" stared down at them from the first landing.

"It's all right," Sam told him. "Go back to bed. It's the wife of an old friend."

Didier did as he was told, but Sam saw the look cross Christina Hunt's face. The distaste. The hint of contempt. It was something that had never crossed Adrien's face. Adrien had never been judgmental. Not of anyone. Over anything. Except perhaps toward himself. Sam felt a sudden, surprising stab of loss. Well, then, he thought, he would have his own mourning to do. So much for the "mature acceptance" he had credited himself with weeks ago over the loss of his friend.

"Come sit down." He tried to lead Christina into the sitting room.

"No. We haven't much time." She drew a breath.

God, she looked harried. Half-mad, he thought.

"Thomas left my house half an hour ago. He knows where Adrien is and, I'm sure, has gone to find him. He's going to kill him, Samuel."

Sam drew back, trying hard not to show surprise or disbelief. "Christina, I'm sure . . . If you'll just come in and have a drink—"

She pulled on his arm. "Sam—" Her eyes filled with tears. She gave his arm another pull; strong, as if she might lead him out the door in his nightshirt. "I know we've never been the best of friends. But I beg of you, listen to me. We found the wrong body in the grave today." Sam had already heard of this mix-up. "And Thomas spoke, or kind of spoke, to the doctor—the one who took the musket balls out of Adrien's living, breathing body. And Thomas *knows.* If he knows, then you must. Surely—"

"You're confused, Christina. Just come sit—"

"No, damn you." She hit his chest with her fist. "Thomas came to me. He told me. And he hates him, Samuel. He *hates* him. He's going to kill him if we don't stop him!"

"I know Thomas was not too fond of Adrien recently. I believe I'm the one who tried to explain this to you. But I hardly think Thomas—"

She leveled her eyes at him. "He tried to rape me tonight." She said this without hysteria. It was a quiet, insistent voice that demanded to be believed.

Sam was shocked. But she had, he realized, said something that was plausible. For some reason, he believed her. It explained her appearance and manner, considering the graveside facts, better than grief-stricken insanity.

"Thomas knows Adrien is alive," Christina continued. "And he knows where he is. If we don't come up with a very good guess as to just where Claybourne could be keeping Adrien, Thomas has an absolutely clear path to

426

him. Don't you understand? Adrien will trust him. Thomas can get as close as he needs. There will be no mistakes this time, no guessing, no trying to keep him alive. Thomas will walk up to him and take his life.

"Think, Samuel! You must have some idea if Thomas does! Where could Edward Claybourne hold a man he had decided to keep as—as a private prisoner—no—" she changed her mind, "as a pet." She looked up at him. Her pale face, her liquid, radiant eyes were filled with the conviction, the look of divine revelation, that might come over a saint, a visionary. "Where could Edward Claybourne keep a man he wanted to keep forever, a man he hated and loved, a man he wanted both to beat and fondle? Like a kennel hound?"

Chapter 38

Edward Claybourne went down the cellar stairs carefully. One or two boards were loose. It was beginning to get dark. As he took hold of the banister, he noticed he was trembling. Horror. Delight. He knew he didn't want to kill Adrien Hunt. He wanted to keep him; to touch him and hurt him indefinitely. But he knew now there was no choice but to kill him, and that brought its own excitement. It would be the final proof, Edward told himself, of his ultimate control over this interesting wayward man.

Gregory, behind him, stumbled on a loose step. Edward gripped the banister and pulled to the wall for fear he would be tumbled over and sent to the bottom of the stairs. He hated large men, he thought. Always bumbling around; never so graceful as his own small figure. In fact, the only large man he had ever felt something for was the one in the room at the foot of the stairs.

They came to the cellar door. Gregory had the keys. Edward stood back to let the giant find the right one. There was not a sound from within. But Edward knew Adrien was there. He could feel it. The presence of his wonderful prize. The ritual of opening this door was like opening a glass show case, a vitrine where one kept some rare collectible. A leather-bound first edition. A bright South American orchid. An unusual butterfly. Owning the clever, handsome earl was like owning all these things; it made Edward special, cultured, learned; discriminating beyond the ordinary man. It made life hum.

Especially this evening. Tonight, Edward told himself, he planned to do things — things to remember. He would prove how much he loved and respected Adrien by doing for him what he had never done for anyone else before: He was going to save Adrien from the most awful, filthy humiliation of death —

For a minute, as the door swung open, the room looked empty. Then Edward released his breath. Adrien was only lying down. The faint, fading light from the window revealed one leg and a shoe. Edward frowned. His prisoner, his "guest" was lying on the floor.

"Adrien?"

No response.

Edward scowled. "Get the lantern," he said peevishly to Gregory. He backed up a step, into the doorway; cautious. Still, the figure on the floor didn't move. "What the devil does he think he's doing?"

Gregory returned, a minute later, with the lantern. He was hustling, trying to keep Edward happy. His eagerness to please made him awkward with the flint. For some seconds, there was just that sound; Gregory scraping, scratching flint on metal. Everything else was quiet. Nothing moved. The light flickered, then blazed. The damp room opened up. Adrien was lying, face down, in the dirt of the floor. There was something white, white scraps of paper, all around him.

Edward picked one up. It took several moments to comprehend. "Oh, my God," he murmured. "Where did he get all this?"

He caught a glimpse of something at the window. More white. He went to investigate. "Sweet God." The man had been caching, in the high window bed, all the opium they had been giving him, for who knew how long. Saving it, judging by all the papers, for this one stupendous gesture.

The imbecile —

Edward bent down to the still body. What to do? he wondered. He felt for a pulse. The man was still living, breathing. Edward stood erect suddenly, and backed away. If the scoundrel had been faking before this. . . .

"Gregory. Break his finger."

The oaf grunted dully in response.

"His finger. Reach down and break one."

"Don' seem right," Gregory said in his slow, low voice, "a man lyin' there like that —"

Edward pushed him out of the way. One long-fingered hand lay relaxed on the floor by Adrien's head. Edward took his heel and stomped on it. Hard.

The man stirred, but that was all. Not much of a reaction.

Edward did it again. A different finger.

The reaction was less. The inert body didn't respond to pain.

Edward sighed and sat down heavily on the bed. He had had so many nice plans — He had wanted to tell Adrien about them — before administering the lethal dose, then helping him, as it took hold, to clean himself and prepare. . . .

"Well," he said at last. He looked up at Gregory. "He's still breathing, at least. We'll just do what we were planning, then drag the body out that hole. There's no point in lugging him up the stairs. You have the key to the kennel door, don't you?"

Gregory responded in the affirmative.

Then, suddenly realizing Gregory was only holding the light, Edward stood up, angry. "Where's the enema can?" he asked.

The giant flinched.

"My God, can't you do anything right?" Edward made a huff; he would get it himself. When a man died, his body lost all control of his muscles, including those of his

430

bowels—he must move quickly, before his dear Adrien shat himself. Edward began up the stairs. "You must have left it up here," he told Gergory, "when you went to get the lantern."

Adrien didn't wait. He gave the giant's leg a hard jerk. The man lost his balance—he was heavier than Adrien had imagined. But a second yank brought Gregory down. Adrien shoved him hard—backward. The giant's head hit the wall. He didn't move.

Adrien climbed to his feet. He was a little unsteady. He had hidden most of the opium in a pile, in the nether shadows of the far side of the cellar. But a large quantity of it was in him: He had guessed that Claybourne would try something to verify his comatose state. He wasn't comatose now. Not yet. He was only beginning to feel the rise. Luckily, though, there was enough opium in him—and will power—to smother the pain inflicted on innocent fingers lying on the ground.

Adrien cursed under his breath, putting his fingers to his mouth. Then he gave a shudder. Enema can? God, he needed to get out of here.

Quickly, he went over the giant's clothes for the keys. There was the possibility of a pistol upstairs, as well as Claybourne's appliance for his bizarre call to personal hygiene. Adrien preferred to go out the kennel door—is that what he'd called it?—than confront the Old Man upstairs.

Adrien found the keys and took them to the far side of the cellar. He began rolling, tossing the rocks away from the door, as fast as he could. He could hear Claybourne overhead, walking across the floorboards, clanking with something. Then, at the top of the cellar steps, the upstairs door opened.

"Gregory? Is everything all right? I thought I would also

431

bring down the warm water, while I'm up here—"

The last rock moved away. But which damn key?

The fourth turned the tumbler; the lock fell open. Adrien slid the wood bolt.

"Gregory? What's all that noise?"

Claybourne was coming down.

Adrien scooted on his stomach through the opening; it was barely large enough to accommodate a man. He slid out onto the other side. It was the outside of the building. He felt a wave of relief. Then he saw.

"Oh, bloody fine."

A kennel. Of course. He hadn't been kept in a cellar, but in a dog pound. It was the Rice estate. Gone to rack and ruin. Dog breeders, long back; William Rice dead, the heirs without money, the dogs long escaped.

But the wire fences—on all sides and above—still existed. Within this, Adrien could see the distant housing; bitch housing where the foxhounds bore and nursed their young. It was the selfsame, dilapidated manor house where he had met Claybourne months ago. The day of the greenhouse; the day the note had come, with Charles and Thomas and Sam standing around gawking as Christina came in—

Adrien leaned back against the cold brick wall. He had escaped into a cage; a labyrinth of fenced-in, narrow corridors. The dog runs.

When Edward Claybourne came out, Adrien Hunt was nowhere to be seen.

The sun had set. The moon was out. Just a sliver. Soon, it would be totally dark.

"You're out here!" Edward called. He laughed and waved the pistol he'd brought from the house—his flag of triumph. He would kill this man yet. "You're out here," he declared, "because there's nowhere else to go.

Edward began to walk leisurely down the first stretch of

dog run. How clever, he thought; this had been used to exercise pedigreed hounds. Now he would exercise his pedigreed earl. Gregory was unconscious on the cellar floor. But this didn't bother him. He had the pistol. A small, elegant gun. It made him physically Adrien's equal. And, of course, the other part — that was the fun; he would match wits with clever Adrien and beat him again. Fatally, this time. Edward laughed and turned toward the small housing for the female dogs. There was no other place he could be.

The opium was affecting Adrien more and more. He gave a shake to his head, trying to clear it. Trying to concentrate.

He watched Claybourne. Slowly, the old minister was winding his way through the paths which, just moments before, Adrien had come through on a dead run. What then? Adrien wondered; when the Old Man got to him, when he got to the blockade of dog houses? He could play a game of hiding, round and round; seeing to it that he was always one corner away from a straight shot. But, eventually, Gregory would get up. The two of them could fox that game; one going to one side, one to the other. Adrien had to find a way out.

He looked around him. He couldn't go over the damn fencing; it was roofed — more ingenious wire to keep the jumpers from getting out. He couldn't go through the fencing; the wire was too thick, made out of steel. But, from experience, he knew that in every pack there were always one or two foxhounds who were aggravatingly good at digging *under* fences. All traces of the dogs were gone. They had surely escaped. Somewhere, there ought to be hole, somewhere along the outer periphery of fencing —

"Adrien! Can you hear me?"

Claybourne was at the far corner of the dog houses.

No time like the present, Adrien thought. Adrien poised

himself to run, then didn't. He had to brace his hand on the building. His head swam for a second. And his eyesight had narrowed, he realized: one of the effects of the opium. The pupils of his eyes, at the peak of the first rush, always contracted. His vision dimmed. If there was an opening, he thought irritably, he wasn't going to be able to see it.

After a second, he was able to move. He broke away from the building, in a perpendicular direction, using the dog houses for a screen. He ran for the fence.

"Why don't you come in, like a good little lamb?" Claybourne continued to call. "We'll make new terms. I don't really want to kill you, anyway . . . . "

Adrien moved, quick and low, along the fence. He was feeling for an upturned piece, a hole in the ground. But all he could feel was solid fencing; they had buried it in the ground on heavy posts. The fence ran yards and yards, around the whole circumference of the pound. It was going to take forever, he thought, to check every foot of it.

A noise near the house made him turn for a second. Gregory, he thought; dear God—Then, in front of him, worse. A dead end. The corridor he'd been running along ended suddenly in a wire wall. He could see the next run, the next stretch that walled off the outside and freedom, but he couldn't get to it. He would have to go back through the maze if he wanted to continue to search—

"You can stop right there." Fifty feet off, Claybourne had come around the dog houses. And Claybourne's vision was good; he aimed the pistol directly at Adrien.

A shot rang out, just as Adrien dived for the earth. He went flat. A ball whizzed over his head. He leaped up, thinking he had time while the Old Man reloaded. Then, another unpleasant surprise. A second pistol ball nearly grazed him.

"What the—" He realized. The Old Man was using a double-barreled flintlock—small balls, but the gun held two charges.

434

Claybourne bent over the gun to quickly reprime. Adrien turned; he would charge him in the interval. But he caught a glimpse of a figure coming—running—from the house. Gregory? It didn't seem large enough for Gregory. But Adrien couldn't get to Claybourne and subdue him in time to find out. He turned back; he would play the maze instead. Poor, dim Gregory would be no help there.

Adrien darted through two quick turns in the tracking, then down a long corridor. It took a U-bend before he was back along the outside fence. He continued running, bent low, pulling at the fence now, hoping for a loose piece, a weak spot; anything.

Another voice called out. "Claybourne!"

It was Thomas! Adrien almost tripped in relief. Help. And none too soon.

"Watch out, Thomas!" Adrien called. "He's just reloaded the pistol!"

But Thomas was on him.

"Get out of here—" he heard Claybourne yell, "don't meddle—"

There was a struggle, then a sharp thud. Adrien crouched, not sure what had happened, who had won.

"It's all right, Adrien." Thomas' voice called through the night. "I've knocked him out."

"God, am I glad you are here." Adrien stood up.

Thomas was winding his way toward him.

"There's another one," Adrien called to him, "unconscious in the cellar."

"I saw him," Thomas said.

Adrien wanted to laugh, to cry for joy. "How the blazes did you find me?"

"I remembered the note. I remembered Claybourne had used this place once before—"

Distantly, horses could be heard. More riders. More company. Adrien welcomed the sound. People at last; God, the wonderful sound of horses and people.

435

Then Thomas rounded the last bend to face Adrien. He was holding Claybourne's pistol. Adrien stopped, not ten feet away; once more, the gun was pointed at him.

Adrien was dumbfounded. Thomas didn't look like himself. His clothes were a mess, his hair a tangle. He was unsteady; either drunk or crazy or both. "What's wrong with you, Thomas? Point that gun down. It's going to hurt someone."

"It damn well is." He took a deep, addled breath. "God, Adrien. Look at you. Six musket balls. Enough blood lost to bath the whole ship's deck in red. And there you stand. Are you bloody human?"

Adrien held out his hand. "Give me the gun, Thomas. It doesn't matter. I know you told him. And I understand why—"

"Do you? Do you understand what it's like to live in the shadow of someone who has everything? Who does everything perfectly!"

Adrien laughed. "You can't possibly be talking about me. Look at the mess—"

"Stay back," Thomas warned. He cocked the hammer. The riders were at the front of the house. People were calling. Adrien thought for a moment he even heard Christina—

Then it was Christina. Once more saving him, from an awful opium dream. "Adrien!" she called.

He answered. "Here, Christina!"

"Too bloody late," Thomas said through his teeth. He fired the gun.

Christina screamed and tried to run headlong to Adrien. Wire fencing stopped her. She could see through it, but couldn't get around it. Frantically, she ran into one wall, then the next, screaming at Thomas.

"Don't!" He had fired, but Adrien hadn't fallen. "Don't

shoot again! Thomas!"

The others were coming up behind her. They came out the back servants' door into the same confusion as she: A dark grid of fencing. What was this?

She could hear Thomas yelling.

"Fall!" he screamed. "Cry out! Do something! I've shot you, you bloody bastard!"

Christina managed to get closer, by running down one narrow corridor. She could just make out Adrien, standing. He seemed to be looking down at his own chest.

While Thomas seemed to be crumpling. He fell to his knees. He was crying. "You're not human. . . . " he said in gasps. "You don't even feel it. I can't fight a bloody devil. . . . "

Then he turned the gun, put it into his own mouth and blew away the back of his head.

Epilogue

Adrien's wound had not been as bad as it could have been. The ball lodged in his chest, but was deflected by one of his ribs. They had brought him, by horseback, back to London where Dr. Townsend had removed the ball.

The doctor had left several hours ago. But this didn't seem to stop the commotion. At four in the morning, the house was still filled with people coming and going. Friends trying to help. And, of course, all the official delegations.

Christina herself had spent the better part of the last hours telling her story to two chief constables; one from Hampshire, one from London. Sam, all the men — for they had gathered together most of the old group to rescue Adrien — had been questioned as well. There was going to be quite a stink, a huge investigation; since the criminal in question was a king's minister.

Claybourne was in custody; he had lost his career and his freedom this past night. He and Gregory were receiving medical attention courtesy of the London Public Police. Sam had left with the coroner to bring back Thomas' body. There would be letters to write, his family to reach. But, all and all, things were getting straightened out. Everything except Adrien, Christina thought. She had yet to have more than a few minutes with him alone.

Christina was worried about him. They had brought him home, but he had been so quiet. So unlike himself. So strangely dulled by the drug. It was time to remove everyone but the most necessary officials out of her house.

The nursemaid came down to tell her someone else was disturbed by the all-night noise: Christina had just fed Xavier an hour ago, but he was up again, inconsolable. She sighed. She would have to delay putting an end to the chaos in her house.

Then on the stairs, she ran into Adrien's grandfather. "Philippe," she said, "Xavier is crying again. The nursemaid can't do anything with him. Do you suppose—?"

His eyes lit. *"Pas de problème. I go immédiatement."* He turned with almost a bounce to his old man's gait.

Christina had forgotten how much he liked to feel useful. And he loved Xavier; he was good with him. She reminded herself she must let him help more often with his greatgrandson.

This left her free to attend to her busy house. There was a conclave of men upstairs. Mostly friends. She would start with them. Christina headed for the upstairs reception salon, thinking to begin turning people out.

Then she noticed the door to the earl's apartments was ajar. She hesitated a moment, though why, she didn't know. These were her rooms, too. All her things were in there. Her whole life. She pushed open the door. No one in the sitting room. At the bedchamber, she paused again. Still a little daunted, she knocked.

"Come in."

The voice sounded strong; the same gentle, deep sound that had, from the beginning, so entranced her. She went in.

At first she didn't see him. There were only two bedside candles for light. He wasn't in the bed.

"Adrien?"

He moved. A slight stirring of an elaborate, loose robe in the corner of the room; she had never seen it before, except hanging in his wardrobe. He had folded it around him. He

439

was sitting in a large wing-back chair in the darkest corner of the room. She couldn't even see his face.

"Let me get a light," she said. She started out to fetch a lantern —

"No, don't."

She paused.

"Would you mind just pulling a chair over here?" As further explanation, he sighed, "It's the drug, Christina. As it wears on, the light hurts. My eyes dilate."

She brought a chair and sat opposite him, frowning, searching for hints of the old Adrien. They were there in disjointed bits. The slouch. One long leg stretched out. The voice.

"I want to see our son."

A day later, Christina brought Adrien's afternoon tea tray up to a much brighter, more cheerful room. The curtains were open, the canopy drapes of the bed turned back. Adrien was sitting up in bed with a writing table in front of him.

"What are you doing?" Christina asked. "You need to move that so I can set this down."

He smiled up at her. "Someone," he said, "has been over my books — very ably, I might add. You?"

"Of course."

He took the table — it held one of his ledgers — and the tray and pushed them aside. He took Christina's hand and pulled her down on the bed.

"This is nice," he said. He was looking, smiling at her hand. At the ring she wore there.

"Oh, Adrien. It came at the worst time. The day of the funeral —" She paused. "It's the diamond from the stickpin, isn't it?" He nodded. "Thank you. It made me feel you were alive, every time I looked at it" — she laughed — "though everyone else thought I was crazy —"

440

"You are crazy." He drew her to him, against his chest. "Thank God." He didn't speak for some moments, then he dove in. "The king would like to know," he said, "if I would fill Claybourne's post. The men who came this morning — they were envoys: To see, if he asked, would I accept." He laughed softly. "One is given the opportunity to avoid rebuffing the king."

"Would you?" she asked.

"I don't know. It's all too soon." He paused. "I have a seat in the House of Lords, as well. Some members of Parliament were up at noon encouraging me to fill it. They want me to argue human rights on the floor of Parliament; they claim I will have more influence, by the end of the week, than the prime minister himself."

"They shouldn't have bothered you —"

"It's all right. It's better than being up here alone. Thinking of Thomas."

She looked at the buttons of his nightshirt, began playing with them. "You're supposed to be sleeping," she said. He stopped her hand with his. She touched his fingers. "How did this happen?" Two fingers had been bandaged. They were an awful blue-black by the time they had gotten home.

"Someone danced on them a little."

"I hate when you do that."

"What?"

"Be flip. I was serious. Was it Claybourne?"

"Of course." Then, out of the blue, he asked, "Did he hurt you?"

"Who?"

"Thomas." She was going to deny it, but he added, "Sam told me. He thought I should know."

"He didn't really do anything —" she offered.

"What he did was enough." He touched her face, brought it up to look at him.

The sweet warmth, the starchy smell of his clean night-

441

shirt coupled with his touch, the look in his eyes; all so familiar. They sent a shot through her. A longing. For more touching, more tenderness. . .

"But he didn't hurt you?" Adrien asked. "You're all right?"

"I am now," she murmured.

After a time, he asked, "So what do you think? The king needs an answer. He can't go the week with a war in France and no foreign minister."

"I don't think it would be good for you." Christina paused at hearing the frankness of her own remark. Then she continued, speaking against his chest. "I don't think your heart wants to make war on France."

He laughed. "And the floor of the Parliament?"

"It sounds opportunistic and crass and politic. And, yes, I think you would love it. You would be a great success at it."

He made a satisfied sound. "Exactly what I was thinking. Except for one problem." She waited. "Could you live in London? Much of the year, at least?" His voice went lower, more tentative. "You weren't thinking of rescuing me only to turn around and leave, like you so meanly promised?"

"No," she whispered. "I wasn't."

His arms gave her an overall, general hug. He made a deep, slightly wicked laugh. "Good. Then I won't be having to waste all my time trying to find you and bring you back—"

"I thought the promise was, you wouldn't do that in any event."

"I'm a liar. So I've been told."

She gave him a little shove. "Well, don't lie to me, Adrien Hunt. I have no sympathy—"

He groaned, reached for his sore chest. "Hitting an injured man," he moaned.

Christina frowned down at him. "Adrien—" She bit her lip. Then she caught a glimpse of his cast-down expression.

442

The angular, perfect, slightly wicked-looking grin.

She hit him more earnestly. "Oh, you're not hurt."

"I am, I am," he insisted as he pulled her onto him. "I'm so injured. And there's only one cure," he said. He kissed her, rolling onto his good side. "Only one cure," he repeated.